Don't you mas~

Brian Zunca

Front Cover Art and Cover Design:
Jenn St-Onge Illustration
http://www.jennstonge.ca/

Typesetting & Layout:
Peter Liethen
http://www.deverishworkshop.com/

Briana Lawrence

DEDICATION

To the ones who know they are, and the ones who are still learning, don't forget: You Are Magical.

ACKNOWLEDGEMENTS

To the muses who decided that creating a purple haired, plus size magical girl and her friends was a better idea than convention prep. To Jessica Walsh and Chealsey Thomas, who braved a wild snowstorm with me and helped me flesh out this idea in-between belting out the Pokémon theme. To every single person who backed the ambitious Kickstarter that didn't go the way I wanted. To my mother, who encouraged me to get back up and let the Black Girl Magic shine on. To the Indiegogo backers and supporters who made the campaign overfund and reduce me to a sobbing mess. To my good friend Peter Liethen, who is always helping me with book projects and responding to messages at all hours of the day. To every single artist who has contributed to this project, whether I reached out to you or you reached out to me. To the cosplayers, fanartists, those who cheer me on at conventions or online, those who continue to show love and support to a fat, black, queer woman and her big ol' dreams.

To everyone who told me that these girls are necessary, I'm here to tell you that they've finally arrived.

EPISODE ONE:

THERE'S THESE THINGS. CALLED PRIORITIES

After twenty-seven tries Bree should've been better at this.

Each new attempt should've been another chance to improve but now she was screwing up the basics. Run and Jump. Duck and Dodge. These were maneuvers that she could do in her gamer girl sleep, the most basic of functions of the A and B buttons… had she not reached the point of utter frustration.

"Damnit! I pushed the button, why didn't it work?!" Then, in a moment of true brilliance, she declared, "This controller's busted!" That had to be it. Her gameplay was immaculate so it had to be her controller, right? She sighed. Even as she spoke – yelled – the words, she knew they weren't true. The controller had been in its charge station all day and was perfectly synced to the console. Maybe she could blame the game itself? It was cheating, somehow, or perhaps it wasn't a fan of cute, black girls. Discrimination. That's what this was, plain and simple. She should tweet at the developers and-

Pause.

Deep, calming breath.

There was no need to take her frustrations to social media. All she had to do was avoid the onslaught of traps, the fast moving enemies, and the bottomless pits. She'd managed to dodge the first two spiky foes, but the third? The third one just had to touch her, didn't it? Why didn't this level believe in power-ups?! Then again, that shouldn't have mattered, because Bree Danvers – certified gamer girl and Let's Play aficionado – should've been better at this!

"I can do this," Bree said as she brushed a stray lock of green hair from in front of her eyes. If she wanted to, she could blame her hair for momentarily blocking her view, but that would be another lie. Her failure was one hundred perfect skill-based, or lack thereof, as they say. All she had to do was concentrate and get to that flagpole.

Unpause.

In front of Bree was a bright, cheerful background where the clouds wore smiles on their faces. They reminded her of happier times, back when she'd been good at this game. Getting this far had been a fun filled breeze full of catchy music, gold coins, and a series of well-timed jumps. Now? Now she was in a demented, 8-bit version of hell. The blue skies made her eyes sore and the music was worse than the tired jingles in department stores – especially when she stumbled into bottomless pits.

Speaking of bottomless pits…

"Damnit!!!"

After *twenty-eight tries!* She *should've been better at this!*

Bree gripped onto the controller and grit her teeth. She wanted to end it all and throw the controller into the TV screen. Sure, it would be an instant kill for the flat screen she loved so much, and her tablet-shaped controller wouldn't survive, but such things could be replaced, right? Bree squeezed her eyes shut and shook her head. What kind of logic was that? Breaking something out of rage? Besides, she didn't really want to deal with a pushy electronics salesperson who'd try to convince her to upgrade to the next big thing?

Breathe. Just breathe. It was just a game, and games could be beaten. Perhaps a prayer would come in handy. Her mother did teach her the ways of calling to a higher power when times were tough.

"In Arin Hanson I trust," she whispered, because if anyone understood frustrating video game levels, it was the "Hey I'm Grump" half of the Game Grumps Let's Play channel. Not that the Grump would hear her, but she could pretend, right? Besides, he'd been able to do this after fifty-eight tries and hadn't lost his sanity until try number thirty-two. She was getting close to that point since this level didn't believe in checkpoints. Seriously, what video game company thought it'd be a good idea to let fans make their own levels?

She was supposed to be breathing or something, right?

"All right. Let's do this."

Ticking clock. 500 seconds. Spiked enemies. Bottomless pits. And that damn cheerful background with clouds she now wanted to punch in the face. How dare they smile at a time like this. Didn't they realize how soul-sucking this level was? Bree decided to work out the intricacies of cloud punching later. Just a few well-timed jumps and she'd be grabbing onto that flagpole and trotting into the castle. Run. Jump. Duck and-

WAM!

Well, at least she'd almost gotten to try number thirty.

"WHO MAKES A CANON FIRE TURTLE SHELLS INSTEAD OF BULLETS?!"

In hindsight, despite her high pitched screech, she hadn't completely lost her sanity. She hadn't flat out smashed her controller the way Markiplier had done during that one Let's Play video where he'd tried to become toast. So, in a way, she had won. Nothing was broken and she hadn't resorted to saying things that would make a censor bar weep.

"Sorry about that," she said as she set down her controller and readjusted her headset. "I just... I need a minute," then she closed her eyes and slumped back in her chair. The game was still playing its bright, catchy tune as the timer counted down the seconds. Not that it mattered. The stage could be beaten in thirty seconds if done perfectly – according to the world record. "You don't understand, this level isn't even remotely fair! I've had an easier time taking on monsters twice my size. Real monsters!"

Finally, the anger was slipping away in favor of something she was an expert in.

Magical Girl Storytelling in front of a live studio audience.

Internet audience.

A recording that would be presented to an internet audience once uploaded. Not only was this game irritating, but she was going to have to relive it multiple times while editing the video.

"You know, like that thing that showed up two nights ago… assuming you're local," she said. Bree opened her eyes and spread her arms out to emphasize how monstrous said creature was. Hm. She wondered if she could use her magical powers on the creator of this torturous level. Naw, she had a feeling that would be against some kind of Magical Girl Code of Conduct. "Actually, my arms don't do it justice, and the camera doesn't reach that far. Picture… Godzilla. Not the remakes, though, cuz he's only onscreen for like ten minutes. Actually, I take it back, picture Akira, because this thing was hella gross," she said with a shudder. All these years later and that mutation scene still made her feel nauseous. "If you live near the science museum you probably heard the commotion, especially when its flesh started to ooze over buildings and-"

"BREE!"

Bree's bedroom door swung open and there stood her good friend and roommate, Marianna Jacobs. She wore a purple polka-dotted apron that complimented her rich, brown skin. She was chubby and adorable even if she was frowning at her – though the stern look was ruined by the flour at the tip of her nose. A cute girl who loved to bake was almost the perfect living situation.

Almost.

"Don't yell! I'm recording!" Bree snapped as she pointed to her camera.

"How is you yelling while recording any better?" Marianna asked.

"Well… you started it…"

Magic Girl

Up Next   Autop

Magical Girl Day Ca
Part 10 - Game Gru
354,211 Views

Bishoujo Soldier Sa
Part 1 - Markiplier
625,222 Views

Sailor Moon: Anotl
(7/?) - Rainbow
4,380 Views

Girl Power Movie -
Review - Black Ner
77,254 Views

Cosmic Power -
Part 3 - KittyKatC
22,132 Views

Magnifique Noir - Part 1 - Cosmickaze Bree

Cosmickaze Bree

✓ Subscribed | 100,245   22,432 views

COSMiCKAZE BREE
Jessica Walsh • www.sewntogetherreflections.com

"Oh that's real mature, Bree."

"Hold on," Bree said to the camera before she pressed the pause button. Didn't she go to college to get away from parental units? Oh, and education, or something along those lines. Marianna was dangerously close to feeling like her mother – minus the need to spend Sunday praising Him. Bree spun around in her chair and asked, "Why were you yelling, anyway? Please say it was to get me to come and try one of your baked concoctions."

"No."

"Was it to tell me to believe in Danny instead of Arin?"

"Huh?"

"Come now, Mari." Bree slipped the cute nickname into the conversation in an attempt to get her to simmer down. The tactic never worked, but Bree was, if nothing else, persistent. "We've lived together long enough for you to know who the Game Grumps are."

Marianna raised an eyebrow at Bree. It was scary how intimidating an eyebrow could be. "Stop playing dumb. You know why I was yelling."

"Is this the Magical Girl Lecture again?" Bree asked, even if she knew the answer. Somehow, Marianna always knew the exact moment when Bree began to talk about her "other life" in her videos.

"Huh. It's like we've had this talk before." The sarcasm was thick in Marianna's voice. She crossed her arms, a wooden mixing spoon in her hand that looked more threatening than the weapons any of those monsters used against them.

Bree prepared for the words that had been drilled into her head several times before. Talking about magical girl stuff on camera is dangerous. Revealing yourself to strangers can be disastrous. All that sparkly jazz.

"As magical girls we have… priorities."

Bree blinked, then blinked again. This was a new direction that Marianna was taking her patented lecture. Usually, she would already be scolding her, practically wagging her finger at her as if she had tracked mud into a freshly carpeted house. "Priorities?" Bree asked.

"That's right. Priorities. It's our job to protect the city, and to do so as discreetly as possible."

"Discreet? How discreet is a monster whose flesh envelopes entire buildings?"

"Flesh? Enveloping buildings? What?"

Bree let out a nervous laugh and said, "I may have made our latest fight sound a bit more… exciting."

Marianna looked less than impressed with her friend. "You think our battles aren't exciting?"

"They are! But gross monster with skin that oozes onto things like a cheese pizza sounds more riveting than an average-sized acid spitter."

Marianna couldn't decide what was worse: Bree calling one of their battles average… or Bree vilifying something as delicious as cheese pizza. "Average? It was twice our size, Bree…"

"Yeah but I've told that story already!" When Bree saw the look on Marianna's face she knew she'd said too much. "N-not that I tell these stories often…"

"Which brings me to my point: you can't let people know who we are."

"People know who we are, Mari. We defend the city on a regular basis."

If Marianna could, she'd roll her eyes into outer space. "They know about **magnifiquenoir**, but they don't know who we really are outside of our magical girl name. That's what I mean when I say *discreet*."

"Oooo," then Bree gave Marianna a bright smile. "Don't worry, people don't know who I really am."

"Your channel is called *Cosmickaze Bree* and you're in your transformed state! On camera! On the Internet!"

And there was the yelling again. Bree had a feeling it wouldn't take long. She tugged at a strand of her green hair and said, "No one thinks this is my real hair." Just like Marianna, her hair was brown until she transformed. Most people, according to the comments on her videos, assumed that Bree wore a really convincing wig.

"And your clothes?"

"What, this?" Bree pointed to the dress she was wearing: all black with green stripes and a skirt that flared out to display what looked to be an entire galaxy on fabric. "People think it's cosplay. You know, just like Ella."

Marianna knew this would happen. She knew the girl would compare herself to her friend, Ella. Because of course Bree had a friend who cosplayed for her YouTube channel. "You can't compare your channel to Ella's! She's not a magical girl!"

"Hey now, Ella is pretty magical," Bree proclaimed in defense of her friend. Sure Ella couldn't pull off devastating attacks via sparkles, glitter, and glamorous poses, but she really knew how to style a wig before going on camera. "In fact, I tell people I learned how to style my 'wig' through one of her tutorial videos."

"Don't play games with me, Bree."

"I'm not! I'm being serious! No one thinks I'm Cosmic Green! I can show you the comments to prove it!"

"You're. Sparkling!"

"I tell people it's an after effect, you know, an editing trick?" Bree shrugged her shoulders and added, "See? Everything I do has a logical explanation."

"That's debatable," Marianna muttered.

"Fine. What if I change clothes, will that make you happy?" Before Marianna could answer Bree walked over to her dresser and proceeded to pull out various shirts and toss them onto the floor. "I can find a geeky look, no problem."

Marianna would've commented on Bree's actions being similar to a child throwing a tantrum, but she was considering this a victory of sorts. Still, there was one thing left for Bree to do. "Your hair."

"What?"

"You need to change it back to normal."

"Oh no, I'm keeping the hair."

"Bree…"

"Do you know how beneficial it is for a black girl's hair to be instantly done for the camera?"

Marianna let those words sink in. No maintaining hair with a particular set of products that had a fraction of a section at every retail store. No scouring the streets for a beauty supply store that took your hair texture into account. No sleeping with hair bonnets. No combing out tangles and straightening, or trying to perfect natural curls if that was the mood she was in. "Fine," Marianna said, "But only for your channel. No green, sparkling hair at school."

"Deal."

"And no talking about our battles online."

"Whoa, wait a minute-"

Before the two could continue their argument a loud alarm began to sound from the living room. Even with hearing it go off at least twice a week – double that if the monsters were feeling extra feisty – the loud sound made both girls jump in surprise. Bree covered her ears and shouted, "Can't she just come downstairs and tell us when there's trouble!? She lives on the floor above us, do we really need a monster alert that echoes through my ears!?"

"Now that's something we can both agree on," Marianna yelled back.

Bree smiled. Despite Marianna's terrible fondness of lecturing her, she still had enough positive qualities to make her friend worthy. Besides, she didn't want to do this magical girl thing on her own.

As soon as the girls stepped into the living room, the TV flipped on and they were greeted by their leader, Golden Blaze. Bree would've complained about wasting the gaming potential of a gloriously large, hi definition TV to communicate with the purveyor of their magical abilities, but the stern look on Blaze's face kept her quiet. Bantering back and forth with Marianna was one thing, but Blaze always meant business when it came to keeping the city safe. True to the name, Blaze's buzz cut was a blend of oranges and yellows, with her piercing eyes and full lips matching the fiery colors. She wore a silver lip ring, the look adding to the hard edge of the woman's appearance.

"There's trouble a few miles north of here," Blaze said. If the alarm hadn't brought the girls to attention, Blaze's commanding voice would've. "I'm sure if you look out your window, you'll see what I mean."

The girls turned and could see a cloud of smoke billowing into the air from their window. "Well then, I guess we need to get to work,"

Marianna said as she pushed the window open. Their building wasn't the tallest in the city but it was still an impressive height, one that Marianna conquered by leaping out and free-falling toward the ground below.

"Oh right, because that's not the least bit suspicious!" Bree yelled. How could Marianna be concerned about her YouTube channel when she was busy jumping out of windows? Bree could hear Blaze chuckling from the television screen before it shut off. At least someone was amused at Marianna's antics.

"It's the magical girl way!" Marianna yelled back as a flash of purple light surrounded her body.

Bree knew Marianna couldn't see her sticking her tongue out, but that didn't stop her from doing it. Soon, she jumped out the window to join her, nailing the landing in a flash of colors and sparkles. How Marianna could question why Bree would want to tell these cool stories was beyond her.

EPISODE TWO:

MAGICAL MOTIVATION

Alarms were meant to be broken.

This was probably why Marianna insisted that Bree use a "real" alarm clock instead of relying on her phone. The grating noise was much more irritating than whatever pre-programmed sound her phone would make. That, and Bree would've just grabbed her phone, flipped it to silent, and lay in bed checking every social media account she had.

Bree wondered if it would be frowned upon to use a fantastical special attack against her clock. One good blast of cosmic power and her alarm would meet its doom in a perfectly clock shaped scorch mark on the wall. The downside would be the potential damage to the various pieces of fanart she'd purchased at her hometown anime convention. Was alarm clock destruction worth putting her favorite pairings in harm's way? Harley and Ivy would understand, right? Harley would laugh it off while Ivy gave some speech about the cruelty of man's world making a girl miss her beauty sleep. Besides, art could technically be replaced. There was so much art of the Iwatobi Swim Club, and her ice skating husbands were making their presence known in artist alleys across the country.

Before Bree could muster up the strength to completely misuse her abilities, she remembered the tried and true SNOOZE button. Just one push and Bree was back to burying herself in her self-made blanket co-coon – much to the relief of her wall and its posters.

With the obnoxious buzzing put to rest Bree drifted off into a pleas-ant dream where she'd conquered a certain video game and earned the respect of the YouTube comment section – minus any irritating com-mentary about black girl gamers on the Internet. Unfortunately, said notion of dreaming was shattered when Bree's bedroom door slammed open for a rude awakening. Bree groaned in protest and curled up under the blankets more. She already knew who was at the door, but maybe her Poké Ball scattered bedding could protect her until she found a Mari-anna-proof door lock.

"Get up," Marianna said as she walked over to the bed, her high heels clicking against the floor. Bree didn't have to look up from her covers to know that her magical companion was already dressed for the day, probably in one of her pinstriped skirts or a floral patterned dress. Marianna was the girl who always looked like she came out of a plus size clothing ad. As cute as it was, Bree felt it was way too early to put that much effort into your appearance.

"Go away," Bree muttered from beneath the covers. "I'm going back to bed."

"We have to get to class."

"Come on! We were up late last night! Remember? Monster attack? You jumping out the window?"

"You mean you were up late last night. I went to bed right after the battle, you decided to stay up playing video games."

"I have a channel to run!"

"Pretty sure your fans would understand you not recording since you insist on telling them that you're a magical girl."

Bree poked her head out from under the covers and asked, "So you're okay with it now?"

"Did I say that?"

"No," then Bree smiled a little. "You look cute today, Mari."

"Don't change the subject. Get out of bed."

"Hey! I meant that," Bree said. She'd been right about the pinstripe skirt and it curved around Marianna's body nicely. "And I'm not getting up. There's no point in going to school." It was such a bizarre concept when you thought about it. They kept the city safe on a daily basis, why did they need to bother attending college? Especially this early in the morning?

"Nope."

"Nope? Wait… you agree with me?"

"No. I mean *nope* as in *I'm not having this conversation with you again,*" Marianna said, hands on her hips to compliment the exasperated look on her face.

"We've discussed this before?" A sharp glare from Marianna made Bree stop with that train of thought. Joking around was not the way to go about this, but maybe whining would help Bree win the day. "It's so dumb, Mari! We already have a job to do!"

"It's important to have an education, Bree. Attending classes sharpen the mind and–"

"Oh god can we not? Please?" Bree ducked her head back under the covers, determined to stay in bed for the entire day. All she had to do was invoke her childhood logic of *if I can't see it, it's not there.*

Unfortunately, Marianna had other plans. She reached down and yanked the blanket away. "I said get…" then Marianna's voice trailed off, her eyes widening at the sight in front of her. "W-why are you naked?!"

"Because I sleep naked," Bree said, as if reporting the weather to her stuttering friend.

"Why?!"

"Because I like being naked! You *know* that!"

Marianna let the blanket fall out of her hands as she shouted, "But other people live here!"

Bree sat up and looked Marianna dead in the eye, more than ready to have a debate about her sleeping preferences. "This is my room! I can be naked in my room if I want! You're the one who came in here uninvited!"

Marianna turned away from Bree, not just over the nudity, but over the fact that she was right. She *did* come into her space uninvited, but she wasn't about to give her the satisfaction of winning an argument. "J-just put some clothes on so we can go," Marianna said as she headed for the door. "And think about other people's feelings in the future!"

"Oh trust me, I will. If I invite a boy or girl to my room they'll probably be naked, too."

"Damnit Bree!"

Bree chuckled to herself as she stretched her arms above her head. She still thought being up this early was borderline offensive, but Marianna's cute, flustered, chubby cheeks made it worth it.

There was a certain kind of comfort in her textbook. The pages, when stacked together with the smooth and glossy cover, made for a decent pillow.

"Bree," Marianna quietly nudged her friend with her elbow. "Bree, wake up."

Bree lifted her head to make another groggy attempt at listening to their professor. Some kind of Math? Letters and numbers? Didn't she learn this back in high school? Why was this her required course instead of something useful like *How to Win at Unfair Video Games*? Bree glanced over at Marianna and gave her a sleepy glare. Of course she was solving every equation that had been written on the board. Of course she didn't feel the need to complain about taking early morning Math classes when her career goals had nothing to do with x and y equaling some arbitrary number.

And of course, she was nudging her again when she started to drift off. "Don't you dare fall asleep again," Marianna whispered.

"I'm trying," Bree whispered back, but she was already laying her head back on her makeshift pillow again. Wasn't getting out of bed and throwing together an outfit enough? Granted, she'd gotten the jeans from off the floor and the shirt from her laundry basket, but it was still an honest to goodness effort. Did she have to stay awake, too?

"Try. Harder."

Bree yawned in response, which earned her another sharp nudge in her side to get her to finally sit up straight. "Fine, fine! I'm awake!" She whispered harshly.

"Good."

Bree let out her best overdramatic sigh as she focused on their professor. She imagined that, outside of class, the man was probably fun to be around. His attempt to look professional was earnest, but not too successful. His tennis shoes were scruffy with the laces untied and his shirt looked like it was scared of the iron. The best part, however, was the muscled, founding fathers tie around his neck. Either their professor had an amazing sense of humor, or he was trying to seem quirkily charming to his students. Had Bree not spent the night doing magical things and gaming she would've appreciated it more. In fact, she'd be sneaking a picture to post online.

"Bree!"

Bree shot up and quickly turned to look at Marianna, surprised that the girl had been willing to yell her name. Wouldn't she be worried about disrupting class? "Huh? Wha-?"

"Get up. Class is over," Marianna said as she stood from her seat.

Bree looked around to see that, yes, lecture had ended and the students were filing out of the classroom. Had she fallen asleep again? She couldn't even remember doing it this time. "How long was I asleep?"

"You shouldn't have been asleep at all!"

"Look, I can't help it, all right? Seriously, lectures this early shouldn't be allowed," Bree said as she grabbed her pillow-book.

"It's 10 o'clock in the morning!"

"Well yeah, it is now. Lecture started at 9, which is entirely too early."

"You realize normal work days start at 9, right?"

Bree shrugged as she stood up, letting out a loud yawn for good measure. "Good thing I'm not normal."

There was the sound of laughter behind them, an almost sultry sound that drew Bree in like a gamer girl to a midnight launch. She turned to see a tall, light skinned girl with black hair decorated in streaks of blue. Pink, yellow, and blue stars dangled from her ears and she smiled a blue lipsticked smile at Bree. She was wearing a loose shirt with cosmic leggings that made her legs look otherworldly.

Bree suddenly wondered what she'd been missing out on by sleeping through lecture.

"I like the way you think," the girl said to Bree. "Required classes are the worst, especially this early."

All Bree could do was smile and nod in agreement. She wanted to say something but her brain sputtered like a malfunctioning robot, as if pretty girls did not compute. Fortunately – or unfortunately – Marianna was there, and she grabbed onto Bree's arm and said, "We should get going."

Those words snapped Bree back to life. "What? Going? But..." she was busy not-talking to the pretty girl!

"We have to get to our next class."

"But–" And that was it. Marianna was pulling Bree away, the girl of her short-lived dreams smiling and waving to the both of them. Bree hadn't been able to talk much before, but once the two were outside the room the words came easily. "Oh my god, Marianna!"

"What, no *Mari* this time?"

Bree glared at her. "You don't deserve a cute nickname right now. I was in the middle of a conversation!"

"No you weren't."

For such a cute girl Marianna could be harsh when she put her mind to it. "Aren't you supposed to be the sweet one in our magical girl circle?" Bree asked.

"It's not a circle. There are only two of us."

"Stop with your analytical-"

"And do not talk about you know what while we're in public." Marianna kept her voice down as she nodded toward the students walking past them. It'd be easy for anyone to eavesdrop on a conversation in the middle of the hallway.

"My point still stands! I was in the middle of… **something**… with that girl!"

"We don't have time for this, Bree. We have to get to our next class."

"Next class? You mean yet another basic course you won't remember next semester?"

If there were a reset button, Bree would've hit it in that very moment. It wasn't that Marianna looked upset or angry, no, nothing like that. Instead, she was smirking a dangerous little smirk that let Bree know just how much trouble she was about to be in. "I wonder what Blaze is going to think about you falling asleep in class." And there it was. The not-so-subtle threat of bringing in the woman they reported to. Marianna only resorted to this tactic when she wanted a discussion with Bree to come to an end. She could've used this statement when Bree had fallen asleep the first time, but no, she was saving it for this very moment.

"You wouldn't…"

Marianna's lectures were one thing, but Blaze had perfected the fine art of the disappointed black mom frown. As much as Bree liked to push all the metaphorical buttons, she didn't actually want to upset the woman who'd turned her into a full-fledged superheroine. They'd had a time management talk before – ok, *multiple times* before – and Bree swore that she'd be able to keep up with the demands of being her normal, and magical, self. And she *could*, and *did*… most of the time.

Seriously, who thought Math was the subject to tackle early in the morning!?

Marianna shrugged her shoulders. "I dunno, I might," then she stepped outside the building to start the walk across campus to their next class.

"I hate you!" Bree clenched her fists and shouted the words as loud as she could. She hoped that Marianna would somehow hear them even if she was long gone.

Two lectures, a lunch break, and another 101 class later, the girls were finished with their day. Bree wondered why their class structure was so similar to what it had been in high school. When would they be able to have the legendary schedule of only having classes two days a week? That cute girl from earlier had been right: required classes were the worst.

It was that awkward time of year where summer had ended but autumn couldn't decide between being too warm or too cold. It wasn't tank top and shorts weather – depending on who you asked – but it wasn't time to bust out the thick jackets and gloves, either. For now, the student body enjoyed tossing Frisbees in the grassy parts of campus, wearing open-toed shoes until the weather shifted to early sunsets and frost on car windows.

Now that the day was done Marianna and Bree headed to what served as their home base. Unlike many first year students, this required going off campus instead of residing in a dormitory where Ramen noodles were treated like a fine dining experience. Campus stopped at the giant stadium in the middle of downtown, but it still made its presence known with buses sporting the college colors and the occasional storefront supporting their football team. It took two buses to get them out of school mascot territory, and soon they were riding past nightclubs and restaurants that were only affordable with the help of Groupon. Bus number three brought them into the last leg of the trip as it ventured through the business district. Traffic was unforgiving as the city's 9 to 5 crowd made the trek home to discard the corporate world's suit and tie dress code. Bree settled for checking her phone and muttering about more unnecessary trips. They'd be home by now if they didn't bother going to class in the first place. Marianna didn't bother responding, but there was a hint of an amused smile on her face. Bree was, if nothing else, persistent with her opinions, and said opinions were entertaining in the afternoon versus hearing them first thing in the morning.

After trudging through traffic the bus dropped the ladies off at the very last stop. It wasn't a dangerous part of town to walk through, but it still put the two girls on edge. Something about the area felt off, like an unfinished thought at the tip of someone's tongue. The closer they got to their building, the quieter the city became. The few buildings they passed were struggling shops and foreclosed businesses whose For Sale signs had been put up in vain. The occasional person they'd walk past was going in the opposite direction, away from what felt like a ghost town to join the rest of civilization. Once they reached their destination there was no one to be found. The entire building was left to stand like a quiet relic that had been left behind by the rest of the city.

"I don't think I'll ever get used to this," Bree said.

"She's doing it on purpose, to make sure no one knows that we're here."

"Isn't that a bit… unsettling?"

"Which part? The quiet? Or her having enough power to ward off this area?"

"…both."

"We have a lot of power, too," Marianna said as she walked up to the door and pressed her hand against it. The beads in her bracelet shimmered as a purple light surrounded her fingers, the door slowly sliding open for her.

"Yeah… not sure if we have enough to quarantine a building," Bree muttered as she followed Marianna inside.

The bleakness of the outside was nothing compared to the inside. It had been an office building once upon a time. The furnishings were still intact, from the couches in the front lobby, to the fake plants by the elevator. The colors were all muted and dull, making the girls feel like they were walking through a black and white painting where the only bits of color were their own clothes and skin. There was history here, they could feel it, but Blaze had deemed their curiosity over the building as nothing to worry about.

Bree, of course, had felt that it was cause for, at the very least, a bit of experimentation. What was the point of having a mysterious command center if you didn't test its limits? So she walked over to one of the plants and knocked it over by giving it a swift kick. "See?"

"See what?"

Bree pointed to the fake, potted greenery and asked, "Why can we hear our voices but nothing else?"

Instead of answering the question, Marianna countered with another question. "Do you have to do this all the time?" It was an ongoing conversation between the two girls: the silent void of the office building they called home. For a moment Marianna wondered if this was how Bree felt whenever she was getting yet another lecture.

Bree sat down in one of the office chairs and used her feet to push herself across the floor. "I've done this numerous times and it never, ever makes any noise. No wheels sliding across the floor. No squeak from the chair. Nothing."

"Bree…"

"You won't let me ask her about it anymore, so I have to figure this whole thing out myself."

"We already know she's doing it so people won't know that we're here."

"Yes, but *how* is she able to do this?"

"Same way you can create pixels with the palms of your hand," Marianna pointed out. "Same way this bracelet around my wrist transforms me into a purple haired magical girl."

"Her name is *Golden Blaze*, not *Golden Void Creator*. And why this particular building? Why not a house or something like that?"

Marianna shrugged as she pushed the button to the elevator. "And here I thought you'd be the one pointing out how all heroes have a secret hideout…"

Bree stood up from the chair to walk over to Marianna as the elevator doors opened. "They do, but there's always an explanation to them. Discovering the secrets of this one keeps me motivated."

"Uh huh. So the arcade center where talking cats guide five planetary defenders of love and justice makes sense?"

Bree chuckled and said, "That's just a normal day in Japan, Mari, but I'm glad you remembered one of my fandoms."

"You have an answer for everything, huh?"

"Almost everything," then Bree turned and gestured toward the office.

"You could at least put the chair back and pick the plant up."

"Why bother? You know they'll be back in place when we come through here again."

Marianna stepped onto the elevator with Bree and let the doors slide shut. Instead of hitting the button to the top floor, she pressed the button to open the elevator doors again. Just as Bree had predicated, the plant and the office chair were back in their original positions. "I never

said it wasn't odd," Marianna pointed out to her friend. "I just trust Blaze, that's all."

The elevator brought them to the top floor of the building. Blaze was sitting in a chair, dressed in a simple white shirt with a long, orange skirt that flowed over her legs like water. While the other floors in the building were lifeless and void of color – beyond their own living quarters on the floor below – the top floor felt like they were walking into a private solar system. The walls were made up of galactic skies and bright stars that twinkled around them, with Blaze settled in the center of it all like a supreme sorceress waiting for her students to arrive. Despite Blaze contacting them via a television screen whenever the city was in need of a good saving, there were no signs of any equipment. There was no sign of any doors that could lead to a bedroom, or space for a kitchen or any kind of living arrangements. Bree had once asked where the woman slept and was met with a playful smirk and a nod to the right. Had that meant that there was a door, somewhere, in the middle of what felt like outer space? Or did their leader sleep among the stars?

Did their leader sleep at all?

"Good afternoon, girls."

"Good afternoon, Blaze," both girls said in unison.

Blaze smiled at both of them. Despite her intimidating appearance, it only took one smile to make the girls feel welcome in her presence. "First of all, good job stopping that creature last night."

"Thank you, ma'am." Marianna was the first to speak up, always happy to receive praise from Blaze.

Blaze let out a frustrated sigh. "Marianna, how many times have I told you that ma'am isn't necessary?"

"Nine hundred and ninety nine," Bree said as if she'd actually been keeping count. "I'm pretty sure you'll hit a thousand soon."

GOLDEN BLAZE'S CHAMBERS
Ann Uland • www.annulandart.com

"It hasn't been that many!" Marianna snapped at Bree, then she turned to Blaze and said, "Sorry for my outburst, ma'am-... I-I mean Blaze!"

"See? A thousand. Told you."

"Just for that I'm telling her that you fell asleep in class."

Blaze raised an eyebrow at Bree. "Oh? Did you now?"

"Oops? You heard that?" Marianna asked. "I'm sorry, I didn't mean to say it out loud."

It was amazing, Bree thought, how bitchy Marianna could be when she put her mind to it. The cute smiles and penchant for baking sweets were a clever disguise, though. "All right, I fell asleep in class," Bree said. "But! We were up really late last night defending the city!"

"Hm. Did Marianna fall asleep in class, too?" Not only did Blaze rock the patented black mom frown, but she came equipped with black mom questions.

"Nope, she sure didn't," Marianna said with a smug little smile on her face.

"It was pretty late, though," Bree muttered. "These creatures don't consider the life of a college student when they attack." Not that they had any idea what these creatures were or where they came from. That'd be much too easy. "Do we reeeeeally need to take classes while we're fighting them?"

"Yes. And this is why you girls need to budget your time properly. You have to balance the work with the fun. Emphasis on the word *balance*."

Of course Blaze knew that Bree had stayed up playing video games. That wasn't a magical thing, that was a black woman thing. "I mean... i-it's technically work..."

"Oh, that whole YouTube thing?" They'd had this conversation before, too, but it was still a concept that Blaze couldn't quite wrap her head around.

"There's actually a lot of work that goes into it."

Bree wasn't expecting Marianna to defend her. Hadn't she been giving her a hard time? "Mari…"

"It's true. You put a lot of work into your channel… you just have to know when to stop so you can focus on other important things."

"Says the one who has a part-time job on top of everything else."

"Yes. *Part-time.* It's not the primary focus of my day."

"That wasn't always the case," Blaze said with a knowing smile. "You used to work more hours at the bakery than you do now."

"You did?"

"Blaze!" Marianna let out a loud whine of her name. There was no time for polite mannerisms when she was about to be thoroughly embarrassed. "Don't tell her that!"

"Oh no, please, tell me." Bree was aching to find a hint of imperfection in Marianna.

Sadly, Blaze wasn't taking the bait. "The point is you have to learn how to balance everything… but I do understand that it's a hard lesson to learn. It took us a while to figure it out, too." There was a sweet smile on Blaze's face now as the stars above twinkled and swirled together, forming several constellations in the shape of different women. Both Marianna and Bree knew who she was referring to: the previous members of **magnifiquenoir.** Blaze had been part of a team several years ago, before Marianna and Bree were even born. She didn't talk about them much, but when she did, it was always with the utmost respect.

The upside of having a leader with past magical girl experience was the wealth of knowledge she had. She could relate to them on the cool, yet bizarre, feeling of doing things that defied all logic. Transformations, monstrous battles, jumping out of windows and landing perfectly on your feet – Blaze had done the dance before and could relate to the two of them. Unfortunately, that was also the downside of having Blaze as their guide. Bree wouldn't be able to get any sympathy points from someone who'd successfully juggled a normal life with an abnormal existence... but she could at least try, right? "So you know it's difficult to do, right? Because it took you awhile to get a handle on it."

"Yes, but I *did* learn. We all did." A thoughtful look crossed Blaze's face as she crossed her arms at her chest and said, "Of course, if it proves to be too difficult..."

Bree interrupted her with an enthusiastic cry of, "No no no! I can do it! I can stay awake in class and balance all of the things!" Damn that *I gave you this thing and I can take it away* trump card.

Blaze nodded her head, satisfied with Bree's answer. "Good."

"But can I at least have my midnight launches?"

"Bree!"

The good news of the following morning was that there hadn't been another attack that night. This gave Bree plenty of time to record for her channel and get a decent night's sleep. She'd even managed to beat the pesky level she'd been stuck on after only five tries.

The bad news was that there had been yet another difficult level in Bree's soon-to-be least favorite video game. She knew she shouldn't have clicked on it, but she'd had so much extra time that she figured she could, at least, take a peek at it. The level had lured her into a false sense of security with checkpoints and power ups, but the tricky jumps and impossible bosses led to almost sixty tries and plenty of swearing. Eventually, she'd managed to beat the level, but her triumph happened at around 3 in the morning. Now she was sitting in class, yawning loud enough to make tears sting the corners of her eyes.

"Did you learn nothing from yesterday?" Marianna asked. There was a biting edge to her voice, one that let Bree know that she was much angrier today than she had been yesterday. It didn't help that Bree had let out a loud, victorious shriek when she finally conquered the level.

Marianna was not a friendly person at 3 in the morning. Bree learned that the hard way when the girl stormed into her room and demanded that she take her ass to bed!

"I learned a lot yesterday," Bree said with another loud yawn. "But, in my defense, that level had way too many-"

"I don't care."

"But-"

"I really don't care." Normally, Marianna would attempt to have some patience with her friend, but losing out on sleep when she had to work later on that afternoon was beyond irritating.

"Oh. Well if you don't care, I'm sleeping."

That did the trick. "What?"

"If you don't care, I'm going to take a nap."

"That is **not** what I meant at **all**!"

This sent Marianna into a long series of rants about responsibility, priorities, and other words that Bree had become accustomed to hearing. Just as Marianna began to demand that Bree listen to her, the smell of freshly brewed coffee interrupted their one-sided argument. "It's dangerous to lecture alone. Take this."

Bree knew that voice. She'd been not-so-secretly thinking about it all day yesterday – well, almost all day, since she had to spend part of the day dealing with Marianna tattling about her classroom naptime. She looked up to see the cute girl from yesterday, dressed in bright colors and a pair of shorts that showed off legs that went on for days. Bless the autumn gods and goddesses for fluctuating weather and the occasional warm day.

"I-..." but just like yesterday, Bree couldn't form any coherent sentences.

The girl took pity on her and spoke again. "I'm Kayla. You fell asleep in class yesterday so I thought I'd bring you some coffee," then she winked and added, "Gotta help out a cute girl in distress, you know? And you're as cute as they come."

"Ah… u-um… uh huh…"

After a moment of uncomfortable silence Marianna decided to do her friend a solid and speak up for her. "She's Bree, and I'm Marianna. Nice to meet you."

"Nice to meet you, too," then Kayla walked off to go to her desk.

"Well that was nice of her, to bring you coffee." When Bree didn't say anything Marianna poked her in her arm. "Hey. Bree? She's gone, you can talk now-"

"OMG! I am so awake right now!"

Marianna didn't have the heart to tell her friend that Kayla probably heard that excited outburst over her presence, so she settled on saying, "Well, that's good."

"In fact, I'm gonna be awake in class from now on."

Marianna smiled. "Even better. I'm glad you're so set on focusing on your studies."

"Studies. Yeah. Right," Bree said, her eyes lingering on Kayla. The blue in her hair was such a bold color and went perfectly with her jet black curls and the shaved sides of her head. She hadn't noticed yesterday, but she had piercings on the side of her lips, adding to her edgy look.

"Bree… that isn't why you should be staying awake. You should be staying awake because-"

"She was flirting with me, right? I mean she called me cute. She brought me coffee. She even made a classic video game reference. That's a sign, right?"

"We can talk about this later. Right now-"

"Man Mari, you were right. School is so important!"

Marianna let out a deep sigh. She could feel a headache coming on but she had a feeling it wouldn't go away with two aspirin. With Bree practically bouncing in her seat, Marianna knew that this was a headache she'd be dealing with for a long while.

At least the nickname had returned? That was something, she guessed.

EPISODE THREE:

PROPER STORYTELLING

When Marianna was little, she heard someone say that baking was like science. She hadn't understood what that meant back then. Bakers didn't work in a laboratory surrounded in chemical vials like the lab-coated men and women in the movies. Science was for the kids who asked for microscopes for Christmas and conducted experiments with kits that made various forms of slime. Now that she was older and taking the necessary steps to turn her sprinkle and whipped cream dreams into a reality, she finally understood. Combining the right amount of ingredients, cooking them at the right temperature for just the right amount of time, and constantly tweaking them to her liking? Yes, Marianna was definitely a chemist in a purple polka-dotted apron.

"Mari!!!"

And like any good chemist, there were always outside variables to take into account. The Bree equation had become a constant in her life, one she could handle without even having to look up from her mixing bowl. "Yes, Bree?"

"I just came to see what you were up to..."

Step one in the Bree equation: pretend like you came over for no reason. Marianna chuckled to herself as she continued to stir the ingredients in her bowl.

"What was that for?"

"Hm?"

"That laugh."

"Oh. Nothing," Marianna said as she reached over and added a pinch of sugar to the bowl. Maybe two pinches was the way to go? Marianna quietly contemplated this and-

"Why do you always think the worst of me?"

Step two in the Bree equation: the guilt trip. Marianna looked up at her friend and smiled. "I don't, I just know you."

"I don't ask you favors that often... do I?"

"No, you just ask in the same way. *I don't want anything... ok actually I dooooo.*"

"Hm. I should change my approach."

Marianna giggled as she stopped stirring her now creamy batter. Bree had made a similar comment the last time she'd asked for a favor. "How about this. When you ask me for a favor, you have to do something for me."

"Oh? Like what?"

Marianna nodded over to the drawer and said, "Grab a tasting spoon and tell me how this tastes."

Bree was more than happy to oblige. "It's about that girl from the other day," she said as she grabbed a spoon, walked back over, and dipped it into the bowl. "What are you making?"

"Cheesecake," Marianna said. "Is it sweet enough?"

"Mmmm..."

"Is that an actual answer?" Marianna laughed as she watched Bree completely clean off her spoon with her tongue. Before she could reach over for another taste, Marianna moved the bowl out of the way and shook her head. "I've told you about double dipping, Bree."

"Awwwww, come on! It's just us, it's not like you're at work!"

"Still no," Mariana said as she set the bowl away from Bree. "Besides, you get one taste, otherwise you'd eat the whole bowl."

Bree gave Marianna her very best pout, then it immediately turned into a sour frown when Marianna didn't budge. "You're so mean…"

"Should you be saying that to someone you're about to ask a favor of?"

"Oh! Right! So… the girl from the other day…"

"Kayla, right?"

Bree nodded as she continued. "Well I was thinking of maybe bringing her something, you know, since she brought me coffee?"

"And how do I factor into this?"

"Weeeeell… I thought cupcakes would be amazing!"

Marianna raised an eyebrow at Bree as she reached step three in the equation: the outlandish favor. Granted, this wasn't as odd as being asked to make cupcakes for the staff of Bree's favorite video game store during a midnight launch. At least it wouldn't require color coded frosting based on various balls used to catch all the poke-creatures. Right? "You want me to make cupcakes for your potential girlfriend?"

Bree practically exploded into tiny little hearts at the word *girlfriend*. "I'll help!"

"You could just bring her a slice of cheesecake tomorrow," Marianna said as she poured the batter onto the graham cracker crust. "This will be done in plenty of time."

"I mean I guess, but… I dunno if she's cheesecake worthy yet…"

"Cheesecake… worthy?"

"Cheesecake is a huge step in a relationship," Bree said as she pointed her spoon at Marianna. "Especially homemade, fresh baked cheesecake."

Marianna didn't claim to be an expert in relationships, but this was a new one. "How is cheesecake a huge step?"

"Well, I mean… you can get cupcakes anywhere, but good cheese-cake takes effort."

"So cupcakes don't take effort?"

"No, they do! Just not *as much* effort."

"Uh huh." Marianna had a feeling this relationship rule had been made up on the spot. "It sounds like you're looking for an excuse to be selfish and keep the cheesecake for yourself."

"I'm just not ready to share your cheesecake yet! But cupcakes… cupcakes are fine."

Marianna smiled. "All right, I'll make you cupcakes, but it'll be to-morrow morning at the bakery before class starts. I've gotta get some things prepped for the shop."

"…isn't that… really early?"

"At least I'm not making you go with me. Just meet me there around seven then we can go to class together."

Normally, Bree would protest. Getting to the bakery required a dif-ferent bus route than the one that went to campus, then they'd have to wait for the right combination of buses to get them to lecture on time. However, since Marianna was willing to do her a favor, Bree smiled and said, "Thank you. Besides, I figured you'd be good at the *baking for a crush* thing."

"Huh?" Marianna looked up from where she was putting the cheesecake into the oven. "What do you mean?"

"Don't be modest, Mari. I'm sure you've made plenty of cupcakes for boys… or girls, depending on your preferences," Bree said with a wide grin similar to a strange, striped cat.

"Not really…"

"Did someone make them for you, then? Oh! Maybe a high school romance in Home Ec?"

"You're mentally writing the fanfic, aren't you?" Marianna asked as she set the timer. While many women of color had perfected the fine art of not needing timers, baked cheesecake was a finicky thing that needed proper maintenance.

"Maaaaaybe," Bree said, bouncing in her seat. "Come on, you never talk about crushes or anything like that."

"I haven't really had any."

"What?!"

"That is possible, you know," Marianna said defensively. "It's not *that* odd."

"I didn't mean it like that…" Bree stood up and began to grab the dishes that had been used to make the cheesecake, helping Marianna bring them to the sink. "Just… no one? Really?"

Marianna shrugged her shoulders as she began to put the dishes in the dishwasher. "… it is odd, isn't it? Girls my age are dating all the time, right?"

There was a tightness in Marianna's voice when she said the word *odd*. It was obvious she'd had this conversation before, probably before magical girls, part-time jobs, and college lectures. Bree didn't have all the details to Marianna's life before they became a two-person team, but she knew how it felt to be labeled as *odd*. So she smiled, clasped her hand on Marianna's shoulder, and said, "Naw, besides, I have enough crushes for both of us."

"…you're counting fictional ones in that, aren't you?"

"Yep!"

Marianna gave Bree a quiet smile as her friend grabbed the dish detergent. As she watched Bree start the machine she decided that making cupcakes for her crush was fine because she didn't want her sharing cheesecake with anyone else, either.

"Should I just give it to her?"

"You're asking the wrong person," Marianna said with a tired yawn. In retrospect, having Bree meet her at the bakery hadn't been the best idea. Bree had actually shown up earlier than expected. At six in the morning she had been knocking on the door, wide awake and full of nervous energy as she asked about the status of her cupcakes while simultaneously questioning her outfit of choice. She'd toned down the geeky flare, having decided to not overwhelm Kayla with anime girls and video games. Upon closer inspection, Marianna had sworn that she'd seen a certain defender of love and justice wear a similar striped shirt and pink skirt combo. Marianna had wanted to point out that Kayla probably wouldn't care about her geeky stylings – obvious or subtle – but she feared that Bree would run back home and bring her entire closet back with her.

To Marianna's relief, Bree couldn't debate the flawless execution of the cupcake. Instead of making a tiny arrangement of treats, Marianna had made one large, well-decorated masterpiece, complete with frosting and cute heart-shaped sprinkles.

"Mariiiiii!" Ah, extra i's for a more impactful whine. "You have to help me!"

"I did help. I made the cupcake."

"I need more help than that!"

"Well you have about ten more seconds to decide," Marianna pointed out. Class had ended, and Kayla was gathering her books.

"Damnit damnit damnit damnit-"

"Excuse me!" Marianna stood from her seat and waved Kayla over. "Kayla, right?"

"No no no no no-"

Marianna ignored Bree's pleas as she continued to wave to Kayla. As the leader of their magical duo – because a group implied more than two – Marianna had to often make the tough decisions... like embarrassing her friend as her crush walked over to the both of them.

"Good morning, Marianna," then Kayla graced Bree with a bright smile. "Good morning, Bree."

"Morning. Um… here!"

Kayla blinked in surprise as the cupcake was shoved into her unsuspecting hands. At least it was in a container. "Oh wow, this looks good! Is this for me?"

Bree nodded. "You know… because of the coffee…"

"That's sweet of you but it was just a cup of coffee. That's not really an equal exchange…"

Bree's eyes lit up at those words. Was she making an anime reference? Every anime fan knew all about the Elric brothers and the law of equal exchange and… no, no that probably wasn't it. It was probably her way of saying that the cupcake had been too much. "Should I not have brought a cupcake? Do you not like cupcakes? I can bring you something else!"

Marianna shot Bree a look. Had she forgotten that she wasn't the one who made the cupcake? Desserts didn't appear out of thin air.

Sometimes.

"No no, I definitely want it," Kayla said, quickly reassuring Bree that the cupcake was fine. "I'll eat it, for sure."

"Good! You should! Mari makes really good desserts."

"Mari?" Kayla asked.

"Oh, it's just a nickname," Marianna said. "Bree does that sometimes."

"I see… so… you made this?" Kayla asked as she looked down at the cupcake then back up at Marianna.

Marianna smiled and nodded her head. "Bree wanted to bring you something that she thought you'd like."

"Ah… I hope it wasn't much trouble."

"No trouble at all," then Marianna added, "I'll wait outside so you two can talk."

Bree's eyes widened. Outside meant… *outside* – a location that was not here in the classroom. "Wait, outside? As in… not here?"

"Yep," then Marianna leaned in and whispered to Bree, "You'll be fine."

"You can't prove that," Bree whispered back, but Marianna smiled that annoying smile of hers and walked off. Some magical girl leader she was. Didn't she realize that Bree couldn't do this on her own? After a nervous chuckle, Bree tried to come up with something to say. For someone who ran a YouTube channel where she rambled about video games, some kind of dialogue should've come naturally to her. Instead, all she could do was smile and hope that Kayla would say something.

Finally, Kayla did speak up, and asked, "So… how long have you two been together?"

Bree, in her frazzled glory, didn't realize the implications of the question. "A couple of months," she said. "But it feels like it's been forever, you know?" And she meant that in the best – and worst – way possible. She valued her friendship with Marianna, but sometimes she was so… *Marianna*.

"Ah, one of those relationships, huh?"

"To be fair, we did meet in a rather unconventional way."

"Oh?"

It was here that Bree realized that in her flustered state, she may have said too much. Maybe this was why Marianna always lectured her about revealing too much about their magical secret. "Well… she kinda saved me."

"What?"

"From a creeper," Bree said. "Some pushy guy who wouldn't take no for an answer," and that was the truth.

For the most part.

FLASHBACK

In typical fashion, it decided to rain as soon as Bree hopped off the bus. She'd hoped that it'd have the decency to wait until she got back to her dormitory, but luck wasn't on her side that evening. The city was proving to be most unkind to its newest resident. Granted, the city had many new residents in the new school year, but Bree had traveled two whole hours from home to attend college here. She'd decided to follow in her older brother's footsteps – if, by *follow*, you meant *make her mother stop hounding her*. Bree wasn't the type who believed the televised hype of college. To her, it was an over-glorified high school, but her mother had insisted that she continue her education. It wasn't like Bree lacked intelligence, she just wasn't interested in pursuing extended versions of the lessons she'd learned in high school. If she had to label where her passions lay, she supposed the easiest word would be "Entertainment." It definitely sounded better than "YouTuber" "Internet Celebrity" or "Cute Black Girl who Likes to Play Video Games and Bitch about Their Difficulty Online."

To think, her mother believed in praying to a magic man in the sky, but not playing video games for a living.

Bree supposed that was one perk to moving away from home. It wasn't that she had a problem with religion, but there was something to be said about her mother's *over-religion* – especially when it came to Bree. Big brother Trey had been spared from any warnings about the world, but Bree? Oh no, she had been told time and time again not to fall into any nefarious temptations now that she was out on her own. Bree didn't need scripture to know that her mother meant sex. Of course, Trey had had plenty of partners before, during, and after college. Meanwhile Bree had been labeled as *fast* for even mentioning a cute boy. She knew the double standard wasn't solely religion based. Her mother had been young once upon a time and had been in two different relationships with two different men who'd decided that pregnancy was something worth abandoning. That being said, people's various interpretations of "The Good Book" certainly didn't help. Neither did the gossipy women of her mother's church – praise them, Amen.

If only they knew Bree wasn't only attracted to the opposite sex. Another perk of being away from home: she could further explore the whole *sexuality* thing.

Bree sighed as she continued her unwanted walk in the rain. Her hair would regret it later, but she was, if nothing else, stubborn. She wasn't about to run the few blocks it took to get back to her dorm room, nor was she going to wait until the rain stopped. Had her mom been here, she could've called her for a ride home. Bree frowned to herself as that thought crossed her mind. Hadn't she just been thankful for being off on her own? Was she really missing her overbearing mother over something as basic as bad weather? It was true, though. Her mother would've stopped what she was doing to pick her up. Meanwhile, Trey lived in the same city as Bree and she knew he'd refuse to interrupt his Saturday night because of a little bit of rain. In fact, he'd call her a brat for even wasting his time on something so trivial.

So Bree resigned herself to her wet walk.

Despite the pounding of the rain and the sound of students frantically running to their destinations, Bree swore she heard footsteps splashing directly behind her. She shook her head and mentally chided herself for being paranoid. Of course she heard footsteps, there were people trekking through the rain. But Bree couldn't shake the uncomfortable feeling that crept up the back of her neck. The steps were a bit too close for comfort. It wouldn't hurt to look back, right? Then she could laugh it off and keep walking. So Bree glanced over her shoulder and-

"Hey baby girl."

All she had wanted was to have an uneventful, dry walk home, but the universe decided that she had to deal with some unwanted company. Not just any ol' unwanted company, oh no, it had to be a random man on a self-appointed side quest where he mistook *stalking a young woman* as a charming character trait. If Bree had to guess, she'd say that the man was old enough to be her father – whoever or wherever he was. This fully grown man had no business making eye contact with an eighteen year old girl's chest. Where was her mother now to condemn this man to hell? Then again, her mother would potentially blame this on her state of dress, as if she could stop the weather from forcing her into a wet T-shirt contest. "I'm not a toddler, sir."

"You know that ain't what I meant," he said as he stepped closer. "What's your name?"

"Unnamed protagonist," Bree muttered, hoping her dry humor would make him lose interest.

Unfortunately, it made him persist. "That ain't a name," he laughed.

"I don't have a name. My parents didn't bother entering one into the select screen."

The man's smile immediately faded, the amused look draining from his face. "I'm just tryin' to be nice, you don't have to be such a-"

"Bitch?"

The man snorted this time. "Y'all black girls are too much, sometimes. Y'all always gotta have an attitude."

"I guess so," then Bree turned and walked off.

"I ain't done with you yet!"

Bree rolled her eyes and kept walking. What a perfect way to end the evening. Not that she thought she'd gotten away from the creeps who referred to her as their baby. She knew that was a worldwide phenomenon, but did she have to face it now?

"I said I ain't done with you!"

Bree had become accustomed to being labeled as *unfriendly* or, in this case, a *bitch*, but it never went any further than that. Hearing the sound of someone running after her caught her completely off guard. She felt the man grab her and force her to turn and face him, his eyes wild and chapped lips curled in pure malice toward her. In seconds he had her on the ground, the back of her head crashing into a puddle on the sidewalk with a wet thud.

"W-what the hell are you doing?! Get off of me!" Maybe, if she screamed loud enough, someone would hear her. There had been people outside before, someone had to come to her aid.

Right?

Not patient enough to find out, Bree started to struggle against him, but he was faster and had her hands pinned above her head in seconds. "Stay still," he growled at her. His voice had a much rougher edge to it and Bree was about to chalk it up to pure rage, but then something peculiar happened.

His teeth shifted into sharp fangs.

She'd seen this kind of thing before in television series about teenage wolves, but such bizarre transformations were reserved for the world of fantasy and make believe. Men's eyes didn't glow in a blood red hue in real life. Men also didn't drool like rabid animals, the saliva dripping onto her cheek before it was washed away by the rain. Bree wanted to scream but she was too shocked to make any sound come out of her mouth.

The man – *creature?* – stood up, and with a sickening pop its hand was detached from its arm to keep her trembling wrists pinned down to the ground. The sight of fresh blood leaking out from where its hand should've been was what did it. Bree screamed, the sound combining with the sudden rush of thunder that rumbled above them.

"Shut. Up!" Then its other arm stretched forward, its hand clamping around Bree's mouth to muffle her cries. Its skin felt slimy against her lips and she could taste something sour on her tongue as she kept trying to scream. Bree could finally hear a few people, but they were making the situation worse with their terrified screams as they loudly proclaimed the obvious: there was some kind of ravenous creature attacking a girl in the middle of campus!!! All the monster had to do was look at them to send them all running, leaving Bree all alone with the looming threat.

In that moment, as her attacker looked down at her, many thoughts circulated through Bree's head. The first thought was one she shut down immediately: this never would've happened if she'd been nicer. Maybe she could've smiled more, or told the gentlemen her name. She wasn't about to blame herself for the horrible situation she was facing, even when the creature sneered at her and asked, "Bet you wish you would've been more agreeable, huh?"

The second thought she let linger: the danger her mother had warned her about. Granted, she was sure her mother hadn't meant that a literal monster would be leering at her right now. She was also sure that this wasn't the temptation that her mother had told her to resist.

The third, and final thought, was one that made the tears flow down her face.

She was about to die, and all she could do was shut her eyes and wait for the inevitable.

But the moment never came.

Bree slowly opened her eyes when she heard her would be killer stumble away from her. She was still being pinned down by its detached hand, but the other that had been covering her mouth was now frantically wiping something from its face. It was a fluffy, purple substance, and there was a sweet smell to it that reminded Bree of fresh baked goods.

"Why can't monsters like you take no for an answer?"

At most, Bree had hoped for some kind of law enforcement to show up and attempt to fight the creature. Whether or not their bullets would work was debatable, but if they were able to get her to safety that was all that mattered. Instead of men and women in uniform, Bree got a lone girl dressed in purple, white, black, and gray, complete with purple hair that sparkled like its own little galaxy.

Was this actually real life right now? The rain had even stopped in favor of letting this girl sparkle – literally *sparkle*!

"Who the hell are-" but before the monster could finish, something was thrown at its face again.

Were those... cupcakes?

Was she throwing cupcakes?!

While the creature was distracted, the young woman walked over to Bree and asked, "Are you all right?"

"I..." The short answer was *no*. The long answer was *hell no!* Bree hoped that her face conveyed her feelings on the situation because there was no time to explain her absolute fear and confusion. Being attacked by an inhuman creature was one thing, but being saved by a sparkly girl in purple?

"You fat bitch!"

The girl in purple smiled sweetly at the monster in front of her. Unrealistic situation or not, Bree had seen people smile like that after having insults hurled at them. This creature was twice the size of the girl in front of her, but that smile made one thing clear.

This creature was about to die. *Painfully.*

"What was that?" The girl asked, watching as her opponent got the last bit of frosting off of its face. There were nasty welts in its skin now due to the sweet, acidic frosting.

Acidic frosting? What?

"You heard me! No one told you to interfere!"

Bree swore that everything was moving in slow motion now. The girl in purple held out her hand, a bright, purple energy swirling between her fingers. The power came together and created what was, indeed, a cupcake. The girl giggled and threw it at the monster, the delicious treat smacking it dead in its face for the third time.

"I don't mean to criticize your technique, but I don't think that's doing anything," Bree said. Was she trying to throw enough cupcakes to melt its face off? That would take a long time, and Bree was sure that her assailant would retaliate eventually.

The girl smiled and knelt down beside her. She ran her finger across the detached hand that was keeping Bree pinned to the ground, that sweet smell perfuming the area around them. There was now frosting smeared over Bree's gruesome handcuffs, and soon, they melted away into clumps of skin and sugary cream.

"H-how did you-"

"I want you to get up and run."

"What?"

"Get up. And run. Now."

Bree wished she were brave enough to insist that she could help, but after the night she had, she had no problem with leaving. To think, she'd been so against running to her dorm before, but now she was running as fast as she could. Behind her, she could hear the girl shouting the words, "**CUPCAKE BOMB**," followed by a loud cry of anguish from the monster. There was a loud sound – an explosion, of all things – and the ground rumbled from the force of the attack. Bree stopped to look behind her, completely ignoring the girl's demands to get away from the scene. There was a purple cloud of smoke spreading across the sky and it made the area smell like a bakery first thing in the morning.

Did that... come from that girl?

Bree's anxiousness to leave was giving way to curiosity. Despite all of her movie marathon training where black folks never survived these situations, she was running back to the scene. The remains of her attacker were now scattered about the sidewalk, complete with frosting and colorful sprinkles. The frosting was dissolving the monster as if wiping away any evidence of there being a monster to begin with.

And there she stood. Her purple rescuer. Complete with high heels and sass as she asked, "Who's the fat bitch, now?"

CUPCAKE BOMB!
Jenn St-Onge Illustration • www.jennstonge.ca

END FLASHBACK

"You didn't actually tell her that story, did you?!"

"No, of course not! I told her the tl;dr version of it." When Marianna responded with a blank stare Bree elaborated her statement. "Too long; didn't read?"

"I know what it means," Marianna said as she slid a fresh tray of cookies into the display case.

Somewhere between the college campus and the hustle and bustle of downtown laid a somewhat trendy part of the city. The streets were lined with clothing shops, a handful of bookstores, and restaurants that specialized in various cuisines. One of those eateries was "Fabu-Cakes," a cute little bakery that filled the delicious dessert requirement for birthday parties, after dinner treats, and those moments when something sweet fixed all of life's problems.

The shop was owned by a large firecracker of a woman named Renee Green. Ms. Green was an older woman who was well past the point of caring about her gray hair. She was the type of woman who hummed and danced around her kitchen, her short hair bobbing along with her. She embodied everything Marianna wanted to be as a baker: a lovable woman who was damn talented in the kitchen. Marianna wore the store's chef jacket with pride, the name stitched into the corner pocket in an elegant font.

"I just told her you saved me from an old creep in the middle of a thunderstorm, that's all."

"Thunderstorm? What thunderstorm? It didn't even rain that day!"

"It didn't?"

Marianna rolled her eyes. "You know it didn't."

"Oh… well, that made it sound-"

"More exciting? I know. You always do that."

Bree put her hands on her hips and asked, "What's your problem with adding some spice to the story?"

"You mean besides the fact that it's a flat out lie?"

Bree's eyes widen and she pointed an accusing finger at Marianna. "Are you calling me a liar?!"

"Um… yeah."

"How dare you! I'm just a good storyteller, is all!"

"What are you two yellin' about?"

The two turned to see Ms. Green walking out of the backroom, armed with a tray of small, square-shaped cakes decorated in what she dubbed as her *famous* buttercream frosting.

"Bree and her wild stories," Marianna said.

"Oh, I got a bone to pick with you, young lady," Ms. Green said to Bree after she put the cakes in the display case.

"What did I do?!" The last thing Bree needed was for Marianna and her boss to double team her.

"You ain't tell me you had someone you liked!"

Oh, so that's what she was mad about. Bree could handle that. "It just happened, Ms. Green. I was gonna tell you."

Ms. Green was very much like an old grandmother who got excited at the prospect of relationships. Relationships could mean marriage, and marriage could mean grandbabies. Since Ms. Green didn't have any children of her own she zeroed in on Marianna and her friends.

"So? What's the boy's name?"

"Um… it's not a boy…" Bree muttered.

"A girl, then? Huh…" there was a thoughtful look on the older woman's face as she let the word *girl* circulate through her head. Girls could still grant her the gift of grandbabies. They could adopt an adorable baby girl who could be showered with grandmotherly love. "You know they say the way to a man's heart is through his stomach… but I ain't sure how that works for a woman."

"Ms. Green!" Marianna could barely contain her laughter while Bree settled for staring at the woman in shock. She was never sure what to expect from the older generation when it came to non-heterosexual romance.

"What? I ain't never tried to get a woman but I sure did get my Leonard with food!"

Marianna smiled. There was such fondness in the woman's voice when she spoke of her late husband. A couple that had been married for decades, Ms. Green had named the bakery after the nickname he'd given her *world famous cakes.*

Well… neighborhood famous, at least.

"Well I'm sure it works the same way," Bree said. "She gave me coffee and she was very happy to get the cupcake."

"That's good. Now if only a certain someone would bake cupcakes and get herself a man," then she quickly added, "Or woman. That's what you kids do now, right?"

"Pretty sure it was being done before…"

Ms. Green gave Bree a hard frown. "Don't sass me, young lady."

Bree rose her hands up in defense and took a step away from the counter. "Sorry."

"That's better. Now, about them cupcakes," then Ms. Green set her sights on Marianna. "Who you gonna make them for?"

Damn. And here Marianna thought she'd be spared from Ms. Green's dating advice with Bree there to deflect it. "I'm not interested in anyone, Ms. Green. I've told you that."

"What about that girl that comes by all the time?"

Bree's eyes lit up when she heard that. "There's a girl?"

"No," Marianna said. "She's talking about Dana."

"Oh, well that one is obvious, I thought you meant someone else."

"It's not *obvious*. She's just a friend," but Marianna didn't sound completely certain about it.

Both Bree and Ms. Green exchanged knowing looks. "Suuuuure she is," Ms. Green said before she turned and headed for the backroom. "I gotta grab some more stuff, you two behave yourselves."

"Yes Ms. Green," they said in unison. As soon as she was gone Marianna narrowed her eyes at Bree and said, "Don't encourage her wild ideas. It's bad enough you over exaggerate everything."

"How did you circle back to that?!"

Marianna ignored her question and continued. "You know, there's a much simpler story you could've told."

"Oh? Well enlighten me, then."

FLASHBACK

Marianna Jacobs was no stranger to facing huge dilemmas. As someone who used baked goods to defend truth, justice, and the almighty sweet tooth, she'd come across all sorts of... *interesting* situations.

But this was the biggest dilemma she'd faced all week.

In front of Marianna sat the new selection of bath bombs that she'd seen in the store's email last night. A silent battle went on in the back of her mind. She'd already gotten the pinstriped heels that had gone on sale so she knew she had no business buying anything else. But the various colors and scents were calling to her, and they were on sale for *This Weekend Only!*

"Just get them, Marianna!"

Dana Santiago, the world's biggest enabler, was already grabbing the bath bombs for her. Brown skinned with a face full of freckles, the girl lived in patterned clothing that shouldn't have worked well together, yet was perfect for her exuberant personality. The two had been friends since high school and were now roommates in college. It meant that Marianna had a never-ending supply of a girl who encouraged her to, quote, *treat herself*, unquote.

"Dana... I don't need them," she whispered to the girl.

"Hey now, we survived our first week of college, we can splurge on some bath products."

That was a good point.

Marianna and Dana were among the few students who lived in the extravagant condominiums on campus. Such was the perk of a full-ride scholarship and lightning fast fingers to secure a spot in the best student housing the college had to offer. The two girls' families only lived half an hour away, but they decided to live on campus instead of commuting everyday – much to Marianna's delight. If her mother had had her way, she'd be taking online courses and never leaving the house. With a luxurious place to call their own, it meant that there was actually a bathtub where Marianna could relax after a week of lectures, working at the bakery, and the awful monster battle two nights ago. She'd already spent enough on books, a few bath bombs wouldn't hurt, right? Especially ones that looked like cute desserts.

"If you don't get them I'm gonna get them for you."

"Dana..."

"Nope, I've made up my mind," then Dana walked up to the counter to make her purchase.

"Dana! I can buy my own bath stuff!"

"Let me spoil you a little bit." Dana smiled as she whipped out her credit card, holding it out like some kind of Holy Grail. "That's what I have this for."

"I'm pretty sure your parents gave you that for emergencies." The Santiago family was wealthy enough to live in a gated community full of large, dreamy houses, but Marianna had a feeling that they were trying to teach their daughter a lesson in responsibility.

"Oh relax," Dana said as she handed the card to the cashier. "If Carlos can use his card on video games, I can use mine on bath bombs."

Marianna chuckled to herself. Dana had perfected the art of throwing her twin brother under the bus. "You're hopeless."

"And you, my dear, are the proud owner of several bath bombs… and a few new soaps."

Soaps? Wait, what? "… when did you add soap to this?"

"They were sitting on the counter!" Dana pointed to the small basket by the register that had, once upon a time, had five decorative soaps in them. The cashier gave Marianna her best customer service smile, looking quite happy with Dana's impulse buy.

"I suppose it's required with the bath, right?"

"Now isn't it much better when you give into me?" Dana draped an arm around Marianna's shoulders and said, "Come on, let's go get something to eat."

"I'm at least paying for that."

"Nope!"

"Dana!"

"Nooooope!" Dana exaggerated the word to further make her point, then she left the store before Marianna could say anything else. Marianna let out the exasperated sigh of a friend who knew that there was no point in arguing. Dana had had eighteen years to perfect her flawless logic of *nooooope* – complete with a twin brother to practice it on.

"You two are so cute together." The comment came from the cashier, and Marianna just now noticed the rainbow earrings in her ears. It was a common misconception back in high school, one that resulted in whispered rumors and the occasional sneer. It was almost comforting to see someone smile at the possibility, even if it wasn't true.

"Mari! Let's go!" Dana yelled from the store entrance.

Marianna waved to the woman behind the counter, grabbed her bag, and met Dana outside. There wasn't a point to go into the *we're not dating* explanation she'd perfected in high school, not with a complete stranger, especially one who was so happy about seeing a queer couple in the store.

"Why are you smiling so much? I was right to get the soap after all, huh?"

"Huh? Oh… she thought we were together. She seemed really happy about it, actually."

"Awwwww, how cute! We probably made her day."

"What? How?"

Dana stopped walking and pointed to Marianna. "Cuz you're cute, and I'm *definitely* cute. People don't see enough cute girl couples debating the importance of bath bombs."

"OK…"

"Oh my god, Marianna, you're so adorable!"

"What?!"

"Not everyone is open about the whole queer thing, so seeing it casually out in the open is great for some people."

"Ah… but… we're not a couple," Marianna said.

Was that a hint of disappointment on Dana's face? Before Marianna could even attempt to ask, Dana was talking again. "Well no, but *she* doesn't know that, right?"

"I didn't see the point in telling her so-"

"Well there ya go!" Then Dana was walking again, heading for the mall directory so they could pick a place to eat.

It occurred to Marianna that this wasn't the first time they'd had a conversation like this. As always, Dana ended it with a smile and a mad dash away before Marianna could question the solemn look in her eyes. Marianna hadn't ever thought much about it, but with the two of them living together and spending more time together, it was becoming more noticeable. Though honestly, between college life and monster battles, would there ever be time to tackle the difference between friendship and everyone else's assumptions? It wasn't like Marianna was an expert on the subject, in fact, she hadn't ever been interested in the subject… and she wasn't sure if she ever would be. Was she really supposed to figure all of this out on top of syllabuses, lectures, and protecting the city? Jeez, that whole "no time for a life" superheroine trope was definitely ringing true.

"Hey, is that man watching that girl?"

Marianna pulled herself away from her wandering thoughts when she heard Dana whispering to her. Hadn't she been looking at the directory? When did she walk back over? "Huh?"

"Over there," then Dana nodded over toward the entrance of the mall's video game shop. Dressed in jeans and a wrinkled top, he didn't even attempt to hide the fact that he was gleefully watching a young woman as she walked through the store.

"I know her. She's in one of my classes." Marianna hadn't actually talked to the girl before, but she recognized her from her geek-themed clothing and high, poofy ponytail. Marianna watched as the man decided to make a move and step into the store. He approached the girl as she read the back of one of the game boxes and stood uncomfortably close to her. "Ugh, that poor girl."

"Let's help her."

"Huh?"

"Let's help her," then Dana walked toward the store, shopping bags in hand from her outing with Marianna, as if she was about to use them as weapons.

"Dana!" Marianna quickly went after her. It was amazing, she thought, that she could stand toe to toe against fantastical creatures twice her size, but helping out a classmate in her everyday life made her feel anxious. It wasn't like she could blow up the guy with a decadent explosive, this would require some kind of-

"Hey girl!"

Or… Dana could shout at the top of her lungs.

Everyone in the store looked toward Dana, including the girl dealing with the man who didn't believe in personal space. All Marianna could do now was go along with the plan Dana had set in motion and hope that it would work. "Hey!" It didn't work. The girl – and the rest of the store – looked bewildered at best, and annoyed at their loudness at worst. But a magical girl, beyond all else, was able to think quick on her feet. "You ran off without us, silly!"

"You're always in such a rush, we were only in the bath shop for a few minutes," Dana added as she walked toward the girl. Marianna followed suit until they were both standing right in front of her. Everything clicked into place as the pushy man took a step back, not at all comfortable with the two young women approaching and the sudden amount of eyes focused on them. Both Marianna and Dana stayed close until the man slunk out of the store, keeping his head lowered as if suddenly ashamed of himself.

As soon as he was gone the girl let out a huge sigh of relief. "Thank you. That creep had been following me since I got here."

"We noticed," Marianna said. "Are you all right?"

"Yeah… hey, we have class together, don't we?"

"Yeah, we do. I'm Marianna, and this is my friend, Dana."

"I'm Bree. It's nice to meet the both of you."

"That was so cool!" All three girls turned to see one of the employees standing near them, holding a stack of games to put back on the shelf. He was a bit chubby and was armed with a cute smile and wide-rimmed glasses that rested against his freckle-faced cheeks. "I… sorry, just… i-it was really great that you girls did that."

"It wasn't that big of a deal," Dana said, but the proud little smirk on her face said otherwise.

"I wish we didn't have to step in at all," Marianna added.

"Same," the clerk said. "Men ain't shit."

Bree tilted her head and asked, "Aren't you a man?"

The clerk shrugged his shoulders and said, "Didn't say I was proud of it," then he stepped past them to put a few of the games back on the shelf. "If you ladies need anything, let me know."

"I think I need this," Bree said as she grabbed one of the games he put away. "A small reward for surviving the first week of college and meeting cute new bodyguards."

"That's us! Protecting cute girls all over the city!" Dana ended the statement with a wink.

"You sound like *The Girl in Purple*," the employee said as he put away another game.

"The... who?" Bree asked.

"It's nothing important," Marianna said. "Come on, Dana. We were gonna get food?"

Thank goodness for Dana's one track mind when it came to food. "Oh! Right! See ya around, Bree!"

"Yeah, see you..."

As Marianna and Dana headed for the door Marianna glanced back at Bree. She was now talking with the store clerk, and she was sure she was asking what the whole *Girl in Purple* thing meant. In hindsight, she probably didn't have to rush off like that, after all, it wasn't like they knew *who* the girl was. Bree would hear about her eventually. The stories had started over the summer and were whispered about whenever something out of the ordinary happened. Marianna decided that Bree's curiosity was nothing worth worrying about. Chances were, she'd only see Bree in class, and nothing else would come of it.

END FLASHBACK

"You mean to tell me that was all Dana's idea?!"

"Shhh," Marianna urged Bree to lower her voice. The two were sitting on the bus together, headed home at the end of Marianna's shift. The exhaustion of working two shifts and going to class was hitting Marianna hard. She'd been hoping for a quiet trip home and, so far, the gruesome creatures of the city had stayed put.

Bree, on the other hand…

Not that she didn't enjoy her company, in fact, she was happy that Bree had hung out in the bakery until her shift was over. The middle of the week tended to be slow, and as much as Marianna loved talking with Ms. Green, the two would eventually run out of things to say.

Her relationship status could only be commented on so many times.

As soon as they'd gotten on the bus, the wear and tear of the day hit Marianna like a whirlwind. For once, she didn't mind the traffic in the city. It meant the trip home would be longer and she'd have time to close her eyes and-

"You never told me that," Bree whispered.

Close her eyes and have a conversation with Bree. "Did it really matter who made the first move?"

"Well… no, not really, I guess… but your story isn't nearly as exciting as mine."

Marianna cracked an eye open to look over at Bree. "It's the same story. In fact, it's the story that comes before yours."

"I still don't see why you're so anti-cool story, especially considering all the stories about *you*."

"Now you know the bus is **not** the place to have that conversation," Marianna hissed.

Bree wanted to point out how no one on the bus was paying attention to them. They were listening to headphones, checking their phones, or reading the next chapter of that new book until they reached their stop. She decided to keep that commentary to herself and go back to looking out the window. She could give Marianna the proper amount of prodding during the quiet walk home.

And she proceeded to do just that.

As soon as they got off at their stop Bree went on the offensive. "How can you say you hate my stories when you let your own stories go on for so long?"

Marianna knew this was coming. Fortunately, she'd been able to recharge on the bus for about half an hour after Bree had stopped talking. "Did I? I'm not the one who came up with all those stories."

"But you didn't correct them, either!"

"What was I supposed to do? Hold a press conference for the city and explain who I was?"

"Sure! Tony Stark did!"

"Oh yeah? And how'd that work out for him?"

Bree wondered how she should answer that. She could attempt to lie and say that everything went swimmingly for the iron-suited genius, billionaire, playboy, philanthropist, but she had a feeling that Marianna would whip out her phone and read the entire history of *Ironman* just to see if Bree was being honest. "All right... maybe not the best example, but you get what I mean!"

"Don't your heroes have secret identities for a reason? Did you really want me to tell everyone who I was?"

"No no no, not that! Just something beyond *The Girl in Purple*, that's all! Had I not figured it all out then no one would know how amazing you are!"

"You mean had you not run headfirst into danger and stumbled onto something you weren't meant to see," Marianna corrected as she pressed her hand against the front door of their building.

"I like my take better..." Bree muttered as she stepped inside with Marianna.

FLASHBACK

Out of all the nights for Bree's roommate to be gone, this was the worst.

Not that the two of them talked much beyond a courteous *good morning* or *good night*, but Bree could've used some company – even if it involved a quiet dinner of Easy Mac with a roommate who she didn't have much in common with.

The first thing she did was take a long shower. The advantage of it being Saturday night was that most of the girls on her floor were out. It meant that the single bathroom was empty and she didn't have to wait to take a shower. Bree scrubbed her body down as much as she could, particularly around her cheek where she could still feel the drop of drool that'd landed there. No matter how much face cleanser she used, her face still felt sticky and violated, and she swore that there was something holding onto her wrists. Finally, when the water turned cold, she shut the shower off and dried herself off. Maybe she'd go back to her room and her roommate would be back.

No such luck.

Bree changed into a fresh set of pajamas and hoped that the clean clothes would comfort her. These hadn't been touched by a pushy man-beast who couldn't take no for an answer, but for some reason, sitting around in a small top and underwear felt… uncomfortable. With her roommate gone, she could sleep in as little clothing as she wanted, but she suddenly felt the need to throw on a pair of sweatpants and the big-gest shirt she could find. It occurred to her that she didn't have many options when it came to nighttime clothing that covered her body, as she was a firm believer in the fewer clothing pieces, the better. No wonder why she gave men the idea that she was-

Bree forced herself to stop that train of thought.

This was exactly why she didn't want to be alone. She'd tried calling Trey on her way home and was greeted by his answering machine. She imagined that he was enjoying his Saturday night, as everyone should, but it meant that he probably wouldn't check his phone until tomorrow. Suddenly, her being out here on her own was more terrifying than it was cool. All her hang ups about having a mom who wore a cross around her neck felt meaningless. Even if it meant being lectured on not being so sarcastic and being more polite, the potential yelling match was better than the silence of her dorm room.

Not that her mother ever raised her voice, but Bree could, at least, yell until her mother told her to change her tone. So, with a lump in her throat, Bree made the call.

The first question her mother asked was, "Why are you calling so late?"

In her panicked state Bree had forgotten that her mother went to bed pretty early on Saturdays. She'd need plenty of sleep for her all day church-a-thon of gospel and scripture. Bree shook her head and said, "N-nothing, it's nothing. Sorry I-"

"Bree? What's wrong?"

Bree blinked away the tears in her eyes. "I... something happened."

"What happened?" Followed by, "Are you all right?"

Bree supposed that, technically, she was all right. She'd been rescued and her assailant had been taken care of. In hindsight, all that had happened was her being pinned down for a few excruciatingly slow seconds before she was taken out of harm's way. But the side of her face still felt unclean and she could still taste that thing, fresh memories of it clamping her mouth shut still thumping against the back of her mind. "Not really," she admitted quietly. "S-someone attacked me."

There was silence, then, "What do you mean *attacked*?"

"I mean some random douchebag followed me and attacked me!" Were her emotions supposed to go from zero to angry so quickly?

"Why did he follow you?" It wasn't exactly victim blaming, but it came dangerously close.

"Because I told him no and he got pissed at me," Bree snapped.

Silence again. Bree could feel her heart hammering in her chest. She imagined every dreadful response her mother was likely to give. Asking for it. Leading him on. Having too much of an attitude while she addressed him. Bree remembered all the warnings and the guilt trips of not being the cause of her own pain. She already knew how she was going to respond to any of her mother's toxic assumptions: yelling, with a healthy dose of crying and, potentially, hanging up the phone and not talking to her again until Trey talked her into it because *mom means well.*

The last thing Bree expected was to hear her mother humming. It was a soft and relaxing tune, some song Bree had vague memories of hearing in church, back when her mother dressed her up on Sunday morning. "What are you doing?" Bree asked, but she didn't get a response. Instead, her mother kept humming into the phone, and after a while, Bree closed her eyes and listened. She let her mother's voice comfort her in a way that, under normal circumstances, she'd roll her eyes at, but in that moment, the familiar sound of Ahna Danvers' soft voice made her feel safe. She'd grown up with this voice. It chased away the nightmares and fed her soup when she was sick. It worked two jobs to take care of her and her brother. It went to the department store and stood in line just to get the latest gaming console she wanted.

So Bree sat and listened, wiping at her eyes as all the negativity of the evening melted away. "And here I thought you were gonna blame me," she whispered.

"You said no," Ahna said. "No isn't an open invitation." The harsh edge in her voice proved to Bree that her assumptions about whose side her mother would've been on had been beyond inaccurate.

"… thank you, mom."

"Have you called the police?"

"Oh… I-"

"Bree, you should call them. I can come down there and–"

"You're two hours away, mom!"

"So?"

"You don't even drive…"

"There are buses for a reason," then, "And have you called your brother? Why isn't he there with you?"

Bree could feel herself calm down as her mother became more determined to make sure she was ok. "The… authorities have taken care of everything," she said, and that was as close to the truth as she was going to get. "And I left a message for Trey, I'm sure he'll be here when he gets it."

"That boy needs to answer his damn phone," Ahna muttered.

"Mom!" Such language from her mother was unheard of, even a simple curse like damn.

"Lord forgive me, but that boy…"

"It's all right, honest," even if part of Bree was enjoying her mother giving Trey a hard time. "I'll be sure to tell him that you're disappointed in him when he finally calls."

"Don't worry yourself over it, I'll call him myself."

"Mom…" but Bree wasn't terribly upset about it. Like every little sister in the known universe, there was a special kind of joy when the older sibling was being scolded… even if there was no way Trey could've known how serious the situation was. "I love you, mom."

"I love you, too. Now are you sure I don't need to come out there? I can be on the first bus tomorrow morning."

"I'm sure. Honest. But if I change my mind I'll let you know."

"All right. Goodnight, Bree."

"Goodnight mom." Bree ended the call and set her phone down. The relief washed across her and made her feel better than the shower she'd taken. Now that she was less frazzled, the pure insanity of the situation was becoming clearer. Much like a video game or some streaming anime series, she'd been hunted down by a supernatural creature. That creature was then eradicated by a lone girl dressed in purple.

Wait.

A girl… in purple?

"The video game store!" Bree turned on her computer, silently praised her current background of one hell of a butler, and clicked on her web browser. That boy at the store had mentioned a girl in purple. THE *Girl in Purple*, to be exact, who was out there protecting the city from the things that lurked in the shadows. It had all sounded like an urban legend, or an original character in an ongoing fanfic, but Bree had just seen it firsthand. There was an actual, real life girl dressed in purple who slayed dastardly creatures… with cupcakes, of all things.

Typing in the words *Girl in Purple* brought about a myriad of pictures of girls wearing purple, mainly for department stores trying to lure people in with bargains. Bree let out a frustrated sigh. Of course that would be the case. How was she going to find any information on a cupcake throwing warrior with such vague terms? Would adding "cupcake throwing" get her better results? No, that was just as fruitless as the last search, as she was greeted with stock photos of food fights, an array of dresses with cupcakes printed on them, and a not-safe-for-work video on a website with a lot of x's in its name.

Ella-Uchi has signed on

Ella-Uchi
Congrats on surviving your first week, college girl!

Bree didn't realize how jumpy she still was about the entire situation until the ping of her messenger made her heart stop. After reminding herself that her dorm room had nothing to be afraid of, she clicked on the box to respond to the message. Ella Yamauchi was a friend Bree had made at a convention over the summer. The creator of YAMA-

CHANnel, she'd become a source of inspiration for Bree's own YouTube dreams. She had a cute, anime girl persona online, often wearing colorful wigs and spewing out pop culture references in every other sentence. She was as close to a magical girl as Bree had seen... until tonight.

> **Bree-Dan**
> Thanks. It's been an... interesting week.

> **Ella-Uchi**
> Oh? Have you had to run to class with toast in your mouth?

> **Bree-Dan**
> Ugh. WHY are classes so EARLY? >.<

> **Ella-Uchi**
> Consider it part of your training, young one.

> **Bree-Dan**
> I'm flipping off the computer screen right now.

> **Ella-Uchi**
> Hey don't blame me, I don't make the rules I just break them ;)

> **Ella-Uchi**
> So is that why your week has been interesting? Cuz you better get used to it, my friend.

> **Bree-Dan**
> No... I was attacked by some asshole guy.

> **Ella-Uchi**
> WHAT?! Shit, are you all right?

> **Bree-Dan**
> Yeah, I'm fine. He was dealt with before it could get really bad.

Ella-Uchi
Thank god. I'm really sorry, Bree.

Bree-Dan
It's fine.

Ella-Uchi
No, it's not!

Bree-Dan
Well no, of course not. I didn't mean... you get what I mean, right?

Ella-Uchi
Yeah. But um... I wouldn't call this interesting.

Ella-Uchi
It's more alarming than interesting, we gotta work on your vocab skills.

Bree-Dan
There's... more...

Ella-Uchi
Oh?

Why did she just type that? Was she really about to tell the other part of the story? While it was interesting, it sounded like it came straight from the depths of her imagination.

Ella-Uchi:
Hey. You gonna tell me or what? Don't do the cliffhanger episode drag out thing, Bree. I don't need a "Next time on Dragon Ball Z" here.

Bree could try and weave together some kind of story but Ella had a knack for knowing when she was lying – even on messenger. She supposed she could just tell her the unbelievable tale. Ella would probably assume that she'd spent too much time scrolling through Tumblr and, hopefully, leave it at that.

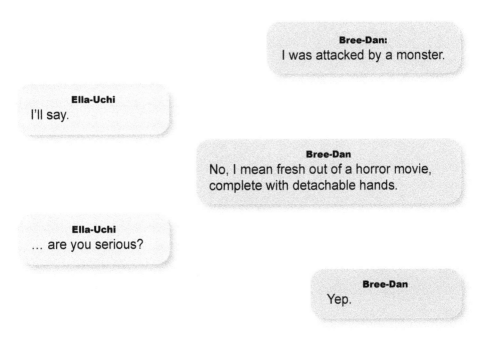

Bree-Dan:
I was attacked by a monster.

Ella-Uchi
I'll say.

Bree-Dan
No, I mean fresh out of a horror movie, complete with detachable hands.

Ella-Uchi
... are you serious?

Bree-Dan
Yep.

Bree waited for the inevitable disbelief. She wouldn't blame Ella, in fact, Bree wouldn't believe it, either, had she not been there to experience it.

Ella-Uchi
Did it spawn from a strange orb?

That... was not the response she'd been expecting.

Bree-Dan
LOL whut?

Ella-Uchi
You know, like an orb? Not a Rita Repulsa crystal ball, but an orb? With some weird projection coming out of it? A bad one. Not an R2-D2 one.

Bree-Dan
No.......... what the hell are you talking about?

Ella-Uchi
LOL! Nothing, just trying to lighten the mood. You know me...

Bree-Dan
Ah... well, I know this all sounds weird, but I'm telling the truth.

Ella-Uchi
Oh, I believe you.

Bree-Dan
... really?

Ella-Uchi
Let's just say it's been a long day.

Bree-Dan
Long enough to believe that I was saved by a girl with cupcakes?

Ella-Uchi
LOL WHAT?!

Bree-Dan
Yeah. Some girl showed up, with purple hair and clothes, and threw cupcakes at the monster.

Ella-Uchi
So you were saved by Strawberry Shortcake?
But purple?

Bree-Dan
There were too many sparkles for that.

Ella-Uchi
Lisa Frank with an Easy Bake Oven?

Bree-Dan
Your references are so outdated.

Ella-Uchi
Not outdated. Retro.

Bree-Dan
Well I'd say she's like Sailor Moon, but black,
and plus size, and dressed in purple... so Sailor
Saturn? Only she can't destroy the world... well,
maybe her exploding cupcakes can...

Ella-Uchi
Her... what?

Bree-Dan
There were monster bits and frosting everywhere.

Ella-Uchi
... all right, I've got nothin'...

Bree-Dan
She wanted me to run but I ended up going
back when I heard the explosion. She even said
a badass line and everything.

Ella-Uchi
Lay it on me.

Bree-Dan
"Who's the fat bitch, now?"

Ella-Uchi
Damn, that IS a good line. Girl crush activated.

Bree-Dan
RIGHT?! How cool is that?! But then she just… left. Purple heels and all.

Ella-Uchi
She Batman'd you, huh, Commissioner?

Bree-Dan
Yeah… except I didn't have my back turned. She jumped away, landed on one of the buildings on campus, and took off.

Ella-Uchi
Well it sounds like you have a superheroine on your hands.

Bree-Dan
Yeah… you'd think people would be talking about her more.

Ella-Uchi
Well… I guess they kinda are?

Bree-Dan
The boy at the video game store mentioned her, and the girls I met seemed to know what he was talking about?

Bree-Dan
But he didn't have much information and I can't find anything online.

Ella-Uchi
Do you know her name?

Bree-Dan
Nope, just that people call her "The Girl in Purple."

Ella-Uchi
Mmmm, so mysterious.

Ella-Uchi
Maybe ask the guy at the store more questions? Or maybe even your brother? He lives in the city, right?

Bree-Dan
Yeah... that's if my mom doesn't curse him out and send his soul to the Heavens above.

Ella-Uchi
LOL! Your mom doesn't curse.

Bree-Dan
She did tonight :)

Ella-Uchi
Huh. It's like she's concerned for your well-being or something. I wonder who told you that...

Bree-Dan
I got it, I got it. You're psychic.

Ella-Uchi
Just don't tell Charles Xavier.
I dunno if I'm ready for all that.

Bree-Dan
Is anyone?

Ella-Uchi
You're purple friend might be.

Bree-Dan
You mean "The Purple Wonder?"

Ella-Uchi
... is that really the name you're giving her?

Bree-Dan
Until I know her actual name. Why?

Ella-Uchi
She deserves better than that, Bree -_-

Bree-Dan
Then YOU come up with a name!

Ella-Uchi
Nope, this is something you must do on your own.

Bree-Dan
:P

Ella-Uchi
LOL! Let me know how it turns out. Oh, and Bree?

Bree-Dan
Hm?

Ella-Uchi
Just... be careful about strange orbs, ok?

Bree-Dan
Again with the orbs, Ella? Really

Ella-Uchi
Hahahahaha, yeah. I'm just
being silly. Goodnight, Bree.

Bree-Dan
Goodnight.

Ella-Uchi has signed off.

Bree had a feeling there was something going on with Ella, but she obviously didn't want to delve into it. Whatever it was, it was bizarre enough for her cupcake wielding heroine to be believable. Not that Bree had time to ask about the workings of Ella and these *orbs*, not when there were monsters and magical girls to look into. Ella did bring up a good point, though. Maybe Trey had heard something, or maybe even Marianna and Dana. If there wasn't any information available online, then she'd have to talk to people directly. At the very least, maybe they could tell her what to search for online, because *purple* and *cupcakes* weren't getting her anywhere.

In the end, Bree decided that this was something for future Bree to figure out. Exhaustion was finally setting in after everything that had happened, and present day Bree needed sleep.

Sunday was Trey's favorite day of the week. While it wasn't *technically* for its religious connotations, Trey would tell you that it was, since to him, sports were as sacred as any holy entity. At most, Bree expected a phone call, but to her surprise he'd shown up to check on her in the middle of his Sunday game-a-thon. He was standing on the other side of her door, out-of-breath and dressed in the sweatpants he'd worn to

bed. He'd thrown on a shirt at the last second, the white top wrinkled and in need of washing. "Trey? What are you-"

Trey cut her off by stepping into the room and hugging her, having to hunch down since he was a full foot taller. "Are you all right?"

Bree thought she'd gotten all the tears out last night, but there she was, crying against his shirt. After a minute of hiccups and soft sobbing she said, "I'm fine. I didn't mean for you to come over, I just-"

"I should've answered the phone."

Bree wiped at her eyes as she shook her head. "You didn't know, Trey. You-"

"Then mom called."

Oh.

While it had been amusing to think about last night, seeing the worry on Trey's face made Bree feel bad. "Do I wanna know what she said?"

Trey let Bree go and took a deep breath before explaining his not-so-lovely conversation with their mother. "Well she'd left about three messages last night and I didn't get to check them til this morning, then she called again before going to church. I managed to talk her out of coming up here because I was on my way to check on you. Did you know mom swears now?"

"I'm really sorry," but there was a bit of an amused smile on Bree's face. So much for feeling bad for her brother.

"You don't look sorry."

"I am! Just... the image of mom in her church clothes cursin' you out..."

"...all right, that's kinda funny," Trey admitted. "Still... I'll answer next time."

"What were you even doing last night?" When Bree saw the sly smile on her brother's face she rolled her eyes and said, "Never mind. I don't need to know," then, "She's not in the car or something, right?"

"Naw, I took her back home. Apparently my concern for you makes me even more attractive."

"Glad to be the equivalent of a puppy," Bree muttered as she finally closed the door to her dorm.

"Puppies are cuter," Trey laughed as he sat down in Bree's computer chair. "So... you gonna tell me what happened?"

"Not if you're gonna keep being a jerk." Seriously, hadn't he been concerned for her safety seconds ago?

"Pass, next question."

"Ugh, whatever. I was attacked by a monster last night."

"...what?"

Oops. Had she just blurted that out? Bree had meant to ease Trey into it but, as usual, the older Danvers had frustrated her to the point of abandoning her plan in favor of getting it out the way.

"Now when you say *monster*, you mean figuratively, right?"

"Um... kinda? I mean he was human at first, but..."

It was at this point that Bree's roommate made her presence known, Trey nodding to the girl when she spun around in her computer chair to face them. Jackie Brooks had been sitting at her desk across from Bree, having come back that morning in the same school mascot themed clothes she'd been wearing the night before. Bree hadn't said anything, she didn't know the girl well enough to make any kind of late night activities comments, and Jackie had looked grateful for it. She'd been playing one of those candy matching, time waster games, not paying too much attention to the conversation between the siblings until the word monster came up. "So you're talking about an actual monster?" Jackie asked.

Bree nodded. "I know it sounds weird, but-"

"Actually, it doesn't," she said as she adjusted her glasses.

It was the most Jackie had ever said to Bree in the entire week. She explained that she'd heard things, *crazy* things, about monsters attacking people around town. With the first story, she'd ruled it as some bizarre tale akin to alien sightings or Bigfoot. Many cities had tales of ghosts, demons, and other supernatural beings, so hearing about a "monster" wasn't that big of a deal. With the second story, she'd become mildly curious. Another monster, another attack, but this time there were whispers about a black girl dressed in purple fighting the monster and disappearing into the night once the battle was over.

The third story? That was the one she said she'd witnessed firsthand.

"Did something happen to you?" Bree asked.

"Not to me directly. But I was there. Some monster was on the loose near the library. We all stayed inside, and then there was an explosion. When we finally walked outside the monster was gone." Jackie turned and started typing on her computer. "There are stories of attacks, but no one has been around to catch who stops them," then she pushed her chair out of the way so Bree could see one of the stories she'd pulled up. Just as she said, the story focused on the library attack, followed by an explosion and then… silence. "There are other stories of attacks that happened over the summer." Jackie closed the story and opened up another one. "And something about a girl in purple-"

"That! That was what I was looking for last night!" She should've added the word *monster* in her search engine. "I saw her! She saved me last night! She threw cupcakes at my attacker then there was an explosion!"

"Exploding cupcakes? Really?" Trey chuckled. "That's far-fetched, even for you, sis."

"I'm not making it up! There's a girl out there fighting monsters!"

"Look, I'm glad you're all right, but-"

"But nothing! This is real, Trey! You've lived here for how long and you've never heard anything?"

"I mean... yeah, sure, I've heard stuff, all right?" Trey shoved his hands into his pockets, suddenly looking uneasy with the conversation. "But I didn't say I believed it, and it's not even the same."

"What do you mean?" Jackie asked.

Trey sighed as he leaned back against the wall. He didn't want to feed into this. He knew how Bree was when she got excited about something, and this was the last thing she needed to be excited about. But as his little sister looked up at him, eyes wide and waiting for answers, he knew that it was already too late. "When I went to school here there were stories about a group of women, but they weren't around anymore."

"An entire group? Really?" Bree was bouncing up and down in excitement.

Trey nodded and spoke the group's name. "**magnifiquenoir.**"

Jackie turned and typed in the name. Her eyes widened as a few articles popped up about a group of women who had, once upon a time, defended their city. "This article is over twenty years old."

"What?!" Bree stepped closer to look at Jackie's computer screen. Right in front of them, in blurry photographed glory, was an article about a group of black women fighting monsters on their college campus. "They were around before I was even born?"

"Yeah. When I went to school here I heard some stuff, but nothing ever came of it. Just some whispers here and there," Trey said with a shrug. "Like you said... alien sightings. Bigfoot. Whatever."

"Why didn't you tell me?!"

"What, you mean when I was a first year student ten years ago and you were eight?!"

That was a good point, but Bree could still be huffy about it. "Bottom line is I saw a girl last night, who took out a monster for me, with magical powers that shouldn't be possible. Maybe she's a part of this group."

"What did she look like?" Jackie asked.

"She was black, and plus size, and beautiful. She looked like she was our age, though, so she couldn't be part of the old group... oh! Maybe there's a new one! Maybe she's-"

Trey quickly interrupted Bree before she could spiral out of control. "Sis... you're investing too much in this. You were just attacked yesterday."

"Yeah, and there's some girl out there defending girls like me. She deserves some credit, don't you think?"

"Is that what she wants, though?" Trey asked.

"I told you to run. What are you doing back here?"

"I just... y-you just... that was incredible!"

"Go home."

"What? But I-"

"Go. Home."

Bree frowned as she remembered their brief conversation before the girl pulled a Batman – as Ella would call it. Trey had a point. It was clear that this girl wanted to do this alone. She wouldn't even stick around long enough for a compliment. "But... she doesn't have to keep this to herself."

"Sis..."

"I mean it, Trey. I want to find out who she is. Besides, don't you wanna know who saved your little sister?"

Trey frowned. "That ain't fair."

"All I'm asking is that you take me to the mall. That's where this whole thing started. The guy who attacked me had followed me into the video game store."

"You better hope I'm not missing a good game for this," then Trey fished his keys out of his pocket.

"Whatever. You know you're recording it."

"That's beside the point!"

And that was that. The two headed to the mall together like some kind of black detective duo. If Bree were to be completely honest, she didn't know where to start in regards to finding out who her purple heroine was. She had a feeling that the mall had some kind of clue. It at least had the store clerk who had mentioned *The Girl in Purple* in the first place. Besides, being out of her dorm and actually doing something made Bree feel better.

As Bree retraced her steps she decided to tell Trey what happened. The man who'd followed her into the store. The fact that he'd followed her even after he'd been chased away. Bree could see Trey clenching his fists in anger, upset about not being able to at least get one punch in. He wasn't much of a fighter, but he could definitely give someone a black eye if he put his mind to it. "If it makes you feel better that thing that attacked me was completely eradicated."

"Define *completely*."

"Limbs scattered all over the sidewalk."

"Whoa. I wonder who got the fun job of cleaning that up in the morning."

"Um… that part was taken care of, too," Bree said as the two walked into the store. "The frosting kinda… dissolved the body parts away like acid."

Trey could only respond in stunned silence. Bree couldn't blame him. *Acidic frosting* was probably the strangest concoction she'd ever seen.

"Hey, welcome back!"

Bree looked up to see the boy from yesterday doing the same thing he'd been doing before – putting away games. "Hi, um… I didn't get your name yesterday."

"Torrence. Are your heroic friends not with you today?"

"Naw, just my lump of an older brother."

"Thanks," Trey said, though he probably deserved it because of that puppy comment earlier. "Wait, what heroic friends?"

"Oh, the man who followed me, he-"

"Was completely owned by these two girls," Torrence said, finishing Bree's sentence. "It was pretty awesome."

"It was just like *The Girl in Purple*, right?" Bree asked, remembering Torrence's excitement from yesterday. "Can you… tell me anything else about her?"

Torrence shook his head as he put away one of the games in his stack. "I pretty much told you all I know. She shows up, fights monsters, then leaves."

"Anything in there about exploding cupcakes?" Trey asked.

"I'm sorry… what?"

"I saw her last night." Bree leaned in close to whisper to Torrence, "That creep from before? Was cosplaying an adult human."

"Bree. Do you have to geek up everything?" Trey knew the answer to that, but there was a time and a place for his sister's geek references. "What she means is that he was a monster of some kind."

"W-what?!" Torrence nearly dropped the games in his arms, his shout startling some of the customers around them. "Are you all right?! What the hell are you doin' at the mall?!"

"That's what I said." At least someone understood logic and reason. No wonder why their mother was willing to get on a bus, she probably wanted to make sure that Bree actually recovered from her harrowing experience.

Bree urged Torrence to quiet down then spoke again. "I'm fine because she saved me."

"She? As in… r-really?! Who is she? Did you find out?"

"No, but I did see her up close." Bree suddenly felt like she was talking about a unicorn or the elusive leprechaun at the end of the rainbow. "Black. Plus sized. Dressed in purple. Able to take out monsters with baked goods. She's flawless." Well, *almost* flawless, because she didn't stick around long enough to have a conversation. At this rate, Bree would only see her again if another monster attacked in an area where she just so happened to be.

Apparently, there was a monster around to answer the call.

Had they been on the West Coast of the country, feeling the ground rumble wouldn't have been as odd. Since they were smack in the middle of the Midwest, the ground shaking enough for the games to fall from their shelves was peculiar. The customers all looked perplexed, not quite sure if this was cause for concern or if something normal was going on near the mall to create the quakes.

The screams from outside assured everyone that it was time to panic.

Torrence set the games down and walked to the door, trying to figure out what was going on. People were being led downstairs by mall security, heading to the lower level that served as a shelter during natural disasters. Torrence managed to catch the words *monster* and *parking lot* before he turned to address everyone. "We need to go downstairs." To his credit, he sounded relatively calm, but his hands were trembling as he urged people to leave the store.

Trey reached over and grabbed Bree's hand, his palms sweaty as he gave it a reassuring squeeze. "It'll be all right," he said, but she could tell he wasn't only saying that for her benefit.

Bree nodded her agreement, even if her stomach felt a sick familiarity in the situation. As she stepped outside to join everyone else, she caught a glimpse of a girl watching them. Bree tilted her head, trying to place where she'd seen her, then her eyes widened in realization. "Marianna?"

"Hm?" Trey asked. "What did you say?"

"There's a girl, I know her." Bree was about to shout her name to get her to join them, but then Marianna did the oddest thing. She ran in the opposite direction. "Marianna!" Bree acted on pure instinct and let go of Trey's hand, pushing past the people in her way so she could pursue Marianna.

"Bree! Wait, where are you going?!" Trey tried to follow his sister, but there were too many people in his way and he couldn't get through them as fast as she could. "Bree!!!" He tried to get the attention of the cops standing near the stairwell, but they were too busy trying to reassure everyone that things would be fine. "Damnit!"

Bree could hear her brother calling out to her, but she was out of the pack now and she could see Marianna running down the now empty hallway. What was she doing?! Why wasn't she going downstairs with them? Bree would deal with any anger Trey hurled her way later, but right now, something told her to run after the girl.

Marianna turned a corner and Bree rushed after her, mentally hoping that the girl would stop running so she could actually catch up to her. Fortunately, Marianna did stop running, but before Bree could approach her she watched the girl roll up the sleeve of her dress to reveal a glowing bracelet. Bree's mouth dropped open as she watched her thrust her hand in the air and-

"galactic purple! Rise up!"

And there was her answer.

The purple bracelet flashed one more time before it snapped apart. The pieces swirled around Marianna as a purple light enveloped her body. Bree watched in stunned silence as the girl she met yesterday transformed before her eyes. Her brown hair shifted into a shimmering purple, the ends twisting into perfect curls. A splash of purple gently caressed her lips to match with her new, magical hair. The sparkles around Marianna's body melded together to create the outfit Bree saw last night, right down to the cute, purple heels. Finally, Bree was able to whisper a breathless, "No way," as *The Girl in Purple* stood in front of her. Suddenly, Marianna's hurried response when Torrence had mentioned the city's urban legend made sense. She was that girl protecting the city. She was the girl that saved Bree. "Y-you're…"

The purple heroine turned to face Bree, her eyes narrowing when she saw her. She hadn't realize she'd been followed. "Go." Her voice was as cold as it had been last night. She may have rescued her, but she didn't want Bree to be any part of this.

"Marianna...? You're her? You're the girl who saved me last night! You're *The Girl in Purple!*" But no, that wasn't her name, was it? She'd said something before that transformation happened. "Galactic Purple...? Is that your name?" That was so much better than *The Purple Wonder.* "That's so cool! I can't believe you-"

"I said go!"

Bree ignored her irritated yell and pushed on. "I wanted to thank you for saving my life. I-"

"I don't have time for this," then she turned her back to Bree.

"W-wait! Are there more of you?"

"...what?"

"My brother used to go to school here," Bree said as she stepped closer. "He mentioned a group. **magnifiquenoir.**"

"Now's not the time to talk about that."

While it sounded like a cop out, Bree knew she was telling the truth. There was a monster to deal with, and if something wasn't done there was a chance it would do damage to the mall.

"When can we talk-"

"Never," and just like last time, she was gone in a flash. By the time Bree got down the escalator and outside, the monster was in the same disastrous state as the last one. But at least, this time, Bree had a name.

Galactic Purple.

GALACTIC PURPLE RISE UP
Ashleigh Beever • www.ashleighbeeversart.com

magnifiquenoir

Player Select

NAME: marianna jacobs
AGE: 18
OCCUPATION: Baker
FIRST SEASON ATTACK: CUPCAKE BOMB!

THE LEADER OF THE GROUP AND THE FIRST TO GAIN HER POWERS, THIS PLUS SIZE CUTIE USES HER SWEETS TO ERADICATE EVIL ONE SPRINKLE AT A TIME & TOPS IT OFF WITH DECADENT FROSTING!

galactic PURPLE

"DON'T LET ANYONE TELL YOU THAT YOU'RE NOT MAGICAL!"

GALACTIC PURPLE PROFILE
Briana Lawrence • www.magnifiquenoir.com
Musetap Studios • www.musetapstudios.com

As Bree expected, Trey wasn't happy with her running off. She showed up downstairs and let everyone know that the situation had been taken care of. The mall officers were a mix of irritated that Bree had gone outside when everyone was supposed to remain indoors, and relieved that the situation had been resolved without any need of their help. After all, none of them were trained for this kind of thing. When Bree saw Trey he was practically shaking from how angry he was, but to her surprise, it was Torrence who snapped at her first. "What the hell did you think you were doing?! Running off like that, oh my GOD, what is WRONG with you?! Don't be out here actin' like those dumb white girls in the horror movies, out there lookin' for Billy when Billy's ass is DEAD!"

Trey looked just as surprised at his outburst and added a quiet, "What he said." There wasn't anything he could say that would top the death of the fictional Billy.

Bree was trying to find the right words after being told off in such a spectacular way. Torrence had been loud enough for the crowd to hear him, and even mall security looked impressed with how savage he was. "Well?" Torrence asked, a stern look on his face. "You gonna say somethin'?"

Finally, Bree spoke up. "That girl I mentioned, she…" then she stopped herself. Superheroine etiquette – and Marianna's cold shoulder – dictated that she didn't want everyone knowing her secret. Even if Bree had been anxious to learn the truth, she didn't want to overstep her boundaries in such a way. Granted, she had chased after her, but was it really her fault that she'd learned more than she bargained for? Ok… yes, it was totally her fault, but Bree wasn't going to think about that right now. "I wanted to make sure she was safe," Bree said.

"Well you gave me and your poor brother a heart attack! Don't you EVER do that again!"

Bree knew she deserved it, but she didn't expect to hear it from someone other than Trey. Speaking of Trey, he was busy nodding his head in agreement with everything Torrence was saying. Why waste his vocal cords when Torrence was checking off all the *concerned older brother* bullet points for him?

"I'm sorry," Bree whispered, but she wasn't quite sure if she needed to direct her sorrowful eyes at Trey or Torrence. She settled for looking up at both of them.

"Don't give me that look," Trey said. He'd fallen victim to Bree's pout before, but this was more serious than her wanting a new game or passes to a geeky convention.

"I mean it! I'm sorry!"

"Is that girl ok, at least?" Torrence asked.

"Yeah, she's fine. In fact... she got mad at me for following after her."

"Good, because it was incredibly-"

"Stupid," Bree said, finishing Torrence's sentence for him.

Trey put a hand on Bree's shoulder. It was clear that she got the message, and at least she didn't seem interested in solving the mystery behind that whole *Girl in Purple* thing anymore. "Don't do anything that stupid ever again."

"I won't."

And she meant that.

Sort of.

After they said goodbye to Torrence, Trey dropped Bree off at her dorm room where she reassured him – for the umpteenth time – that she wasn't going to do anything reckless. Jackie greeted her with a smile and asked, "Did you find out anything?"

"Not really," Bree lied. "Guess it'll take a bit more research." That part wasn't that much of a lie. Bree did have more questions, but she had a feeling Marianna wouldn't be that forthcoming with the answers. As Jackie settled down in her bed to go back to reading her book, Bree sat at her computer and proceeded to have a staring contest with the blank screen.

What now?

This felt worse than any of her high school relationships where she knew she had been in the wrong and tried her best to make it up to her partners. Granted, she only had three people she'd considered as partners in her high school career: two boyfriends and a girlfriend that her mother hadn't known about. Though honestly, she didn't feel too wrong about this situation with Marianna. Yes, she knew she invaded her privacy, in a way, but she was also trying to give the girl props for her heroism. Was that so wrong? Didn't people deserve to know who was out there fighting these battles? More importantly… did Marianna have to fight alone? In fact, why was she fighting by herself? Everything Bree had heard about **magnifiquenoir** described them as a group, not a single person. So why was Galactic Purple the only one? Shouldn't there be more girls?

Could there be more girls?

Bree shook her head as she turned on her monitor. What in the world was she thinking? This was exactly what Trey – and Torrence – had been talking about. In a city where creepy men could transform into actual, full blown nightmare fuel, the last thing she should've been doing was chasing after a superheroine. With that in mind, Bree settled on treating Marianna like a normal girl. She'd address her as such in class and that would be the end of it.

That was the plan… until the knock on her door.

Bree glanced over at Jackie to see if she was going to answer, but her roommate had drifted off. That was fine, it was probably Trey again, anyway. He'd probably thought of something else to say while he was driving home and decided to turn the car around to say his piece in person. Bree would be sure to tell him that her Lois Lane days were over. She'd leave the monster slaying to the Galactic Superwoman.

When Bree opened the door she was surprised to see that no one was standing there, but there was definitely something worth staring at. Bree's first thought was that she was dreaming. She'd fallen asleep at her desk just like Jackie had fallen asleep in bed. In front of her eyes was what looked to be an entire solar system. The pitch black sky was lined with stars, comets, and what could've been planets. While that in itself was odd, the dark skinned woman sitting in the middle of it all added the icing to the strange cake. Dressed in a white top with a long, fiery orange skirt, her lips curved into an amused smile as she watched the perplexed look on Bree's face. Bree glanced behind her to see that her dorm room was still the same as always: sleeping roommate, computer screensaver of various fictional husbandos and waifus. "Am I dreaming?" Bree asked.

The woman chuckled and said, "No, you are not."

Bree's second thought was that she was hallucinating, but she wasn't sure how. She hadn't gotten drunk last night, but she did get attacked by a monster, so her third thought was that this was some wonky side effect to that entire fiasco.

"You look like you're not believing what you're seeing."

"So you're saying this is real?"

"Come now," the woman said with a smile. "You believe in magical girls and monsters, how could you possibly question this?"

"How do you know what I believe in?"

"Because you've been asking questions about my girls. The ladies of **magnifiquenoir**."

Bree's eyes widened. "So… there are more?"

"Currently? No. But there could be."

It was exactly what Bree told herself not to think about, but she couldn't help but ask, "What exactly does that mean?"

The woman's smile turned into a playful smirk as she held her hand out. "Why don't you step inside and find out?"

In that moment Bree knew that her life was about to change. In that moment, she knew she had to make a decision. She could close the door and pretend like this never happened. She could go to class tomorrow morning, say hi to Marianna, and never think about the monsters hidden among them again.

Or.

She could step into this odd little galaxy, get all the answers to her questions, and piss her brother off by diving headfirst into a situation he didn't want her to be involved in.

Bree closed her eyes and took a deep breath. Did she really want to do this? Last night had been horrifying, to say the least, but something about Marianna doing this alone didn't sit well with her. Did she really have to deal with these grotesque creatures by herself?

"Ah, what the hell," Bree said to herself. "Little sisters are supposed to make their big brothers panic, right?" And as she stepped forward, she let one last thought linger in the back of her mind.

Thank goodness her mother hadn't caught that bus.

END FLASHBACK

"Why hasn't she said anything to me?"

Marianna looked up from her notebook to see herself on the receiving end of Bree's patented pout. She was glad that Bree had moved on from yesterday's conversation about proper storytelling, but she didn't much care for this alternative: Bree being convinced that she'd ruined things with Kayla.

"Maybe she'll talk to you after class," Marianna said.

"How did we go from her bringing me coffee to her not even saying good morning?"

Marianna frowned sadly at the question. While this wasn't exactly the time for this conversation, Bree did have a point. Kayla had given Bree the cold, frigid shoulder this morning. The last thing Marianna wanted was for Bree to be upset, so she placed her hand on top of Bree's and smiled. "Maybe she's trying to figure out what to say after you brought her the cupcake. It was a really nice gesture."

"Yeah… maybe…" but Bree didn't sound too sure. Kayla had been so confident when she approached her, she didn't seem like the shy type.

The rest of lecture was spent with Bree fidgeting in her seat and Marianna going between taking notes and watching Kayla, hoping she'd at least glance back at Bree and put her mind at ease. By the time the bell rang, Marianna was feeling an irrational amount of anger on behalf of her friend. From her perspective, the two had really hit it off, and Kayla was definitely, at the very least, attracted to Bree. But now the girl was packing up her books and heading to the door, not even bothering to acknowledge Bree's presence. Bree slumped down in her seat and in seconds, Marianna was on the move, quickly following after Kayla. "Excuse me?"

Kayla stopped at the door and looked back at Marianna, then gave her a thin smile. "Ah, good morning. Mari, right?"

"Marianna," she corrected coldly. "I don't mean to be rude," that was a lie, she absolutely meant to be rude, "But… what happened?"

"What do you mean?"

"With Bree. You seemed so interested yesterday, why aren't you talking to her today?" Surely Bree hadn't done anything so abysmal that Kayla felt the need to ignore her, right?

Kayla raised an eyebrow at Marianna then said, "Wait… you want me to talk to her?"

"Of course, why wouldn't I want that?"

"Aren't you two dating?"

"Huh?!"

"You two. Dating," Kayla said as she bitterly added more salt to the wound. "She went on and on about how amazing you are, so I thought-" Kayla was interrupted by Marianna's sudden burst of laughter – more like a cackle, actually. "Um… did I say something funny?"

"Y-you think… oh my god, really?!" Marianna asked between her giggle fits. So much for thinking that Bree hadn't flubbed this up.

"She talked you up so much so I thought… I mean, unless you don't mind sharing? You did make that bomb-ass cupcake, after all. I'm not super knowledgeable about polygamy but-"

"Hold that thought, I'll be right back," then Marianna walked back over to Bree with a huge grin on her face. "Oh Breeeee…"

Bree finally looked up from her self-appointed state of *I can't get a cute girl to like me.* She was a bit startled by the look on Marianna's face. That combined with the cheerful exaggeration of her name was cause for concern. Marianna looked so pleased with herself that it was almost sinister. "…what?"

"So remember our talk about those grand stories you tell?"

"Yeah? Why are you bringing that up now?"

"Weeeeell… Kayla thinks we're dating."

"She… wait, what?!"

"I mean I guess I appreciate you praising me so much, but it looks like it cost you your crush."

Bree shot up from her seat. Why would Kayla think they were dating? She mentally hit the replay button on their conversation from yesterday, trying to find any signs of-

"So… how long have you two been together?"

"Oh god oh god oh god!" How had Bree not put two and two together when Kayla asked that question? Instead, she'd spent the whole time talking about Marianna and how great she was. Bree could see the smug little smirk on Marianna's face. That was the *I told you so* smirk, complete with a little twinkle in her eye that took pride in how right she had been. Bree wouldn't be in this mess if she hadn't been so set on telling an exciting story.

"You better go," Marianna said as she nodded over to Kayla. "And this time, get straight to the point."

Bree didn't need to be told twice. She ran over to Kayla, frantically screaming, "I can explain!" Followed by, "It's not like that! She don't even like me that much!"

Marianna nearly choked on the air around her. "Bree!"

"I get on her nerves all the time! We're always at each other's throats, I swear!"

Marianna watched Bree chase after Kayla, who had stepped out of the classroom with an amused look on her face. She should've known that Bree wouldn't learn anything from this, then again, her words weren't a complete lie. Once upon a time, the two hadn't gotten along so well – a continuation of sorts from Bree's fantastical tale of their first encounter.

But that was an entirely different story.

EPISODE FOUR:

AN ENTIRELY DIFFERENT STORY

FLASHBACK

Bree wasn't sure how it had come to this.

What she had wanted was an explanation.

What she got was an invitation.

Golden Blaze. That was the woman's name. She was the one Marianna reported to in her quest to keep their city out of supernatural harm. A former member of the original group, Blaze now acted as an adviser of sorts because she'd seen it all before. Now, she was imparting her knowledge on the younger generation: the new **magnifiquenoir**. Despite remaining on the sidelines, Bree was sure that Blaze was dangerous when she decided to stand up and join the action. A woman who could open a door to an entire galaxy was not to be trifled with.

Blaze confirmed everything that Bree had discovered during her research. **magnifiquenoir** had been a group of women who protected the city with fantastical powers and glorious hair. The group had been out of commission for several years, becoming a bit of a hidden legend in the city. With the monstrous threats resurfacing, Blaze had decided that it was time for the group to return.

"But it's not much of a group," Bree had said to Blaze. *"Not if Marianna's the only one out there."*

Unbeknownst to Bree, that was exactly what Blaze had wanted to hear.

Which led to Bree's current situation: standing on top of a tall building, watching a terrifying creature stomp through the streets as several people played the part of frightened bystanders. As a kid, Bree remembered loving heights. She used to be the girl who would climb trees in her Sunday best – much to her mother's dismay. She was also the only kid in junior high who didn't cry when riding all the tall roller coasters at their great American theme park. Standing on top of the building brought those feelings back to the surface, the adrenaline coursing through her veins.

"Don't overdo it," Marianna said as she stepped up next to her.

Was that really the first thing Marianna was going to say to her? Couldn't she be a little bit more encouraging? "I know that. Besides, once upon a time, you weren't ready, either."

Marianna frowned at her as she remembered Blaze's words to the both of them before this mission. Marianna wasn't a big fan of having a second girl on the team all the sudden. This led to Blaze reminding her of two things: there was no *I* in *team*, and Bree would need time to adjust – just like Marianna did when she first started. "Touché," she muttered. "Now, the first thing we should do is-"

"Jump in and kick that thing's ass?"

"No. We should come up with a plan."

"How about this for a plan," then Bree pointed to the large creature as it continued its destruction below. "Kill the thing before it pins some girl down and traumatizes her for life."

Marianna remembered the distressed look on Bree's face when she'd been attacked. It was clear her determination stemmed from that moment. She could sympathize, but running in without a plan was foolish, at best, and deadly if things took a turn for the worst. "Listen, I get it, but-"

"I'm going in," then without missing a beat, Bree jumped off the building.

"Bree!"

Despite her anxiousness to jump into the fray, free falling from a building wasn't the smartest thing to cross off of her *to do* list. Bree let out a loud scream that echoed around her, as if to remind her of how incredibly stupid this was. The thoughts in her head were working overtime as she desperately tried to remember what came next. They'd talked about this before they left. Blaze had given her something but Bree's heart was pounding too fast for her to remember what it was. All she could do was scream until her voice got hoarse, loose strands of her hair flying into her face and-

Hair.

Her hair!

Bree reached into her hair and clasped onto the green bow that Blaze had given her before they left. As she fell, she squeezed her eyes shut and remembered watching Marianna transform at the mall. She remembered her bracelet snapping apart and a purple energy emitting from the pieces. Something like that would happen right now, right? Blaze had said as much, anyway, after giving one of those *the power is inside of you* speeches. The words had sounded so cheesy at the time, but as Bree held onto the bow in her hair, she swore she could feel something bubbling up inside her chest. It was a warm energy, something that was eager to come out and show that terrible monster what she could do. She wished with every fiber of her being that she could've felt something like this with her own attack. All she'd felt that day was a cold sense of fear that left her shaking and crying until Marianna had come to her rescue. She was definitely thankful for Marianna's presence, but Bree wished that she could've protected herself. No, it was more than that. She wished she could've shown that thing why no truly meant no.

"**cosmic green**," Bree whispered, her voice low and deadly serious. She had been falling at a dangerously high speed, but as the power welled up inside of her, it felt like she was floating. It was hot and angry, ready to burst, ready to annihilate whoever dared to put their hands on her without her consent. "**press start!**"

Just like Marianna's bracelet, Bree's hair bow shattered with the pieces swirling around her. The pieces digitized into several bits, looking like they came out of an old video game. *Retro.* The word was *retro*, that's what Ella would say. Bree closed her eyes as she fell through the bits of green.

This was it.

This was really happening.

Bree's hair tie broke as her hair flowed around her, the brown shifting into a shimmering green. Her clothes dissolved away as the power washed over her, creating a new look.

Not just a new look: a new Bree.

Black and green stripes with a hint of sparkling stars enveloped her body. A matching, fluffy skirt puffed up around her hips. Her legs were decorated in black and white tights that ended in a pair of knee-high, chunky black boots. The entire sequence ended with a splash of green hitting her lips as a stylish choker appeared around her neck. In that moment, Bree felt like she could've taken on an entire army of monsters as she landed on the ground with a simple step. Bree suddenly understood why her favorite magical heroines struck poses after transforming. There was something empowering about this, and she felt the urge to give a twirl, point an accusing finger at the terrible fiend in front of her, and recite a dramatic speech about punishing it. She decided to save it for later. Maybe after she practiced in her room and came up with the epic line the moment deserved.

Player Select

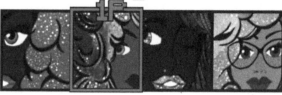

NAME: Bree Danvers
AGE: 18
OCCUPATION: Let's Player
FIRST SEASON ATTACK: 8-BITS and Pieces!

THE SECOND IN COMMAND & RESIDENT GAMER GIRL, IF YOU DARE DELAY HER DUNGEON CRAWLING BY ATTACKING HER CITY, THEN IT'S AN INSTANT GAME OVER FOR YOU — NO CONTINUES!

cosmic GREEN

"I'LL SHOW YOU HOW MAGICAL I AM!"

COSMIC GREEN PROFILE
Briana Lawrence • www.magnifiquenoir.com
Musetap Studios • www.musetapstudios.com

The monster in question turned its attention away from small shop number three in its rampage to focus on Bree. It was covered in too much hair, hair that had become matted and smelled like a moldy basement. Bree wrinkled her nose in disgust. She shouldn't have been able to smell it from where she was standing, but the stench was overtaking the entire block like a rotten cologne. The creature took a step toward Bree and smirked a gruesome smirk. "That was an impressive entrance, *cutie*."

That single word set Bree off. It was another person, another *thing* that thought it had the right to be so familiar with her. There was such a lack of respect in its voice. She was sure that if she allowed their interaction to go on any longer, it would pin her down and tell her to be nicer. "I'm gonna make you regret saying that," she hissed.

"Is that so? Well I'm right here, show me what you can do."

"Oh trust me. I'll show you how magical I am," and with that, Bree – no, *Cosmic Green* – was on the move. She was so focused on her adversary that she didn't realize that she'd come up with the perfect line.

Bree Danvers was never very fast. In high school she could, at least, run fast enough for the bus driver to notice her when she was running late. She wasn't the type to break any records in gym class. That was for the sporty girls who didn't mind running a couple of laps. Cosmic Green, on the other hand, was fast – not fast enough to create a time paradox or save woodland creatures with speedy, red shoes, but fast in a sense that made her feel like she could outrun a large cat on the hunt. There was a tingle in the palm of her hand that grew warmer and warmer as she got closer to her target. She was relying on pure instinct to guide her forward as she slapped the palm of her hand against her opponent's chest. Bree would've been satisfied with the creature stumbling back or letting out a cry of pain, but it appeared that, as Cosmic Green, she could do so much more. A green energy hummed around her fingers and, without warning, blasted through the monster's body. She watched as the pixelated energy left a large, sizzling hole in its wake. Cosmic Green pulled her hand back as the monster's eyes widened to a comical size. With a weak, blood stained cough, it collapsed to the ground.

"W-what did you do?!"

In all the frenzy she'd forgotten that Marianna was around, now transformed and staring at the hairy remains of the city's latest threat. Cosmic Green looked down at her hand and smiled at the energy surrounding it.

It wasn't every day that Bree returned to outer space after a giant monster fight, but there she was, standing in Blaze's cosmic chambers. She knew she should've been paying attention to the woman, but all she could think about was the battle that had taken place.

Though, not to brag, it hadn't been much of a battle.

Bree had utterly destroyed that creature in a single hit. It was like she'd waited for her Super Meter to fill before inputting the right button combinations to release the ultimate Hadoken. Did she really have this kind of power inside of her? The command she shouted out to transform. The attack she used. It was all real. Cosmic Green was all hers, and she could use that power in any way she wanted.

"You're too reckless."

Almost in any way she wanted.

Bree glanced over at Marianna. The girl was standing next to her, arms crossed like a disapproving parent. Not even Blaze looked as irritated as she did, in fact, the look on Blaze's face was completely neutral. "What's your problem?" Bree asked. "The monster was killed. We won. End of story."

"It's not that simple! There's a technique to this! You can't just run in like that and-"

"And what? Save the day? Isn't that what *you* did when you saved me?"

Marianna frowned. "I had a plan. If you'd stayed a second longer on the roof I could have told it to you. It was foolish to run in like that when you didn't know what you were doing."

"Oh? Exactly how long were you gonna stand there before we went in and attacked that thing?"

"I know more than you do," Marianna said. "I know what those creatures can do."

"And I don't?!"

"Enough! Both of you!"

Both girls turned to face Blaze, whose neutral look had turned into one of disappointment as the stars dimmed down around her. "You two shouldn't be arguing like this. You two should be working together."

Marianna sighed and said, "Yes ma'am."

Bree nodded her agreement, but she still wasn't thrilled with Marianna's attitude toward her. However, it wouldn't do any good to keep the argument going, not when Blaze looked so displeased with them.

"It's true that the situation was handled, but you two should've worked together. Neither of you need to fight alone."

"Tell Marianna that. She doesn't trust me."

"You didn't even give me a chance to-"

"Ladies! I said enough!" There were asteroids floating around high above Blaze now, colliding into one another in loud, chaotic crashes as she gripped onto the arms of her chair.

Both Marianna and Bree turned away from each other.

"Well this team is going to be a disaster if you two keep arguing like this."

Marianna opened her mouth to say something, but decided to stay quiet when she saw the harsh look on Blaze's face. Bree had a feeling what the girl was going to say, something along the lines of not asking for this "team" to begin with. To be fair, Marianna was right. This had been Blaze's idea, not hers.

"I think you two need to learn how to work with one another."

Bree didn't like the sound of that, and neither did Marianna. "So what, are we gonna train together or something?" Bree asked.

"More like *or something*," Blaze said, an amused smirk on her face as the stars around her grew brighter. "You two are going to live together."

Marianna and Bree's eyes widened and they both shouted, "What?!"

Jackie wasn't too heartbroken about Bree moving out. The two had barely gotten to know each other, so there were no hurt feelings as Bree boxed up her side of the room. Still, she did voice her concern and asked, "Is this because of the attack?"

The answer, of course, was yes, but it wasn't like Bree could go into detail. So instead she said, "No, just moving in with a friend."

Jackie nodded, and Bree had a feeling she didn't believe that. She probably thought Bree was too scared to stay on campus, which she supposed was fine. It was kind of lousy that she couldn't talk about how she'd become a badass who could smash green pixels into monsters, but she knew that Marianna would throw a fit.

Which led to the real annoyance of the situation.

Having to repack so soon? That in itself was annoying. But packing to move in with Marianna? How did her opinion of the girl sour so quickly? She'd gone from being the sweet girl who'd kept an unsettling man at bay, to the teammate she wanted to launch a few pixels at.

Though Bree was certain that Galactic Purple could easily stop them with cupcakes or sprinkles or something.

A knock on the door interrupted Bree's magical battle thoughts. Jackie answered and was greeted by Blaze, who offered her and Bree a smile. "Almost ready, Bree?"

"Yeah. Jackie, this is my... aunt."

"Nice to meet you," Jackie said.

"Nice to meet you, too." It was odd to see Blaze outside of that orbital room of hers. There was no grand outfit, no skirt that flared out like flames. She was dressed in a simple pair of jeans with a tank top – which still managed to look remarkable on her. "So, shall we get everything into the car?"

"I guess..." Bree was a bit disappointed that they were actually going to have to take the boxes to a car. Bree had been able to step into a different plane of existence because of Blaze, so she thought moving in with the woman would be a bit more mystical.

Blaze chuckled at the look on her face and whispered, "Even magical girls have to do normal things sometimes."

"Wonderful," Bree whispered back, then, "So where's *you know who?*"

"You mean Marianna? We'll be picking her up."

"Great." So she'd have to sit in a packed vehicle with her. Terrific.

With the both of them working together, it didn't take that long to load up the car – or rather, van. Blaze had come prepared, and there was plenty of space for Bree's belongings with room to spare. It helped that they didn't have to take the mini-fridge or microwave, and Jackie had no issue with keeping both of those items. As they got into the van to pick up Marianna, Bree asked, "What exactly am I supposed to tell my brother about this?" Bree wasn't too worried about her mother's opinion. She wasn't worried because she wasn't going to tell her anything. While the woman hadn't blamed the attack on her, she'd definitely have issue with Bree running around fighting monsters.

Blaze smiled and said, "Tell him the truth, if you want."

"Seriously?!"

"Yes. Marianna's parents know. It's much better if they know what's going on instead of being caught off guard if something happens to her."

"I guess I thought it had to be kept secret. Marianna doesn't like sharing this information."

"Well don't go around telling *everyone*, just those who you feel need to know. Marianna's parents needed to know, and if you feel like your family needs to know, tell them."

"All right." It was comforting knowing that she didn't have to put on this secret identity charade. She knew she wouldn't be able to keep this from Trey, not when he had been so worried about her. That being said, he was going to be beyond pissed when she told him.

Eventually.

Blaze drove off and headed to the lavish buildings across campus where Marianna lived. "Wait... she lives in those?!" Bree had not-so-secretly made fun the housing units when she first saw them. They looked more like luxurious condominiums then dorm rooms. Bree could only imagine how disillusioned the students would be when they graduated. There was no way they'd be able to afford a place so nice without a six-figure salary. "Are her parents rich or something?"

"They do well enough, but it helps that she got a scholarship," Blaze said as she parked in the visitor's spot.

"Somehow I'm not surprised," Bree muttered as she got out the van. In the short time they'd known each other Bree could already tell that Marianna was an overachiever.

As the two ladies stepped inside the building Bree took a moment to look around the lobby area. It looked like it belonged in a multiple-star hotel instead of a college campus. She almost expected a bellhop to come over and ask if they needed help. "You're gonna make her leave a place this nice?" She may have made fun of it, but she realized she wouldn't mind living in a place with a fitness center and pool – not that she was going to work out, but she'd take any excuse she could to laze around in a bikini.

"It'll be better if you lived together," Blaze said as she led Bree over to the elevator.

"I guess..." but Bree had her doubts. In hindsight, Marianna had every right to be bitter about the situation. On top of having to leave the spoiled anime protagonist version of student housing, she was leaving to move in with Bree, of all people. Not that Bree was hard to live with – though she was biased about that opinion – but Marianna had been doing the whole magical girl thing on her own. While it was certainly dangerous, it probably didn't feel good to have to change her routine in favor of a new girl who leapt off of buildings without any kind of warning.

That being said... Bree still didn't much care for her attitude and wasn't looking forward to them trying to live together.

The two got off on the third floor and walked toward the room at the end of the hallway. It was odd, Bree thought, to be walking through an air conditioned hallway that didn't have one lone bathroom for a floor of sixty-some girls. Blaze knocked on the door and smiled at the girl who answered. Bree recognized her as the other "heroic friend" from the mall, and said friend didn't look too happy to see Blaze. "Why are you making my Marianna leave me?"

Bree raised an eyebrow at that. *Her* Marianna? "You're making her leave her girlfriend?"

Dana sidestepped the question by asking a question of her own. "Aren't you the girl from the mall?"

"Ah, um... y-yeah," Bree said. "Crazy coincidence, huh?"

"Yeah. Marianna didn't say she was moving in with you..." Dana forced the disappointment away in exchange for holding the door open for Blaze and Bree. "I suppose you two can come in."

"Thank you Dana," then Blaze walked in, not at all phased by how Dana was responding.

"So... you two just met a few days ago and you're moving in together?" Dana asked as she closed the door.

"Uh... well..."

"Bree came here on her own and could stand to live with someone she knows," Blaze said. "I'm good friends with her mother, and we thought it would be a good idea."

Bree was impressed with Blaze's quick thinking. There was no way she would've been able to put together such a well-crafted lie so fast, but she could at least add to it. "Especially considering what happened before... my mom's a bit of a worrier."

The hard look on Dana's face softened. "That dude who followed you?"

"Yeah... he was a bit more persistent after you two left."

"He came back?! Ugh, gross!"

"Indeed," Blaze said as she sat on the couch with Bree. "So you can understand her mother's concern, yes?"

"Yeah..." then Dana pouted and said, "I'm gonna miss Marianna, though. Hey! What if you moved in here with us?"

"Now now, Dana, there's only two bedrooms here... unless you don't mind sharing with Marianna? She might have room in her bed-"

Dana interrupted the woman with a loud, nervous laugh. "N-no, that's quite all right! Let me go get her for you!"

Bree didn't think it was possible to blush that much. It was quite the adorable sight to behold as the hint of red shaded across her freckles. As Dana hurried off, Bree shook her head at Blaze and said, "Isn't it against some magical girl code to exploit someone's obvious crush like that?"

Blaze shrugged her shoulders. "I've heard of no such code."

"Of course," Bree chuckled. "So is this a one-sided crush thing or..."

"Marianna won't believe you if you tell her, and Dana goes along with whatever she says."

"Ah, one of those." Bree had seen it – and felt it – plenty of times before.

"Even so, the two have been friends since high school. *Best* friends, in fact. Marianna didn't have many friends before coming here." Blaze leaned back against the couch and frowned up at the ceiling. She almost expected it to shift into an orbital backdrop, but it remained its bland, white self. "This should put things in perspective for you. You aren't the only one who has to make an unwanted adjustment."

"You know, if neither of us want to do this maybe it's a bad idea."

Blaze shook her head. "I told you, you two need to get used to each other. This is the best way to do that."

"Did the girls live together before?"

"No... but perhaps they should have."

There was a story there, Bree could tell. She wanted to ask what Blaze meant by that, but from the pained look on her face, she decided to keep quiet. In the last few days she'd already stumbled into enough information to last a lifetime, she didn't need to learn anything else. Not yet, at least.

"Hello," Marianna said as she walked into the living room. She looked as stylish as always with an off-the-shoulder top and capris. She was even wearing cute heels despite having to move boxes soon. "I'm all packed and ready to go."

"Good. Shall we?"

Bree was surprised that Marianna wasn't putting up more of a fight. Maybe she'd given in to the inevitable: they were going to live together, whether they liked it or not.

"Marianna!!! Don't leave me!!!"

At this point Bree wondered why Blaze wasn't recruiting Dana. She apparently had the ability to appear out of nowhere and launch herself like a human rocket at unsuspecting targets. Marianna handled the situation with the expertise of a friend who was used to their bestie being a bit over-dramatic, laughing as Dana latched herself onto her. "We'll still keep in touch," Marianna said as she combed her fingers through Dana's hair. "It's not like I'm leaving the city."

"But who's gonna bake me cupcakes?"

Bree almost snorted when she heard that. She had vivid images of Marianna's cupcakes and the effects they had on her enemies.

"You can come by the bakery and get cupcakes, I promise."

"But Mariaaaaaaannaaaaaa!!!"

Bree glanced over at Blaze. "You sure about this? I don't think you can separate these two."

"It'll be fine. Trust me. This will work out."

Marianna finally managed to convince Dana to let her go after including shopping days – within reason – to her bakery promise. Dana gave her one last pout before she turned her attention to Bree and Blaze. "You'd better take good care of her," then she turned and walked off, saying something about not being able to watch Marianna leave her.

"Does she know? About... *you know?*" Bree asked.

Marianna shook her head. "No, she doesn't, and I'd like to keep it that way."

"So what did you tell her?"

Marianna shrugged her shoulders and said, "That it was Blaze's idea. I'm sure you came up with something, right?"

"I did."

"Good, then it's settled."

The tension between the two was thick enough to suffocate Bree. Marianna might not have been protesting the situation directly, but the snippiness in her voice was biting enough to illustrate her disdain over the situation. Blaze took it in stride and walked down the hallway with Marianna to help carry her boxes.

Bree sighed and followed after them. She wondered if magical pixel powers was going to be worth all of this.

"Where is everyone?" Bree asked. It was the first question that came to mind as Blaze drove them toward what looked to be a shell of an old financial building. The city had been so full of life when they left campus, especially in the middle of a bright and sunny Friday afternoon. Students had been prepping for the weekend with promises of parties and other social gatherings, thrilled to have survived the second full week of college. But now? In this part of the city? Everything just seemed to... stop. Wherever they were now was empty, like something apocalyptic had happened that left only the buildings intact.

"This is where you're going to live," Blaze said as she parked the van.

"Here?" Bree asked. This wasn't at all what she expected, not when Blaze's chambers were so spectacular. "But it's so..."

"It's like that on purpose," Blaze said. "To protect you girls."

Bree was sure that if she were a cartoon character, her jaw would drop low enough to hit the ground. "Wait... you're doing this? You can just close off an entire area in the city?"

Blaze laughed and shook her head. "It's mostly this building and the block around it."

Bree wasn't sure what was more intimidating: the fact that Blaze had this kind of power, or the fact that she was so nonchalant about it. "Still... that must take a lot of power..."

"I suppose it does. But remember, I'm one of you, too, and have been for quite some time."

Before grabbing any boxes, Blaze escorted Marianna and Bree into the building. As they headed to the elevator, Bree could feel herself having second thoughts. A woman she barely knew had picked them up in a van and brought them to an abandoned part of town. The magical powers were nice, but it was starting to feel like a clever ruse via an ongoing television series about the criminal justice system and its two separate, yet equally important groups. What had her mother said about not giving into temptation? Bree glanced over at Marianna, who had been oddly quiet for most of the trip. "Hey," Bree whispered to her. "Have... you been here before?"

"No, just her chambers, just like you."

"Ah..." she had hoped that Marianna had a bit of insight to this place. "Listen, it may be too late to ask, but... we can trust her, right?"

Marianna stopped walking and raised an eyebrow at Bree. "You're asking that now?"

Yeah, definitely too late to ask, but Bree pushed on anyway. "It seemed fine before, but... I dunno, this whole thing feels..."

Marianna smiled and placed a hand on her shoulder. "You can trust Blaze."

There was a voice in the back of Bree's mind whispering to her about the dangers of blind devotion. This seemed especially relevant because of the animosity between her and Marianna. But something about the girl's smile was putting her mind at ease. Despite their differences, there was something so reassuring about that smile. If Marianna trusted this woman then Bree could, at least, attempt to do the same. After all, she did already step into a bizarre, galactic world, put on a magical hair bow, and leap off a building.

"Ladies? Shall we head up?"

Marianna and Bree stepped into the elevator with Blaze and went up to the very top floor. Both of the girls let out audible gasps when the doors opened to reveal the room Blaze had taken them to before. "This place is here?! In this building?!"

"That's incredible," Marianna whispered.

"You ladies will be on the floor below this one. I wanted to show you something familiar to put your mind at ease."

"I wasn't... I-I mean..." then Bree stopped. There was no use denying it. She recognized that knowing look on Blaze's face. "... sorry."

"No need to apologize. I'd worry if you didn't have any questions. Marianna certainly had plenty when she first got her powers."

"That's how I know I can trust her," Marianna said.

Huh. So did all her earlier disdain wear off during the car ride? Bree had a feeling that wasn't the case. Nobody got over something that quickly. Marianna may have trusted Blaze, but that didn't mean she agreed with everything she did. Still, Bree would settle for Marianna stifling her feelings if it meant she could have an easier time moving in. They could tackle the whole *working together* thing after she made sure she had a decent Wi-Fi connection.

The elevator doors slid shut and Blaze brought them to the floor below. The girls would've compared it to a studio apartment, but it was so spacious that it felt more like a one story house that was ready to complete that two kids and a dog dream – minus the picket fence. "Is this all... for us?" Marianna asked.

"It is."

Unlike the room upstairs, this area had walls and doors to section it off. While it was cool that Blaze's room felt like it went on forever, the girls didn't want to live somewhere they'd get lost in. Still, when Blaze had suggested they move in together, Bree had been expecting a dorm room or, at best, an apartment-like space as big as Marianna's had been. This went far beyond that. Bree felt like she'd stepped into a home with so much potential that Home and Garden enthusiasts would weep. "This is insane," she whispered as Blaze showed them around.

"Well, I want you ladies to live comfortably. Marianna could have her large kitchen, and you-"

"I can have an entire recording space!"

"Recording space? For what? Are you filming something?"

"Something like that," Bree said in response to Blaze's questions. She wasn't sure if she was ready to explain the whole Let's Play thing – not that she had a good amount of space in her dorm to attempt to do any proper updates. The equipment she'd managed to get via birthdays and Christmases was still packed away in boxes for a reason. "Wait... what do you need a large kitchen for?" Bree asked, remembering Blaze's comment toward Marianna.

"Oh... I do a bit of baking."

"And you'll have plenty of space to do more. Let me know what you need. Same for you, Bree. Whatever you need for your recording space."

There were two kinds of people in the world. Marianna was the type to smile, shake her head, and say, "You don't have to do that for us, ma'am."

"Naw, you can if you want to." Bree, on the other hand, was already planning multiple trips to the mall for electronics and games. If she was going to be a superheroine who risked her life for the sake of the city, she was going to, at least, take Blaze up on her offer to spoil the both of them.

"Bree!"

"It's my pleasure to take care of both of you," Blaze said. "If we're going to be together here, we need to bond with one another. So, first thing's first. Marianna? Don't call me *ma'am.*"

Marianna hesitated, then finally said, "Oh... right. Blaze it is, then."

Bree was certain that Marianna would forget and slip back into formalities. "So... what do we do, now?"

"Well first, we grab boxes. Then, we decorate."

Everything was perfectly fine.

At first.

The large amount of space had definitely won Bree over. Now she had a bedroom to call her own instead of a tiny living space she had to share with another girl. She'd decorated it the way she wanted, filling her walls with posters and filling shelves with figurines and cute plushies. Blaze had even let her upgrade her consoles and computer, complete with a camera, headset, and other equipment to create high quality videos of her swearing at video games. When the woman said she'd take care of her girls, she meant it. She never blinked at the price of one of Bree's games or Marianna's cookware. She didn't even flinch when Bree finally explained the kind of content she was planning on creating, though she did make an amused comment about *kids these days* and the creative choices they made.

But as Bree sat in her room a week after moving in, surrounded by all the things her little gamer heart dreamed of, she realized that it felt kind of... lonely.

The dorm rooms may have been small, but there was always some kind of activity going on, whether it was from the girls running down the halls for whatever reason, or even Jackie reading a book. It didn't feel nearly as empty as her new living space did.

She couldn't even invite her brother over.

Blaze had no problem with Bree telling Trey the truth – which she still hadn't done yet. However, since the building served as a headquarters, it was dangerous to bring anyone inside who wasn't part of the group. Bree could understand the logic, but it didn't solve the problem of feeling completely alone.

"Why don't you try talking to your new roommate?"

Bree sighed as she looked into the camera on her computer. Now that she had one, she was eager to try it out, and fortunately, Ella had been around to video chat with.

"I have. Well... sort of..."

It was a real downer. She hadn't talked to Marianna much before the whole magical girl thing, but there was a definite warmth to her. Bree had hoped that they could talk more, especially after she'd found out about Galactic Purple. But now? Now there was tension between them. Marianna wasn't hard to live with while, at the same time, extremely difficult to live with. She spoke to Bree when she had to, which boiled down to morning interactions and polite smiles. But beyond that? Silence. Marianna clearly didn't want Bree around and wanted to work alone, or at least, work with someone who she thought was competent enough to be a magical girl. And that was what hurt the most, knowing that the girl she'd been so thankful for felt so poorly toward her. Sure, she'd rushed into that first fight and made a poor impression, but she could adjust and actually follow a plan.

Maybe?

Not that Marianna would ever want to. Well, actually, she'd feel that she *had* to since Blaze was so set on this *team* thing. Marianna would go along with it because Blaze would tell her to. "That's her other annoying habit," Bree said. "She pretends like things are fine when they actually bother her." She'd almost prefer Marianna snap at her the way she'd done before Blaze interfered. The cold shoulder routine was driving her nuts.

"Ah, one of those. Then it'll all explode like Vash the Stampede or something," then Ella spread her arms out to illustrate said explosion.

"I can't let that happen. I can't deal with that much angst... even if she can bake her own doughnuts." Whether or not they exploded was up for debate.

"Then go and talk to her. Maybe bond over some doughnuts."

"But when I talk to her she acts like things are fine! I need her to admit that they're **not** fine!"

"Bree, why did you move in with this girl anyway?"

Bree let out a loud sigh as she slumped back in her chair. "It seemed like a good idea at the time..." That was partially true, after all, decorating her room had been fun.

"If it's that bad then move out."

"And find an open dorm space during the semester? Yeah right." Not that Bree could move out, anyway, but Ella didn't need to know that.

"Wish I could help you out," Ella said. "Somehow, this is more complicated than that whole monster thing you were dealing with before."

"Tell me about it," then Bree sat up in her chair and asked, "Oh hey, did that whole strange orb thing get figured out?"

Ella's let out a chorus of uneasy laughter. "Bree, I told you, I was kidding about that."

"Uh huh."

Ella sighed. "It's a long story, but next time you're in town, maybe I'll explain it."

"Mario Kart rematch?"

"You know it! A nice, normal gaming experience would be great."

Before Bree could ask what that meant, a loud siren rang throughout the entire building to interrupt their conversation. Bree winced and covered her ears. "Argh! That's really annoying!"

"Someone pull the fire alarm?"

"Yeah, something like that. Guess I should go."

"Hey, at least you're not at a convention where you have to stand outside in costume until the fire department shows up."

"Then you have to take the stairs back to your room? No thanks."

Ella laughed as she waved into the camera before logging off. Bree followed suit before she turned off her camera and computer screen. When she stepped out of her room she could see Marianna already waiting for her, looking just as annoyed over the siren. "I take it this is something we're gonna have to get used to?" Bree asked.

"I guess so," Marianna muttered, not a fan of the piercing noise.

"You know, a phone call can be just as effective."

"That's what she used to do with me. I guess this is much easier since there are more of us now..."

"You reeeeeally hate that, don't you?"

Marianna's eyes widened and she frowned at Bree. "I never said-"

"Good evening, ladies. I see my alarm worked." Behind them, the large television in the living room turned on to show that Blaze was now watching the both of them. At least the siren had finally stopped. "The break's over. There's been a monster spotted in the middle of the city. Marianna... it's near the bakery."

"W-what?"

"The bakery?" Bree asked.

"It's where she works," Blaze said.

Bree knew that Marianna had mentioned doing a little baking, and she'd mentioned a bakery to Dana, but she'd said nothing about working at one. Bree noticed the disappointed look on Blaze's face. She couldn't blame the woman. After a week of living together the two hadn't talked to each other enough for Bree to know something as basic as a part-time job.

"I need to go," then Marianna ran over to the window.

"Marianna!" Blaze snapped. "Wait for her."

Marianna stopped at the window and looked back at Bree. She must've been really worried about the attack because she didn't bother trying to hide her irritation, even with Blaze watching. With a sharp eye roll Marianna said, "Yes ma'am. Bree, let's go."

"If you don't want me to go-"

"We don't have time for this. Come on," then Marianna turned and jumped out the window. Bree glanced back at the TV and tried to find comfort in Blaze's smile, but as she ran after Marianna, she somehow felt more unsure of herself than she had the first time.

It was the biggest monster she'd ever faced as Cosmic Green. Then again, she'd only fought one monster before. Still, if she had to guess, it was about eight feet tall and easily loomed over her and Galactic Purple. It also looked more like a blob of black ooze than an actual being, bits of it pooling over the sidewalks.

When the girls had arrived on the scene, transformed and ready to go, it all felt so very familiar. People were running and screaming, ducking into any shops that had room. The bakery wasn't very big, but people were doing their best to find somewhere to stand as the two magical girls faced off against the large creature. Galactic Purple felt her heart stop when she spotted Dana holding the door open for everyone to run inside. "Dana..."

"Crap." The situation had gone from bad to cruel in an instant. Cosmic Green couldn't imagine having to keep such a big threat away from a good friend. "All right, we need-"

"I need you to make sure the people in the bakery are all right."

Oh. Right. That whole *I don't want you here* thing was still in full effect. And here Cosmic Green thought that maybe, just maybe, Galactic Purple would be more reasonable now that her friend's life was at risk. "What? No way! You're gonna try and fight this thing alone? Are you crazy?!"

"I have a plan, unlike you."

Had it not been an emergency, she may have let that slide, but as it stood there was no time for repetitive lectures on past mistakes. "Damnit, it was **one** time!" Cosmic Green clenched her fists as she stomped her foot in frustration. "This isn't the time to throw that in my face!"

"Protecting people is our number one priority. I need you to go and do that while I take care of this."

"What do you expect me to do? Sing them a lullaby or something? They're in the building, and they're-" but before she could finish, the creature sent a large clump of black ooze after them, as if reminding them that it was still here and still very much interested in killing them. Both ladies managed to jump out the way and watched the substance stick to the street like glue being spread across someone's skin. In seconds, the black gunk hardened in place, the ground beneath it cracking in web-like lines across the pavement. "Well, guess we know what it can do now," Cosmic Green muttered.

"Go and check on the people!" Then Galactic Purple ran forward, one of her signature cupcakes forming in the palm of her hand.

More than anything, Cosmic Green wanted to yell some more, maybe throw an end all, be all, tantrum. But as she watched the girl she'd once praised for her heroics, her eyes widened in realization. Those cupcakes exploded. They exploded and she could imagine black bits flying around in a grotesque shower that hardened into jagged little rocks. Those rocks would smash into everything, including the bakery and any other shops in their way.

They'd probably hit Dana first, though, since she was still closest to the door.

"Mari-" She stopped herself from yelling the girl's real name and tried again. "Galactic Purple! Stop!" But she didn't get a response. Galactic Purple didn't think she had a reason to listen to the newest member of the team.

"Cupcake..."

Cosmic Green only had seconds to come up with something and did the first thing that came to mind.

She attacked Galactic Purple.

"8-Bits and Pieces!"

The green bits flew out of the palms of her hands and rushed after Galactic Purple, who looked back just in time to see what was coming. The energy in her hands disappeared as she quickly rolled out of the way, the green bits flying forward and shooting into the monster and leaving small holes in its body. The creature roared in protest as the holes began to close and reform its blubbery shape.

"What the hell are you doing?!" Galactic Purple snapped as she got up and walked toward Cosmic Green, heels clicking against the ground to emphasize her anger.

Cosmic Green could feel her heart pounding from the furious look on the girl's face, but she needed to stand her ground, especially if she was going to be part of this team. "You can't attack it like that."

Galactic Purple stood in front of her, shaking from how angry she was. "Stay out of this! You don't know what you're doing!"

"Look, I don't know what your problem with me is, but I'm here whether you like it or not." This was the worst possible time an argument, but if Marianna wasn't going to listen to her at home, then Galactic Purple was going to listen to her in battle.

"My problem? My problem is that you're reckless and you think this is a game."

"Excuse me?! When did I say this was a game?!"

Galactic Purple scoffed in Cosmic Green's face and said, "Oh please. You jumping off a building without a plan? You actually bantering with that last monster, telling it that you'd show it how *magical* you are? You don't take this seriously at all."

"How dare you! I was attacked by one of these *things*! You have no idea how threatening they really are! You're just out here playing the heroine and are pissed off because you have to share the spotlight!"

"...what?"

"You heard me," though, to be honest, Cosmic Green had a feeling that wasn't true. From their few interactions the plus size warrior didn't seem like the type who wanted a flood of attention. However, the accusation had at least gotten her to stop yelling. Besides, if she could make such damning assumptions about her motivations, then Cosmic Green would do the same thing. "You were some myth in this city, and you

loved that, didn't you? But Blaze knows you can't handle it by yourself, not when these creatures are getting stronger. Not when they're attacking more frequently, and more brazenly."

The horrified look on Galactic Purple's face said it all, but, in that moment, Cosmic Green didn't care. The girl she'd been so impressed with had not only belittled her, but she belittled what had happened to her.

"No! Get away!"

The shrill sound of Dana's scream caught both of their attention. Their adversary had decided to shift its focus and was now approaching the bakery. Galactic Purple completely froze, watching in horror as a glob of the tar-like substance was sent after Dana, a hand forming out of it to try and grab her. Fortunately, Cosmic Green was on the move and shot another wave of green bits to cut into the arm. Chunks of it fell onto the sidewalk, right in front of Dana, and Cosmic Green yelled, "Get inside!"

"R-right," then Dana stumbled inside and slammed the door shut.

"D-Dana, she..."

And just like that, all of her anger melted away. Cosmic Green grabbed hold of Galactic Purple's shoulders and said, "Snap out of it! I need you!" Because now the creature was lurking toward them.

"I... I froze, I-"

"You're allowed to freeze up! But I need you to get a hold of yourself! Now!"

Galactic Purple took a deep breath and nodded her head, trying her best to calm down. "I'm not... i-it's not about being in the spotlight," she whispered.

"We can discuss that later. Right now, we need to stop this thing."

BAKING BITS OF TROUBLE
Dave Branch • www.facebook.com/Artbydavethewave/

"...you stopped me before because if I blow it up, the pieces will harden."

"Yeah."

"And when you shoot it, it reforms."

"Yeah... so, I'm not sure what to do," Cosmic Green admitted, bracing herself for a round of harsh judgment.

Instead, Galactic Purple looked over at the monster, watching as the bits it lost from Cosmic Green's attack molded themselves back together. She nodded to herself and said, "I know what we have to do."

"We?"

Galactic Purple nodded. "How long do you think you can shoot it? It's pretty big, can you shoot it down completely?"

"I have no idea. I've never tried something like that before."

"To be fair, you've only been in one fight."

"True... but if I shoot it down, won't it just reform?"

"I won't let it."

Cosmic Green wasn't sure what Galactic Purple was going to do, but she could tell from the determination in her eyes that she was serious. With a deep breath, Cosmic Green closed her eyes and pushed both of her hands out. "**8-Bits and Pieces!**" It was a continuous stream, like endless bullets trying desperately to shoot down their target. She imagined herself mashing buttons on her controller when a video game prompted her to do so. With a determined yell, Cosmic Green forced herself to keep going. She ignored the hot burn at the back of her throat. She ignored how badly her hands were shaking. The monster was screaming and falling apart into black chunks, and instead of hardening, the pieces were crawling toward each other in an attempt to reform.

"Keep going," Galactic Purple said from behind her. "It's almost completely broken."

Cosmic Green wanted to tell her that it wouldn't matter. She knew how this scenario played out. Television taught her that the monster would reform or, even worse, each blotch would turn into a different creature. Not that it mattered, because she was now out of energy. Cosmic Green dropped to her knees. She could feel the sweat on her forehead, her hair damp from it as she panted harshly for air.

"Good job."

Cosmic Green glanced up to see that Galactic Purple was now standing in front of her. The purple haired girl glanced back at her and offered a smile – a sincere smile – and in that moment Cosmic Green remembered why she'd been so enamored with her in the first place. Galactic Purple faced their enemy and launched one of her cupcakes into the sky. The cupcake was twice the size as her normal ones, and when she cried out, "**CUPCAKE BOMB**," it exploded in the air. A small rainstorm of frosting and sprinkles hit the black chunks, and Cosmic Green suddenly realized what the magical baker was doing. It was the same thing that had happened with that very first monster that had attacked her. The frosting was dissolving the putrid chunks of the monster until there was nothing left.

Her plan had worked.

With the battle over, Galactic Purple turned to leave, but Cosmic Green got a burst of a second wind, stood up, and grabbed onto her hand. "Look. Over there."

Galactic Purple turned to see Dana slowly stepping out the bakery along with a few others. They all whispered amongst themselves, marveling at the fact that they were now safe, their vicious attacker nowhere to be found. Dana locked eyes with Galactic Purple and said, "You're her. You're *The Girl in Purple*."

As the rest of the crowd began to put the pieces together, Galactic Purple took a step back. "We shouldn't be here. They shouldn't see us."

"They already know about you. About *us*," Cosmic Green said. "We should let them know who we are, officially, so they know that they'll be protected."

Galactic Purple looked a bit uneasy, but then she saw the look on Dana's face. She looked so relieved, but more importantly, she was safe.

She'd protected her. No, *they'd* protected her. Together. "My name is Galactic Purple."

"And I'm Cosmic Green."

Then together, they spoke as a team. "We're **magnifiquenoir!**"

There was a hesitant knock on Bree's door later on that night. When Bree answered she was greeted by Marianna, who was dressed in a pair of cute, cat themed pajamas. The normal loose braid in her hair undone for maximum comfort after the battle. Marianna held up a plate of freshly baked cupcakes topped with a healthy dose of buttercream frosting and sprinkles. "Good evening."

Bree said the first thing that came to mind. "These won't kill me, right?"

"Huh? O-oh, no, they're normal cupcakes. Some are chocolate. Some are vanilla. I wasn't sure what kind you liked..."

"I was kidding," Bree said, then she held the door open for Marianna to step inside her room.

"Oh! Right, of course." Marianna took a moment to look around her room. "Was I interrupting something?"

"Huh?"

Marianna nodded over to the television where Bree had been playing one of her video games. "I can come back-"

"Naw, it's fine. I was about to lose anyway. You can have a seat on the bed."

Marianna glanced over at the bed, which still hadn't been made from that morning. Somehow, she wasn't surprised as she took a seat on the messy blanket. "What's all the other stuff for?" She asked as she set the plate of cupcakes down next to her.

"You mean the mic and camera and stuff? For my channel. Thinking of giving it a makeover, though, but I'm not sure yet." Bree paused as she shut her game off. She'd take down the villainous Shao Kahn later... assuming he didn't resort to cheap tactics like he usually did. "But... you're not here to talk about that, are you?"

Marianna sighed and shook her head. "No, I'm not."

Bree sat next to her and grabbed a cupcake. She knew this talk was going to happen and had a feeling that the cupcakes were an attempt at an icebreaker. Bree's stomach was more than happy to accept Marianna's offer as she took a big bite. "Oh my god this is orgasmic," she said around a mouthful of the cake.

"W-what?"

"This. This cupcake. It's really good!"

"Ah... thank you," Marianna said, flustered over Bree's choice of words.

"I mean it!" Bree took another bite and made sure to lick up any of the frosting from her lips. "Why didn't you tell me you could throw down like this in the kitchen?"

"Well... I did tell you I did a bit of baking."

"*A bit* sounds like my mom when she feels like getting those premade cookie cubes. This is like elderly black church lady who has all her recipes memorized."

Marianna laughed. "I dunno if it's *that* good, but it's definitely what I'm aiming for. I'm gonna have my own bakery someday."

"Yeah? I'll definitely sign up for your loyalty card."

Marianna smiled sadly as she watched Bree take a second cupcake. This was exactly what Blaze had wanted to happen, but the two had been so stubborn... no, that wasn't right. *She* had been the stubborn one, not Bree. Marianna grabbed a cupcake for herself but couldn't come to eat it. Instead, she poked her finger into the frosting and whispered, "I'm sorry."

"Hm?"

"I'm sorry for what I said out there. I had no right to trivialize what happened to you. And I'm sorry I've been so difficult."

Had this been days ago, or even a few hours ago, Bree would've relished in the apology. But now she knew that if this partnership was going to work, she'd have to actually listen. "Why?"

"Why what?"

"Why were you so harsh on me? I mean, I know I went about things the wrong way with that one monster, but-"

"That's not the reason. I suppose I could say it is, but it's not. I understand why you were so eager to fight. Being attacked like that and gaining the strength to do something about it? I understand."

"...it was still pretty dumb to jump off a building like that."

"Yeah... kinda. How did you even know it would work?"

Bree shrugged her shoulders and said, "I dunno, that's what the heroic characters do."

"You know, I'm really trying not to criticize your actions..."

"I know I know! I'll shut up now!" To prove it, she stuffed the remainder of her second cupcake into her mouth.

"It's a mix of things. I've been doing this on my own and I thought I was doing a good job, but Blaze... she wants to reform the group. And that's fine, I just... everything happened so fast! She recruited you, we had to move in together, I... liked things the way they were."

Bree nodded her head as she quietly swallowed the rest of her cupcake. She had a feeling that was part of Marianna's problem with her. She'd obviously had a routine, and a life, before Bree came along. Unlike Bree's relationship with her roommate, Marianna and Dana had, at the very least, a friendship. "Why didn't you tell Blaze any of this?"

"I don't like to cause trouble."

Bree stopped herself from laughing out loud. "Really? Because you were fine with telling me off, and you were definitely snippy with Blaze."

"You're different from her. She's done a lot for me and I didn't want to sound like I didn't appreciate it. I know how important this is to Blaze, so I didn't say anything to her. Not directly, at least."

Bree eyed a third cupcake, debating if she should eat it, especially since Marianna was still poking at her first one. "You shouldn't bottle stuff in like that."

Marianna sighed. "That's hard for me. I didn't exactly grow up with a lot of encouragement."

"Oh?"

Marianna finally gave up on poking at her cupcake in favor of setting it back on the plate. "It's primarily my mother. She's always worried that if I do anything, I'll stand out too much. I want to show her that it's okay to stand up for yourself. That's why I took on this power. I thought that if I stood up for others and protected them, she'd see that it was a good thing. Blaze has been nothing but encouraging, but my actual mother? Not so much."

Bree decided to pass on the third cupcake and completely focus on Marianna. It was obviously hard for her to talk about this and she deserved her undivided attention. "So you want to protect people and show your mother what you're capable of… but you didn't even tell people your name so they'd know who was protecting them. Why?"

Marianna lowered her head, her voice cracking as she whispered, "… because… my mother hates that I'm a magical girl."

Bree felt a pain in her chest when she heard those words. She couldn't imagine anyone hating this, not when the main goal was to defend others who couldn't defend themselves from the monstrosities that roamed about. No matter how much Bree feared her brother's reaction to this, she knew that, deep down, he wouldn't hate it. He'd be worried about her safety, but eventually, he'd see the good in it. And when Bree really thought about it, her own mother would feel the same way. She'd be preached to about the dangers of it all, but she'd never be made to feel as low as Marianna felt right now. "A-are you sure she hates it? Maybe she-"

"She told me, Bree. She hates it." Marianna brushed her hand across her eyes, trying to hold back the tears. She'd already cried far too many times about this topic. She'd hoped she'd moved passed it by now, but talking about it with Bree was stirring up all those emotions again.

Bree really hated the fact that she was a sympathy crier. She could already feel her eyes watering as she watched Marianna. "... d-did she say why?" Bree asked.

"The group before us? They were around back when my mother went to college here. One day, she was paralyzed by an attack. I guess **magnifiquenoir** didn't get there in time."

"So she hates all magical girls now?" Bree hated when people used that kind of logic. "I'm sure they tried their best to get there."

"She doesn't want the same thing to happen to me. Because I might get hurt, and because... I might not show up in time, and I might see someone else get hurt. So when I saw Dana at the bakery...."

"Jeez... I'm sorry, Marianna. And I'm sorry I accused you of being upset because I was stealing the spotlight."

"I remember how scared you looked when that thing was pinning you down. I didn't want to see that happen to you again. I thought if I did this alone, and could do it well enough, that I'd always get there in time."

Bree smiled as she reached over and took Marianna's hand. "I jumped because I needed to do something."

Marianna looked up at Bree, confused by her words. "What? I thought you said-"

"I know what I said, but since you're being honest with me, I'll be honest with you," then Bree took a deep breath and continued. "When I was attacked, I was so scared, but worse than that? I felt completely helpless. That creature made me feel so helpless and I absolutely hated it. Then you showed up and just... you dominated it so effortlessly! I wanted to be able to do that, but at the time, I couldn't."

"So when Blaze gave you the power..."

Bree nodded. "I had to do something. There was another monster terrorizing people and I just... had to."

Marianna smiled and said, "I felt the same way the first time I transformed. I spent so much time with a mother who told me to just sit down and stay quiet, and suddenly... I was loud, and powerful, and people needed me."

Bree smiled back and said, "You are magical. And so am I."

And just like that, things were resolved. With the tension fading between them, they could talk the way friends did. Marianna gushed about the size of the kitchen and how she may have gone overboard with baking. Bree had definitely noticed that there was a steady supply of sweet treats in their living space. She, of course, didn't mind at all. She'd steal a few cookies late at night before she went about taking on the imaginary threats of the gaming world.

"So what's your channel like? What kind of changes are you planning?" Marianna asked as she finally took a bite out of the cupcake she'd grabbed before. It was pretty good, but not at all close to *orgasmic* levels. She had a feeling that Bree liked to over-exaggerate, either that, or she was easy to please when it came to food.

"Oh! It's a gaming channel. I'm thinking with the whole magical girl thing I got goin' on, I should use it to my advantage. Re-brand it into something really cool, put *Cosmic* in the name somewhere and-"

"No."

"What?"

Marianna set her cupcake down and shook her head. "You can't do that."

"What? Why?"

"Are you seriously gonna put your name out there like that? Do you have any idea how stupid that is?"

Bree scooted away from Marianna and the plate of cupcakes. "I thought you were done being mean to me..."

"This isn't being mean, this is being logical!"

Bree pouted. "Can I at least be transformed?"

"Absolutely not! And I better not catch you recording while transformed! Now, I'm gonna go get some Kleenex. Do NOT eat all the cupcakes," then Marianna stood up and left the room.

Bree actually smiled as she watched Marianna leave. She had a feeling, as she took her third and not at all final cupcake, that this would work out just fine.

EPISODE FIVE:

MAGICAL KICKBOXER LONNIE KNOX

PRESENT DAY

"What are you doing today?"

Bree looked up from where she was packing up her books to see Kayla standing in front of her. It had been another dull lecture, but she did, at least, manage to stay awake. Kayla's occasional smile from her seat and gorgeous blue lipstick certainly helped. "Oh... going to the mall," Bree said.

"Ah. Sounds like fun. Don't suppose you want some company, do ya?"

"O-oh! Um... it's just for some boring stuff..."

"Boring? Aren't you picking up your game tonight?" Marianna cut in with her patented raised eyebrow from where she was sitting. She knew there was a midnight launch for a game and she knew every intricate detail about it. How Bree had to transfer her reserve when she went off to college. How she'd convinced – *begged* – her brother to finish paying off the Collector's Edition as a *congratulations for getting into college* gift. How she'd been spending the entire week playing the previous installments in the series on her channel. Boring? That was *not* the word Bree should've been using.

"Huh? O-oh! Right, that!"

"Game?" Kayla asked curiously. "Like a video game?"

"Ah, yeah... i-it's kinda silly, huh?"

"Did I say it was silly?" Kayla asked.

"Well no..." Bree frowned as she struggled to find the right words. While she took great pride in her steadily growing YouTube channel, she wasn't sure how anyone outside of the geek sphere would look at it. Under normal circumstances, this wouldn't be a big deal and she'd sashay away from anyone who judged her. But she was trying to make a good impression on Kayla. She didn't want to do anything too startling to the attractive Muggle and... Lord, did she *actually* refer to her as a *MUGGLE*? What was this, Hogwarts? Was she so accustomed to geek speak that she couldn't even refer to her crush as a normal person? Bree glanced over at Marianna and sighed. She had that look on her face, that *don't be ashamed of who you are* and *if she doesn't like it she's not worth it* look.

"I already know you're a geek if that's what you're worried about," Kayla said. "You're wearing *Pokémon* earrings."

"You recognize them?!" Did that mean that Kayla was a gamer, too? Then again, she had made that subtle Zelda reference when she brought her coffee before. But that quote had been on enough memes that she could've picked it up from there. Still, knowing *Pokémon* showed some geek cred, didn't it? Maybe she watched the anime. Bree could show her *PokéRap* skills and-

"Yeah. Kinda hard not to. *Pokémon* is everywhere these days."

Oh. Yeah, that was a good point. "Well... I'm going to a midnight launch for a video game..."

"So?"

"In costume..."

"So like cosplay?"

"All right, are you sure you're not a geek?" Bree asked with a suspicious grin, much like a great detective who'd gotten closer to solving the big case.

Kayla laughed and said, "I dabble in a few things," then she added, "I work with people who cosplay."

"Oh. Is it that coffee place you brought me coffee from?"

"You mean *Pandasaur Cafe*? Naw, I just like their coffee."

"I thought I recognized the place," Marianna said. "It's close to where I used to live on campus."

"Isn't that from a TV show?" Bree asked. She hadn't connected the dots before. She'd been too busy forgetting her own name whenever Kayla breathed the same air as her. "Oh duh! That's what your shirt is from!"

"This?" Kayla looked down at the shirt she was wearing: a cute hybrid of a snail and an octopus with a large, cartoonish smile. "Yeah, it's kinda silly, huh?" The show was aimed at a much younger audience than her.

"It's cute! The Pandasaur runs a cafe and has all sorts of odd little friends, right?"

"Yeah, something like that..."

Marianna watched the two of them and chuckled to herself. Bree hadn't realized that Kayla's normal confidence had slipped away. She also hadn't realized that she was actually speaking to her crush in complete sentences. "So... midnight launch?" Marianna asked, deciding to grant the two mercy from each other's embarrassment.

"Right! I'll bring some coffee for our midnight get together."

"W-wait! You're coming with me?"

Marianna sighed. At least Kayla wasn't flustered anymore. She could at least carry them in the right direction, but Bree? Poor Bree could barely get through classroom conversations.

Lucky for Bree, Kayla found her flustered state of affairs adorable. "Sure, why not? I'm usually up around that time anyway."

"You do know that a midnight release doesn't start at midnight, right? That's more like the end. I'm sure a line has started already."

"Already?" Kayla glanced at her cellphone. "It's only 10 in the morning."

"Yeah... people are reeeeeeally looking forward to this game. I was gonna head over when all my classes were done."

"Well give me a call when you're on the way and I'll meet you there. This is the only class I have today."

"It is?" Marianna asked. "How'd you manage that?"

"By being a senior and only having one semester left after this one."

"Wait, you're a senior?" As if her being gorgeous wasn't intimidating enough, she was older, too? Was the taboo of a senior dating a freshman not a thing in college? "How old are you?"

"Twenty-one. I procrastinated in taking this class because it's a dumb requirement."

"Ha! See, Mari! I'm not the only one!"

Marianna hung her head in shame. She couldn't believe an older classmate was validating Bree's terrible attitude toward early morning Math classes.

"Anyhow, I'll see you tonight. Don't stand me up, cutie," then Kayla headed for the door.

"But... I don't have your phone number..."

Kayla smirked and walked back over to Bree, leaning in kissably close. "Should I do it the old fashioned way and write my number on the palm of your hand? Or can we make it easy and you give me your phone so I can put my number in?"

When Bree didn't say anything Marianna reached over and pulled her phone out of her pocket. "Here, I'll do it for her," she said.

"A baker and a wing woman, you're pretty good."

"Someone has to be," though she did find it amusingly ironic that it was the one who had very little interest in relationships. Then again, her lack of interest didn't mean she was incapable of interacting with people. Dana was solid proof of that.

Meanwhile, Bree still wasn't sure what was happening. She knew Marianna had her phone for a reason, and Kayla was telling her something. Midnight launch. Get together. Phone number... ah, that was it! Kayla was giving her her phone number.

Wait, what?!

But it was too late. Kayla was already out the door and Marianna was handing her back her phone. "That went well," Marianna said. "We should get going."

"Get going? Are you serious?! I have to get ready for tonight!"

"It's 10 in the morning, you've got plenty of time."

"But..."

"Relax. There's no reason to panic."

"ELLA!!! HELP ME!!!"

Ella sighed as she watched Bree pace back and forth in her room via her computer's camera. "I fail to see what the problem is," Ella said as she took a bite from what passed as a burrito. Just because it was microwavable didn't mean it had to be so lackluster. At least it wasn't the bowl of healthy greenery that her roommate was trying to force everyone to eat. Then again, there was a chance that Sean was right outside her door, armed with a bowl of salad and no Ranch dressing.

"This wasn't supposed to be a date!"

"You're just going to pick up your game," Marianna said from where she was sitting on Bree's bed, scrolling through her phone as she listened to her friend's personal crisis. Classes had ended fairly early, and since it was her day off, Marianna had planned on spending the afternoon relaxing. Friendship, Roommate-hood, and Magical Girl Loyalty had other plans. Instead of soaking in a nice bubble bath, Marianna was sentenced to sitting on the bed and trying to calm Bree down.

"In. Costume!"

"She doesn't care about that. Remember?" Marianna wondered if Bree was suffering from memory loss. Kayla had clearly stated that she had no issues with cosplay. In fact, hadn't Kayla been worried about Bree's relationship status before? That should've been a sign of Kayla's interest in her.

"Yeah. So you've got nothing to worry about. Besides, you look cute as hell in that costume," Ella said after swallowing another mouthful of food. "It's all Nikola could talk about when he saw the picture on your page." Ella felt a bit sorry for her good friend, Nikola. His whole quirky nerd bit was definitely lovable, but it wouldn't get him any closer to his not-so-secret crush. Ella didn't have the heart to tell him, no matter how many times he asked her to put in a good word for him.

"That's great, but what is *Kayla* going to think when she sees it? And finds out I'm going to livestream the whole thing for my channel? Ugh, I didn't even get to tell her about my channel!" Bree had, at least, stopped pacing, and had decided to flop down on the bed next to Marianna. She was so anxious that she was bouncing up and down, the bed squeaking along with her.

"I don't think she's going to care," Marianna said, forced to bounce along with Bree since she was moving so much. "She doesn't seem like the type."

"But she's twenty-one! She's an older woman! I've never dated an older woman before!" Bree let out one last desperate whine before she laid back, grabbed one of her pillows, and used it to hide her face.

Ella knew she shouldn't laugh at Bree's state of panic but she couldn't help herself. "You've had, like, one girlfriend..."

Bree shot up in the bed and tossed the pillow aside. "That's beside the point, Ella!"

"Would it make you feel better if I came with you?" Marianna asked. "I suppose going to pick up a game isn't much of a date. This could be the trial run to see if you two are compatible enough to go on a real date."

"Careful, FOX might take your idea and turn it into a reality show," Ella said.

"You'd stand in line for hours with me?"

It was hard to look into Bree's eyes and not melt from cuteness. They looked shockingly similar to that cat in the movie with the ogre. Marianna smiled at her friend and said, "Sure," then added, "Well... not the whole time... I'll probably wander around-"

"Just wander?" Bree smirked at Marianna. "Or shop?"

"There's a sale somewhere, I'm sure."

"Don't pretend like you don't have coupons loaded up on your phone already."

"You want me to come with you or not?"

"No! I do! Thank you!" Then Bree gave Marianna a big hug.

Ella smiled at the two girls. "Marianna, the date buffer- Oh! That's a great name for the reality show! Trademarked by Ella Yamauchi."

"Ha ha, Ella," Bree said, then, "I should get ready."

"You gonna wear your cosplay with your green wig to represent your channel?"

"I sure am!" Bree glanced over at Marianna and gave her a big smile, after all, she was the one who said her green hair was fine as long as she didn't go full-blown magical girl.

Marianna responded with her typical *Frustrated at Bree UGH why are we Friends?!* look, but nodded her head in agreement. She so loved how Bree only remembered their talks when it was most convenient to her.

"I'm looking forward to seeing the livestream! Take lots of pictures! Oh, and I hope the game is good. For your sake... and Chevy's."

Bree's eyes lit up when she heard that name. Chevy was filed under future life goals as she was a bit of a legend when it came to the gaming community. Not everyone appreciated her former gaming child prodigy status, but Bree did. "Chevy's picking it up, too?"

"She has to write a review for her blog. She hated the last install-ment and went on this whole rant about how the old school games were much better."

"Well, I mean, she's right. Lightning's cool and all but-"

"Bree. Get ready," Marianna cut in. "Otherwise you'll sit here all day talking to Ella about this supposed *Final Fantasy*."

"Right, right. Time to sign off. Ella, let Chevy know that if the game sucks, there's always room on the *Persona* train."

"She doesn't have the patience for Social Links. Dungeon crawl-ing, yes, but actually talking to people? That's apparently too much work gaming wise," Ella laughed.

Bree got up and walked over to her closet to grab the pieces of her costume. "Tell her she's missing out!"

"Will do!"

"It was nice talking to you, Ella," Marianna said.

"You too, Marianna. And next time, you should wear something cute to match!"

"Oh please cosplay with me, Mari. Please please please!" It was pretty last minute, but she was sure a fashionista like Marianna had something in her closet that, with a few creative tweaks, could be a cos-tume for a character who lived in a fantastical setting.

Marianna watched as Bree jumped up and down like a kid hopped up on too much sugar. Did Bree think her excitement would convince

Marianna to play dress-up with her? "Bree. Get dressed," Marianna said in an attempt to once again remind her friend of her end goal of cosplaying at the event.

"You're no fun," Bree muttered.

"Again, I don't *have* to go-" Marianna was cut off by another hug, this one much stronger than the last one. In that moment Marianna wondered if Bree could use the death grip as another magical attack. "All right, all right! I'm coming with, don't worry!"

"Have fun you two," then Ella signed off.

As the two girls stood outside the mall to wait for Kayla, Bree gave the fall weather a mental high-five. It decided to cut her a break with its lack of cold air, as if sympathizing with her cosplay choice. After scoring big at the local thrift store, Bree had found the belt, goggles, yellow jacket, and red baseball cap she needed for her character. Combined with the tiny shorts she already owned and her cute, pink bra, she was ready to go. The only thing off about the outfit was her green hair instead of the character's blonde, but she looked terrible in a blonde wig, anyway. Besides, *Cosmickaze Bree* most certainly had to livestream the event.

"So this is your cosplay?"

Bree and Marianna turned as Kayla approached them, armed with two cups of coffee in a clear sign that she'd thought this get together would be just her and Bree – minus the line full of eager gamers. Marianna gave Kayla a sympathetic smile. "It's fine," she said. "I'm not much of a coffee drinker."

"I'm sorry, I thought..."

"Yeah, I know." Marianna glanced over at Bree, who still hadn't said anything yet. "Bree? She asked about your cosplay, you should say something."

Bree mentally told herself to not be a bundle of nerves, but instead, she blurted out, "It's not the best." At Marianna's loud groan Bree tried to adjust her sentence. "I-I mean! I've worn more complicated costumes before, I just-"

Kayla cut her off. "It looks great. Then again I might be biased because I'm a sucker for pretty girls in small shorts who rock green hair."

"Oh, well, the hair isn't part of the costume. That's... well, it-"

"She has a YouTube channel," Marianna said, ripping the Band-Aid off for Bree, as they say.

"You do? That's cool! I've been looking into having a channel myself. What do you do for yours?"

"Play video games while partially dressed as a magical girl." There. She said it. She said it and it was now out in the open. What happened next was up to Kayla and whatever higher power heard her silent prayer. Bree could imagine the disapproving look on her mother's face. If only she knew that her daughter was trying to use the power of prayer to get a girl to like her.

"Magical girl? Oh, wait! Is the green hair for my girl Cosmic Green?" So you're combining two costumes right now?"

"Your... girl?" Marianna asked.

"Oh come on. **magnifiquenoir**? Galactic Purple and Cosmic Green? They're pretty amazing."

Both Marianna and Bree stared at Kayla for what felt like an eternity. They were aware that people in the city knew about their magical alter egos, but it was odd having someone talk to them about it directly. Marianna still remembered how awkward it had been to introduce herself as Galactic Purple to Dana after the bakery attack. That awkwardness had increased tenfold when Dana regaled her of her harrowing tale the very next day, complete with elaborate details about the two women who had saved her.

"You two got quiet all of the sudden..."

"Oh... sorry, just... I was worried you'd think this whole thing was weird," Bree said.

"It's all right, I've seen weirder."

"Oh?"

"You kinda see a lot of things when you're a dancer."

"Dancer?" Marianna asked. "Why would that be weird?"

Kayla smirked. "I'm not talking about ballet."

The girls were reduced to staring at Kayla for a second time in the span of a few minutes. Bree wondered if she was taking on more than she'd bargained for. She tried her best not to imagine Kayla dancing, but her mind was already becoming cluttered with breathtaking imagery of the light-skinned girl moving to the music.

"So... can one of you hold the door open? My hands are kinda full," then Kayla held up the two cups of coffee.

"O-oh! Right!" Bree rushed over and opened the door for Kayla. "Sorry about that."

"It's all right." Once all the girls were inside the mall Kayla handed Bree one of the cups of coffee. "So do you wanna ask about my dancing? Or maybe Marianna does?"

Marianna and Bree looked at each other as the three of them walked through the mall. Finally, Marianna decided to speak up. She didn't want to assume, so she asked, "What... kind of dancing?"

"I suppose it's kinda mixed bag but my passion is in burlesque. That's how I know about cosplay, I've seen performers do nerdlesque."

"Nerdlesque?" Bree asked.

"It's a combination of geek culture and burlesque. I got introduced to it when I saw a girl do an act as Storm from *X-Men*."

"People do that?!" How had that slipped past Bree's radar? "That's cool!"

Kayla smiled at Bree's excitement. "I've been thinking of doing a **magnifiquenoir** act of some sort, but I'm still working on it."

Bree could feel her breath catch in her throat while Marianna tried her best not to look so flustered. "That would be amazing," Bree finally managed to say once the shock wore off.

"You're gonna have to tell me where you got that green wig, though. It's perfect."

"Yeah, um... just at a booth at a convention. *Arda*, I believe? They have great wigs." Thank goodness for giant geek fests with wig booths for Bree to walk past and make note of.

"Nice save," Marianna whispered to Bree, still trying to get over a potential burlesque act of their magical adventures.

The trio headed up to the video game store where a line of people were already sitting outside. Both Marianna and Kayla were left speechless at the number of people. One group had even brought lawn chairs to sit in and a cooler full of drinks and snacks. Bree, on the other hand, took it all in stride. She'd expected this kind of turnout and would've been disappointed if such a big release had a small crowd.

Finally, Kayla managed to say something. "All this for a game?"

What Bree wanted to say was that this was more than just a game. This was a legacy. Well, at least, it *used* to be. The last series of games had been decent, at best, but nowhere near the masterpieces they should've been. So this newest release was about redemption. A long awaited redemption that had been delayed time and time again, and now, it was here.

Bree wanted to say all those things, but instead, she said, "Weird, huh?" And honestly, it was kinda weird, wasn't it? Standing in a mall for hours dressed as a fictional character just so she could pick up a video game? A video game that, deep down, she was hesitant about because of her love/hate relationship with its previous installments. Hopefully, she wouldn't end up sobbing in the arms of *Shin Megami Tensei* later. When in doubt: *Persona*.

"Hey, I dream of the day I have a line of people waiting to see me. I'd say this is pretty admirable."

"So not *too* weird?"

"Naw," then Kayla smirked at Bree and whispered into her ear, "I like weird."

Bree, somehow, managed to not squee in delight.

Before the group moved to the back of the line, Bree looked into the store and waved to Torrence. He smiled at her and mouthed the words *nice cosplay* followed by *save me*. There was a separate line of people in the store as customers tried to reserve the last available copies of the game. Poor Torrence looked like he'd been standing in the middle of a war zone. His coworker had called to say that she was stuck in traffic, but that she'd be there as soon as possible. There was no time to attempt to put back any of the display cases for the game, nor was there time to organize any of the games that had been traded in toward the upcoming title. "Poor guy," Kayla said.

"I should've brought him something," Marianna added, always the one to feel bad when others were clearly suffering. "I could've whipped up some cookies in no time."

"I can give him my coffee. I'm gonna be hyper enough as it is."

"That's nice of you, Bree. I can share mine with you if you want."

Bree smiled at Kayla and ignored the childish voice in her head that commented about indirect kisses. Instead, she walked inside with the girls and set her coffee drink on the counter. "For when you get a break," she said to Torrence.

"So never, then," Torrence whispered back to her when he finished ringing up one of the customers. "I'm in hell."

"Coffee is known to calm down the flames of hell," Bree said.

Torrence managed to smile at that, then he turned his attention to Kayla. "Is this the girl?"

Kayla raised an eyebrow. "*The girl?*"

Bree wished that she was cosplaying a ninja who could melt back into the crowd as Marianna spoke for her. Again. "Yeah, this is Kayla."

"Nice to meet you, Kayla, though I wish it were under calmer circumstances."

Kayla shrugged. "This is fine. And you are?"

"Bree's dealer, also known as the provider of video games."

"Um, hello? I need to be rung up."

Without missing a beat, Torrence faced the woman in line and smiled. "Right away, ma'am," then he began typing on the computer. "*Final Fantasy* reserve?"

"Yeah, I guess," she said. She had one of those voices that sounded like it was permanently smacking on bubble gum, complete with an overabundance of make-up on her face. "Whatever popular game is coming out, my boyfriend wants it. The Collector's Edition with the figurine," then she turned her attention to the phone in her hand, no longer feeling the need to look at Torrence.

Torrence may have appreciated her eyeliner game if she hadn't been so rude. "The version with the figurine is only available on the Square Enix website," he said with practiced ease, having had to say that numerous times. "And the Collector's Edition available in stores has been sold out for months. We still have copies of the standard edition." Torrence kept the smile on his face even if he knew something akin to a nuclear warhead was about to go off on him.

"That's a lie, he says you employees always got copies in back."

Torrence wished he could find the mystical employee who spread that rumor. "Ma'am, I'm sorry, but-"

"Look, Terrance, could you just work with me here? My boyfriend really wants this stupid game."

Torrence sighed. It wasn't worth correcting her about his name even if it was spelled out on his name tag. "There's nothing I can do."

"What kind of customer service is this?! I want to speak to your manager!"

"I'm the manager on duty…"

"Well I just can't believe you all weren't more prepared for this!"

Torrence could've pointed out how they'd been reserving the game for over a year, but there wasn't a point in adding more fuel to the fire. So instead he said, "I'm sorry," for what felt like the millionth time.

"Whatever," she said. "Get me the standard or whatever."

"You shouldn't get her ass nothin'," Kayla said.

Marianna and Bree looked at each other, sharing a silent look along the lines of *dayum*. They'd both been thinking it, but neither one was going to say it. Kayla, on the other hand, didn't seem to believe in filters. Her clear disdain for the irate woman was written all over her pretty face. Meanwhile, Torrence looked like he wanted to hug the girl for saying exactly what he'd been thinking and wasn't allowed to say. Dealing with this much attitude wasn't worth the subpar pay, especially since he hadn't had a break yet.

"Excuse me?" The woman hadn't bothered to give her full attention to Torrence, but she was more than ready to narrow her eyes at Kayla.

"I know you heard me." Kayla crossed her arms and looked the woman straight in the eye. "Or maybe not, since you don't seem big on actually listening to people."

"How dare you talk to me in such a way!"

"And how dare you talk down to someone over a game."

"They're the ones not selling me what I want!"

"They're sold out of the version you want." Kayla tilted her head and gave the woman a questioning look. "You do know what *sold out* means, right?"

"Listen honey," the woman said as she stepped closer to Kayla. "You should keep your nose out of other people's business."

Kayla raised an eyebrow at her, not at all bothered by how close the woman was standing. "Says the one making a scene over a video game that she procrastinated on buying."

It was here that the woman realized just how many people were around her. The line behind her went to the back of the store while people from the line outside were looking in to see what all the commotion was about. She could hear a few people whispering about her. They were talking about how unreasonable she was being and how they felt bad for her boyfriend dating such a venomous woman. The woman let out a low growl of, "Bitch," before she turned and stomped out of the store. The customers erupted into a round of applause as the tension in the air was immediately lifted.

"If Bree weren't trying to date you, I'd kiss you," Torrence said.

"I think Bree gets the first kiss, you know, when we reach that point."

Bree kept cheering with the crowd as she said, "How quickly can we get to that point, because that was awesome!" A good looking woman who didn't take crap from anyone had stood up for Torrence – one of the most important people in her life. Bree wanted to throw herself into Kayla's arms and be whisked away into the sunset... or at least to the back of the line outside.

Kayla laughed. "I guess we'll see."

After the commotion died down the girls stepped out of the store. Bree went right to work and asked the people in line if they had any issue with her recording them, happily explaining the workings of her channel and who she was. Neither Marianna nor Kayla were surprised with the crowd's enthusiastic agreement. Bree was a hard person to say no to – cute outfit or not.

Marianna took Bree's phone and began recording the livestream. Bree faced her and Kayla and mentally forced her nerves away, trying her best to not let Kayla's presence get to her. If anything, she needed to put on an even better show now that her crush was watching. Bree took a deep breath and belted out the best deliver she could. "Hi, everyone!

Cosmickaze Bree here at the *Final Fantasy* launch!" Right on cue, the line behind her erupted into screams, Marianna recording everyone: the cosplayers, the ones in Chocobo shirts, and ones sitting with their portable systems and playing older titles. The ones who'd been sitting in lawn chairs were extra excitable, clanking their cans of pop together in a toast to the game's release.

Even if Marianna and Kayla weren't familiar with the game series, there was a positive energy in the air that felt so welcoming. They watched as Bree talked to people in line, a natural performer as she bounced around in-character. Her energy was contagious and brought smiles to everyone she spoke with.

"She's really in her element," Kayla said.

Marianna nodded as Bree easily slipped into posing for pictures. After recording her interactions for a few more seconds, Marianna paused to talk to Kayla. "And you're okay with that, right?"

"You're pretty protective of her, aren't you? You sure you two aren't dating?"

"Very sure, but I have to look out for my friend."

"Fair enough," Kayla said with an understanding nod. "And yes, I'm okay with all this, why wouldn't I be?"

"She was worried about it. Not everyone is cool with the whole geek thing."

"Well, not everyone is cool with burlesque, either. I say as long as you're enjoying what you're doing and not hurting anyone, then by all means."

"Hey! Mari! It's a livestream! You're supposed to be recording!"

"You know, I didn't sign up for this. I was gonna go shopping," but Marianna hit the record button anyway, just in time to catch Bree's pouty face. She wondered what Bree's recording plan would've been had she not gone with. She had a feeling that getting her to tag along had been the plan all along. She certainly wouldn't put it past her.

"Ah! Marianna! This night just got better!"

Marianna blinked in surprise at the familiar call of her name. There, near the back of the line, was a bored Dana who looked more than ready to leave. Marianna quickly handed Bree the phone and braced herself for the impending hug. Dana, true to form, practically flew over to Marianna, her arms around her in seconds.

"What in the world are you doing here?" Bree asked as she stopped recording. "You're interrupting my livestream!"

"I'm here with Carlos," Dana said with a loud groan. "He's in the bathroom right now."

"You actually volunteered to sit in line with him for this?" Marianna knew that this wasn't Dana's kind of scene.

Dana shrugged her shoulders and said, "He doesn't have any friends so I'm doing him a favor."

"You were bored because your only friend doesn't live with you anymore."

Dana turned and delivered a sisterly glare at her twin. He was taller than her, his face not covered in quite as many freckles. He had an annoying habit of taking joy in getting on her nerves and Dana wanted to smack that smile off of his face. "Whatever, Carlos. Get back in line for your stupid game."

"You know, you were supposed to be holding my spot in line," Carlos pointed out. Not that he had been close to the front, but he'd still given her a job to do.

"Was I? Oops, silly me."

"You know, sis, this whole *stupid game* thing is about as stupid as buying a handbag that costs more than someone's rent."

"You take that back!" Dana snapped.

"I'm only speaking the truth. We all have our vices, sis. I have my games, and you have your crush on-"

Dana clamped her hand over Carlos' mouth. "Sooooo, you all are joining in on the fun, too?"

"Technically I'm trying to do a livestream..." Bree muttered.

"Cool! Sounds fun! Let's focus on that!"

Kayla looked between Dana and Marianna, then glanced over at Bree, her eyes asking a silent question about Dana's uneasiness about her brother revealing a certain crush. Bree simply nodded with a cute little smile on her face. Dana's crush on Marianna was obvious to everyone except Marianna.

"I'm Kayla, by the way," Kayla said as she held her hand out toward Dana for a handshake. "I have lecture with these two."

"She brought me coffee!" In Bree's mind, coffee meant dating, though to some *hot coffee* meant something completely different.

"Coffee, huh?" Carlos, being the gamer that he was, grinned at the reference, then promptly winced when Dana elbowed him in his side. "Ow! What was that for?"

"For being a perv," she hissed at him. "And for the fact that my understanding that reference means that I've been around your dumb games too much."

"Maybe we should get in line," Marianna said as she nodded over to it. It had gotten longer since their conversation started, the excited gamers taking up space in front of the neighboring stores.

"We'd still have a decent spot if someone hadn't jumped out of the line," Carlos muttered. Dana responded by repeating his words in a much whinier tone of voice.

"You should record this part," Marianna said to Bree. Bree whipped out her phone and the two siblings quickly stopped their banter.

The group joined the line without any other hiccups. Marianna took Bree's phone and went back to recording her friend as she chatted with a few others in line. As she recorded, she noticed a familiar, unwelcome woman approaching. "Hey... isn't that the woman who caused a fuss in the store?"

Both Bree and Kayla turned to see that Marianna was right. The woman was walking toward them, looking angrier than she had looked earlier. She was muttering something to herself that they couldn't hear, but they imagined that it wasn't anything good.

"What's she so upset about?" Dana asked.

Bree sighed and answered, "She wanted the Collector's Edition but they were sold out."

"And whose fault is that? She should've reserved it ahead of time, I think Carlos has had it reserved since the dawn of mankind."

Both Bree and Carlos laughed at that. The game had been announced years ago, so Dana wasn't too far off with her assessment.

"Um... guys? Something's happening to her skin," Kayla said.

Marianna slowly lowered the phone and looked over at Bree. They'd seen this happen before – Bree especially. This brought back memories of that horrible transformation Bree's assailant had gone through. The woman's skin was bubbling as if she were in a malfunctioning sauna. Bubbles dotted across her skin like mutated bug bites. A few of the bubbles popped, releasing a murky puss that splattered onto the ground. The angry muttering became louder, leaking into a blood-curdling screech that forced everyone in line to stop and pay attention. The entire line of people began to back away from her, but before they could leave she cried out, "No one is going anywhere!" Her voice was so loud that the floor began to rumble and crack, and everyone made the same terrifying realization.

They were on the second floor.

At best, a few cracks would be an inconvenience for the people on this floor. At worst, with the people and shops below, those cracks could destabilize the entire floor and send them all tumbling to the ground level on top of whoever or whatever was beneath them – rubble, concrete, rebar and all. Marianna and Bree had to think fast on how to handle the situation. The solution, of course, was to get rid of the monster, but how were they supposed to do that when they were surrounded by so many people?

Not just people: friends.

To make matters worse, Dana spoke up before they could decide on a course of action. "You should calm down, sweetie, or the ladies of **magnifiquenoir** are gonna destroy you."

"Dana," Marianna whispered to her. "Don't antagonize her."

"It's true! They're always here when we need them! This creature doesn't stand a chance." There was a smile was on Dana's face but her hands were shaking. Badly. She needed to reassure herself that help was coming and that took the form of calling this transforming lady out. It broke Marianna's heart to think that she didn't have a way to get away, transform, and provide Dana and everyone else the help they needed. She could, of course, throw caution to the wind and take off running so she could find somewhere to transform. Explaining that to Dana and Carlos would be tricky, and she had a feeling that this monster was deadly serious with its demand about no one going anywhere. The last thing she wanted to do was anger it even more.

Meanwhile, Bree was fidgeting, debating on whether or not she should grab onto the bow in her hair and go for it. She was the one who had originally wanted to do her entire channel in her magical girl garb. It wasn't that much of a stretch to just out herself and save the day. But the thought of everyone actually knowing her secret was unsettling. Knowing that people would expect this much out of her, the *real* her, every time something happened didn't sit well with her.

"It'd be great if those ladies showed up now," Kayla whispered. The lady-monster's eyes were twitching about, lingering on Kayla and obviously remembering the confrontation in the store. Part of Kayla regretted talking back to the woman, but the other part? The other part still felt proud for telling off an entitled jerk of a woman – pimply, puss-filled skin and all.

"Yeah…" Bree said to Kayla, but she wasn't quite sure how to make the whole **magnifiquenoir** thing happen without exposing herself. Kayla looked nervous, while Dana was putting on a grand bravado that wasn't fooling anyone. The people in line were chiming in, squashing their fears to cheer for the magical girls who always arrived to save the day.

"**magnifiquenoir** you say?" Then the monster laughed. "I wish they *would* show up so I could put them in the place, just like I'm gonna do with all of you."

"Go ahead and try," Dana said, ignoring Marianna's pleas and Carlos grabbing onto her hand. "They'd wipe the floor with you."

"Well then, let's give them a reason to show up."

Things were about to go from bad to worse and both Marianna and Bree held their breaths. With a piercing screech, cracks spread out from beneath the monster's feet and snaked across the floor. The few seconds of bravery from the people in line became nonexistent. Soon, they began to scatter, forgetting their receipts in favor of their lives. The creature growled angrily and yelled, "I said don't go anywhere!" Its scream caused the floor to shake so much that those who had decided to run ended up tripping over their own feet. Dana stayed close to Marianna and Carlos while Bree stayed close to Kayla. There was no other choice, at this point. Marianna and Bree would have to transform and fight. There was no way they could let this continue for any longer.

Just as Marianna grabbed onto her bracelet, the girls heard someone say, "You need to stop screaming. You're causing a scene."

Up ahead was a young woman who had been listening to a pair of headphones, but had slid them into her pocket in favor of yelling at the grotesque creature. She was tall with flawless, dark skin and braids that went down her back. There was a piercing in her nose and several along one of her eyebrows, her wrists proudly equipped with rainbow armbands. Dressed like she'd just come from the gym, she was built with muscled abs and toned legs.

"Get to safety! Don't provoke it!" Marianna didn't care about how strong this girl appeared to be, the last thing she needed was a casualty from someone trying to play heroine.

"Another stupid little girl who can't keep her mouth shut." But it was too late. The creature already had its sights on the new girl.

As foolish as Marianna thought this girl was being, she realized that she now had an opening. She used the distraction to whisper to the people behind them to start slowly walking into the store. Torrence was at the entrance and ushered the people inside, both him and Marianna working together to use the moment to their advantage.

"Come on, Dana," Carlos whispered, but Dana wouldn't move. She couldn't stop staring at the monster up ahead. "Sis, please?"

"W-why aren't they here? They're supposed to be here."

Marianna winced but forced herself to shove aside the curdled feeling of guilt in her stomach. "We need to get you to safety."

"And make her fight by herself?!"

"I think she'll be all right," Kayla said as she headed toward the store with Bree.

"How can you say that?! That creature is gonna to tear her to shreds!"

Kayla shook her head as she nodded over to the mystery girl, who was eerily calm despite the situation. In fact, she was now standing in a fighting stance. Fists up and ready, legs long and powerful, she was ready for a fight and wasn't at all intimidated by the supernatural creature in front of her. "I know her," Kayla said. "She's in one of my classes."

"Who is she?" Bree asked.

"Her name is Lonnie Knox and she's a kick ass kickboxer."

Everything that happened after that felt like someone had hit the fast-forward button. The monster shouted at Lonnie, the force coming out in a destructive wave that crushed the garbage cans in the walkway and shattered the glass from the stores in its path. Lonnie jumped out of the way, then dodged another attack, and another, making it look as easy as playing a game of hopscotch. As the creature's voice became strained from screaming, Lonnie launched herself forward. With a mighty kick, her foot left an indent in the creature's stomach as if it were as soft as a bean bag. The monster stumbled back and let out a harsh cough, but Lonnie didn't give it a chance to recover. One punch to the face, followed by a second, and a third. All Marianna and Bree could do was stare as Lonnie continued to hit her opponent so hard that they could hear her fists bursting the bubbles, disgusting splashes of puss and blood hitting the ground and covering her fists. Finally, Lonnie landed a swift kick across the monster's cheek. The power in her kick was so hard that the creature was knocked out cold, its body adding a final crack to the floor.

"Holy shit," Bree whispered. The creature's face was now bruised beyond recognition, and it didn't look like it was going to get up anytime soon. Mouth wide open, stomach caved in from Lonnie's knee, Marianna looked just as bewildered as Bree. Neither girl had time to dwell on it. Dana was already cheering for Lonnie, and the group that had gone inside the store was stepping outside to see the aftermath of the one-sided battle. The rest of the crowd joined Dana in cheering for Lonnie, who stood there and smiled an embarrassed little smile. Both Marianna and Bree looked at each other and quietly wondered the same thing.

Had Blaze sent in a new magical girl?

Marianna frowned and shook her head. Blaze would talk to them about it, first. Furthermore, Lonnie wasn't transformed. That meant that she was able to fight this thing by herself. Marianna hadn't been too thrilled to have anyone join her in this crusade to defend the city, but if girls like Lonnie were out there…

"That was amazing!" Dana shouted.

Carlos was never one to enjoy encouraging his sister's outbursts, but he couldn't help himself this time. "I can't believe you did that all by yourself!"

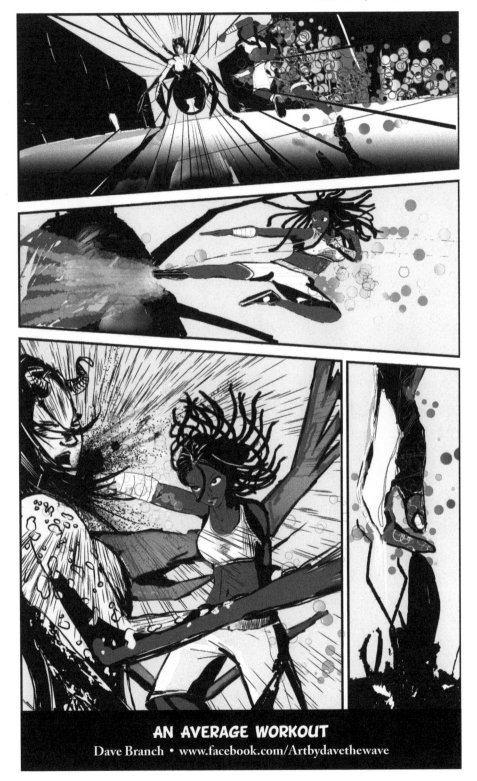

AN AVERAGE WORKOUT
Dave Branch • www.facebook.com/Artbydavethewave

Lonnie shrugged as she looked around for something to wipe her hands with. She had a feeling she wouldn't be able to go to the bathroom anytime soon. "It's not that big of a deal."

"Not a big deal? You just finished off a monster!" Bree had needed an entire magical makeover to do it, but this girl? This girl had done it with her bare hands.

"Now really isn't the time to be modest," Kayla added.

Marianna disappeared inside the video game store then came back out with a roll of paper towels. She handed them to Lonnie and said, "You should be more careful, though. That was extremely dangerous."

Lonnie looked down at the shorter girl in surprise. She smiled as she tore off a couple of sheets from the paper towel roll and did her best to wipe her hands. It would do for now. "I had to do something, I couldn't just let that thing threaten people."

"Are you one of them?" Kayla asked.

Lonnie laughed and shook her head. "I'm assuming you mean **magnifiquenoir**, right? Naw, I'm not with them, but those ladies are incredible."

"Yeah right. They didn't even do anything." The sudden disdain for the group came from someone who'd been in line for the midnight launch. Now that there was no threat of danger, he had something to say about what had taken place.

"What is that supposed to mean?" Dana asked.

"I mean they didn't even show up. Some random girl came to the rescue. They're the ones who are supposed to be out here fighting."

Marianna tried to not look so guilty. She always tried her best when it came to protecting others, but she knew she was far from perfect. Now that Bree was part of the team, it meant that they could get more done through teamwork. Today proved that they couldn't be everywhere at once, no matter how hard they tried.

Bree, on the other hand, looked ready to punch the guy in the face. She especially looked ready for a fight when others in the crowd started to agree with him.

Fortunately for Bree, Lonnie was there to vocalize everything she wanted to say, and everything Marianna needed to hear. "How dare you," Lonnie said through gritted teeth. "Some *random girl*? What do you think those ladies are? They come out of nowhere to protect us. They are the very definition of *random girls* coming to the rescue."

"Well... y-yes, but where are they now?"

"Probably saving someone else, what did you do today?" Lonnie pointed to the complainer in the group. When he didn't respond, she eyed everyone else, looking increasingly annoyed at the fact that she'd saved such an unappreciative group. "In fact, what did **any** of you do today?" When no one said anything in response Lonnie let out a harsh laugh. "That's what I thought."

Someone else in the crowd spoke up, picking up where the man left off. "But... they're heroines," she said, as if that justified everything. "They're magical girls..."

"And you can't expect them to always be here. You can't put this all on them. They're doing the best they can. It's two girls fighting lord knows how many monsters, how dare you get pissed off because they couldn't make it this one time."

"We could've died!" The woman's eyes began to water as she tried to appeal to Lonnie.

Lonnie raised an eyebrow at the woman and asked, "And did you?"

"Well... n-no, but..."

"But nothing. This is our city. If we can do something to protect it, we should. We all have to work together, we all have to take part in this."

"So you expect us to fight monsters, too?!" Another man, this time, from the very back of the crowd. "You can't expect us to do that!"

"No, but I expect you to show some respect to the ones who do fight them. If you can't do that, then you don't deserve their protection." And with those words Lonnie turned and walked away, leaving the group to mull over her words.

"She's incredible," Torrence said, now standing outside with everyone else. "I'm surprised she's not one of them."

"Me too!" Dana said. "She really should be!"

As Marianna and Bree watched mall security make their way upstairs to assess the damage and speak with the crowd, the same thought crossed their minds.

Blaze wanted a group of magical women, and Lonnie definitely fit the bill.

EPISODE SIX:

TWO'S COMPANY, THREE'S MAGNIFIQUE

"*Cosmickaze Bree* here after the midnight launch. I apologize for my livestream being cut short, but our launch was interrupted by a monster attack... as you probably saw."

Bree took a deep breath as she leaned back in her computer chair. The costume was now gone, replaced with a simple crop top and panties. The green hair was also gone, as Bree opted for maximum comfort. She could see people appearing in the comments of her Facetime video, frantically asking if she was okay Marianna had caught part of the attack on film, but everything was a blur after that. The screaming, the frightened people...

And the lone kickboxer who'd saved the day.

"This is gonna be a quick update. I'm all right, in fact, everyone's all right. The launch had to be cancelled, though, so I'll be picking up my copy later." Bree couldn't help but smile at the absurdity of it all. She was certain that whenever she mentioned monsters and magical girls on her channel, no one believed her. Now? **magnifiquenoir** was making quite the name for themselves.

But tonight? Someone else stood out in the crowd.

"I'd love to tell you that we were rescued by Galactic Purple and Cosmic Green, but someone else saved the day. I'm not sure if she wants her name out there though I will tell you this: she was amazing!" Normally, Bree would give full details, but after tonight she was starting to appreciate having things kept secret. "So tonight, my magical girl love goes to her. Thank you for saving this cute gamer girl." Bree curved her hands together to make a heart shape as she smiled brightly into the camera. "On that note, I'm turning in early. It's been a long day," then she waved and closed the video.

As Bree sat in her computer chair, she could hear her instant messenger going off. She didn't have to look at it to know it was Ella, demanding to know more details and to make sure she was all right. Instead of responding right away, she leaned back in her chair and mentally replayed the night's events.

The officers who had arrived on the scene tried their best to deal with the situation. When these attacks happened, the monster would be defeated and its body would be gone by the time any police officer arrived. This time, however, had a lump of a body left broken and beaten to the point of it being barely recognizable. Not quite sure how to approach the situation, the officers did, at the very least, evacuate the mall. Of course, there had been one or two customers who had the nerve to make a fuss because they desperately needed their video game. For the first time in his days of retail, Torrence had the ability to snap at unreasonable people. He demanded that they leave and pick up their damn game somewhere else if it meant *that* much to them. He was sure that they'd have a hard time justifying any kind of complaint to a district manager – it wasn't every day that police had to close a mall because of a monster woman.

In the end, the officers had decided to deal with the dead creature later. They'd return in the morning with a more qualified person at their side – if such a person existed. As the group left the mall, Marianna had ever so discreetly stopped in the bathroom and waited for the mall to clear out. Once it was empty, she went back and dropped a cupcake near the remains of the monster. The sweet smelling frosting leaked off the cake to eat away at its body. She knew things would be easier this way. The police would bring someone to the scene who claimed to specialize in the strange and bizarre. They'd make the situation more complicated when all it took was one cupcake to make the nightmarish creature disappear. They'd probably conclude that the bodies evaporated after a certain amount of time, or someone would point to **magnifiquenoir** or even *The Girl in Purple* if they were one of the ones who listened to the whispered stories about her.

Once outside, Kayla had said something about it being the most interesting non-date she'd ever been on. She especially loved the part where a girl from one of her classes became some kind of boxing heroine. Meanwhile, an exhausted Dana quietly requested to go home. Carlos agreed with her and even volunteered to stay the night at her place. Marianna – after catching up with the group – made Dana promise to call her if she needed to. In true Dana fashion, she promised that she was fine, but the fact that she was letting Carlos stay at her place spoke otherwise.

Now that the dust had settled and she was alone, Bree had time to assess everything that had happened. Somewhere out there was a girl who could take down a monster without any magical enhancements. Not just *out there*, but at her college – Bree remembered that Kayla said she had a class with her. Not only that, but she was definitely pro-magical girl, defending **magnifiquenoir** in their absence when people decided to air their grievances. All and all, Lonnie was beyond qualified, probably more qualified than Bree, to be honest. Bree squeezed her eyes shut and shook her head to clear away the negative thoughts. Now wasn't the time for insecurities, now was the time to work on getting a third member for their group.

Bree's instant messenger pinged again and she finally clicked on it. There Ella was, having sent a long stream of messages asking if she was okay. Each message sounded more frantic than the last as Ella had gone to all-caps mode toward the end. Before Bree could answer, her phone went off, signaling the inevitable phone call from her brother.

Terrific.

Bree had told Trey about her newfound abilities shortly after she'd gotten them... kind of. She did move in with Marianna, first. Oh, and there was the whole jumping off of a building thing followed by a handful of battles against the very creatures Trey had wanted her to avoid.

Marianna had tried her best to respond to Trey's accusations of the task being dangerous, reckless, and downright stupid. Bree, on the other hand, knew that the best way to deal with an irate older brother was to let him yell until he wore himself out, then plead her case. She wanted, no, *needed*, to go out there and protect other girls. She needed to make sure no one else ended up into the same kind of situation her dreadful attacker had forced her into. It was the only way she'd feel better about what happened to her. It was the only way to keep anything like that from happening to someone else.

In the end, the two had come to an agreement: Trey was going to call more often, whether Bree liked it or not. On top of that, Bree had to let him know that she survived her battles via phone call, text message, smoke signal – whatever means necessary.

But just because Bree agreed didn't mean she looked forward to the phone calls.

"Hey Trey," she said as she typed a response to Ella to let her know she was fine.

"*Hey Trey?* That's all I get?"

"Well… I'm still alive and kicking, as always after one of these attacks. And hey! This time, I wasn't even directly involved!"

Meanwhile, Ella was sending her an array of questions. What happened? Your livestream was cut short, did a monster really attack at the launch? Are you all right?! Bree tried her best to type a response but it was hard when Trey was yelling at her. "That's still not an excuse to be so nonchalant about it!"

Bree sighed. It was actually the perfect reason to be so calm, but she knew now wasn't the time to argue with her brother. "Trey, I'm fine. Honest."

"It's just… when this happens, you're usually…"

"Fighting?"

"Yeah…"

Bree smiled a little. She could've pointed out how Trey was so against her fighting, but she knew now wasn't the time for that, either. "So how'd you find out?"

"Besides the fact that your livestream was cut short? It's been all over social media. *Mysterious Magical Girl* and *Kickboxing Savior*, stuff like that."

"Awwwww, you were watching my livestream?"

"Bree..."

"Sorry, sorry, I just... wait, there's stuff online?"

"Oh yeah, definitely."

Bree did a quick search of the phrases Trey had mentioned. There, right in front of her, were all kinds of stories via social media, blogs, and websites that had hastily put together a list of the "best" tweets about the kickboxer. "Oh boy..." Bree wasn't sure if Lonnie would like that. She was so quiet about her victory, she wasn't sure if she'd like the extra attention.

"Do you know who the girl is?"

"Yeah, Kayla has a class with her. Her name's Lonnie Knox."

"Who's Kayla?"

Bree's eyes widened. Crap. She hadn't mentioned Kayla to Trey yet. "Just a friend," Bree said, then she mentally kicked herself for the high pitch in her voice. She knew exactly what Trey was about to do.

"A friend, you say? Are you sure it's not more than that?"

"Aren't you a little too old to pick on your sister about her crushes?" Double crap. She hadn't meant to say *crushes*.

"Ah, so she *is* more than a friend."

"I'm hanging up!"

"Tell Kayla I said hellooooo," Trey said as he gleefully sang that last word.

"Goodbye, Trey!" Bree hung up the phone before she could hear Trey's obnoxious laughter. She supposed him giving her a hard time about a crush was better than him yelling about her safety. Still, like most things about him, she didn't have to like it. Bree sent Ella one last message to reassure her that she was okay before signing off. She'd give her more details tomorrow after she got some much needed sleep.

At least that was the plan until she smelled brownies.

Like a chocoholic after Valentine's Day, Bree was up and on the move, gaining a second, third, and fourth wind in favor of baked goods. When she got to the kitchen she saw Marianna pulling a tray of chocolate chip brownies out of the oven. Dressed in her standard kitty pajamas, it was obvious that the girl had been planning on going to bed. But late night baking never hurt anyone, right? And one tray was never enough. Marianna moved over to the marble counter and began mixing together another batch – this time, with caramel.

"Mari?"

"Oh good, you're still awake. I know you like licking the spoon," then Marianna held up the chocolate covered spoon in question.

As true as that statement was, Bree didn't like how frazzled the girl sounded. "Mari... why are you baking so late at night?" Granted, it wasn't *that* late, in Bree's opinion, but Marianna should've definitely been in bed by now.

"I felt like it."

Bree walked over and took hold of Marianna's hand, urging her to lower the spoon. "You mean you can't sleep because you can't stop thinking about what happened."

Marianna sighed. "... yeah... that."

Bree smiled at her. "Join the club, I can't sleep, either."

"You were actually going to go to bed before midnight?"

"It's rare, but it happens sometimes."

Marianna smiled back. "Wanna watch me make an insane amount of brownies then help me eat them?"

"Girl. Yes."

The two were silent as Marianna poured her brownie batter into the pan. As promised, Bree was given the spoon to lick clean as Marianna put the newest batch into the oven. After Marianna cut up the chocolate chip brownies, she brought Bree one to try. "Now you know I'm gonna need more than one," Bree said.

"Trust me, there's gonna be more. I'm making a brownie cheesecake batter next."

"Stress baking sounds way too labor intensive for me."

Marianna let out an almost bitter laugh and said, "I'm too stressed to notice."

Bree took a bite out of her brownie and made a happy little sound. Not that she wanted Marianna to be stressed out, but she was definitely reaping the benefits of it. She was torn between eating a second brownie or waiting for the next batch to cook... particularly the heavenly sounding cheesecake batch that Marianna was now putting together.

"So... where do we start?" Marianna asked.

Bree frowned down at the remaining half of her brownie. She knew there was something she was trying to avoid. "I suppose we have two options: the guilt of not being able to do anything, or the Amazonian warrior who saved the day."

"I'm not sure if we need to delve into the guilt," Marianna said. She was sure she'd have a nice, restless night where she'd remember how much Dana was shaking. She was also sure that, out of nowhere, her concern for Dana would morph into an unwanted reminder from her mother about not being able to save everyone. So, for her own sanity, she decided to focus on something far more important. "We should discuss Lonnie."

Bree was more than happy to leave the guilt buried. "Are you thinking the same thing I am? That she'd be a perfect member of the group?"

172 – Briana Lawrence

"Exactly."

Bree smirked as she finished off her brownie. "I'm impressed. You hated the idea of me joining."

"To be fair, Lonnie did beat a monster all by herself…"

"Good point," Bree said. It was hard to argue with the fact that a girl punched and kicked a monster into submission. "So… what do we do?"

"We tell Blaze and see what she thinks."

"All right," then, "Wait… you mean right now?" But there were brownies to be made and, more importantly, brownies to be eaten.

"…we can wait until after brownies."

And they did exactly that. Once all the brownie batches were baked – and Bree got a chance to sample each one – the two took the elevator to have their impromptu, pajama clad meeting with Blaze. Marianna had insisted on bringing a couple of brownies with despite Bree's very best pout. If they were about to interrupt Blaze's evening, the least they could do was bring treats. As the two rode the elevator up, Bree wondered if they'd actually catch the woman sleeping. Maybe she'd be wearing comfortable pajamas or something more luxurious. Those thoughts were put to rest when the doors slid open to reveal that Blaze was sitting in her normal spot, as if she'd been expecting them.

Neither girl would've been surprised if that were the case.

Marianna started things off by offering the fiery woman her brownie of choice. "That's not necessary," Blaze said, but she wasn't about to turn down fresh baked chocolate. "So what brings you up here this evening?"

Marianna and Bree then proceeded to try and explain the wonder that was Lonnie Knox. Bree went into a wild explanation of Lonnie being a beast who could defeat monsters by simply sneezing on them. Marianna edited the story to make it sound a bit more viable, but made sure to add the important parts. Lonnie already knew how to fight and had managed to beat a monster all by herself without any powers.

Blaze quietly ate a cheesecake brownie as she listened to the two girls. Part of her was entertained at how animated Bree was with her storytelling compared to the more reserved Marianna. The other part? Concerned. *Definitely* concerned. The entire point of the group was to protect people so that they wouldn't have to do something as foolish as this Lonnie girl had done. "Was there a reason why you ladies couldn't deal with the situation?"

So much for not dealing with the guilt. "We were in the crowd when the attack happened, but we didn't have a chance to transform," Marianna said.

"Not just the crowd, but our friends. Even if that thing gave us a chance to leave and transform, there's no way we would've abandoned them. We're not Superman."

Marianna shot Bree a sharp glare. Now wasn't the time for her geek references. "What she means is that it would've looked suspicious if we up and disappeared, only to have **magnifiquenoir** show up." Marianna stopped and realized that Bree was absolutely right. It was like Superman.

"I know the situation must've been hard for you ladies, but there are times when you're going to have to make tough decisions in regards to those closest to you."

Bree frowned at the woman in front of her. Leave it to Blaze to take the joy out of eating brownies. "We've already done that. My brother doesn't want me here because he worries about me all the time, and Marianna's mother hates her doing this."

"Are you saying you no longer what to do this?"

"N-no, of course not!" Marianna shouted. The last thing she wanted was for Blaze to think that she wasn't grateful for the opportunity to do this. She knew in that moment it would be best to apologize, but the thought of doing that didn't sit well with her. So instead, she took a deep breath and said, "But... Bree is right. I didn't want to leave Dana because of how scared she was and-"

"And sometimes…you might have to." There was a sympathetic look on Blaze's face now. She understood what this felt like, but, "Once you both decided to do this, you made a promise to put this above all else."

"Did we?" Marianna asked, still determined to make her point, even as the sky around Blaze got gloomier. "We promised to protect the people here. By staying with our friends, that's exactly what we did. They needed us."

"And by doing that, the threat escalated."

"No, it didn't," Bree pointed out.

"Because of the random girl that showed up? You two can't rely on that all the time."

"Why not? The rest of the city does. We're random girls, aren't we?" Bree remembered what Lonnie had said earlier and decided to bring up the same point she'd made.

"No. You're *my* girls. There's nothing random about you." Blaze smiled at the two of them, the sky around her growing brighter and no longer looking as dismal. "You're **magnifiquenoir**."

"Yes, we are. And maybe she could be, too."

Blaze raised an eyebrow at Marianna. Suddenly, it made sense that the girl had brought her brownies. "That was a pretty low tactic, wasn't it? Buttering me up with brownies?"

"Not at all. I know you're too smart for that kind of thing," Marianna said smoothly, not letting Blaze's accusation phase her. She had to push through this and get Blaze to see things their way. "I do think that Lonnie should join us in our fight. Anyone who stands up to that kind of threat is definitely magical."

"Or they're a normal girl who's a bit too reckless," Blaze said as she laced her fingers together, her eyes hard and serious. "Or, even worse, a girl who got lucky this time. She might not be so lucky the next time."

"No offense, Blaze, but weren't the both of us normal girls until you came along?" Bree asked.

Blaze shook her head and spoke sincerely to the both of them. "There is nothing normal about the two of you. You two are extraordinary."

Marianna appreciated the compliment, but she and Bree weren't the only ones who deserved it. "Well, to us, Lonnie is extraordinary."

And that was that. Both of them had said their piece. Now all they could do was wait and see if Blaze agreed with them or not. Neither one was certain about how much time had passed. What they did know was that the area around Blaze was constantly changing. The stars fluctuated between dimming to growing brighter as the magical woman thought things through. One minute, she looked contemplative. The next? She looked concerned, hesitant, almost angry as she mulled everything over. Bree was about to plead with her to say something, *anything*, but then Blaze stood up and said, "I hope you two are right about this."

"If we aren't, we'll take full responsibility."

Bree didn't like the idea of Marianna speaking for both of them, especially in regards to who would take responsibility for what. She especially felt uneasy when Blaze said, "Oh, I'd expect nothing less from you."

The two watched as Blaze turned and started walking toward what they assumed to be the back of the room... assuming the room had any sort of end to it. She stood in front of what looked to be a planet, but when she touched it, it actually opened up to reveal a small shelf. Before either girl could make out everything that was on the shelf, Blaze grabbed what appeared to be a rainbow anklet and walked back toward them. The planet-shaped shelf closed back up and went back to rotating like a normal planet would. "Take good care of this," she said, then she handed Marianna the anklet.

Marianna stared down at the piece of jewelry and asked, "Whose is this?"

"According to you, it belongs to Lonnie," Blaze said, "And she'll use it to become Radical Rainbow."

Bree grinned and said, "That's a cool name."

"It is, and she was an amazing woman. Hopefully, Lonnie does her proud."

In that moment both Marianna and Bree realized how serious this was. Up until that point, Blaze had picked who she wanted on the team herself. This time, the two of them were the ones making the decision. Blaze had always been part of **magnifiquenoir** and it never occurred to the girls that she had probably been very close to the previous team members. She never really talked about them, but the few times she did, she spoke fondly of them. Bree wanted to ask about the previous Cosmic Green and Galactic Purple, but knew now wasn't the time.

"She will," Marianna said with a firm nod. "Lonnie will be a perfect fit."

"All right. I'm trusting you. Both of you."

Both girls nodded, Marianna looking down at the anklet in her hand one more time.

Radical Rainbow's anklet.

No, *Lonnie's* anklet.

This would belong to Lonnie, she just knew it.

Finding Lonnie on campus was much easier than they thought. It helped that she was surrounded by a crowd of students eagerly trying to talk to her.

"Poor girl," Marianna said. They were both standing in the food court on campus, watching as Lonnie tried her best to eat lunch in peace. The crowd was peppering her with questions in-between her bites of food. Some had even pulled out their phones and asked to take selfies with her, asking if they could tag her various social media handles. That part seemed to make Lonnie a bit uneasy, but she at least took the pictures and left it at that.

"They could at least wait until she finishes with her sandwich, damn," Bree muttered.

Word had spread on campus fast. Stories of Lonnie's heroism were whispered about among the students and even some faculty members. To Lonnie's credit, she responded to all the questions with a smile, but both Marianna and Bree could tell that the smile was wearing thin.

"Bree?"

Bree turned, surprised to see her old roommate from her pre-magical girl days. Bree hadn't spoken to Jackie since she'd left. It was a shame since she'd gotten used to her in those last few days of being in the dorms, but they hadn't gotten close enough to have a reason to exchange contact info. "Hey Jackie."

"I haven't seen you in a while... h-how have you been?"

There was a hint of hesitation in Jackie's voice. Bree realized that the last time they'd talked was right after her attack. She wondered if Jackie thought she was still suffering from the effects of such a traumatic experience. In a way, Bree supposed that she was, only now she had a way to fight back. "I've been fine," Bree said, then she nodded over to Marianna. "This is Marianna, the girl I moved in with."

Marianna smiled and said, "Nice to meet you."

"Nice to meet you, too," then Jackie glanced over to where the crowd was gathered. "Did you hear about what happened?"

"Huh? Oh, you mean attack at the mall?" Bree asked. She didn't need to tell Jackie that she was there when it happened.

Jackie nodded. "That girl over there? She defeated a monster all by herself."

"That's pretty impressive," Marianna said, easily playing along and pretending like this was news to her.

"I was hoping to be able to talk to her, but it looks like she's busy."

"I have a feeling she's gonna be busy for a while," Bree said. "Maybe you should leave her be."

"I'm surprised you'd say something like that considering how curious you were about *The Girl in Purple*, though I suppose we do know her name now."

Jackie did have a good point. Bree had jumped at the chance to learn everything she could about her purple savior. There was also the fact that they were going to ask Lonnie to join them, but to Bree, that was different.

After all, she and Marianna would at least let the girl eat her lunch.

"Things change, Jackie."

"Yeah... I suppose they do. Take care of yourself, Bree."

"You too," Bree said as she watched Jackie walk over to the crowd.

"That was pretty mature of you."

Bree shrugged her shoulders. "I have my moments. Besides, she's got enough people to deal with."

"It's going to be impossible to talk to her alone."

"Who knows, maybe an opportunity will present itself."

Marianna nodded as the two of them walked over to grab lunch. Bree made a beeline toward the college's best attempt at Chinese cuisine, Marianna reluctantly following after her. "I should start making us lunch," Marianna muttered as she stared down the fried rice behind the glass. It was dangerous being a person who enjoyed cooking. All she could do was think about how she'd make everything so much better.

"Not that I'd object... but when would you have time?"

"Probably never, but when has that stopped me in the past?"

Bree smiled as she walked up to the counter to order while Marianna glanced around the food court one more time. If she tried hard enough, maybe she'd find something other than cheap sub-sandwiches and pizza with a cracker like crust. As she continued her fruitless search she saw Lonnie stand up from her table near the food court entrance.

The kickboxer politely excused herself before she headed toward the bathrooms.

"So about that opportunity you spoke of..." Marianna whispered to Bree.

"Hm?"

"Lonnie left and headed for the bathroom."

Bree set her tray of fried rice and orange chicken down to deliver her most judgmental look. "Mari... are we really gonna interrupt the girl peeing?"

"No!" Marianna quickly lowered her voice when the man behind the counter turned his attention toward her. "But... if we just so happen to be outside the door..."

"Isn't that... creepy?"

"Was it creepy when you opened your dorm room door and saw Blaze's room?"

"Yes, but... it ended up being cool."

Marianna smiled at Bree. "How about this, I'll go so we don't both bombard her. You just ordered food, anyway."

Bree slid her tray over to the register, making sure to order her required liquid sugar rush before she paid for her meal. "So are you gonna flat out ask her?"

"Not right away," Marianna said as the two walked out the food court to find somewhere to sit. "I want to get a feel for what she thinks about the whole thing."

"Didn't yesterday show us what she thinks?"

"I... yes, but... I've been thinking about what Blaze said. I want to make sure we're making the right decision."

Bree nodded as she spotted an empty table near the back of the room. "I'll save a seat for you. Good luck."

"Thanks," then Marianna headed to the bathrooms. As she walked she took a moment to glance over at the table where Lonnie had been sitting. The crowd was still there, waiting for her to get back, anxious to ask her more questions and shower her with praise. Marianna leaned back against the wall outside the bathroom, contemplating what she could possibly say. Before she could come up with something tangible she could hear someone asking Lonnie questions from inside the bathroom.

Wow, had Bree been right? Was the girl not allowed to even pee in peace?

Marianna stepped inside and saw Lonnie standing at the sink, trying to wash her hands as a girl stood next to her. Marianna recognized the girl as Bree's old roommate, who apparently had the same idea she did when Lonnie went into the bathroom. Lonnie's smile looked tacked on as Jackie asked the same series of questions that she'd been answering.

This... was the right thing to do, wasn't it? Someone like Lonnie was born for this. But as Marianna watched her she felt terrible for following after her. Marianna knew what it was like to have people talking about her, or at least, a part of her. No one knew she was Galactic Purple, which spared her from moments like this. Even if it was compliments that were being given, they were still invasive.

"Excuse me, Lonnie?"

Both Jackie and Lonnie turned and looked over at Marianna. "Hey, I know you. You're the girl who was with Bree," Jackie said.

Marianna walked up to them and stood in front of Lonnie, smiling up at her. "I'm sorry to interrupt, but Kayla was looking for you."

All Marianna could do was hope that Lonnie caught on to what she was trying to do. Luckily, it dawned on the taller girl and she slapped her forehead. "Argh, I forgot! We were supposed to meet up. Do you know where she is?"

Marianna nodded. "I can take you to her if you'd like."

"Thanks," then Lonnie looked over at Jackie and said, "I'm sorry, but maybe we can talk later?"

"Ah, um... sure..."

"Cool. Let's get going." Lonnie walked out of the bathroom with Marianna and quickly walked down the hallway with her. "Oh man, thanks for doing that."

"No problem. It looked like you needed it."

"This way," Lonnie said as she opened the door to the stairwell. The two walked up a couple of flights together before settling on the fourth floor. Lonnie took a seat on the stairs and sighed. "Sorry, this is the only place I could think of that wasn't surrounded by people."

"It's fine. I'm sorry everyone keeps bugging you."

Lonnie shrugged her shoulders. "It's to be expected, I guess."

Marianna suddenly looked guilty as she said, "I... was gonna do the same thing everyone else is doing, but now isn't the time."

"It's not that I hate talking about it, I just haven't had time to process everything, you know?"

"I can understand that," Marianna said as she sat next to Lonnie. "I should thank you. I was there yesterday."

"You were?" Lonnie looked Marianna up and down then her eyes widened in realization. "Oh yeah! You were with Kayla, weren't you? That explains how you know her name." When Marianna nodded, Lonnie continued. "I think there was another girl there, too? With a guy? And a girl with green hair?"

Marianna nodded. "That was my friend, Dana, with her brother, Carlos. The girl with the green hair is my friend Bree."

"Oooooh, so *that's* Bree? Kayla's mentioned her."

Marianna wondered if she should share that information or not. She was sure Bree's spirit would float out of her body if she knew that Kayla was talking about her with other people. "So you and Kayla are friends? She said you two had a class together."

"We're more like war buddies," Lonnie chuckled. "We had to do a group project and we were the only two who gave a damn."

"Ugh, that's always the worst!" When Lonnie laughed louder Marianna frowned at her. "It is!"

"No no, I agree! Just... your face was really adorable."

"I'm not adorable, I'm frustrated! Slackers are terrible!" And she knew that firsthand. She was losing track of how many times she had to wake Bree up in the morning. At least Bree stayed awake for class, but lately it was only for the benefit of seeing Kayla in the morning.

Once Lonnie's laughter died down she smiled at Marianna and said, "I lied."

"Hm?"

"I remember you. I made it sound like I didn't, but I do. You were the one who brought me paper towels and told me that fighting that thing was dangerous."

"Oh... well, I mean, I was telling the truth," Marianna said as she looked down at her purse. "What you did was dangerous."

"I know, but you were the only one who cared enough to even say that much."

"That's not true. Bree was worried, too. So was Kayla, I'm sure, but she did say that you'd be all right. And she was right."

"Yeah. I just... you reminded me of my trainers," Lonnie said as she took a moment to close her eyes and enjoy the quiet. "They teach me how to fight, but they always tell me to be careful."

Marianna smiled at Lonnie. "Well you don't often see a girl standing up to something like that."

Lonnie shook her head. "That's not true, **magnifiquenoir** does it all the time."

"Yeah... I suppose they do."

"That's why I got so mad at those people. Those girls protect us all the time."

"But those people were right. They weren't there..."

"Look, I'm glad they're around, but I don't expect them to do it all, you know? That's impossible, and frankly, it's unfair to put that much pressure on anyone. So I figured since I was there, I could step in."

"That's very nice of you."

"Naw, it's not nice. It's realistic. We're in this together," then Lonnie stood up and stretched. "Like right now? You've definitely helped me out."

"How? All I did was talk with you."

"Yeah, like a *person*, and not an icon."

"I... oh," then Marianna smiled and stood up. "Well... what you did was amazing, but you're still a person."

"And so are those other ladies. Sure, we look up to them and depend on them, but they're allowed to be people sometimes. If they can't make it everywhere, that's fine, because I'm here. And I'm sure others would step up, too."

"Yeah, you're right. Thanks, Lonnie."

"Hey, I didn't do anything," Lonnie said with a shrug.

Marianna supposed that, to Lonnie, she hadn't said anything groundbreaking. It wasn't like she knew who she was actually talking to. But, to Marianna, it was a gentle reminder that she didn't have to carry this responsibility by herself. Even after Bree joined her, she still had a nasty habit of putting too much pressure on herself. Yesterday was a reminder that she wasn't alone. She was part of a team, and that team had plenty of time to grow. "I suppose we should get going. I have to get to class soon."

"Ah, yeah, I need to get to the gym. Hey! You should come down sometime, I'd love to talk with you more. It's *Handsome Rodney and Madame Raye's.*"

"I might stop by. Bree might be with me, if that's okay"

"Sure, I don't mind. Tell her Kayla might be around, too. She comes by and works out sometimes, being a dancer and all."

Marianna nodded as Lonnie waved to her and ran down the stairs to get back to the bottom floor. After talking with her, Marianna felt even more confident in their decision to ask Lonnie to join them. She was absolutely perfect, and she would help them to create a well-rounded team.

"Radical Rainbow..." that was the name of the girl before her. Marianna smiled as she walked downstairs. She'd been hesitant about Bree, but Lonnie? Lonnie was going to be a fantastic member of **mag·nifiquenoir**.

All that was left to do was ask.

It wasn't one of those fancy gyms with memberships and commercials on television. *Handsome Rodney and Madame Raye's* only existed in one tiny location. There was just enough room for a boxing ring, punching bag, bits of exercise equipment, a locker room, and an office that felt more like a glorified closet – but the paperwork wasn't going to do itself. What it lacked in size it made up for in character. The walls were lined with cheesy motivational posters that looked like they belonged in an old school training montage. One of the posters even had the couple on it. It was something they'd gotten done at a print shop for fun, their names in bubble font as they flexed their muscles together. There was a whiteboard in the corner of the room where the trainers kept a list of important tips: don't forget to stretch, take breaks, drink water, and respect one another.

Stepping into the gym felt like coming home, though that may have been because Lonnie lived above the gym with the two owners. Rodney and Raye were old family friends and were especially close to her grandmother. Her grandmother always made enough food for an entire colony, and they never shied away from grabbing a plate.

Rodney had been a bit of a legend once upon a time. Tall, with rich, brown skin and a charming smile framed by his goatee, he'd been damn near unstoppable in the ring. He'd earned the *Handsome* nickname because he'd still maintain his good looks when fighting. He was known for his bold claims of becoming more attractive with each hit he took, the bruises adding to his award winning smile. Those days may have been long gone, but he still took great pride in keeping himself fit. He walked around without a shirt as much as possible, after all, why cover a perfectly good body with fabric?

There was only one person who could stand toe-to-toe with Rodney: his wife, Raye. Stereotypically speaking, this would be attributed to their marriage and Raye having Rodney wrapped around her finger. Anyone who entered the gym knew the truth: Raye was even more ferocious in the ring. She was one of those women whose small stature made people underestimate her, though her muscled, dark skin should've been a clear sign of her ability to bench press the naysayers with ease. While she hadn't pursued a full-fledged career, she did help train Rodney, and he had no problem telling people that he wouldn't be where he was if it wasn't for her.

Lonnie stepped inside, not at all surprised to see all eyes on her. She let out a loud sigh and said, "Go on. Make your comments, I've been hearing it all day."

"Well look who it is. The magical girl graces us with her presence."

That was Braydon Carmichael, leaning against the side of the ring as if he'd been waiting all day to say that line to her. As far as rivals went, he was the most annoying. He looked like he came right out of a Disney movie, armed with dashing good looks and a smile that Lonnie wanted to smash with her fist. He was taller than her – but barely – and had perfected the white boy habit of wearing bed hair as an actual style. He always found a reason to pick on her for something, and unfortunately, he could back up his arrogance in the ring.

"You know, only you would give someone a hard time for helping people," Lonnie said as she tried to step past Braydon. He wouldn't let her, blocking her way to the locker rooms. "Move, Braydon. I'm not in the mood."

"Is this your attempt to be girlier?"

"That doesn't even make sense!"

"Sure it does. When the magical girls didn't show up, you decided to become one yourself. Do you spin around and sparkle, too?" Braydon asked, giving a twirl and speaking in a higher pitched tone of voice.

"I'll show you want I can do in the ring," Lonnie hissed.

"Jesus, Braydon! Knock it off!"

And there she was. Braydon's one weakness – though he'd never admit it. Kendra Sanders had been doing push-ups on one of the work-out mats, her warm, brown skin covered in a light sheen of sweat. She was smaller than Raye, with long hair that she kept in a ponytail while working out. The girl was lightning fast and armed with a wicked kick that could knock you out of it connected in just the right way. Instead of using that kick on Braydon – like Lonnie wished she would – she settled for walking over and lightly pushing him.

"I'm only messing around," Braydon said with a laugh.

"Well you're not being funny," Kendra said as she crossed her arms and frowned up at the boy. "You're being an asshole."

"All right all right, jeez. Calm your tits, short-stuff," because Braydon was secretly a five-year-old boy who could only talk to his crushes with insults.

Kendra raised an eyebrow at Braydon. Though she would never say it out loud, part of her appreciated the jabs he made toward her femininity. It meant that he saw her as a woman, something that not everyone could accept about her.

The other part of her? That part of her cracked her knuckles and said, "Excuse me?"

Lonnie took a step back. "You've gone and done it now."

"Come on, bro. You could definitely take out that little girl."

While the three of them didn't always see eye to eye on things, they were all in agreement about one thing: Jeremy Richards was a douchebag. He was a mixture of muscles, beach blond hair, and a terrible attitude that he boasted about by proudly calling himself an asshole. Braydon may have said problematic things but he knew how to reign it in. He was one of those guys who spoke to his friends in insults and he'd back off if you told him that his words actually hurt.

Jeremy was the exact opposite.

"Didn't this *little girl* wipe the floor with you yesterday?" Kendra asked.

"Whatever," Jeremy said, denying his humiliation from yesterday. "You don't really count as a girl, anyway. I should've said *little boy*."

"You watch your mouth," Braydon snapped. He took a step forward but Lonnie placed a hand on his shoulder and shook her head.

"He ain't worth it," Lonnie said. "Save that energy on someone who's worth your time."

"Like who? You? You're just as bad as *her*." Jeremy made sure to look over Lonnie's body as he said that, clearly trying to make a statement against her build.

"Is that supposed to be an insult?" Lonnie asked, not at all phased by the way Jeremy was looking at her. "Because at least she wins her matches."

That set Jeremy off. He walked over to Lonnie and stood so close that she could feel his breath on her face. "Careful what you say to me, Knox."

"Oh? What are you gonna do? Take a nap in the ring like you did yesterday when Kendra knocked yo ass out? Or maybe I'll knock you out this time, I've certainly done it before."

"I'd expect a man like you to do it," Jeremy sneered at her.

There was pure malice in his voice, not at all like the lighthearted tone Braydon used. Lonnie brushed it aside and said, "I'm more of a man than you'll ever be, Richards."

"Guys, enough," Kendra said, then she nodded over to the whiteboard to remind them of the fourth rule written on it.

Lonnie took a deep breath to calm herself down. As much as she didn't think Jeremy deserved anything that resembled respect, she knew it was a requirement in the gym. No matter how much shit an adversary talked, when it came to the ring, there had to be a level of respect. Jeremy seemed to agree and unclenched his fists, but still didn't look happy to be sharing the same space as Lonnie.

"Good to see that someone remembers the rules." Everyone turned to see Raye walking toward them. Even in a loose tank top and sweatpants, Raye looked like she could knock them all out just by breathing on them.

"She started it," Jeremy said, very much the whiny child who didn't want to be punished. Lonnie didn't say a word in response. She didn't have to. She knew that Raye knew about the kind of comments Jeremy made and the bad temper that came along with them. Lonnie wished that Rodney and Raye weren't the type of people to give everyone a chance. To them, Jeremy needed guidance and a place to channel his anger. To Lonnie, he needed to take himself to another gym.

"Jeremy." Then again, it was impressive how motherly Raye could be even if she didn't have children of her own. All she had to do was speak his name to get him to step away from Lonnie. "Go and lift some weights, work off some of that energy. Braydon, go and be his spotter."

Braydon tried his best to not look irritated. He may have bantered back and forth with Lonnie and Kendra, but he knew better than to do that with Raye. "Yes ma'am."

"I should hit the weights, too," Kendra said, and it made Braydon smile immediately.

As Braydon and Kendra followed after Jeremy, Lonnie finally dropped her guard and said, "God he's such a dick."

"You weren't egging him on, were you?"

"Why is it always my fault?!" She didn't mean to sound so defensive, but, "He was being a complete jackass to Kendra, and to me. He shouldn't be able to say that kind of garbage to us."

"And you know you're gonna hear worse. Both of you are."

Lonnie had had this conversation with Raye before. Raye knew firsthand what people said to women who possessed even the slightest iota of physical strength. That was the exact reason why Raye hadn't sought out a professional career in kickboxing, no matter how many times Rodney told her she could. While Raye loved supporting Rodney, she did admit to Lonnie that part of her regretted not taking the chance. Lonnie knew that was why she pushed her so hard. She didn't sugarcoat things and was always brutally honest, feeling a need to prepare her for what was going to come her way.

"I know people are gonna say bad things to me and Kendra, but that doesn't mean I have to like it," Lonnie said.

"Oh no, of course not. It just means you have to hit harder and be smarter."

"But you stopped that from happening."

"For now. I might *accidentally* put you two in the ring even if it's supposed to be you and Braydon today."

"Please, pleeeeeeeease do this."

Raye chuckled and said, "Jeremy very much needs a lesson in humility, but not when you're angry at him over his personal comments. If it's personal, he'll lump your strength up as an emotional woman and nothing else."

"Maybe he needs an *emotional woman* to show him a thing or two," Lonnie muttered.

"If that's the case then prove it in the ring... or, you know, the middle of the mall..."

Lonnie let out a nervous laugh. "So you heard about that?" Braydon may have joked around about it, but Lonnie knew there was no way that Raye would see it as being humorous.

"Of course we did."

And there Rodney was, walking over to join his wife so they could come together and scold Lonnie. There was a gentle smile on his face, but Lonnie knew it was deceptive. He could chew her out with just as much skill as Raye.

"Braydon said something, didn't he?" Lonnie asked.

"No. Your grandmother did."

Lonnie's eyes widened when she heard Raye say that. Damn social media for allowing relatives to keep track of her life. And damn her grandma for being motivated enough to learn how to use it. "How mad was she?"

"*I sent my baby out there and this is what y'all do?*" Rodney said, doing his best impression of an elderly, angry black woman. There was nothing scarier than that, to be honest.

"Care to explain why you decided to take on a monstrous creature by yourself?" Raye asked.

Couldn't they go back to talking about Jeremy? As much as Lonnie hated the guy, he was a much better topic of conversation than this. Then again, she knew she'd have to talk about it with them eventually, she just didn't think her grandmother would bring it up before she did. "That thing was holding a bunch of people hostage. I couldn't stand there and do nothing."

Rodney shook his head and said, "You can't just rush into situations like that, Lonnie."

"I didn't!" When Rodney and Raye gave her a stern frown Lonnie lowered her voice. "I didn't," she repeated quieter. "I accessed the situation and I felt like I could handle it. So I did."

Rodney sighed, not at all liking the fact that Lonnie was using their teachings against him. The knowing look on Raye's face didn't help much, either. He and his wife didn't exactly teach their students to sit back and do nothing. If they were capable of assisting others, they should. But neither one expected a student to take on a supernatural creature, especially when said student was the granddaughter of a close family friend and under their care. In the end, all Rodney could say was, "Be careful out there. If it's something you can't handle…"

"I know."

"Rodney, sweetie? Will you go and grab us some water?"

"Of course," Rodney said with a smile, then he turned and walked off, leaving the two alone.

Lonnie knew what was about to happen. She'd seen the couple use this tactic before. Rodney would step away for whatever reason so Raye could speak to Lonnie woman to woman. "I know you think you have to take on the world and prove yourself, but-"

"That's not it at all." Lonnie wasn't sure why she said that. She knew that Raye could see through her.

"Lonnie." Raye watched as Lonnie fidgeted and did everything in her power to not look her in the eye. "Lonnie, look at me."

Lonnie didn't want to. She wanted to watch Jeremy lift weights. She wanted to watch Braydon try to keep his focus on Jeremy when he really wanted to watch Kendra curl dumbbells. When Raye cleared her throat Lonnie finally looked at her and said, "I really did think I could handle it, and I did handle it. Why am I in trouble for that?"

"You're not in trouble," Raye said, smiling. "We just don't want you to jump into dangerous situations because you think you have to be the strong one."

"T-that's not…" Lonnie cut herself off. There was no point denying it, not with Raye. "… I hate talking to you," she muttered.

Raye laughed and reached up to rest a hand on Lonnie's shoulder. "You can't hide your feelings from me. I've felt the same way. Many women do, Lonnie. You don't have to take on the world by yourself."

"Easier said than done," Lonnie muttered.

"I hear ya on that one. Just try and keep that in mind when you're doing your *Magical Kickboxer* thing."

Lonnie let out a loud groan and rolled her eyes. "Don't. Please don't."

"What? I had to check out at least one of the articles after your grandmother called."

"School was a nightmare today."

"That's the price of fame, my dear magical one." When Raye saw the look on Lonnie's face she decided to back off. For now. "All right all right, I'll go easy on ya."

Before Raye could turn and walk away, Lonnie spoke up and said, "I did mean what I said, though."

"Hm?"

"I do think that if I can help, I should. But... I promise to be more careful."

Raye nodded her head because she knew that was all she could do. Once Lonnie was set on something, there was no arguing with her. "Good," then, "Have fun explaining that to your grandmother," because there was no way Raye was going to deal with the woman's wrath by herself.

In seconds, Lonnie was reduced to being the scrawny five-year-old with beads in her hair. "Raaaaaaye! Come on, you already talked to her!

"And she expects you to call."

Lonnie pouted as Rodney came back over with two bottles of water. "Are you two done talking yet?" He asked.

"Yes dear. Lonnie's upset because she has to call her grandmother."

Rodney gave a low whistle and said, "It was nice knowing ya, kid."

"That ain't funny!"

Lonnie waved to Braydon and Kendra as they left the gym. Braydon suggested that the two walk home, claiming that his house was in the same direction as Kendra's. Lonnie knew he was lying, but she was kind of proud of him for actually making an attempt to spend time with the girl outside the gym. Braydon may have worked Lonnie's nerves on a daily basis, but deep down, the two were like siblings... siblings who could beat the crap out of each other if they were unsupervised.

"Good match, Knox."

Lonnie looked over as Jeremy put his shirt on and grabbed his bag. The two had had the practice match that Lonnie wanted. Not to toot her own horn, but the match had went about as well as she'd expected. Jeremy let anger guide his movements, which made him terribly easy to read. She had him on the floor in less than a minute. "Thanks," Lonnie said, but she didn't really mean it. A good match would've been more entertaining.

Raye was right. She definitely did egg Jeremy on, but he deserved it.

"We'll have to have a rematch sometime."

"Sure, whenever you want."

Jeremy smirked. "You won't be so lucky next time."

Lonnie should've let it go, but, "Luck?"

"Yep. I always feel bad for hitting girls."

"What happened to all the *man* comments?"

Jeremy shrugged his shoulders as he headed for the door. "Men aren't as cute as you when they get pissed off."

Lonnie imagined herself hitting him hard enough that he lost some teeth – mouth guard be damned. She tucked the image in the back of her mind, remembering Raye's words about not making things personal in the ring.

Now that day was turning to night, Lonnie finally had a real chance to think about everything that had happened. She was certain the buzz would die down soon enough, and people would forget all about her heroism. She wasn't too heartbroken about that. She hadn't done it for any sort of fame, she genuinely did want to help. Lonnie wasn't the type to stand by when people were being hurt. She also wasn't the type to, well, have a boxing match against a monstrous creature.

So what sparked the urge today?

Lonnie couldn't put it into words, and she knew she'd have to when she eventually called her grandmother. Penny Knox was as tough as they came. She was one of those women who could make you feel bad about yourself with words alone. She'd ask her granddaughter for an explanation, and she'd have no problem cursing her out via old lady sass if the explanation wasn't good enough. Lonnie couldn't imagine anything she said justifying her running headfirst into danger. Maybe she could prolong that phone call for just a little longer. Besides, the gym wasn't going to lock itself up. There was trash to take out and towels to put in the washing machine.

Lonnie stepped out the back door to enter the alley and toss the trash into the large dumpster by the gym. She took a moment to enjoy the breeze to cool off after hours of training. Just as she was about to step back inside, she caught sight of what appeared to be two girls standing on top of the building across from the gym. They may have been standing several feet above her, but Lonnie swore she could see them sparkling, their purple and green hair blowing in the wind.

Purple? And green?

Lonnie had never seen **magnifiquenoir** in person. She'd heard plenty about them and had seen a couple of pictures online. "No way..." Lonnie watched as the two girls jumped from atop of the building to land in front of her. They looked even more majestic up close. Their dazzling clothes were lined in stars that Lonnie had only been able to see at night. "You're **magnifiquenoir**!" Lonnie didn't mean to sound like a fangirl, but she couldn't help herself. Galactic Purple's smile was much lovelier in person, and Cosmic Green looked just as radiant.

"We've heard about you, Lonnie Knox," Galactic Purple said. "We need to thank you for what you did yesterday."

Cosmic Green nodded her agreement. "It was incredible."

"You two... jeez, you don't have to thank me!" Lonnie didn't get flustered easily, but there she was, tripping over her words as she rubbed the back of her head. "It's the same thing you two would've done. It's the same thing *anyone* should do if they're able to."

"That's actually what we want to discuss with you," Cosmic Green said.

Galactic Purple stepped closer to Lonnie and held an anklet toward her. Lonnie watched the jewelry shimmer in her hand, the rainbow colors humming with energy. "We'd like for you to join us."

"...what?"

"We want to strengthen our team, and we think we can do that with you."

Lonnie stared at the woman in front of her. Was she being serious? Was this actually happening? It was difficult enough to grasp the concept of a team of magical black girls, but overtime, she'd managed to do so. It was even more difficult to accept that monsters could just appear at a mall and interrupt your shopping day, but Lonnie had slowly been coming to terms with that.

But this?

"What... is that?" Even as Lonnie asked the question, she had a feeling she knew what the answer was.

Cosmic Green answered her. "It's how we get our power. We each have something. This would be yours."

Yep. That's what she thought it was.

"It seems like you want to help defend the people of this city. We want you to join us. We can all work together on this."

Lonnie looked at the purple haired woman in front of her. She'd heard about her before people came to call her Galactic Purple. She'd been fighting alone, the same way Lonnie had done yesterday. Eventually, Cosmic Green came into the picture, and both girls had been defending the city ever since. It was a tall task to take on – Lonnie had even admitted that much yesterday. She wondered if both girls had jumped into this without any sort of hesitation.

Or did either of them do what Lonnie was about to do. "I'm flattered, but... I can't accept this."

Galactic Purple's eyes widen as Lonnie stepped away from her. "W-what?"

Lonnie shook her head and said, "I appreciate what you two do, but... I'm not interested in working with others. I want to rely on my own strength." It was everything Raye was telling her not to do. Lonnie knew it was. She wanted to believe everything the woman told her, but no matter how hard she tried, she couldn't. All she could do was think of Jeremy's words and the words from countless others just like him. Too many people didn't give her credit for what she had rightfully earned.

Taking some magical anklet would just prove them right.

She'd defeated that monster on her own and she'd become that strong on her own. She'd lose all that effort if she accepted some magical power from someone else.

So Lonnie nodded to the two girls in front of her, turned, and walked back inside the gym, leaving the anklet behind.

EPISODE SEVEN:

BE RADICAL

When Marianna was upset about something, she'd turn to cooking. She'd dance across the hardwood floor and throw together a multi-layered cake. To be fair, that had been her go-to solution, and she'd even pulled out the ingredients to make said cake... but her heart wasn't in it. The thought of baking felt tedious, at best, so she quietly put everything back in its place. Milk and eggs in the fridge. Flour, baking powder, and cocoa back in the pantry. Hand in the cookie jar for a quick, pity me snack, combined with a glass of milk for dipping.

Where had she gone wrong?

Marianna sat down at the kitchen table and sighed as she dipped one of her cookies into the milk. Their meeting with Lonnie had been an hour ago and it was the only thing on her mind right now. She swore that she'd read Lonnie right, but if that was the case, why had she say no? She was so occupied with that single question that she didn't notice that the cookie had gotten soggy in the milk, breaking apart to drop to the bottom of the glass. Marianna sighed. Yeah. That explained her feelings right now: a soggy cookie. She reached across the table and poked at the anklet, which she'd slammed down in frustration when she first came into the kitchen. It should've been resting around Lonnie's leg, but no.

Lonnie had said no.

She supposed that their first mistake was assuming that Lonnie would agree. Just because she had defeated a monster didn't mean she wanted to be part of the group. They'd only gotten a snippet of who Lonnie was, that didn't necessarily mean that she was a shoe-in for their group. They didn't know anything about her personality, her beliefs. They didn't really know anything beyond the fact that she kicked ass. Was this what Blaze had meant? Why she had been hesitating? Was this all to teach them some sort of lesson with planning and being careful to not waste efforts? Even so... Marianna couldn't help remembering the conversation in the stairwell. She was sure Lonnie was right for this. It couldn't end like this, right? There had to be something more.

Marianna took a deep breath and pulled her phone out of her pocket. She needed a distraction. If she sat here and kept thinking about it, she wouldn't figure anything out. Baking was out of the question, but there was something else she could do.

"Marianna! Hey!"

Marianna smiled as soon as she heard Dana's voice. She knew her friend would be able to cheer her up. "Hey you," then, "What are you up to?"

"Nothing. Literally nothing. I'm sitting in my room bored."

"That sounds lovely..."

"Is everything okay? You sound a bit upset."

Even over the phone, Dana could tell when something was bothering Marianna. "It's been a long day," she said. "I think I could use some retail therapy. We should go out tomorrow." While Marianna knew that Bree would be up for a shopping excursion, the two of them were interested in very different things. There was nothing wrong with wanting to splurge in the video game store or the dark and moody store full of fishnets and geeky T-shirts, but Marianna needed a shopping buddy who wanted to try on high heels that turned any surface into a runway. That's where Dana came in, and it had been too long since the two played with decorative shoes and handbags. So tonight, Marianna would relax in a nice, warm, grape soda scented bath and mentally map out what stores they should hit up tomorrow. That was definitely better than remembering how she'd failed.

"I see…"

Marianna frowned. It wasn't like Dana to sound so hesitant about shopping. "What's wrong? Did you max out a credit card again?" Marianna wouldn't be surprised. Even if her parents threatened that this card would be *the last one*, Dana could pout her way to another shiny piece of plastic. Or she could, at the very least, point to Carlos' spending and throw him under the bus with a smile.

"No no, nothing like that. I just…" Dana paused, trying to find the right words. "You really want to go back to the mall? Not that it matters, I guess, since it's probably still closed down…"

Marianna's eyes widened in realization. The attack had only been a day ago. "Oh… I guess I hadn't thought of that." She was so busy trying to recruit Lonnie that she hadn't thought about Dana's feelings. Her friend wasn't used to encountering monsters on a weekly basis, of course she wouldn't want to return to the mall so soon. Besides, Dana was right: there was no way the mall would even be open. "I'm sorry… we don't have to go."

"No no no, it's fine! We'll go to a different mall! I'm letting stupid things get to me, you need a shopping day!"

"Dana…" Even if they could travel out to a different mall, who in their right mind would trust any shopping center right now – save for a girl who could blow things up with cupcakes. It had taken Dana a week to return to the bakery back when Marianna and Bree had fought together for the first time.

"Hey, if you can be so calm about it, I can, too."

Calm wasn't the word she'd use, but it wasn't like she wanted to tell Dana the truth: she was used to these attacks. "Dana… you don't have to be calm."

"I can't let some *thing* stop me from doing what I love. We should totally go shopping tomorrow!"

There was no way Dana was going to let this go, but Marianna knew what would happen if she agreed. They'd end up going out and Dana would be on edge the entire time. "Actually... let's do something else."

"Like what?"

"You pick," Marianna said, smiling. "Anything you want."

"Well... you could always come over here tomorrow after class and we can hang out. Oh! You know what? Just come over here right now! We could have a girl's night! Pajamas, popcorn, make-up, movies, the works! And if you're in need of some shoes, you can try on some of mine."

"A girl's night? Tonight?"

"Yeah! Right now!"

As tempting as that sounded, Marianna knew she should spend the evening figuring out their next move. "Dana, it's late, and we have class–"

"Oh my god, just go already!"

Marianna looked over to see Bree standing at the kitchen door, an exasperated look on her face. "Hold on," Marianna said into the phone before she pulled it away from her ear. "Bree, we should–"

"No."

"No?"

Bree walked over, took the phone from Marianna, and said, "She'll call you right back," before she hung up. She could imagine Dana's perplexed look and she'd probably be calling back in a few seconds. Bree worked to make this conversation as short as possible. "Take a night off, Mari."

"After everything that's happened, you think I can–"

"Yes. And you should. We can discuss this whole Radical Rainbow thing when you get back. Not like that's going anywhere," Bree said as she nodded to the anklet on the table.

Marianna debated on putting up a fight, but honestly, what was the point? Why waste her energy when she was already exhausted? Besides, was there any harm in waiting a day? "And what are you gonna do while I'm gone?"

"Chat with Ella. Record for the channel," then Bree walked over and grabbed the covered plate of leftover brownies. "I also have these to keep me company."

Marianna opened her mouth to protest but stopped when her phone started ringing. It was no surprise to see Dana's name appear on the screen. "All right, but you better save me some," she said. Without even realizing it, she grabbed the anklet and quickly headed to her room to pack an overnight bag, answering the phone on her way.

"No promises," Bree shouted.

"I heard that!" Marianna yelled back to her. Not that she really cared, she could always make more brownies.

It didn't take long for her to pack, and soon, Marianna was going down the elevator to leave. As she walked through the muted office area she was surprised to see Blaze wandering through the rows of cubicles, quietly looking over the various desks and colorless plant life. "Blaze?"

Blaze paused in her walk to look over at Marianna. "Ah, good evening. What brings you down here so late?"

What Marianna wanted to do was ask what the woman was doing down here. It was like she was patrolling the area – even if there was no way anyone could get in the building. She supposed it made sense for Blaze to be extra careful, but it was a little unsettling to see the woman down here when they generally saw each other in a more spectacular place. "I was going to spend the night with Dana, if that's all right."

"Of course it is. I can give you a ride, if you want."

"Oh... um, that's okay, I-"

"I'm not going to bring up Lonnie, I promise."

Marianna frowned. "You already know, don't you?"

Blaze gave Marianna a knowing look as she walked over to her. "You'd be in a much better mood if she'd said yes."

"... I guess I should give you back the anklet," which she'd tossed in her purse before she left. She wasn't sure why she felt the need to have it with her.

Blaze smiled and placed a hand on Marianna's shoulder. "Why don't you hold onto it for a bit longer."

"Really?"

"Marianna, it's not like you to give up so easily."

"But... you were so opposed to Lonnie before..."

"True... but you girls made it clear you wanted this. If you think she's a good fit, then you should follow through."

Marianna's frown faded as she asked, "Even if I'm approaching her a second time?"

"Even if you're approaching her a fifth time."

"I'm not gonna be *that* pushy," Marianna laughed.

"You get my point. So, shall I escort you to Dana's place?"

Marianna's original plan had been to take the bus, but if Blaze was willing to drive her then, "Yes please." Not that she was opposed to public transportation, but if she could avoid waiting for bus number one and running to catch bus number two to get to Dana's place, she would happily save herself the time and unwanted jog.

Upon arriving at Dana's, Marianna was immediately greeted by a pile of shoes, a handful of romantic comedies she *really needed to see*, and a large pizza for the both of them to share. "So, what should we do first? I've got plenty of movies with attractive female leads who I can pretend are pining after me instead of some clueless man. We can play with my shoe collection. We can-"

"This is perfect." Marianna would normally tell Dana that she'd gone overboard. Tonight, she was happy to have the girl shoving away her worries with food and movies. Marianna let Dana pull her over to the couch and start up one of the movies in her *must see* pile.

"Did you want to talk about why you had a long day? Or should we just watch the movie?"

"Let's just watch the movie."

"Got it. Oh! One more thing!" Then Dana ran out of the room to disappear into the kitchen, then returned with two bottles of orange cream soda. "We can't have a girl's night without these."

Marianna couldn't stop smiling as Dana sat next to her and handed her a bottle. All she wanted – no, *needed* – was a chance to be a normal girl hanging out with her friend, and Dana was doing exactly that. Marianna clinked her bottle against Dana's and said, "Thank you."

"What are you thanking me for? This is what I'm here for."

"Dana..."

"I mean it. I'm here for you."

There was a bit more weight to those words, weight that sounded deeper than friendship. Marianna had thought about it before, a brief idea that she let slip away because of the complicated mess that was her life. Now, things were more complicated than ever, and she wasn't sure it would be fair to pull Dana into it. Although, technically, she *could* pull Dana in, as revealing herself was ultimately her decision, but the truth was... she didn't want to. Marianna liked having something normal. She liked being seen as *normal*, and if she told Dana how abnormal she was that normality would be gone.

So Marianna settled on sipping her drink, eating pizza, and rubbing Dana's back when she started crying during the required *I love you* scene of the movie – even if she'd been calling the lead guy a moron for most of it.

What in the world had possessed her to wear a dress to school today?

Bree knew the answer to that question, actually. The dress was cute, curved around her body in all the right places, and had a print of the stained glass window designs from *The Legend of Zelda*. Bree couldn't turn down the cute, geeky things that were becoming more available in stores and she'd bought it as soon as she'd found her size. Unfortunately, she never considered that she'd be wearing the dress to meet up with a cute girl. Granted, she'd gone out with Kayla in the tiniest shorts she owned, but that was cosplay. Something about a dress felt much more personal.

As Bree leaned back against the wall outside of Kayla's class, she looked down at her phone for what felt like the millionth time that morning. Kayla had sent a text with a simple question: did she have any plans for lunch? Bree absentmindedly responded with a no, which led to Kayla asking if she wanted to meet up. Bree, in all her oblivious glory, not only responded with a "yes" but had added a smiley face emoji to the end of the statement. Had she been thinking she'd realize that she needed time to fix her hair and analyze her wardrobe. As it stood, she'd come straight out of class and was now waiting for Kayla.

At least lunch with Kayla would take her mind off of the situation with Lonnie.

Soon, Bree could hear the students getting up from their seats. The door opened and the first few walked out, some complaining about their professor's nasty habit of talking past the bell. Kayla was one of the last to leave and made Bree's heart skip a beat in just a pair of cosmic leggings and a loose, white shirt. "*Legend of Zelda* today?" Kayla asked.

"Seriously, are you sure you're not a nerd?"

"'It's dangerous to lecture alone. Take this.' Did you forget I said that?"

Bree almost blurted out that she had that entire moment committed to memory, but she managed to stop the words from tumbling out of her mouth. Instead, she said, "Well no, but... memes..."

"I explained the *nerdlesque* thing to you the other day..."

"Oh my god! Did someone do a Zelda act?" Bree shoved the nervousness away in favor of bouncing up and down at the thought of a cool, burlesque act for one of her favorite games.

"Not Zelda. Sheik. Well... I guess that's Zelda, or something? I dunno, I need to brush up on my gamer geek," then Kayla smirked and added, "You know, so I can pick up the cute girl with the YouTube channel."

"A-ah, I..." Why did she have to get so flustered?! Bree supposed it was fine since Kayla seemed so pleased with herself.

"Come on, I'll treat ya to lunch. Where'd you wanna go?"

"Oh... the food court is fine."

Kayla almost looked as disgusted as Marianna had looked when she saw that fried rice before. "For real? The food court?"

"Why, what were you thinking?"

"I was thinking that maybe we could go to an actual restaurant. You know, where we can sit and talk without midnight launches and monsters?"

Bree smiled. Achievement unlocked. "I think that's called a date."

"Ah, yes," then Kayla rubbed her chin as if she were a scientist making a new hypothesis. "I believe it's pretty popular among girls our age."

Bree finally felt herself loosening up as she started laughing over Kayla's analysis. "Not that I don't wanna eat something besides the campus fast food options... but I have a class later."

"Damn. I suppose campus food court will have to do. But someday I'll take you on a real date."

"Hey, it's real as long as we're going somewhere together." Bree instantly regretted the words as soon as she said. She wished she could grab onto them and toss them in the garbage before they were able to be heard. Why did she get so sappy? In seconds she felt uneasy, quietly squirming as she waited for Kayla to respond to her corny-

"You have these moments of absolute romantic perfection."

Corny? More like perfect, apparently. Bree wasn't sure if she'd ever smiled such a large smile before. "It offsets my awkwardness, I'm sure."

The two girls smiled at one another and were about to head to lunch when they heard a few more students leaving the classroom. They were excitedly speaking to one another, something about not believing that they had class with the *Magical Kickboxer*. "I can't believe people are still buggin' her," Kayla said as soon as the two students were out of earshot.

Bree looked into the classroom and frowned. Class was over, but there were students clustered around Lonnie's desk. They were asking questions about the mall attack and making it near impossible for her to leave. Bree wondered if this was part of the reason why Lonnie had said no. Maybe she was tired of the attention. But that wouldn't make much sense. As a magical girl, all the attention would be directed at that persona and not her. It'd be the perfect way to escape from it.

So why had she said no?

As Bree watched Lonnie she couldn't shake the feeling that she absolutely had to know. Saying that she wanted to rely on her own strength didn't feel like a complete explanation. Bree had told Marianna that they should wait to discuss it. She'd even convinced Marianna to take a night off, but that didn't mean she didn't have her own questions and thoughts. And now those thoughts came flooding back, completely ruining the perfect date setup that had fallen into her lap.

"I wanna talk to her." Bree immediately regretted the words, but she couldn't deny them. She winced when she saw the look on Kayla's face – a mix of amusement and frustration. It occurred to Bree that if Kayla had class with Lonnie, it meant that she'd been seeing people trip over themselves in their attempts to talk to her. It had to be more than a little annoying.

If Kayla was irritated, she didn't say. Instead, she shrugged her shoulders and said, "Good luck with that. I don't know if her fans are gonna let her leave."

"They have to eventually, right?"

"Are you saying you want to wait to talk to another woman when I'm trying to take you out to lunch?"

"T-that's not it!" Oh god, Kayla didn't really believe that, did she? "I just-"

Kayla interrupted her with a soft laugh. "Relax, I'm kidding. I get wanting to talk to her. What she did was pretty amazing."

Bree wasn't sure if Kayla meant that. She didn't sound too happy a few seconds ago. "It's more than that..."

"Oh?"

Bree realized that she'd said too much. Again. She'd done this once before with Kayla and it was becoming a troubling bad habit where she'd slip and say things she shouldn't. All she wanted was for Kayla to understand where she was coming from. At this rate, she was going to end up transforming in front of her and blurting out her magical girl status. "I was attacked by one of those things shortly after coming here for school."

"W-what?!"

Bree nodded. She could at least say that much. "Remember when I said that Mari saved me from a creepy guy? That... was the creepy guy."

"She beat up a monster for you?"

She'd done more than that. She'd completely obliterated the thing, but Bree couldn't reveal that information. So instead she said, "No, nothing like that, but she did help me get away."

"Why did you say it was a creepy guy?"

"Because it was, originally. He transformed in front of me, or rather, he transformed *on top* of me." She wanted to stop talking but she couldn't. Talking about it was bringing all those old feelings back. Bree thought she'd gotten rid of those helpless trembles, but she could still remember what it felt like to have her hands pinned down like that. It was annoyingly terrifying. "Everything was kind of a blur, but when the dust settled... Mari was there."

"Shit..." Kayla whispered, because what else could she say to something like that?

"So I guess I want to thank Lonnie for saving all of us," among other things, "You know, because of... that."

"Well that's easy enough," then Kayla turned and stepped into the classroom. "Yo! Lonnie!"

"K-Kayla!" Bree's eyes widen and she stared at Kayla. She hadn't expected her to do anything like that! She watched as Lonnie excused herself from the one-sided conversation to squeeze past the students and walk over to Kayla.

"You realize I love you right now, right?" Lonnie whispered to her.

Kayla waved it off then looked back at the lingering students. They were all standing there, waiting to see if Lonnie would come back and not talk to them. "Don't y'all have to get to class or something?" In seconds, the remaining students jumped to attention and left the classroom, some of them whispering to each other about how they hoped they'd get a chance to see Lonnie again. Kayla rolled her eyes. Were they so starstruck that they didn't realize they'd see her the next time they had class? "That must be exhausting," Kayla said.

Lonnie shrugged her shoulders and said, "It is, but they're slowly becoming less invasive. No more bathroom encounters. Yet."

"Well I hope you don't mind talking to one more person," then Kayla nodded over to Bree. "This is Bree."

"Ah, the infamous Bree."

Bree blinked, not at all expecting such a title. Meanwhile, Kayla coughed and looked away from both of them. Was she blushing? Holy crap, she was blushing! Had she talked about her to Lonnie? Bree wanted to process this newest development in their... whatever it was they were doing... but she knew she had more important things to do.

But she filed it in the back of her mind for the future.

"I was hoping we could talk. Alone."

Lonnie looked a bit surprised at that. Most of the people who wanted to admire her came in packs. Lonnie glanced over at Kayla who nodded and went along with it. Bree had already shared enough about what happened to her, Kayla didn't want to stick around and pry. "It's ok, I'd rather take her out to a real restaurant then the college food court."

"Definitely. I'm infamous, after all." Bree mentally patted herself on the back for saying something so clever, especially since it looked like Kayla was close to blushing again. Lonnie chuckled as Kayla turned and walked off, muttering something about wishing her classmates kept their mouths shut.

"Look, if you wanna thank me about what happened at the mall, it's not necessary. Besides, your friend already did."

"You mean Mari? Yeah, she told me. But I actually wanna talk about something else."

"Oh?"

Bree realized the situation she just put herself in. There was no way to talk about this without revealing who she was. But maybe if she approached her as herself and not her magical persona, Lonnie would be more willing to join them. Behind the transformations and astonishing attacks they were normal girls, just like Lonnie. Maybe she'd come around if she saw that.

So Bree took a deep breath and went for it, her heart drumming as hard as it had been back when she'd jumped off that building. "Why... did you say no?"

"What?" Lonnie asked, confused by Bree's question.

"To us... last night. Why did you say no?"

Lonnie didn't know what the girl was talking about. She hadn't even spoken to her until now. The only girls she'd said no to about anything were...

No.

It couldn't be.

Before Lonnie could say anything Bree pointed to the bow in her hair as if it held all the answers. And, in a way, it did, because as soon as Bree poked it it began to shimmer, as if coming to life. A few sparkles drifted off of the bow and into Bree's hair. The brown strands they touched shifted to that iconic, bright green, for just a moment. Lonnie's eyes widened in realization as she slowly shook her head, not believing what she was seeing. "You're..."

Bree nodded and lowered her hand away from her bow. "Yeah, I am."

"Why would you tell me this? Shouldn't you be keeping it a secret? What if I told everyone?"

"I don't know you very well, but I can already tell that you're not the type to do that."

"But I *could* be."

"But you're not."

"What do you want from me?" Lonnie asked, the frustration clear in her voice as she narrowed her eyes at Bree. "I said I didn't want to join, why won't you let it go?"

Bree slammed her hand down on the desk. She could feel her entire body getting warm from how angry she felt. Why was this so hard? Why couldn't Lonnie see how much she needed to be a part of this? "Because I can't! *We* can't! You... y-you seemed like the perfect fit! You wanna help people, this would be the way to do it!"

Lonnie clenched her fists and tried her best to stay calm, but she ended up snapping back at Bree. "I can do it on my own!"

"There is no way in hell you can do something like this alone," Bree whispered. She knew it was probably the wrong thing to say, but it was the absolute truth. "What you did yesterday was great, but there's no way you can keep at it by yourself."

Lonnie scoffed at Bree and asked, "Says who?"

"Says me! I've seen what they can do! You can't honestly want to take them on by yourself!"

"Your other friend did. Galactic Purple. Or should I assume that's Marianna since she cornered me the same way yesterday?"

Bree wasn't going to respond to that. Instead she said, "And she thought she had to do it alone and she was wrong. She needed me."

Lonnie walked up to Bree, standing uncomfortably close as she looked down at her and said, "Well I don't. If I *choose* to help you two, it'll be on my own terms. I don't need power from anyone else."

"But-"

"Are we done? I have a class to get to."

Bree frowned sadly and said, "Yeah... I guess we are."

As Lonnie walked off Bree took a seat at the desk she'd been standing next to. Revealing herself hadn't worked at all, and Lonnie was probably more set on her *no* than she had been before. "Terrific," Bree muttered to herself. A lunch opportunity with Kayla wasted because she was so sure that she could reason with Lonnie. Maybe they were wrong about her. Maybe she wasn't the one meant to inherit that anklet.

Bree decided to head home and play a video game. Skipping the class she had after lunch in favor of gaming would be the perfect way to cure her sorrowful mood. She could execute some over-the-top fatalities on multi-colored ninjas – though not the yellow one, that one was her favorite. She'd mull over how she'd tell Marianna about her encounter with Lonnie after ripping off a couple of heads.

There was something truly therapeutic about punching and kicking something, even if it was an inanimate object.

Armed with her headphones and a playlist full of loud, aggressive music, Lonnie slammed her foot into the punching bag. She'd told Bree

212 – BRIANA LAWRENCE

that she had a class to get to. Technically, she did, but she'd skipped it in favor of kicking a bag until she felt better. Raye had looked displeased with her ditching and promised to talk to her once she was done finishing up the work she had in the office – bless the paperwork for prolonging that inevitable lecture.

"There's no way in hell you can do something like this alone."

Punch.

It wasn't that Lonnie wanted to fight these things on a normal basis, but if she wanted to, she definitely could. She meant what she said about wanting to help, but why did that have to mean that she wanted to join them?

Punch. Kick.

What was so wrong about wanting to fight in her own way?

Punch. Kick. Kick. Punch.

Why did she have to rely on someone else's power?

Kick. Kick. Punch!

Lonnie took a couple of deep breaths and stepped away from the punching bag. She slipped off her headphones and grabbed a nearby towel to wipe her forehead. She'd worked up a good sweat and she could feel the frustration fading away.

"Yo! Lonnie!"

That was until Braydon showed up, armed with his gym bag and a healthy dose of annoyance.

Unfortunately for Lonnie, Braydon didn't attend college. He didn't have a string of classes to distract him from being at the gym at any moment's notice. He worked for his father, if *work* meant *come in whenever he pleased* since it was a family owned business and his mother felt the need to coddle him because he was still her *baby*. How he had enough focus to come to the gym was beyond Lonnie. "I'm not in the mood," she said.

"Whoa, I just got here," Braydon said as he put his hands up. "I didn't even say anything yet."

"No, but you were going to."

"Jeez, what's got your panties in a bunch? Or should I say boxers?"

What happened next was not at all something that Lonnie would normally do. She turned and tried to punch Braydon. *Tried* being the key word, because Braydon had annoyingly good reflexes and was able to block her attack. Lonnie lowered her gloved fist and whispered, "I'm sorry."

"Feeling better now?" Braydon asked as he picked up his bag, having dropped it when Lonnie came at him.

"No."

"Wanna punch me again?"

"Will it actually land this time?"

Braydon smirked and said, "No."

Lonnie smirked back. "You don't know that."

"Sure I do. It never lands."

Lonnie laughed and said, "That's not true and you know it."

"I know, but it got you to laugh."

Lonnie was completely caught off guard by that statement. She rolled her eyes and said, "Why can't you be this nice all the time?"

"Not my style," Braydon said as he walked over and sat on the bench, pulling his gear out of his bag.

Lonnie walked over and sat next to him, taking off her gloves and grabbing the water bottle she'd set out for herself. "I bet Kendra would adore you being nicer," she said before she took a drink.

"Y-you shut up!" Braydon looked away from Lonnie to try and hide the flustered look on his face. "Don't talk about my precious Kendra!"

"I take it walking home together was awkward?"

Braydon sighed the longing sigh of a young man with a crush. "You don't understand what it's like to pine after someone, do you?"

"Nope, cuz I tell people how I feel, unlike you," then Lonnie poked Braydon's shoulder.

"Ugh, you're such a man."

"What does that say about you then?" Lonnie asked before taking another sip of water.

"It... I... shut up!" Braydon shoved Lonnie away from him, doing his best to ignore the way her laughter echoed around them.

"Come on, we should go a round in the ring."

"You mean when you're not all pissed off? I'm not sure which is better," but Braydon was already putting on the necessary equipment.

Lonnie smirked and put her gloves back on. "Let's find out."

Before the two could step into the ring the door to the gym opened. Lonnie frowned as she felt all the tension rise up in her body all over again. She shouldn't have been surprised that Marianna would show up. In fact, Lonnie had told her to stop by at any time. While Bree hadn't confirmed that Marianna was Galactic Purple, it was fairly obvious, and Lonnie wasn't in the mood to have another conversation about her personal decisions.

"Who's the girl? I've never seen her before."

"A friend... or so I thought," Lonnie said as she set her gloves down. "I'll be right back."

"Good luck," Braydon said as Lonnie walked over to Marianna.

Marianna smiled at Lonnie despite the hard frown on her face. Meanwhile, Lonnie fought the urge to return the gesture. The girl's cuteness was infectious, but Lonnie wasn't going to let her use it to her advantage. "What is it?" Lonnie asked.

"You said I should come by sometime so I thought I'd check the place out. It's almost... quaint."

Lonnie shrugged. "It's a gym."

"Yes, but it feels comfortable," Marianna said as she looked around. "There's a lot of love in this place, I can tell."

"It's definitely from the owners. They welcome anyone in who wants to learn."

"It sounds like you're close to them."

"I am... but you didn't come here to talk about Rodney and Raye." It was best to cut to the chase. Lonnie recognized this good cop, bad cop tactic from a mile away. Bree had yelled at her, leading to an argument between the two. Now Marianna was here to be the soothing voice of reason.

"We can if you want to. I did come to talk to you."

"Cut the crap," Lonnie whispered harshly. "Bree already talked to me."

"...what?"

She was kidding, right? The two had planned this, right? "Don't act like you don't know, Marianna. Or should I use your other name?"

The realization slowly dawned on Marianna. "Oh Bree, what have you done?" After listening to Bree's advice and taking the night off, Marianna felt relaxed and ready to tackle the situation. Unfortunately, Bree apparently had the same idea. In retrospect, she should've known that the girl would do something. The least Bree could've done was give her a heads up, especially if she decided to reveal who they really were. "What did she say to you?"

Lonnie blinked, then blinked again. She was actually being serious, wasn't she? "Holy shit, she really didn't tell you?"

Marianna shook her head. "She tends to go off and do things without thinking," then she added, "I'm sorry if either of us have upset you, but... can we just talk? Please?"

Lonnie glanced back at Braydon, who was still standing by the boxing ring, waiting to see where their conversation was going. She wasn't too thrilled with either of the girls, but something about Marianna felt so genuine. She was still very much that girl who had been so nice in the stairwell, that girl who had shown concern for her after that fight. "Let me get my gear off then we can go for a walk."

Marianna smiled. "Thank you."

The neighborhood was surrounded in a comfortable buzz of noise. The gym wasn't too far from a playground, and there were kids outside running around being kids for as long as they could. The sun set came much earlier these days, and every child knew to be inside before the streetlights turned on.

As the two girls walked past the playground fence, Lonnie got tired of the silence and blurted out the first thing that came to mind. "You're okay walking like this, right?"

"Hm?"

Lonnie stopped walking and nodded down to Marianna's shoes. "They're cute, but, they're heels. Don't they hurt?"

Marianna couldn't help but laugh at the thought of a girl who spent her days kicking things wondering if shoes were painful. "Naw, I'm used to them. I even wear them when we're fighting."

"I've noticed. How is that even possible?"

Marianna shrugged her shoulders and said, "It's easy when you wear them all the time. You should see Cosmic Green's boots."

"I have! Those are insane. I'd be such a loser, I'd probably be wearing sneakers or something."

"You can wear whatever you want."

Lonnie frowned at the girl then started walking again, a clear sign of wanting to end that train of thought. Still, as they crossed the street and headed toward the local corner store, Lonnie felt the urge to state something that'd been bothering her. "It's irritating how you do that."

"Do what?"

"Make people so comfortable that they blurt out things they don't mean."

"We were just talking about shoes, Lonnie," Marianna pointed out.

Lonnie stopped walking again and leaned back against the brick wall of the store. People were going in and out, the bell above the door jingling each time. "You know what I'm talking about, Marianna."

"I do, and you know what? I think you do mean it, you just want to deny it for some reason." Even if Marianna was beyond ticked at Bree for acting without her, she had to admit that spending the night with Dana had helped in the long run. She could stand in front of Lonnie now, less stressed and more confident. There had to be more to the kickboxer's line of thinking, and Marianna was going to find out what it was.

"I don't wanna yell at you," Lonnie said. "I actually liked talking to you before, I don't wanna ruin that."

"Maybe yelling is what you need to do. Holding in your feelings isn't doing anyone any favors. Bree actually taught me that."

"Bree had to teach you something?" Lonnie couldn't quite wrap her head around that, not after the exchange she'd had with the girl. "I haven't known you two for very long, but you definitely seem like the more level headed one."

"Generally yes, but I needed a reminder that I didn't have to do this alone. I... wanted to prove to someone that being a magical girl could be a good thing. I wanted to prove that it could help a lot of people," and that was all that Marianna would say about that. Lonnie didn't need to know the details. She hadn't earned them, not yet.

"So you think I'm the same way? That I'm trying to prove myself?"

Marianna nodded her head. "You're the one who said that you wanted to rely on your own strength."

"That's right," Lonnie said as she crossed her arms, not willing to back down. "And there's nothing wrong with that."

"Of course not. What makes you think this isn't your own strength?" Marianna pressed one of her hands over her heart to emphasize her point.

Lonnie understood what she was going for, the whole *inner strength* angle – or something along those lines. She wasn't buying it. "Right. Because exploding cupcakes and green bits of power is something you develop on your own."

Despite Lonnie's skepticism Marianna kept smiling. "I didn't think someone like you would make assumptions."

"Aren't you making assumptions yourself? Assuming I'd join your team?"

"That doesn't change the fact that you'd fit in," then Marianna pulled the anklet out of her purse. "You really would be an amazing Radical Rainbow."

"You already have a name for me?!" Lonnie's laughter was sudden and loud enough to startle Marianna, who was suddenly very much aware of the two of them standing outside. Not that anyone was eaves-dropping on their conversation, too busy grabbing what they needed from the store and heading home.

"It's who owned this before," Marianna explained once Lonnie finally stopped laughing, though laughing over the situation was better than her being angry.

"Ah, so it is someone else's power."

Marianna sighed and tucked the anklet into her pocket. "Why are you so stuck on that?"

"Because I don't want my strength attributed to anything else. I'm either too masculine to be a woman and all my strength is because I'm *like a man*, or I'm too feminine to be strong at all."

Marianna knew there was a bigger reason than the one Lonnie had given her, but hearing it out loud hurt. "Lonnie..."

"Save it," then Lonnie pushed herself off the wall and stepped past Marianna, more than ready to head back to the gym. "You wanted your reason, now you have it."

That was true, but Marianna didn't feel good about it. "Lonnie, you don't-"

"Have to feel like that? I've heard it all before." She'd even heard it from Raye and was honestly trying her best to keep it in mind, but it was much easier said than done. The difference between Raye and Marianna was that Raye knew it took a while. Marianna wanted her to make a decision right now.

"You've heard it, but have you actually listened to it?"

"Is this the part where you lecture me?"

"No. This is the part where I tell you that you're already amazing. That's why we want you to join, because you've already proven you're amazing. The power would be yours to use as you see fit. It's not some-one else's. Radical Rainbow is just a title. It-"

"Stop."

"But I-"

"I said stop! I don't wanna hear it," then Lonnie took off running. It was the most immature reaction to something that she'd ever had, but she knew it was the only way she could end the conversation. Marianna was much more persistent than Bree, and Lonnie had a feeling that if she stuck around long enough, she'd convince her to join them.

So she ran. She ran all the way back to the gym. She needed to hit something again and when she stepped into the gym she saw the perfect target. Jeremy was there, and Lonnie suddenly remembered that he had requested a rematch. True to form, as soon as Jeremy saw her he was raring to go. "Was wondering where you were," he said as he dropped his bag. "Thought you might have gotten scared and-"

"Cut the crap," Lonnie said as she walked up to him. "Let's go."

"Oh, feeling a bit forceful today? I'd say that was a turn on but then people might think I'm attracted to men."

Braydon winced from where he was watching with Kendra, who'd come in a few minutes after Lonnie had left. Both of them knew that they should've directed the two into the ring and have them hash it out via boxing gear, rules, and regulations – it's what Rodney and Raye would've done. Instead, they both watched in stunned silence as Lonnie punched Jeremy right in his face. "Must've been a bad conversation," Braydon muttered. Lonnie hadn't looked too thrilled when that girl came in earlier.

Kendra finally snapped out of it and ran over to Lonnie. "What the hell?! Lonnie, you know better!"

"People need to stop telling me what to do and how to feel!" Lonnie snapped back at her. "This asshole's got it comin'."

Jeremy made the mistake of laughing despite his now busted lip. "It's cool, Sanders," he said to Kendra as he licked at the blood on his lip. "We can go at it right here, Knox."

Kendra quickly grabbed onto Lonnie's arm before she decided to take him up on his offer. "No, you cannot," Kendra insisted. "Both of you, in the ring. Now!"

Jeremy ignored Kendra and gave Lonnie a wicked grin. "I'm not that patient, how about you, Knox?"

Lonnie responded by yanking her arm away from Kendra and cracking her knuckles. Kendra shook her head and said, "No, Lonnie. You're better than this."

"She's right," Braydon said as he walked over to stand in front of Lonnie and block her view of Jeremy. "You need to calm down and-"

"And what? Take it like a *man*? Stop being so emotional like a *woman*?"

Braydon shook his head. "I... shit, Lonnie. You know that's not what I mean..."

"Please, Lonnie. Breathe," Kendra said.

"What's going on out here?"

Lonnie looked over to see Rodney and Raye coming out of the backroom. She turned her back to both of them as the flood of anger finally subsided. This was exactly what they were teaching her not to do and she didn't dare face either of them. "She lashed out at me," Jeremy said, eagerly playing the sympathy card. "I tried to get her to stop."

"Liar!" Kendra yelled. "You provoked her! Like you always do!"

Raye sighed and shook her head in disappointment. "I thought you two learned your lesson yesterday."

"Well *I* did," Jeremy said. "I can't help it if girls like her are always angry."

Raye raised an eyebrow at him and calmly asked, "Girls like her?"

"Oh boy," Rodney whispered.

Lonnie glanced back at Raye and told herself to not take delight in how offended she looked right now. She'd seen that look several times before and was happy to not be on the receiving end of it. While Raye would never allow anyone to belittle the students of her gym, there was a special kind of rage reserved for anyone who belittled the women – *especially* women of color.

Unfortunately, Jeremy didn't notice the warning signs and continued to shove his foot in his mouth. "Yeah, you know, *black girls*. They're always pissed off. That's why no one ever wants to listen to them."

Either Jeremy had forgotten that he was talking to a black woman, or he stopped caring. Either way, Lonnie could tell that Jeremy's lives had run out. "Get out," Raye said, and her voice left no room for argument.

"You serious?" Jeremy asked in disbelief. When Raye didn't say anything he turned his attention to Rodney. "Come on, man, are you serious?"

"Very," Rodney said, standing right at his wife's side.

"This is bullshit!" Jeremy snapped, then he pointed over to Lonnie. "You're gonna kick me out because this bitch-"

It took a few quick steps for Raye to stand right in front of Jeremy. In one fluid motion, her leg was in the air and her foot was fast approaching the side of his face. Jeremy squeezed his eyes shut and braced himself for impact, but the attack never came. The trembling student hesitantly opened his eyes to see that Raye had stopped herself at the last second. Her foot was almost brushing against his cheek as she held her stance, right where he'd left himself open. "Get out," Raye repeated.

Jeremy wisely kept his mouth shut... until he was a few steps away and safely hidden behind his gym bag as he picked it up from the floor. "I thought you were different," he hissed, and his voice sounded much rougher than it should've. "But you're just as dumb as those other bitches."

Raye didn't bother to respond to that. There wasn't a point to waste the energy. She watched as her student – *former* student – headed for the door in a frustrated huff, still muttering to himself about *dumb bitches.* Rodney rested his hand on his wife's shoulder and said, "You did the right thing. He needed to go."

Lonnie had pointed that out a while ago, but she wasn't going to rub it in. Not now. Not ever. She didn't need to make the situation more unpleasant so she settled on standing with everyone else and watching Jeremy leave.

But he didn't leave.

When he reached the door he dropped his gym bag and hunched over with a sickening growl. The muscles in his back rippled and actually began to move across his skin like living rocks. Without warning, he punched the front door right off the hinges with a delighted laugh, sounding very pleased with his new burst of strength. "You want me to leave, huh?" Jeremy whipped around to face the group, his head looking much too small for his new, bulbous chest and back, his legs still somehow retaining their normal shape. "I think I'll stick around."

"What the hell is that?" Braydon asked, a horrified look on his face.

"... Jeremy?" Kendra didn't sound too sure, but whatever it was, it was stalking toward them.

Lonnie couldn't get the words out but she most definitely recognized this. It felt much more malicious than the mall incident. She watched as Rodney and Raye stood in front of them in some vain attempt to offer protection. She wanted to tell them that there was no point but was too shaken to speak.

What had she said before? That should could handle this? It looked like she was going to get her chance... whether she wanted to or not.

The first thing Marianna was going to do when she got home was yell at Bree. Not talk. *Yell*. She'd normally try and keep her composure, but she wasn't too happy with her comrade right now. While she couldn't blame Bree for wanting answers, she should've known to not jump in and do something without a plan of some sort. Marianna couldn't help but wonder if Lonnie's earlier encounter with Bree was a catalyst to her apprehension. Maybe if they spoke to her together, or waited for just a little bit longer...

Marianna sighed as she looked down at the anklet in her hand. At the end of the day, she knew that it wasn't Bree who made Lonnie so angry. Lonnie wasn't interested. Period. Or rather, she *was* interested, but not enough to give it a shot. She was set in her ways and convinced that joining them would somehow devalue what she'd already accomplished. So the second thing Marianna would have to do when she got home was return the anklet.

224 – Briana Lawrence

It was a real shame that it wouldn't be Lonnie.

As Marianna headed home she saw the sidewalk that led to gym. Part of her wanted to walk down there, maybe pass by and even peek in one more time. The other part wanted to give up. At this point she'd be completely dismissing Lonnie's feelings, and that was the last thing she wanted to do.

But it was only a few blocks away.

Marianna shook her head. This was exactly why Lonnie was so frustrated with the two of them. They weren't giving her any time to process the situation. They were acting like the students who surrounded Lonnie and didn't give her a chance to breathe. So no, she wouldn't return to the gym. She would go home and put this behind her.

"Yo, there's something going on at the gym."

Marianna turned to see two teenage boys walking down the sidewalk in the opposite direction of the gym.

"Should we check it out?" The second boy asked, the curiosity clear in his voice.

The first boy shook his head and said, "Hell naw, man. I ain't about to get my ass beat by some monster."

In an attempt to sweeten the deal, the second boy said, "Come on, man. We might get to see **magnifiquenoir!**"

It didn't work. "You can go if you want, but I'm goin' home."

The two boys walked passed Marianna and kept walking. Marianna, on the other hand, was on autopilot and quickly ran toward the gym as fast as she could. As she got closer, she could see more people standing around on the sidewalk. They were talking about some kind of commotion but no one was willing to go and investigate. The kids at the playground had all gathered around the fence, their parents now on the scene and telling them that no, they could **not** go and see the creature. The police had been called and they'd be there soon.

The closer Marianna got to the gym, the fewer people were in the area. That was a small blessing in disguise as she wouldn't have to try and get random onlookers to run to a safe place. She was immediately greeted by the broken door, but when she looked inside she was surprised to see that no one was actually in the building. There were signs of a fight having taken place. The floor was cracked, with one of the benches broken in half and a few holes in the wall from what looked to be vicious punches. Marianna followed the cracks in the floor toward the back room, its door barely hanging by the hinges. When she stepped around it she could see that the back door had suffered the same fate as the front door.

The scene out back was complete chaos. The creature looked like a combination of boulders and flesh, its skin torn apart in a couple of spots that weren't able to handle the massive amount of muscles. Raye was sitting near a large dent in the side of the building, holding Rodney in her arms who was breathing, but barely. "Just breathe, baby," she said, trying to soothe him through the worried tears in her eyes.

Braydon was panting harshly and sporting a couple of bruises that he was trying his best to ignore. He was facing the thing that used to be Jeremy, smirking up at the creature as he asked, "Is that all ya got?" It sounded like it hurt to speak, let alone try and challenge the creature to a fight, but he had to attempt to do something.

"Oh no, I'm just getting started." Even as a grotesque monster, it still retained Jeremy's assholish behavior. Before it could try and hit Braydon, Kendra ran over and kicked it from behind. Normally the kick would do some damage, but Kendra ended up limping away as it felt like she'd just kicked the side of a mountain.

"Awwwww, what's the matter?" The monstrous Jeremy cooed at Kendra and turned to face her. "Am I too strong for the little girl?"

"Screw you!" She cried out.

"Hey, your fight is with me!" Braydon shouted, trying to divert its attention back to him.

Kendra wasn't having any of it and said, "No, it's with *us*, Braydon. We work together."

As the two tried to come up with a way to fight the creature, Lonnie was slowly pushing herself up. She'd been knocked into the dumpster and had been having a hard time getting her bearings back. As she watched Braydon and Kendra attempt to fight together, she forced herself to stand. It wouldn't be long before they became too tired to fight – or worse. In its new state, Jeremy had gone after Raye first. The woman faced him one-on-one and drew him toward the back door away from everyone else. By the time she'd managed to get him outside she'd damn near wore herself out. Despite the monster's hulking size, it managed to maintain Jeremy's speed, only now, there was a cataclysmic amount of strength with the punches and kicks. Just as one of those punches was about to connect, Rodney had shoved Raye out of harm's way to receive the full force of the vicious attack meant for her.

"Lonnie! What the hell are you doing?!" Raye's voice was frantic, much more panicked than Lonnie ever wanted to hear.

"I can't let them fight alone!" Lonnie shouted back to her.

"Stay away from it! All of you stay away!"

"Too late for that," the creature growled out as its large fist smacked Braydon away.

Braydon imagined that this was what it felt like to be hit by a semi-truck at full speed. He felt himself being launched into the air and all he could do was hope to land on some kind of soft surface. Unfortunately, the softest thing that existed outside was the gravel below. When Braydon finally managed to open his eyes, the first person he saw was a concerned Kendra, who'd run over to be by his side. She was calling out his name and pleading with him to say something to her. Despite the dismal situation, he was trying to decide if he should go with snarky or charismatic. In the end, he managed to blurt out, "You shouldn't look so upset. I like it better when you smile," before promptly passing out.

Kendra knew that a full-on attack would be foolish, but in that moment she wanted to hit that thing with enough force to shatter it into a thousand pieces. She had never cared for Jeremy to begin with and this certainly wasn't helping his case. Kendra walked toward the beast, ignoring the pain in her foot from her earlier kick. She could hear Lonnie and Raye screaming at her but she ignored it. Instead she kept moving forward, her fists balled up and ready to do as much damage as she could.

All it had taken was one well-placed kick to send her flying toward the wall.

"Damnit!" There was no way Lonnie would make it to her in time and neither would Raye. Lonnie could just imagine the damage such an impact would do. She squeezed her eyes shut, not wanting to watch, but after a few seconds she realized that she hadn't heard anything hit the wall.

"This isn't how they wanted you to use your fighting abilities."

And there Marianna was, standing before them as Galactic Purple, holding the unconscious Kendra in her arms. The stone-skinned Jeremy let out an obnoxious laugh. "Oh look! Another woman who doesn't know her place! Goodie!"

Galactic Purple carefully set Kendra down and walked toward the creature, small starlights starting to gather in her hand. As Marianna, she'd called Bree to come and help as soon as she could, but there was no harm in getting a couple of early hits in. Especially on an irritating creature like this one.

"Stop!"

Galactic Purple glanced over at Lonnie. The kickboxer still looked completely disheveled but had at least caught her breath. The determination was clear in Lonnie's eyes and Galactic Purple quickly shook her head. "Lonnie, you can't be serious!"

"I've never been more serious in my life," Lonnie said as she walked toward the creature.

Galactic Purple knew that Lonnie wanted to tackle this herself, but she had to realize how dangerous this was. "At least let me help you," she pleaded.

"Yes, let her help you." There was a mocking tone in its voice that was reminiscent of the same boy that always got under Lonnie's skin. "It's not like you can win on your own."

Lonnie knew that she was being antagonized on purpose, but she didn't care. This was all because Jeremy couldn't deal with being defeated by a woman. Several women. He wouldn't dare show them respect. He'd dismiss their strength and do anything he could to push them down. "You wanted a rematch, right?"

"Lonnie!" Raye's voice was hoarse with tears as she screamed the girl's name. "Lonnie, stand down!"

"No! I can handle this!"

Raye shook her head. She hated doing it, but she knew it was true. It was the same conclusion she'd reached when she'd tried to fight that thing. She'd managed to get a couple of hits in, but it was like punching a brick wall. Her hands were still throbbing from her attempted punches, her legs tired and feeling as useless as jello. If Rodney hadn't jumped in to play the part of heroic husband, she'd be the one unconscious right now. "You can't fight," she whispered. "Not like this. Let that girl help you."

"I said no!" Then Lonnie charged forward. Instead of hitting her and knocking her out with one swift blow, the monster that was Jeremy did something worse: it toyed with her. It dodged all her attacks despite its lumbering size and laughed at her the entire time. It took delight in Lonnie's frustrated cries as she worked herself into an exhausted haze.

"Help her!!!"

Galactic Purple wanted to with every fiber of her being. She'd stood on the sidelines back at the mall, watching Lonnie take on that extraordinary challenge. She never wanted to be in that position again even if Lonnie insisted she could handle it, but with Lonnie moving so much, Galactic Purple couldn't get a clear shot. She'd need her to back away enough to be away from the explosion of her cupcake, but Lonnie was too furious in her assault. If Cosmic Green were there, she'd be able to get in close and blast through it... assuming her attack was strong enough. Suddenly, this felt much worse than the mall, because all Galactic Purple could do was wait for Lonnie to wear herself out.

That was until she felt the warm sensation in her pocket.

Galactic Purple reached into it and pulled out the anklet. It was now emitting a rainbow colored glow. Was it reacting to Lonnie? After trying multiple times to get Lonnie to see things her way, Galactic Purple wasn't sure if there was a point to try again. But it was clear that the power was responding to Lonnie's need to beat her opponent.

All she had to do was accept it.

Lonnie stumbled away from her adversary, her entire body shaking as she dropped to her knees. She was sweating, lips dry and throat hoarse as she desperately tried to catch her breath. The monster was standing there, wide open, waiting for her next move. It was so confident in her defeat that it didn't even feel the need to defend itself. "Just get it over with!" Lonnie screamed. "Stop toying with me, you know you've won!"

It still sounded like Jeremy even if its voice was more gravelly. "I want more than that, Knox. I want you to admit that I'm better than you. That you can never be as strong as me." The creature walked over and leaned in close to Lonnie, its hand caressing the side of her face. "You're just another girl, Knox, trying to play in a man's world."

"That's not true! Lonnie, listen to me! You can do this!" Galactic Purple held out the anklet so Lonnie could see it. "This is because of you! This is your power! You're doing this! Don't let anyone tell you that you're not magical!"

Lonnie looked over to see the anklet shimmering in Galactic Purple's hand. "I told you I don't want it," she whispered.

"You should take it. After all, it's the only way you stand a chance against me."

More than anything Galactic Purple wanted to cover the thing in enough frosting to make it disintegrate into nothingness, but she knew if she did that, Lonnie would doubt herself more than she already did. Lonnie had to be the one to win this fight, and there was only one way that was going to happen. "Lonnie..." No, that wasn't the name she should be using. "Radical Rainbow. You can do this."

"I'm not-"

"Yes, you are! It's sparkling like this because it's close to you! I'm not doing it, this is your power! It only has whatever power you put in it! It has nothing on its own without you! This is just a catalyst to who you really are. It wakes up what's already inside of you."

"Enough sentimental garbage," but before Jeremy's monstrous form could make good on its threat, Lonnie closed her eyes and rammed her forehead into its mouth. The pain was excruciating, and she could already feel the blood slipping down her face. The monster reeled back with a cry and Lonnie took a second to enjoy the fact that she'd done exactly what she'd wanted to do earlier: make Jeremy lose a couple of teeth. Lonnie used that time to push herself up and run toward Galactic Purple. She knew she was moving too slowly, her body protesting the entire time and begging her not to move.

A lot of things happened all at once in that moment. Lonnie could hear the monster screaming obscenities at her. She could also hear Raye begging the creature to leave her alone. All the noise melted away as Galactic Purple tossed the shimmering anklet toward her. She could see the purple haired magical girl nodding to her as if that explained everything. And, oddly enough, it did. Lonnie raised her leg in the air and kicked the anklet, the jewelry breaking apart, but instead of hitting the ground the pieces surrounded her in an assortment of rainbow colors.

"Radical Rainbow. Let's Kick It!"

There were colors all around her, and soon, they were melding into her braids. Her injuries became mere afterthoughts as light engulfed her entire body, her clothes changing before her very eyes. She was now wearing a form fitting, all white outfit with a rainbow colored hoop skirt around her waist. The outfit was complemented with a pair of white

RADICAL RAINBOW LET'S KICK IT
Radiant Grey • radiant-grey.deviantart.com

sneakers that had colors splashed around the bottom of them. Lonnie looked down at the ensemble – especially the shoes – then back up at Galactic Purple, who gave her a knowing look. Lonnie had said she'd be wearing sneakers if she were a magical girl, and apparently, she was right.

"What just happened…?" Raye asked.

Galactic Purple was more than happy to answer that question. "Lonnie's true self has emerged."

Lonnie wasn't sure about all that, but she did know one thing. As she turned and looked at what used to be the brash and hotheaded Jeremy she knew, without a shadow of a doubt, that she could beat it. In the blink of an eye she was running forward again. This time there was a power coursing through her body and she knew exactly where to aim it. "**Rainbow Rush!**"

The cocky smile was long gone and replaced with the same pitiful look that Jeremy had on his face when he thought he was about to be kicked in the face by Raye. Unlike Raye, the newly formed Radical Rainbow had no plans of stopping. The creature raised its arms up to try and defend itself from the attack. It was a series of furious punches and kicks, bursts of color dotting its arms in painful bruises. As Radical Rainbow, hitting the creature didn't hurt anymore. The rock-like texture of its skin wasn't an issue as she delivered one last devastating kick to its crossed arms. For a moment nothing happened, then tiny, rainbow colored cracks traveled up its arms. Soon, they grew larger, creating colorful webs that spread across its skin. By the time they reached its shoulders they were large enough to be able to slip your fingers inside, and soon, its arms crumbled away and fell around the creature's feet.

The now armless monster stumbled away from her with a frightened scream. There was no more snarkiness, just hatred, plain and simple. "You bitch!"

"I suppose I am. And this bitch has left you wide open."

"So what are you waiting for, huh? Huh?! Did you tire yourself out already? You can't finish me off yourself, can you?"

Radical Rainbow smiled and glanced behind her. "I don't have to," then she jumped out of the way in time for the creature to see a cupcake flying toward it.

Bree ran as fast as she could down the bland, white halls of the hospital. She'd tried to get to the gym in time, but when she'd arrived there were police officers surveying the building as they put out rolls of bright yellow caution tape. After a quick phone call, she'd learned that Marianna and Lonnie were now at the hospital with the others. Marianna had insisted that she could take her time getting there, but Bree opted to take the Cosmic Green route of hopping across buildings and running at top speed instead of trying to figure out which bus route would get her there faster.

While Bree couldn't run as fast through the hospital corridors, it was fast enough for a couple of nurses to remind her not to run. She shouted out quick apologies, but went right back to running as soon as she turned the next corner. She spotted Marianna by one of the rooms, holding a cup of some kind of warm drink. "Mari!"

Marianna smiled a little as Bree ran toward her. She knew she'd disregard the common rule of being quiet in a hospital. There was something comforting about hearing that familiar voice even if she'd been angry with her earlier. "Bree. Hospital."

"Right, sorry. I just... I'm sorry I couldn't get there in time. Is everyone okay?"

"The owners are fine. One is recovering and his wife is with him. That's whose room this is," Marianna said as she nodded to the door across from them. "Lonnie's friends are fine, too. Kendra's already awake. Braydon's still resting."

"And Lonnie?"

"She went outside to get some fresh air. She's perfectly fine... and she became Radical Rainbow."

Bree's eyes widened. "She did? So she agreed?"

"In the heat of the moment, she did. I'm not sure what she's going to do now that the dust has settled."

"Ah. Um... about Lonnie, I kind of..." Bree rubbed the back of her head in embarrassment as she gave Marianna a hesitant little smile.

"Yeah, I know. She told me. Thanks for the warning, by the way," Marianna said as she took a sip of her drink.

"I'm sorry!"

"Bree..."

Bree covered her mouth. Right. Hospital. She uncovered her mouth and repeated the words, "I'm sorry," in a much quieter tone followed by, "I just... I had to do something, and-"

"I get it. It's fine."

"Really?"

"Well *no*, but I don't have the energy to put together a proper lecture."

Bree nodded and leaned against the wall next to Marianna. "That smells like coffee in your cup."

"It is," Marianna said as she took another sip.

"You're not really a coffee drinker."

"No I'm not, but the vending machine hot chocolate is watery. I put a lot of cream and sugar in this so it's more like brown sugar water," Marianna said with a small laugh. "I just needed something warm to hold, I guess."

"We should hit up *Pandasaur Cafe* later."

"That might be fun. You gonna text Kayla to see if she'll join us? She loves that place."

Bree could feel her cheeks growing warm at the mention of Kayla's name. "Why do you have to do that?"

"Cuz it's fun."

In retaliation, Bree took the cup out of Marianna's hands to take a sip of the coffee. She instantly regretted it. "How much cream and sugar did you put in this?!"

"Enough to make you make that disgusted face."

"I know you said brown sugar water but jeez!"

"Bree. Hospital."

"Yeah yeah yeah," Bree said as she handed Marianna her cup back.

"Oh good, you're both here now."

Marianna and Bree looked up as Lonnie walked over to them. Neither of them knew what to say to her. Marianna felt like there were no words left between them. Lonnie had fought with her, and she had fought well, just as she expected her to. But it came at the cost of several people she cared about lying in the hospital, and Marianna didn't have enough ways to apologize for that. Meanwhile, Bree and Lonnie had parted ways on bad terms. Part of Bree wanted to apologize, but she wasn't quite sure what to apologize for since Lonnie did, indeed, join them, if only for a moment. The other part of her really wanted to know what Radical Rainbow looked like. She wanted to know what sort of kick ass powers she had, which really wasn't the appropriate thing to ask at that moment. Still, she needed to say something, so she took a deep breath and-

"I want to join your group."

Well that was quick.

"You do?" Marianna asked.

Lonnie nodded as she stepped closer to them, keeping her voice low in case anyone walked past and caught what she was saying. "I know I was apprehensive about it, but after that battle... I feel like I need to. I was lucky that I was able to fight that one monster by myself, but there are more powerful ones out there and-"

"Stop," Marianna said as she shook her head. "That wasn't luck before. That was all you."

Bree nodded her agreement. "You shouldn't knock yourself down because you struggled with one thing."

"I struggle with a lot of things, to be honest. It shouldn't have taken me this long to agree, but once I did, I felt what you were talking about. This power... it is mine, not anyone else's."

Marianna smiled brightly and said, "It doesn't matter how long it took you. What matters is that you understand now."

"I do. So... what happens now?"

"Introductions, I suppose."

Blaze's voice came from a door across the hall. The door should've led to a patient's room and not the oddly familiar orbital room where Blaze spent most her time. Lonnie stared at the woman in surprise while Bree nearly jumped out of her skin. "You have got to warn us when you do that!"

"Where's the fun in that? Besides, you know I'm watching you girls."

Lonnie watched Blaze carefully as she approached them, the door closing behind her. Neither of the girls had mentioned her, but Lonnie could easily tell she was who they answered to. Something about the way she carried herself spoke of a woman who demanded the utmost respect. It reminded Lonnie of Raye and her grandmother, and there was something comforting about that.

"Lonnie, this is Blaze. She used to be part of **magnifiquenoir** and is now our leader."

Blaze smiled and held her hand out toward Lonnie. "It's a pleasure meeting you, Ms. Knox."

NAME: Lonnie Knox
AGE: 20
OCCUPATION: Kickboxer
FIRST SEASON ATTACK: Rainbow Rush!

STEPPING INTO THE RING IS A FIERY YOUNG
WOMAN ARMED WITH **STRENGTH, DETERMINATION,**
& A BLAZING RAINBOW KICK THAT SENDS HER
MONSTROUS FOES DOWN FOR THE COUNT – RING
THE BELL, IT'S AN INSTANT TKO!

Radical ★
RAINBOW

"STAND AND FIGHT TO BE MAGICAL!"

RADICAL RAINBOW PROFILE
Briana Lawrence • www.magnifiquenoir.com
Musetap Studios • www.musetapstudios.com

238 - Briana Lawrence

This was it. Lonnie could tell that taking this woman's hand would solidify her decision. There'd be no turning back and she'd be dedicated to this group of incredible women. Lonnie knew she still had some flaws to work through, and in that moment they all came rushing forward to try and hold her back. She had a tendency to push herself too hard and wasn't the type to go along with a group, but with a little bit of time, she could work through it. That anklet was hers now, and it was securely fastened around her foot. It gave her a sense of balance and strength that she didn't realize she was capable of.

She wanted to keep that feeling.

So Lonnie smiled and clasped her hand around Blaze's and said, "It's nice to meet you, too."

EPISODE EIGHT:

FIT RIGHT IN

"Hello?"

"Hi grandma."

Lonnie could hear the deep sigh on the other end of the line. "Now I know this ain't my grandchild callin' me *days* after she was supposed to."

Lonnie winced as she sat down on the bench outside the hospital. "Grand-Penny..." Maybe if she used the nickname she'd come up with as a child the woman would go easy on her.

The idea backfired. "Don't you *Grand-Penny* me Lonnie Octavia Knox."

Crap. She'd used her full name. Lonnie could practically feel the neck swivel her grandmother most likely delivered when saying her name. Lonnie knew she was dead on arrival but she had to try. "What, no Lonnie-Pooh?"

"That girl is dead to me."

"Grandma!"

"You know damn well yo' black ass was supposed to call me!"

The words felt like they'd slapped Lonnie upside her head. She quickly looked around the area as people walked in and out of the hospital. She knew they were talking on the phone, but it felt like everyone could hear the grandmotherly smack down she was receiving. It was like the older woman was there in person, yelling at Lonnie in front of the entire world. "I-I know. And I'm sorry. Just... a lot happened and-"

"Unless the world has come to an end you **know** you supposed to call when I tell you to!"

"No, nothing like that... kinda..."

"Don't get smart with me young lady."

"I'm not, I swear!" Then Lonnie lowered her voice, knowing better than to raise her voice to her grandmother. "Just... s-something happened at the gym yesterday."

Penny got quiet for what felt like an eternity before she spoke again. "Is everything all right?"

"Rodney was hurt," Lonnie said. She debated mentioning Braydon and Kendra, but revealing that many injured parties would put her grandmother in a tizzy. It was bad enough that she had to tell her about Rodney. "He's gonna be fine, but I thought I should let you know."

"What do you mean he was hurt?"

Lonnie tightened her grip on her phone. She had a feeling her grandmother would latch onto the word *hurt* instead of the *fine* part. Lonnie didn't want to go into all the details. She'd already put off calling after the first monster attack, she didn't want to bring up this second one. "I don't have all the details," Lonnie said. It wasn't necessarily a lie. She technically didn't know how much she could, or should, divulge to her family now that she had magical powers. "But Raye is gonna stay at the hospital with him."

Another moment of silence, then, "You know you ain't off the hook for not callin' after that mall incident."

"Yes ma'am."

"Good. Now... how are you doing, Lonnie-Pooh?"

Lonnie felt her heart swell at the use of her grandmother-given nickname. It felt kind of childish to be near tears, but hearing the name said so lovingly after everything that had happened meant everything to her. "I'm... here, I guess. I'm gonna stay with a couple of friends."

"Oh good, you don't need to be there by yourself."

"Agreed." What Lonnie didn't say was that she was going to be staying with those friends indefinitely. She'd bring that up later once she had a handle on all the details. She also needed to tell Raye about this move. In fact, she still had to tell Raye that she'd agree to make this whole magical girl thing permanent – she'd seen the transformation, after all.

"So who are these friends? You only talk about Braydon and Kendra, and I know you can't stand Braydon."

Lonnie laughed even if she felt her heart drop. Just hearing their names brought a fresh wave of memories of that awful creature knocking them around. "Yeah no, not Braydon. Though it's nice to know that you wouldn't be concerned about me moving in with a guy."

"You ain't interested in men, did you think I forgot?"

Sometimes, Lonnie loved how blunt her grandmother was. "Well... it's not Kendra, either, in case you were concerned about me moving in with a girl."

"Nope, cuz there ain't no chance of pregnancy with a girl..."

"Grand-Penny!"

"What? I'm too young to be a *great grand* anything!"

This was why Lonnie needed this phone call. In spite of her grandma's worry, she needed the laughter that a talk with her always brought. As soon as Lonnie stopped laughing Penny asked, "So who are you moving in with? What other friends do you have?"

"Thanks Grand-Penny..."

"That ain't what I meant!" But Penny was laughing into the phone. "Like I said, you ain't never mentioned anyone else."

"I haven't had the chance to. Fighting monsters and all that jazz."

"Lonnie..."

"Sorry, sorry!" Yep, it was definitely too soon to make fun of the situation. Still, she needed to say something about who she was moving in with. "Their names are Marianna and Bree. They go to the same school as me. I met them a little bit ago and they're really nice." Emphasis on the words *little bit ago* as they'd only known each other for a couple of days.

"Two girls?"

"Yes, grandma. I'm living out every male fantasy," Lonnie muttered as if giving a bland weather report.

"Is that not a female fantasy for you?"

Lonnie was sure that any other person would cringe at having such a conversation with their grandparent. However, Penny Knox didn't have any kind of filter, and it was something Lonnie had gotten used to while growing up. "Eh, too complicated. I should at least get one girlfriend before I try having two."

"Well this could be your chance."

"Is it in every grandmother's DNA to try and hook their grandkids up with someone?"

"Yep, so get to it!"

Lonnie smiled and responded with a dutiful, "Yes grandma," followed by, "I love you."

"Love you, too, Lonnie-Pooh."

Lonnie hung up the phone and took a deep breath. The hard part was over... sort of. She closed her eyes and let the wind brush against her as she enjoyed the cool breeze. Sitting outside the hospital gave her the illusion of not being in such a suffocating environment, even if hearing the occasional ambulance reminded her of where she was. One of the nurses had suggested that she go home and rest, and truthfully, Lonnie probably could. There had been very little damage, all things considered. The broken front and back door had been temporarily fixed with that good ol' caution tape until the proper repairs could be made. The dented walls would take longer, but Lonnie could imagine Rodney slapping a poster over the cracks and calling it good. So yes, the space was livable, but going back would make Lonnie relive everything that had happened. She was already thinking about it enough – the added piece of rainbow flare around her ankle made sure of that.

Lonnie tucked her phone back into her pocket and mentally prepared herself for the next part: talking to Raye. As she got up and walked back into the hospital, the stark whiteness hit her harder than her grandmother's yelling. It felt like she was stepping into a sterile haze and it was making her throat itch. She contemplated going back outside for another taste of fresh air, but she knew she couldn't put off this talk any longer. She had decided to join the group and she needed to own up to it and tell Raye.

Or she could go check on her friends.

Braydon's room was on the way so it would be rude of her to not see how he was doing. After everything that had taken place she could admit, without a shadow of a doubt, that Braydon was the dumbest, most annoying, true friend she'd ever had. Despite their constant bickering, he always had a knack for showing up when she needed him to. Unfortunately, this particular instance had landed him in the hospital. With a gentle knocked on the door Lonnie pushed his room door open. She was happy to see him sitting up in bed, looking annoyed as he poked at the rice on his plate. "This sucks," he muttered. "I'd kill for a cheeseburger right now."

"Why didn't you order one? Isn't that on the menu?"

"Well yeah, but it's a *hospital* cheeseburger, not a real one."

Lonnie walked over and sat in the chair next to Braydon's bed. Honestly, the plate of food didn't look all that terrible. Rice, vegetables, and a grilled piece of chicken was better than the typical depictions of the hospital menu. "I thought the whole crappy hospital food thing was just a stereotype."

"I guess," Braydon said as he ate a bit of the rice on his plate. "It's not bad, just... bland."

"I thought your people were used to bland," Lonnie chuckled, then she laughed louder when she saw the irritated look on Braydon's face.

"Really, Lonnie? I expected better from you."

"No you didn't!"

"All right fine, I didn't, but be nice to me! I'm injured!"

"You ain't that injured if you can whine about the food," Lonnie pointed out. "And here I was thinking about smuggling a *real* cheeseburger for you."

"If you do that I'll stop making fun of you."

"Oh? For how long?" Lonnie stood up. "Because if that's the case I'll go and-"

"Naw, too late, changed my mind," then Braydon ate another forkful of rice with a dumb grin on his face.

Lonnie rolled her eyes and sat back down. "Well I guess you're back to normal then, huh?"

"Kinda..." Braydon said, fidgeting a bit as he ate. The hospital gown was hiding the fact that his ribs were wrapped in bandages similar to the ones around both of his arms.

"Braydon-"

He cut Lonnie off before she could voice her concern, surprising her with the words, "I'm sorry."

"Huh?"

"About always giving you a hard time."

For a moment all Lonnie could do was stare at Braydon. After all the chaos, this was the part he wanted to focus on? "W-where is this coming from?"

"Yesterday... at least I think it was yesterday? Jeremy went all monster on us yesterday, right?" When Lonnie nodded, Braydon continued.

"Which... was freaky, really freaky, I mean... what the hell, right?!" Braydon sounded mildly terrified as he recounted Jeremy's monstrous transformation. He even waved his hands around to try and illustrate his point. "Anyway, I'm rambling, because I just... I didn't think that crap I said bothered you so much. I'm sorry."

All Lonnie could think to respond with was, "All right, who are you, and where's the real Braydon?"

"Damnit, I'm being serious!" Then Braydon winced. Even yelling too loudly hurt. "I just... I say stupid shit, a lot, but if it's actually bugging you I should stop."

Lonnie thought about that for a moment. A life without Braydon's unoriginal comments? For some reason, that didn't feel as appealing as it should've. Though it may have been amusing to see him try. He'd probably last five seconds. Ten tops. Hell, he hadn't even lasted long enough to get that cheeseburger. "Don't worry about it," she said. "It was a combination of a lot of things. Besides, I think I've always known that you don't mean it. You're like an annoying, unfunny, simple-minded, hopeless-"

"Is there a point to this, or..."

"Brother. You're like my brother. Except, you know, white. And stupid."

"Thanks sis," Braydon muttered.

"No problem," then Lonnie gave him a huge, overly sweet smile.

"Now when you say *brother* do you mean that in a familial term or like, you know, *brotha*?"

The look on Lonnie's face was the look of someone who had lost faith in humanity – particularly the twenty-something white male demographic. "Please don't ever say that again..."

Behind them, there was a soft knock on the door before Braydon's nurse looked inside the room. "Ah, I see you have a guest. Are you up for having another one?"

246 – B RIANA LAWRENCE

"Sure, long as it's not my mother again," who had cried enough to put Kleenex out of business, or at the very least, enough to make the mascara run down her cheeks.

"It's not, I promise," then the nurse held the door open as Kendra slowly wheeled herself into the room, her leg in a cast as her foot recovered from her attempted attack on Jeremy.

"Kendra! Um, h-hi! You look... um..." Suddenly Braydon had forgotten how to string words together.

"It's fine," she said as the nurse left the room. "It's not as bad as it looks."

"You're not just saying that, are you?" Lonnie asked.

Kendra shook her head. "In hindsight, kicking a rock monster probably wasn't the smartest idea, though it could've been a lot worse," then Kendra glanced over at Braydon who responded with a small blush as he awkwardly went back to eating his vegetables. "Though I'm a bit jealous, Lonnie, you look great... all things considered."

"Yeah... guess I was lucky..."

"What happened to Jeremy, anyway? Was he stopped?" Kendra asked.

Lonnie nodded. "**magnifiquenoir** showed up and beat him."

Kendra frowned a little and asked, "Does that mean he's... dead?"

"I... yeah, I guess it does," Lonnie said. She hadn't even thought of it like that. She'd been so focused on eliminating the threat that she hadn't even considered the aftermath. From what she'd heard, many of the monsters who'd appeared in their city had started out as people. Did that mean they were leaving loved ones behind, or were they just wandering monsters hiding amongst humanity? Lonnie was leaning more toward the latter for her own peace of mind. Jeremy had never spoke of any family, and it was much easier to believe it was because he was some diabolical villain's creation.

"That... sucks?" Braydon wasn't sure if he was that heartbroken about it. It wasn't like there was any other choice once Jeremy had snapped like that. Chances were, he was going to kill them if he hadn't been stopped.

"Does he even have anyone for us to contact? We should contact someone, right?"

"I'll look into it," and Lonnie would. Later. After all, Blaze had to know what these monsters were, right? She and the others probably had a whole process in place or something. "For now we should focus on recovering."

"All right," then Kendra got quieter as she hesitantly asked, "Um... Lonnie? Did you need a place to stay until they go back to the gym?" She knew Lonnie lived with the couple, and she could only imagine what she was going through right now. Not only had Rodney been hurt, but their home had been invaded.

Lonnie smiled and shook her head. "Naw, I got it covered, but thanks."

"What other friends do you have?" Braydon asked.

"First my grandmother, and now you? Seriously, I have other friends!"

"All right all right, I'm sorry. Jeez. Yell at the injured guy, why don'tcha."

Lonnie stood up and smiled sweetly at Braydon. "Fine, I'll leave the injured guy alone," then she headed for the door.

"W-wait. Where are you going?"

"To check on Rodney and Raye. Why? Something wrong?"

Braydon's eyes narrowed as he looked at the girl in front of him. She knew exactly what she was doing. If she left, that meant he was going to be alone with Kendra, and he was in no condition to deal with his crush. He needed to be at his best, but he couldn't even muster up the strength to get out of bed. "I hate you," he quietly mouthed to Lonnie as she giggled and left the room. As soon as she was gone Braydon gave Kendra a shaky smile. "H-hey there..."

"Hey. Did you need anything?"

"Huh? Oh, no, just... enjoying this thing they call food..."

Now that Lonnie was gone Kendra decided to wheel over to Braydon and take up the space where the other girl had been. She looked at the food on Braydon's tray and made a face. "Looks bland."

"I know, right?!" Leave it to bad food to calm Braydon's nerves. "Maybe I'll call my parents and beg them to bring me a steak or something." He'd deal with his mother's tears if it came with the promise of tasty food.

"Or maybe we can order pizza. Can you have pizza delivered to a hospital?"

"I don't think so, but maybe if my mom cries enough they'll give in."

The two fell into a comfortable silence after that, with Kendra sitting by the side of Braydon's bed as he finally decided to try the chicken. It was actually better than he expected and kinda made all of his whining pointless... *kinda*.

"Hey Braydon... about what happened back there..."

"Hm?" Braydon gave Kendra a questioning look.

"Before you passed out, you said-"

"Ah! I... I-I said something?"

"Don't play dumb, Braydon."

"Yes ma'am..." because there was no point in lying, especially to Kendra, so Braydon went about eating his surprisingly delicious chicken.

"You weren't fighting that thing in an attempt to play hero, were you?"

"Hell no," then, "Well... maybe a little. Not that it mattered..."

"Why? Cuz it beat the crap out of you?"

"No... cuz you don't need a hero. Lonnie doesn't either."

"True... but I don't mind having a partner."

Braydon didn't want to read too much into that, but it was hard not to when Kendra reached over and rested her hand on top of his. It wasn't a kiss like in the movies. It was something much more comfortable, much more relaxing. It was the feel of her hand and the smile on her face, and to Braydon, that was more than enough.

And Lonnie thought coming out had been difficult.

Though, to be fair, she hadn't done that on her own terms. Having such a large family meant that it was damn near impossible to keep any secrets. One of her cousins had told another cousin who told the third one, who then proceeded to spread the word to the fourth one and the fourth one's much chattier sister, who then blurted it out to their mother who was **the** serial gossiper of the family. There was no better stage for a good story than one of Penny Knox's patented Sunday dinners. By then, the story had morphed into an otherworldly being where Lonnie had gone from holding a girl's hand on the way to school to having a full-blown make-out session in the locker room of her eighth-grade gym class. A mortified Lonnie had no choice but to tell the true story and reveal her feelings for the cute girl in her class. She should've ratted out her pimple-faced cousin who she'd seen kissing a boy – tongue and all – but Lonnie had been too busy worrying about her Grand-Penny's reaction to her liking girls *that way*. She'd expected some tears and some, *"Where did I go wrong in raising you."* To her surprise, her grandmother told her aunt and loudmouth cousin off for sticking their noses in other people's business. *"You know you way too old to be gossipin' about a little girl,"* she'd said to her aunt, followed by a swift, *"And I know damn well yo' fast ass be out there with them little boys,"* directed at her cousin.

Still, that whole event wasn't nearly as difficult as what she was about to do. Monsters. Fighting said monsters. Transforming into a magical rainbow warrior. Agreeing to become part of **magnifiquenoir**. Being forced out of the closet had been tough, but telling her guardian that she was going to join a group of women who put their lives on the line on a regular basis? Part of Lonnie wished that her pimple-faced cousin and nosy aunt were there to family-splain the situation for her.

Lonnie took a deep breath and stepped into the hospital room. Raye was sitting by Rodney's side, her hands wrapped up from her attempts at hitting Jeremy. Rodney was actually sitting up in bed, but looked like he was going to fall back asleep at any minute. There was a nasty bruise on his cheek and around one of his eyes, his hospital gown covering the bandages that had to be wrapped around his waist. Despite all that, he smiled when he saw Lonnie, and she couldn't help but smile back at him. "You're up," she said, not able to keep the relief out of her voice.

"Yeah... not sure if I wanna be, though. Everything hurts."

"Oh hush, you've been hit harder before and you know it."

Lonnie smiled even more when she heard that. Raye picking on her husband definitely meant that he was on the road to recovery.

"Love you too, dear," then Rodney turned his attention to Lonnie. "And it looks like you're okay, too?"

Lonnie nodded. "So are Braydon and Kendra. I just saw both of them."

"That's a relief. It's a good thing those girls showed up when they did."

Lonnie glanced over at Raye, trying to read the look on her face. Had she... not told him everything? Was she planning to?

"Yes, we're very lucky," Raye said, not meeting Lonnie's look. "Unfortunately... Jeremy wasn't, but I suppose there was no other choice at that point."

"I was gonna see if he had any family to reach out to..."

"That would be nice. Thank you, Lonnie," then Raye stood up, stretched, and said, "I'm gonna grab a cup of coffee. Lonnie, walk with me?"

Uh oh.

"Of course," Lonnie said, but she didn't really mean it. Rodney could tell, and tried his best to give her a comforting smile.

As the two women walked down the hallway, Lonnie tried to get a feel for what Raye was thinking. She'd been living with the two since she was eighteen years old, new to the college scene and away from her grandmother for the first time. Now, at age twenty, she thought she'd be better at reading Raye, but the woman could still hide her feelings when she wanted to. At times, Lonnie could tell when she was angry or upset, but there really was no expression on her trainer's face. In a way, that was much worse than any amount of yelling.

Finally, as Raye got herself a cup of coffee, she said, "The number he had listed for emergency contacts doesn't work."

Lonnie frowned when she heard that. Since there was always a chance of someone being injured at the gym, both Rodney and Raye had required them to fill out forms with emergency contact information – even Lonnie, who they knew personally. "So he lied to us?"

"At least about that part. I didn't think to check because he's an adult. *Was* an adult," Raye said as she took a sip of her coffee. No cream. No sugar. It was bitter but it gave her brain the jolt it needed. "Lesson learned, I guess."

"Not everyone who approaches us is gonna be like Jeremy."

"Still feels pretty shitty. Even if he didn't have anyone, he was still a person... right? Or... was he something else?"

That was the question, wasn't it? What exactly was Jeremy? What were any of these creatures? Had that woman in the mall left behind friends? Family? Or were these rageful creatures set on destroying everything? "I did mean what I said. I am going to look into it."

"Just look into it? Or do more than that?"

This was the part Lonnie was worried about. Raye had been so concerned about her fighting these things, and now Lonnie was going to go dive in head first.

"More," Lonnie whispered.

In that moment Lonnie wished she was old enough to drink, because a stiff glass of *something* would be amazing after this entire ordeal. She envied Kayla for being a year older than her, then again, many college students were partaking in underage drinking, right? But that would probably involve going to one of those keg-filled party spaces or trying to sneak something in a bottle past Raye. Neither of those sounded appealing.

"I had a feeling you'd say that," Raye said as she took another sip of coffee.

"But I won't be fighting alone. Not this time. I'm going to be helping those girls."

"Oh? You mean the thing you should've been doing?"

Wait. Was Raye... smirking at her? That's when Lonnie realized that she didn't need to worry about Raye trying to talk her out of anything, she needed to worry about an, "I told you so," lecture.

"I know what you're gonna say..."

"That I told you to let that girl help you when the fight started?"

"You tried to fight alone, too," Lonnie pointed out.

"Yes, well, you're supposed to do as I say, not as I do."

Ah, yes, that lovely line of black parental logic. "That still doesn't make sense no matter how many times you say it."

"All right, fine, how about this. I know what I did was foolish and it's why my husband is sitting in a hospital bed."

Lonnie felt the words ball up into a fist and slam into her stomach. "You don't have to do that," she whispered. "You don't have to blame-"

"Myself? No, I do, and I don't want you to ever have to do the same thing. Learn from my example. That includes my bad example as well."

And there it was. The truth. "That's why you wanted her to help me."

"You also needed help, but I know you, it's hard for you to accept help. We're the same. I paid for going in alone, and I don't want the same to happen to you."

Lonnie nodded. "**magnifiquenoir** works as a team. I can learn. I want to learn."

Raye smiled. "I have nothing left to teach you, my student."

"Isn't that a bit overdramatic?"

"It's also unrealistic, especially with you."

"Thanks," Lonnie muttered. "Everybody got jokes today."

"Oh?"

"Well... I guess that's the other part to discuss. I'm going to be moving in with them."

"You will?"

Lonnie nodded. "It's something their leader suggested, so that we can get to know each other and bond as a team."

"I wasn't aware they had a leader."

"Neither was I until she showed up at the hospital."

"I see." The tone in Raye's voice had become much more serious. "You do realize that I will be speaking with this woman, right?"

Lonnie nodded. She knew that was coming and she couldn't imagine the group being surprised by it, either. "They actually said I could tell you, then again, you did see it all happen firsthand."

"True." Raye took another long sip of her coffee. Now that the hard part was over she was wishing she had actually added some flavor to it. "How are you gonna tell your grandmother?"

"I... haven't planned that far ahead..."

"Fair enough. I won't say anything, I'll leave that up to you... for now."

"For now?"

"I'm not gonna have another mall incident on my hands, Lonnie. You need to tell her in a *timely* manner. Speaking of which..."

"Yes, I have called her. I told her about what happened at the gym... sort of."

"I assume no talk of monsters and transformations?" When Lonnie nodded her head Raye smiled a little. "That's understandable, just don't keep her in the dark forever, ok?"

Lonnie returned the smile. "I won't, I promise," then she added, "You know, I have to say, you're taking this much better than I thought you would."

"I've had some time to think about it. I'd be more concerned if you were trying to do this on your own."

"I told them no originally. I said I wanted to use my own strength. But I realized that I'm still doing that. This is my power, and I can do some good with it." Lonnie turned to face Raye and lifted her leg to show that she was wearing the anklet.

Raye smiled and said, "This is how I can take it so well, because you finally understand. It's important to stand and fight, but you don't have to do it alone."

"Stand and fight, huh? What exactly am I standing and fighting for?"

"For everything. For other people, for yourself, to be yourself-"

"To be magical?"

Raye shrugged her shoulders and said, "Sure, why not? Anything worth having is gonna require a fight or two."

Lonnie nodded in agreement. Even with these new abilities, it was clear that she still had a lot to learn, particularly from Raye. There was something comforting about that. Things were moving so fast and changing in the blink of an eye, it was nice to know that there was still a familiar voice to keep her grounded. "Thank you, Raye."

Raye smiled. "You're welcome, Radical Rainbow."

Lonnie wondered if it was a bad sign that her music collection took longer to pack than anything else. In an age of iDevices and streaming music, Lonnie still liked having a music selection she could look at and hold in her hands. She supposed her walls were a testament to that since they were decorated with old records and music notes she'd found at the local craft store.

"How many boxes of CDs do you have?" Rodney asked from where he was sitting at Lonnie's desk. What should've taken a week had been reduced to three days since Rodney had invented the word *stubborn*. Fortunately, Raye was standing right by his side, making sure he didn't try to do any heavy lifting. He'd resorted to picking up the CDs on her desk and handing them to Raye who would then go about packing them.

"Never enough," Lonnie said, the response locked and loaded every time they had this conversation.

"Your father loved him some music," Rodney said as he picked up one of the CDs to look it over. "He'd definitely be amused to see all of these."

"Knock it off, Rodney," Raye said as she took the CD out of his hands. "You act like the girl is leaving the country."

"What? I'm gonna miss having her around is all."

Raye shook her head at her giant sap of a husband and handed Lonnie the CD. "She's still gonna come by for practice."

"She better."

Lonnie smiled as she watched the two of them. Rodney had a tendency to bring up her father when he got emotional around her. "Dad's collection was still superior, for sure," though he'd probably be upset at Penny for keeping it boxed up in her attic. Still, it was better than throwing it away. "It drove mom nuts."

Raye smiled and whispered to Lonnie, "Your mother would definitely be proud of you right now."

Lonnie smiled more when she heard that. She had very few memories of her parents, but the one that stood out the most was spending Sunday mornings listening to music. The sounds would seemingly come out of nowhere, interrupting her mother's cooking to mix smooth lyrics with bacon and eggs. Her father would always comment on the artist and the deeper meaning of the lyrics. Meanwhile, her mother would try her best to ignore him as she flipped pancakes. Lonnie – who was missing her two front teeth – would go about setting the table, moving her tiny hips to the beat. Eventually, her father would take her mother by the hand and dance with her through the kitchen – after she made sure the stove was off. The woman would say she was too busy, but the smile on her face and loving look in her eyes gave away her true feelings. And then Lonnie would join them, jumping up and down in her attempt to dance to the music, the beads in her braids clanking against each other.

How Lonnie ended up kickboxing was beyond her, but she had a feeling it was because she wanted to savor the music instead of work with it. Plus, she couldn't deny how epic a good, upbeat song sounded when it was in sync with her fists and feet against a punching bag.

"Now who's worried about who being gone forever?" Rodney asked.

"Oh hush," Raye said as she stuck her tongue out at Rodney. "I was just telling her to enjoy herself."

"Uh huh."

"Shouldn't you be in bed?"

Rodney groaned. "I feel fine."

"Rodney..."

"There's no point arguing with her," Lonnie said in a singsong voice. Raye always came out on top whenever Rodney attempted to make a point.

"I wanted to meet your new friends."

"You can meet them another time," but Lonnie wasn't sure how true that was. Marianna and Bree would surely be around, but Blaze was another story. Raye still hadn't told Rodney the truth, not wanting to add a layer of stress during his recovery. Lonnie was sure she'd tell him, eventually, but one thing was certain: she wasn't gonna tell him today. So Raye walked over and took Rodney's hand, helping him stand up and walk out of the room.

Unfortunately, Rodney wasn't born yesterday and could read both of them better than anyone else. "What are you hiding from me?"

"I'm not hiding anything," Raye said as she stepped into their bedroom with him.

Rodney sat down at the edge of the bed and took a breath. He was more tired than he wanted to admit and definitely had no business moving, but he would never say it out loud. "Fine. What is *Lonnie* hiding?"

"Smart man," Raye said softly.

"Come on, we know you married me for my brain, my astonishing good looks were the bonus prize."

Raye laughed as she sat down next to him. "It's... not my place to say."

"I already know she's gay..."

"*Lesbian*, dear."

"Well I already know about that, so what other secrets could she possibly have? Did she get a girlfriend? Is she dating Kendra?"

Raye laughed louder than she meant to. Somehow he'd manage to figure out that Lonnie was hiding something, yet was so dense that he hadn't figured out Kendra and Braydon. "I love you," she said between her uncontrollable giggle fit.

"Don't mock me, I'm injured."

"Which is why you should be resting. I'll take care of Lonnie, I promise."

Rodney sighed and said, "If anything happens..."

"I'll let you know," then Raye leaned in and kissed his lips.

Rodney hated how much he melted over the feel of Raye's lips. There was still plenty that they needed to discuss – and she *knew* that. But she was kissing him, and he was starting to relax, and suddenly, the idea of resting in bed didn't seem all that bad. So he did just that, and before he knew it, he was falling asleep. "Tell Lonnie I love her," he murmured. "And to be safe out there," then he drifted off.

"I will," Raye said, then she stood up and left the room.

Instead of heading back to Lonnie's room, Raye went downstairs to look over the gym. The doors had, at least, been fixed, but the walls had definitely seen better days. Still, the police tape had been removed and the gym no longer looked like a crime scene where Jeremy had gone ballistic.

Raye frowned. She supposed she should've referred to him as a monster instead of a person.

It was the worst place she could be in that moment: alone with her thoughts. At the hospital she'd agreed to let Lonnie do this, but now that the dust had settled she wasn't so sure. After helping her bring home boxes and watching her start to pack up her room everything became a bit too real. She knew that Lonnie was capable, but did that mean she was ready? Like the rest of the city, Raye had heard whispers about the one girl who'd been defending them. Later, she heard about the second girl who'd come along and how the two had called themselves **magnifiquenoir**. That name had brought up a few memories that had been tucked away in the back of her mind. Once upon a time, she'd heard of a group by that name who definitely had more than two girls at the helm, but those stories had mostly faded. Now, it looked like the group was trying to re-establish itself, which was all well and good...

...until Lonnie got involved.

A knock on the door pulled Raye out of her thoughts and a second confirmed that they were ignoring the "closed" sign on the door. She had a feeling she knew who it was. It was time to meet Lonnie's new friends and teammates along with their leader, the very woman that Raye had been wanting to talk to. Now wasn't the time to sit and worry about Lonnie, now was the time to find out what she was really getting herself into. When she opened the door she greeted everyone with a smile, mentally patting herself on the back for looking so calm.

The two girls did their best to return the gesture, but there was a hint of guilt brimming at the edge of their eyes. Raye had seen Marianna at the hospital but hadn't had a chance to speak to her, too busy getting Rodney taken care of and calling Braydon and Kendra's parents. Now that she was standing in front of her, Raye was certain that she was the one at the gym that day. By process of elimination, the second young lady standing next to her was the green one in the magical group.

They looked so young.

Granted, they had to be around Lonnie's age as she'd said that they went to the same school, but it was hard to believe that these girls were the ones carrying on the task of protecting the city. It was an odd situation to be in. As a woman who was a firm believer in women being able to accomplish anything, part of Raye felt like a hypocrite for wanting Lonnie to stay tucked away in her room. But this wasn't like some kind of difficult match in the ring, this was something that could get Lonnie killed. Raye remembered how vicious Jeremy's monstrous self had been, she could only imagine what else was wandering around out there.

"Perhaps we should talk."

Raye looked up at the woman standing with Marianna and Bree. She'd been so preoccupied with the two young girls that she hadn't even noticed the grown woman standing with them. This had to be the leader Lonnie had mentioned. Tall with brightly colored orange hair that complimented her dark skin, there was something about her that commanded respect. "Yes, we should," then Raye smiled at Marianna and Bree and said, "You two can go upstairs and help Lonnie pack. It's the first door on the left."

Marianna looked uncertain, but Blaze smiled and gave her a reassuring nod. She had a feeling that Raye would want to talk to her alone, out of earshot of Lonnie so she could say what she really wanted to say.

Once the girls went upstairs Raye walked over and took a seat on one of the benches by the ring. Blaze raised an eyebrow and crossed her arms at her chest. "Didn't realize you wanted to talk here. I thought you meant a kitchen or something."

"Don't know you well enough to start makin' cups of tea."

"Fair enough. So... where did you want to start?"

"It sounds like you have experience with this."

"It's better if you know what's going on. It's pretty awful to find out the hard way that someone you care about risks their life so often."

"So you already know how I feel."

Blaze nodded. "More or less. Doesn't mean they aren't valid feelings to have. I'm surprised because Lonnie said you already agreed, in fact, she mentioned something about a lecture?"

Raye laughed. "Ah yes, my patented, 'Stop trying to do things on your own,' lecture."

"That sounds like a somewhat familiar one. Marianna used to do this alone."

"Oh, I've heard several stories," then the lighthearted smile shifted to a more serious look. "I also know that there was a group before. I know there were monsters before, too. Never did figure out what happened to those girls, where those creatures came from, what they are..."

Blaze suddenly looked a bit uncomfortable with the conversation. Raye decided to let her guard down just enough to nod to the space next to her, inviting Blaze to sit with her. Blaze took her up on the offer and sat down, resting her hands in her lap. "You growing up here makes this a little bit easier," she said. "That means you were around when this all started."

"Well... yes and no. I went away to college, met Rodney, stuff like that. I'd call home and hear all these fantastical stories but I didn't think too much of it. It's kind of hard to believe, you know?"

"I can agree to that," Blaze said with a laugh. "I can't say I'd believe any of it unless if I was directly involved," then she closed her eyes and began her story. "Those creatures are an anomaly that showed up back when I was in college. I suppose these abilities are also an anomaly. Even so, I knew those things needed to be stopped. So my friends and I came together and created **magnifiquenoir**."

Raye nodded. "Where did you get Lonnie's anklet? I'm assuming all the girls have something."

"They do," Blaze said. There was an almost cute looking smile on her face as she spoke about the tools the girls used. "I made them. I used to do a bit of crafting and sewing, you know, anything to not be the business woman my parents wanted me to be. They're all small objects that any girl might have, but there's just a little bit of magic mixed in."

Raye couldn't help but chuckle. She wondered what other quote, unquote *girl* products had a magical backstory to them. Though, there was something else that Blaze said that had gotten her attention. She'd actually mentioned her parents, more specifically, their approval. "Ah, good ol' parental approval," she said with an irritated sigh. The lack of it in her life was something she could definitely relate to.

"It's not always worth trying for."

There was more to that. Raye could tell by Blaze's soft tone of voice, but grilling the woman about her personal issues was not the way to go.

Even so, it was nice to see a woman like Blaze act so... human. "So you made the tools they use to transform? Should I be asking where *your* power comes from?" Raye asked, getting back on topic.

"I'd say those tools help bring out what's already there and act as a focal point for their abilities. I'm not trying to sound cheesy, but... black girls are magical."

"I agree, but I don't think most black girls can throw cupcakes that explode."

Blaze laughed and said, "All right, so maaaaaybe those tools *enhance* their capabilities."

Raye raised an eyebrow at that and smirked. "Lonnie's not gonna be kicking rainbows onto her sparring partners now, is she?"

"Depends on if she transforms for her matches."

"Well... it was nice knowing Braydon, I guess," Raye said with an amused smirked. She imagined that the thought of sprinkling a barrage of rainbow attacks over Braydon would cross Lonnie's mind at some point. "Though I gotta say, I'm surprised you came to talk to me. I thought the whole secret identity thing was a big deal."

"To be fair, you saw her transform," Blaze pointed out.

"True..."

"But even if you didn't, I'd encourage her to tell you. I feel that it's important for them to tell their loved ones – when they're ready, of course."

"Even if our feelings fluctuate over whether or not we're okay with this? How do you know I won't change my mind after this conversation?"

"That's why I said I was surprised that you'd already agreed."

"Looking back, I'm surprised, too. I think it was the relief about us being safe, or maybe it was because Lonnie was so determined? Take your pick, really," Raye said, looking up at the ceiling as if it had the answers.

"Got it," then, "I'm sorry that attack happened the way it did. It must've been hard since you knew him."

"We'll repair the damage and move on," but it was clear that Raye meant more than the damage to the gym. "So the monsters... are human?"

"It's... I'm still trying to figure it all out." Blaze sounded frustrated to admit that part. "Back then, it was clearly monsters attacking, and it still is... they just wear human skin, I guess."

Raye scoffed. "You've had all this time to figure it out and you still don't know?"

All Blaze could do was nod at Raye's obvious disbelief. "It's been quiet for years so I stopped looking into it."

"So they just... stopped? Then came back, what, months ago?" Raye shook her head. "I don't buy it."

"Which part?"

"*Your* part. I don't believe that after all this time you know so little about these creatures."

Blaze frowned as she gripped onto the fabric of her skirt. "I never said these creatures made sense, I just said that I knew they needed to be stopped. I thought they *had* been stopped but then they returned."

"So the original group beat them then, what, those monsters waited decades to retaliate?"

"It's not like I believed it right away, but... you get used to the quiet. Guess I got *too* used to it."

"Huh." Raye tried to organize the thoughts in her head. Blaze certainly had an answer for everything, and nothing about the answers felt disingenuous. However, there still seemed to be some missing pieces that had yet to be uncovered. "Must suck to be back at it," Raye said.

Blaze shrugged. "I dunno... kinda missed the rush. You look like the kind of woman who gets that."

"To be honest, I spent a lot of time helping my husband. He was the one in the spotlight. I didn't think I could be. But I suppose I've been training Lonnie to stand proudly in that spotlight, so yeah, I do get what you're saying." Suddenly, Raye's eyes took on a dangerous edge. "But if anything happens to her while she's in that spotlight, you'll have to deal with me. And trust me, you don't want to."

And there it was, the moment Blaze knew had been coming. Raye could've continued to ask her questions. Honestly, she probably wanted to, but Lonnie's safety was more important. This was the kind of woman Blaze liked, and the kind of woman she could respect. So Blaze nodded and said, "Understood," then added, "Have I earned a cup of tea now?"

"Not quite, but I can at least get you a glass of water."

"Can I request something with a bit of flavor? Have I earned that much?"

Raye stood up, smiled, and said, "I'll add a lemon, how about that?"

"Perfect," Blaze said with a laugh.

That had gone better than she expected.

"What do you think they're talking about?"

"Us," Bree said in response to Marianna's question.

"No, I mean... I thought we'd be part of the conversation."

"That's cute," Lonnie said as she put another stack of CDs into a box. "You thought your 'mom' and my 'mom' were gonna talk in front of 'the kids'?"

Marianna sighed. "I guess that was a bit naive..."

"You did say she was okay with the whole thing," Bree said as she sat down on the edge of Lonnie's bed. Bree had thought the dorm rooms were small, but this felt like a closet. Her dorm room had at least been able to fit appliances – albeit *very small* appliances with just enough room for a shared closer. Lonnie's room had a bed, a desk, and a dresser – not even a closet. The dresser served the dual purpose of a shelf for a stereo system. The stereo, in turn, was a shelf for a small, flat screen TV, creating a makeshift entertainment center for what Bree assumed was a Hobbit. It was impressive that Lonnie had managed to fit so much stuff into such a small space, especially all those CDs. She was going to flip out when she saw how big her new living space was.

"Yeah... didn't say I believed it," Lonnie muttered, closing another box of CDs.

"Well it did take you a while to come around, guess we shouldn't be surprised."

Marianna frowned over at Bree. The girl couldn't help herself sometimes, but she supposed she raised a good point. Lonnie did decide to join in the heat of the moment, and she'd sounded pretty determined in the hospital, but now that things had settled... did she still feel the same way?

Lonnie took it all in stride and said, "But I *did* come around, so now, we're a team, right?"

"In theory," Bree said dismissively.

"So you two instantly clicked and agreed on everything?" When neither girl responded Lonnie stood up and grabbed the box she'd just packed up. "That's what I thought. At least give me a chance to screw up before you assume I'm gonna screw up."

Bree opened her mouth to respond but Marianna shot her a harsh look. "That isn't what she meant," Marianna said, always the peacekeeper. "We just wanna be sure you want to do this."

"I wouldn't be packing up my entire life if I didn't," Lonnie said. She was trying to keep the bite out of her voice but it was proving to be difficult. "What else do I have to do to prove myself to you two? I thought you wanted me to join."

"We did. We *do*. But people you care about were hurt, Lonnie. And–"

"And it's not gonna happen again. I'm gonna make sure of it."

"That! That's what I was waiting for!" Bree jumped out of the bed and clapped her hands in excitement.

"What?"

"That determination! That energy!" Bree pumped her fist in the air, cheering for Lonnie now. This was the girl who took on a monster without any magical backup. "That badass *I'm gonna kick a monster's teeth in* response!"

Lonnie set down her box as she watched Bree. For a moment she wondered if her energy came from that bow in her hair or if it was all natural. "Didn't I already do that?"

"Well I mean I suppose there's the mall–"

"No, I mean kick a monster's teeth in," then Lonnie smirked and rubbed her forehead. "Though technically I head-butted the thing."

"Damn, knew I missed a good fight. Nice!"

It was clear to Lonnie that Bree was the wide-eyed, *this is just like the movies* girl. Meanwhile, Marianna was the more level-headed one. One look over at Marianna told Lonnie that her thoughts were accurate. She looked fondly exhausted over her friend. "So I have a few more things on my dresser then we should be good to go," Lonnie said.

Bree nodded then walked over to grab the last stack of CDs. Her eyes widened and she let out a piercing shriek of, "OH MY GOD!"

Lonnie was about to pick her box back up but stopped when she heard Bree's yell. "What?"

"It's *Ninja Sex Party*..."

"Oh god..." Marianna groaned. She already had enough on her mind, she didn't need to add in Bree's fangirling.

Unfortunately, Lonnie had no idea what she was walking into. "Oh yeah, those guys. They're pretty good."

"Pretty good. PRETTY GOOD?! They're AMAZING! Do you have *Starbomb*, too?"

"Huh? Oh, their video game parody band or whatever? Yeah they're in there somewhere," Lonnie said with a shrug. She only knew the bare minimum facts of *Game Grumps* lore. They were Let's Players who also did music, or something like that. In all honesty she'd gotten the CD as a gift from a girl she'd been dating a few months ago. The girl frequently wore NSP shirts and quoted their lyrics in conversation. Finally, the girl got her a copy so Lonnie would understand what she was talking about.

Bree cradled the CD like a precious child and leaned in, looking up at Lonnie with huge, watering eyes. "I didn't know you were a geek," she whispered.

"Well, I wouldn't-"

"WE'RE GETTING ANOTHER GEEK IN THE HOUSE!!!"

Lonnie watched in utter fascination as Bree bounced up and down in delight. While Lonnie did have a major soft spot for cute, bouncy girls, she was too shocked at seeing the girl go from *are you sure you wanna join our club* to *we're best friends now*, all because of a music comedy band.

Marianna stood up and walked over to Lonnie, whispering to her, "She does that. You get used to it."

"Do you?" Lonnie sounded doubtful about that.

"It's endearing, just... spontaneous."

"Got it," Lonnie said as she watched Bree lovingly hug the CD against her chest. "Well it was pretty easy to win her over. Now I gotta work on you."

"Me?" Marianna asked.

"Yep. Just have to figure out what makes you, well... do that." Lonnie nodded over to Bree who was now singing the lyrics to one of the songs on the CD. "Gotta try and fit in, you know?" Then Lonnie grabbed the box and stepped out of the room.

Marianna wasn't quite sure what to think about the whole thing anymore. Before, she'd been so confident about Lonnie, but now? Marianna was having doubts. In the end, Lonnie had come through for them, and her words certainly sounded genuine... but was it enough? Not that she needed Lonnie to be so dedicated that she'd jump off a building the way Bree had done, but she needed a bit more reassurance that she'd be there for them. Fighting to protect her loved ones was one thing, and fighting to protect innocent people was another, but would she fight for the two of them?

"Still on the fence?" Bree asked.

"I know you are, too."

Bree nodded as she set the CD down. "It feels... hypocritical, in a way. We were the ones pushing for her to join, and now..."

"Now we're doubting our choice."

"Well yes... and no. She'll be a great Radical Rainbow, but will she be great for the team?"

"Careful," Marianna said in a warning tone of voice, "You're starting to sound like Blaze."

"How did she trust me so easily?"

"I think she had a plan for the two of us all along. I tried to have one with Lonnie, but we see how well it went. People ended up in the hospital and now we're not sure if Lonnie will... fit in."

Bree smiled a little and poked Marianna's cheek. "Or, we can look at it like this. People are still alive and Radical Rainbow is awesome."

"Yes, but is Lonnie?"

Bree was quiet for a long moment, long enough for Lonnie to come in, grab another box, and leave the room. Finally Bree spoke up and said, "Well... there's only one way to find out?"

"And that is?"

Blaze parked the van and leaned back into the driver's seat. What she had planned to do was go back home, get the car unpacked, and relax after a long day. But for some reason she was now in a supermarket parking lot, further extending her time away from the familiarity of her orbital room. Not that she couldn't keep up with the girls, but some days were a clear reminder of the endless energy that this younger generation had. "So tell me again why you couldn't bake a cake with what you have at home?" Because she knew Marianna kept their kitchen well-stocked.

"Because I'm letting Lonnie pick what kind she wants me to make," Marianna said. She felt like she was channeling Bree, eagerly waiting to go inside and grab all sorts of ingredients.

"That's very sweet of you, but you don't have to go through this much trouble for me."

"It's no trouble at all!" Marianna said as she got out the car, Bree getting out with her. Bree had come to the conclusion that the best ice breaker was a decadent one, and Marianna wasn't going to say no to baking.

Lonnie sighed and looked over at Blaze. The older woman had her eyes closed as she attempted to unwind in the confines of her seat belt. They had all spent most of the day packing and moving, only Blaze had the added pressure of dealing with Raye... even if Raye was rather easy on the eyes.

"I like cake and all, but..."

"It shouldn't take long," Blaze said. "Just don't let Bree loose in the potato chip aisle."

"All right," then Lonnie stepped out the car. She blinked when she realized that Blaze wasn't moving. "Aren't you coming with?"

"Me? Oh, no, I'll wait for you girls out here."

"Lonnie, come on!" Bree shouted. The longer she took, the longer she had to wait for cake. Blaze smiled and waved to the three girls, quite taken with the idea of not moving for a while.

As Lonnie walked into the store she could feel her legs protesting. It was a throbbing reminder that she'd spent the day packing and moving boxes up and down the stairs. Somehow, the two girls in front of her still had enough energy to walk through the store – and Marianna was walking in heels! All that kickboxing training and Lonnie could barely turn the corner into the next aisle. At least she was the one pushing the cart, that way she could lean on it whenever they came to a stop.

"So what kind of cake do you want?" Marianna asked.

"Oh, um... I dunno, anything is fine with me."

"Anything? Well... we can do chocolate, that's a common one. But what *kind* of chocolate? And do we want the cake itself to be chocolate, or the frosting? Oh! Maybe you're the kind who likes fruity cakes, like a nice strawberry shortcake. Or maybe cheesecake, hmmmm... but what flavor..."

"U-um..." Lonnie listened to Marianna rattle off an entire bakery's worth of cakes. Meanwhile, Bree was shaking her head at Lonnie, as if she should've somehow known the full potential of their baking goddess. In an attempt to help Marianna come to a decision, Lonnie grabbed a box of cake mix and asked, "What about this one?"

"Oh no..." Bree debated on backing away and going to the relative safety of the potato chip aisle, but it probably wouldn't be good to leave Lonnie alone. She'd just joined them, after all.

Marianna saw Lonnie with the box and a look of sheer horror crossed her face. "What. Is that?"

"You said to pick a kind of cake, right?"

There was a smile on Marianna's face now, but there was something off about it. "Lonnie. Put the cake box down." Marianna spoke in a slow, uncomfortably friendly tone of voice.

"Yes ma'am," Lonnie whispered. Not that she thought Marianna would ever hurt her, but there was something about her demeanor... "So... I should just... say a flavor?"

"Yes."

"So... just like my grandmother. Got it."

"Good."

"So... um..." Lonnie rubbed the back of her head, feeling an embarrassed sort of nervousness as she tried to think of the kind of cake she was in the mood for. "I like strawberries, if that helps?"

"Excellent!" And just like that Marianna's scary smile shifted into a much happier one. "I can work with that."

Before the three of them could walk off to the next aisle they heard someone laughing. Marianna glanced behind them to see two girls looking at them – or rather, *her*. The laughter had a harsh edge to it, and it didn't take long for Marianna to realize why they were laughing. She'd been privy to this before, along with the whispered, "She know she don't need to be eatin' no cake."

"We should go," Marianna said.

But it was too late. Bree had caught wind of what the girls were saying. The look on her face showed clear signs of being ready to get kicked out of the store for going off on these girls. Bree was about to walk over to them but Marianna grabbed her arm to stop her. "Mari..."

"Let's just go," Marianna said again.

Bree shot the girls a nasty glare. What she wanted to say was that they had some nerve poking fun at someone. If Bree wanted to, she could be just as catty. She could point out how she'd hoped that the girl who'd made the unnecessary comment had gotten a refund for her horribly uneven haircut. She could also point out how the girl laughing with her wasn't the skinniest person in the universe. Then, she could tell her the not-so-secret truth: mocking a fat person didn't negate her own fatness.

Sadly, Bree knew that saying such things would lead to a lecture from Marianna. She'd say that they needed to be better than that, so Bree kept her mouth shut. However, Marianna hadn't said anything to Lonnie, who walked over to the two girls and asked, "You two got a problem?"

The laughter stopped immediately as Lonnie towered over them. The girl who'd been laughing at her friend's awful comment stuttered, "N-no."

"Oh. Okay. Because it sounded like you were making fun of my friend."

The stuttering girl quickly shook her head. "Not at all! Was just looking at a funny picture on my phone..."

Neither of them were holding phones, which was probably for the best. Lonnie looked like she would've smashed them with her foot. "And you?" She asked the second girl. "Were you laughing at a joke of some sort?"

The girl responded with the most dramatic eye roll that Lonnie and the others had ever seen. She put her hands on her hips and was ready to go toe to toe with Lonnie... until Lonnie cracked her knuckles. "Y-yeah, that's it," she muttered.

"Cool. You two ladies have a nice day," then Lonnie walked back over to Marianna and Bree. "Buttercream. I like buttercream frosting."

Not satisfied with how the encounter had played out, the girl with the misshapen haircut decided to keep poking the bear. "Ol' manly lookin' ass," which sent her chubby friend into another giggle fit.

This time Marianna beat Lonnie to the punch. Making unoriginal comments about her weight was one thing, but making fun of her new teammate? "Excuse you?"

274 – Briana Lawrence

Lonnie had to admit that she was pretty impressed. She'd had to lace her words with the prospect of physical violence, but Marianna's smile was so unsettling that the girls, once again, stopped laughing, one coughing in her haste.

"Seriously, who wastes their time making fun of someone in a grocery store?" Bree asked.

"You don't know me!" Haircut girl snapped at Bree, then she turned her attention to Marianna. "None of y'all know me! Don't act like you know me, you fat-"

"Bitch? Whale? Cow? Which one, huh? Which recycled insult are you going to use?"

For a moment the girl was stumped, then she dug deeper to try and come up with more insults to throw at Marianna. "Why don't you go and-"

"Eat a cake? Die? If you're gonna come at me, at least put some more effort into it."

"Let's just go," the other girl said as she grabbed onto her fuming friend's arm. The confrontation was becoming more pointless by the second and they were going to end up making a scene. There were already a handful of onlookers at the end of the aisle and they could hear words like *unruly* being tossed around between them. Her friend yanked her arm away from her and stormed off, muttering more unpleasantries as she pushed past the spectators.

"She'll feel better about herself someday," Marianna said. "You will, too."

The girl had expected Marianna to comment about how she had no business laughing about someone else's size when her shirt was two sizes two small. Instead, there was a knowing look on her face, one that made the girl fidget under her gaze. "Yeah, um... s-sorry we made fun of you," because while she technically hadn't made the comments, she'd been there to laugh at them.

Marianna shrugged her shoulders. "It's nothing new."

A MONSTROUS RETELLING
Briana Lawrence • www.magnifiquenoir.com

"Doesn't make it okay, though."

"You're right, it doesn't. So try not to do it, okay? Everyone has the right to enjoy cake."

"Shay! Let's go!" The other girl had come back to collect her friend, shouting her name from the end of the aisle. She turned to the small group that had gathered to watch her confrontation with Marianna and said, "What are y'all lookin' at?!"

The girl, Shay, shouted, "I'm coming," then she looked at Marianna and said, "I'll try," before she ran to catch up to her friend.

"That was amazing," Lonnie said from where she was watching everything with Bree.

Bree smiled and said, "Yeah, she is."

Lonnie wasn't quite sure where to start.

The room was bigger than she imagined it would be. There was enough space to fit her entire music collection and a couple of shelving units – which she desperately needed. In fact, she could grab her father's collection from her grandmother and set it up alongside hers. Lonnie hadn't ever thought about how small her room was until she walked into this one, now she felt like she didn't have enough stuff to fill the space.

After changing into a comfortable pair of shorts and a tank top, she got her stereo hooked up so she could listen to music while she unpacked. This led to her going through her music collection to try and find the perfect CD to decorate her new room to. By the time it occurred to her to just listen to whatever random station came up on the music streaming app on her phone she was interrupted by the smell of freshly baked cake. Before she knew what was going on, Bree was at her door in a crop top and panties telling her to take a break.

Lonnie almost commented on how this was borderline lesbian fantasy fuel, but she wasn't quite sure if their relationship was one where they could–

"This is pretty ridiculous, huh? Half-naked girl coming to tell you to eat cake with her? Whose erotic fanfiction is this?"

Lonnie nearly fell over and forgot how to breathe when she started laughing. If only Bree could be this confident around Kayla.

Bree led Lonnie into Marianna's room where the girl already had the cake sliced up. Marianna's room was the exact opposite of Bree's. The purple walls were lined with the occasional framed portrait of a fancy city or a chic looking bakery. She even had a small table surrounded by comfortable, multi-colored chairs to create the perfect café atmosphere. Where Bree had an impressive collection of video games, Marianna had a walk-in closet full of various shoes and outfits that ranged from sophisticated stripes to fun polka-dots. Unlike Bree's room, everything was organized and put in its place, right down to the make-up, bath products, scented lotions, and the handful of cat plushies that Marianna had to feed her love for the animal – as if her paw printed pajamas weren't enough of a sign.

Lonnie took a seat at the table with Bree, who happily grabbed herself a plate. After a sharp look from Marianna she refrained from eating it, waiting until Lonnie tried a bite first. Lonnie immediately closed her eyes and let out a happy little sound. "Damn this is good."

Now that Lonnie had tried the cake, Bree took that as a sign to begin eating her own slice. It should've been illegal for food to be that good.

"I'm glad you like it," Marianna said as she ate her own slice. The frosting could've been a little bit sweeter, particularly the pink icing she decorated the edge with. However, it was still good, so good that Lonnie had wolfed down her slice. "Wow Lonnie..."

"I'm sorry," but she wasn't. "It's really good!"

"Well help yourself, that's what it's here for."

Bree had a slight moment of panic when she realized that she was now living with someone who had a sweet tooth as big as hers. She supposed it was worth it for the good of the city or whatever. "And here you said you didn't care what kind of cake she made."

"I didn't! But I guess I didn't realize you could throw down like this."

"I try," Marianna said, always trying to be humble.

Lonnie set her fork down and chuckled as she shook her head. "Are you always like this?"

"Huh?"

"Yep," Bree said as she finished her first slice and reached for a second one.

"What do you mean by that?" Marianna asked.

"I mean the way you handle yourself. You're humble. You're patient. You're clearly a born leader. It's pretty admirable."

Bree smiled as she quietly ate her cake. Maybe if Marianna heard it from someone else she'd start to give herself a little more credit.

"Are you referring to those girls today?" Marianna asked as she finished her slice. Despite her feelings about the frosting not being to her standards, it was definitely tasty enough to grab a second slice like the others.

"I mean in everything I've seen so far!"

Marianna giggled and shook her head. "I'm not always patient. Bree can attest to that."

"True... but you're patient when it matters," Bree said. "Either that or persistent. I can't decide."

Marianna turned her attention to Lonnie who had, at some point, finished her second slice of cake and was now contemplating a third. "I see I'm going to have to increase the amount of baking I do, huh?"

"Mmmhmm! Oh... if that's okay with you..."

Both Marianna and Bree exchanged a silent look of relief. This was a nice side to see from Lonnie, one that made her feel more like a friend than an apprehensive teammate. Speaking of which... "What you did in that store was awesome," Bree said.

"Hm?"

"Standing up to those girls." Bree was no stranger to the kind of comments Marianna would get. She would respond with all the angry friend sass she could muster, but Lonnie definitely had the advantage with her sheer, intimidating presence.

"Those girls had no right saying the things they said. I *almost* thought you were being too nice, Marianna, but I'm glad you stood up for yourself."

"That's usually where the negativity comes from – lashing out because you feel bad about yourself. I... wasn't expecting you to do that," Marianna said.

"Why wouldn't I stick up for you?" Lonnie asked, putting a third slice of cake on her plate. She cut it in half and nodded over to Bree who was more than happy to grab a fork and dig in.

Marianna paused, trying to think of the best way to explain her feelings. Bree, on the other hand, went in headfirst – as always. "We weren't sure if you'd be there for us."

"Bree!"

"No, that's fair," Lonnie said. "I wasn't very... agreeable."

"To be fair, I was extremely agreeable, so I guess I thought anyone who joined would be."

"We both were," Marianna said. "But I was really hesitant about Bree."

"Oh?" Lonnie could see how it was easy to butt heads with Bree. She'd done so herself back in the classroom. But it was hard to believe that Marianna would have a hard time with anyone. "Why's that?"

Marianna set her fork on her empty plate and said, "Because she jumped off a building."

Bree, in all her flustered glory, jumped out of her seat and asked, "Do you HAVE to tell her that story?"

"After getting to know you... I'm not surprised you'd do something so extra," Lonnie said.

Bree pouted as she sat back down. "Is this gonna be our team now? You two picking on me?"

"Naw, I'll let Kayla do that part," Lonnie said with a sly smirk.

In response, Bree got up from her seat again, walked over to Marianna's bed, and dramatically flopped herself onto it. She buried her face into one of the pillows and said something, but her voice was completely muffled out. Both Marianna and Lonnie laughed at her utter embarrassment.

The rest of the night was spent talking and eating. Lonnie learned about Bree's YouTube channel and the bakery where Marianna worked. In return, they learned about Lonnie's kickboxing and how Rodney and Raye were friends of her rather large family. Bree was the first to fall asleep, curled up in Marianna's bed after spending a few minutes denying being tired.

"You'd think someone who games so much would be able to stay awake," Lonnie said as she helped Marianna carry their dishes and leftover cake into the kitchen.

"She conks out pretty hard at least once a week. She'll probably wake up and freak out about not being in her own room."

"I can carry her-"

"Naw, don't bother. It's amusing," Marianna said as she began to load the dishwasher.

"Sit down," Lonnie said as she ushered Marianna over to a chair. "You cooked, that means you shouldn't have to clean."

"Lonnie!"

"Hush. You had time to help me pack, tell some girls off, and bake a cake. I can do dishes."

Marianna watched Lonnie try to go about cleaning the kitchen, opening various drawers and cabinets to try and find the dish pellets for the dishwasher. "Lonnie I can-"

"Nope, found them," Lonnie said after opening the fifth cabinet door. "You're not helping with this no matter how hard you try."

Marianna decided to give up and relax in her seat, watching Lonnie load the dishwasher. "You know what? I think you did it."

"Did what?"

"Fit in with us."

Lonnie stopped and turned to look over at Marianna, dish pellet in hand. "I... oh..." she had been worried about that, hadn't she? But as she looked at Marianna she felt at peace with her decision. To think, she'd been so against joining, but now she couldn't imagine not wearing that anklet and letting the rainbow colors wash over her hair. "I guess I did, didn't I?"

"You did," then Marianna smiled and added, "Welcome to the team, Radical Rainbow."

SLEEPOVER
NamiOki • namioki.deviantart.com

Episode Nine:

Enter Prism Pink

The weather had finally made up its mind and settled on being cold outside. Bree didn't mind the colder temperatures – unless if she was cosplaying a character in tiny shorts. Colder temperatures meant warm, delicious drinks like hot chocolate with an obscene about of whipped cream or caramel apple cider. The downside was that Christmas did invade Halloween's privacy a bit too early for Bree's tastes. On the plus side, it meant that she got to play little sister and kindly ask – *beg* – Trey for expensive gaming gifts.

"Oh I see, you can ask me for things but not take my feelings into consideration."

Of course, this year would be extra annoying, what with the magical girl thing and all. Even weekly phone calls were laced with the occasional jab at Bree's life decisions. Though, to be fair, the phone calls had increased because of said life decisions.

"Are you gonna bring that up every time I ask you for something?" Bree asked.

"I don't bring it up *every* time..."

"Trey."

"You know I don't want you out there, Bree."

"And you know why I'm out there doing it. Mari and I have each other's backs, Lonnie's here now, and Blaze is watching out for us." Lonnie had been with them for a week, and in that week, they had become more efficient at monster killing. Bree assumed it was because they'd hashed it out over Lonnie's refusal to join. After the yelling and frustration, the trio had a girl for all their battle needs. Bree could attack from a distance, Lonnie could attack up close, and Marianna could finish creatures off with effective explosives. "We're good, Trey. I mean it."

Trey sighed. "Fine, fine. Now tell me what god awful thing you want for Christmas so I can **not** get it for you."

"At least I've grown out of those toys that talk, right?"

"You know, some sisters at least wait until Thanksgiving."

"I mean I *could* but you're gonna have to go and reserve it before it sells out," Bree said sweetly.

"Can I tell you what I want for Christmas?"

"I'm not leaving **magnifiquenoir**, Trey."

"That's not it." Trey paused, trying to find the right way to say what he wanted to say. Finally, he decided to just go for it. "I want you to come with me to see mom." When Bree didn't say anything Trey changed his tone of voice, sounding much more serious. "You knew you'd have to go home for the holidays, right?"

"Can't I just stay with you?"

"Keep this up and I'm gonna move the trip to Thanksgiving break."

"Actually, that's a shorter break, so that might be better..." It was also coming up soon. She could treat it like binge watching an emotionally draining anime series and get it over with quickly.

"Why are you so hesitant? I thought you two were getting along better."

"We are," Bree said as she laid back in her bed. Trey was right, her and her mother were getting along better. She still said things from time to time that would irritate her, but after that very first monster attack,

Bree had to admit to not minding a handful of motherly phone calls. "But... I'm not ready to tell her about *you know what.*"

"Well at least the *you know what* isn't just your sexual preference anymore."

"I swear that would be easier to explain." Before Trey could say anything Bree quickly added, "Which I'm **not** going to do!"

"I still don't think she would take it as hard as you think she would."

"I'll tell you what. If things get serious with me and Kayla, I'll tell her."

"Awwwww you didn't stutter that time!"

"Shut up!"

"Are you still bringing her cupcakes? Have you upgraded to cheesecake yet? Did you woo her with another midnight launch?"

"Aren't you almost 30?! How can you still be so immature?" When Trey responded by laughing Bree growled into the phone, "I'm hanging up."

"Love you too, sis."

Bree ended the call and stuck her tongue out at her phone as if Trey was right there to see it. Part of her wished she was born in a time where corded phones were all the rage, then she could slam it down to hang up on her brother instead of pushing a button. Perhaps she could buy a heavy-duty phone case, then she could throw her phone across the room whenever her brother got under her skin.

He did bring up a good point, though. She wasn't stuttering about Kayla that much anymore. So much had happened that she didn't have time to be flustered over a cute girl. That didn't mean she had to like that he brought it up, and she definitely didn't have to like the prospect of going home for the holidays.

"Trey being a jerk again?" Marianna asked as she poked her head into Bree's room. She was dressed in her purple polka-dotted apron, hands dusted in flour from her latest baking foray. "Do I need to let you lick the spoon?"

"Mari, you know I *always* need to lick the spoon."

"Who's Trey?" Lonnie shouted from the living room.

Bree laughed at the somewhat distressed look on Marianna's face. They'd gotten used to Lonnie the Fighter, but Lonnie the Girl Who Lived with Them? In a lot of ways, it was like having a taller, more muscular Bree in the house, complete with her penchant for yelling. She even yelled at the television when someone on one of her reality shows did something particularly scandalous. That trait never made sense to Marianna, but it was especially odd with Lonnie since she could be so calm at times – even in the middle of a battle.

To spare Marianna from a yelling back and forth session, Bree stepped out of her room to interrupt Lonnie's television program. "Trey is my asshole older brother who just signed me up for a trip to see my mother."

Lonnie somehow managed to pay attention to Bree's sentence while watching the head chef on her show smash an entire chicken breast with the palm of his hand before declaring it to be raw. "Do you and your mother not get along?" Followed by, "Damn, Ramsey gonna kick y'all out the kitchen."

For some reason, it was easier to talk about this when there was a chorus of censored beeping coming from the television. "We do and we don't get along," which Bree supposed was better than her automatic response of *hell to the no*. "There's things about my life she doesn't know. Magical things. And Kayla things."

"Ah." As Lonnie watched an entire team of cooks be kicked out the kitchen, she quietly said, "I suppose I should talk to my Grand-Penny when I go home for break…"

"Grand-Penny?" Marianna wiped her hands on her apron and smiled as she sat next to Lonnie. "That's a cute name for your grandmother."

"Yeah," Lonnie said with a gentle smile on her face. "She's been so understanding about everything – even when others in the family haven't been. Still... I'm not sure how she's gonna handle this."

Fortunately, there was a commercial break to cut the intense yelling from the cooking show. "Are they not supportive of you?" Marianna asked.

"They *think* they are," Lonnie muttered, remembering her tattle-tale cousins and nosy aunt – who'd only gotten worse over time. "Thanksgiving will be a day full of good food and *manly* comments that are supposed to be compliments."

"Ick," Bree said, her face twisting into a sour expression as she sat on the arm of the couch. She was starting to appreciate Trey. A little. All right, she still didn't appreciate him, but she did feel bad for Lonnie. "Meanwhile, I'll be wearing a sunflower dress and spending an entire Sunday in church."

"That might not be so bad. There will probably be good food afterwards, meaning you get Thanksgiving and church dinner."

Bree shook her head. "My mom does this whole non-traditional Thanksgiving thing where she makes lasagna."

"What? No macaroni and cheese? No collard greens?" Lonnie looked more appalled than her TV chef did over the raw chicken. She may have hated dealing with certain family members, but they at least provided her with peach cobbler to go alongside her grandmother's sweet potato pie.

"Nope. It's just the three of us so she doesn't want to make a meal that'll feed an entire block of people. That, and my brother likes lasagna, so he got what he wanted when he came back home from college. It's been like that ever since."

"That doesn't sound terrible, Bree," Marianna said.

"I mean it's good lasagna, sure, but... my brother is gonna keep poking me to tell her about... you know..."

"Tell her you're bisexual, first. That'll soften the blow," Lonnie said as the commercials ended. It was time to see who was going to be eliminated this week and she had a feeling raw chicken guy had run out of excuses.

It took a moment for Bree to snap out of her shock over Lonnie's nonchalant comment. "That's not funny!" But Lonnie's focus was on the TV, an amused smile on her face from Bree's yelling. "And here I was feeling bad for the two of you for having crappy families!"

"Wait... two?" Lonnie turned away from her program to look at Marianna, who was busy giving Bree one of her *you talk too damn much* glares. "What does she mean by that?" Lonnie asked.

"It's nothing," Marianna said, then, "It looks like that guy is leaving *Hell's Kitchen*."

"Ha! I knew it!" Lonnie clapped her hands and actually let out an excited cheer as the show played a montage of the contestant's best moments – though she didn't think he had any to begin with. "It's about time he left. And it's about time you explained what Bree meant by her comment."

It was annoying how Lonnie could switch focus so easily, at least when Marianna was trying to not divulge details about her life. Still, it was going to come up eventually, and it was best to talk about it. She'd learned that lesson the hard way when she and Bree had first moved in together. "My mother and I don't see eye to eye about this magical girl thing. Well... at least *one* of my mothers, the other one is more supportive. And my dad is, well, my dad."

Even if Bree had already heard the story, it still made her heart hurt whenever Marianna talked about her mother. But there was something different this time. This time, Marianna was going into more detail, and she revealed something that she hadn't talked about before.

Her other parents.

"It's not exactly the easiest thing to tell a loved one," Lonnie pointed out.

"It's a little more complicated than that," Marianna said. Bree reached over and rested her hand on her shoulder, squeezing it to encourage Marianna to continue. Marianna glanced over at Bree and smiled before she reached up and rested her hand on top of hers. "She was severely injured before I was born, during a monster attack that the original group tried to stop."

"Oh... I'm sorry to hear that."

Marianna almost responded with *it's all right* but she knew that would be a lie because, "I understand where she's coming from, but..."

"But you want to show her what you can do, what *we* can do. People need us."

Marianna nodded. "My second mom, Yolanda, would tell me some great stories about my first mom, you know, before the accident. They were friends back in college, and my Mama Yo was there for her during her recovery. I guess their friendship turned into something more."

"And your first mom? What's her name?"

"Lynn," Marianna whispered, as if it hurt to say the name.

Lonnie moved closer to Marianna and wrapped her arms around her. Marianna let out a surprised cough, then she closed her eyes and rested her head on Lonnie's shoulder. That was something else to get used to: Lonnie was a hugger. "Well I'm sure she's proud of you," Lonnie said.

"And your Grand-Penny will be proud of you," Marianna said in response.

"Ugh. Can we focus on you and not me?" Lonnie let Marianna go and frowned at her.

"Mari does that," Bree said. "You'll get used to it," then she grabbed the remote and began flipping through channels. Now that Lonnie's show was over and the conversation had taken a lighter turn she could find something more fun to watch.

"Well that's too bad because I have more questions." Lonnie leaned back as Bree settled on the cartoon station. She recognized the Crystal Gems immediately thanks to another girl crush she'd had. "So are your mom and dad divorced? And your mom hooked up with your Mama Yo?"

Lonnie was way more blunt than Bree, so blunt that Marianna was too flustered to yell back at her and stuttered, "Um... n-no."

"But you said you had three parents... oh! Did your moms adopt you and then THEY got a divorce, so now your mom is with your dad?" Bree was practically drafting the slice of life anime script in her head.

"No..." Marianna squirmed on the couch as she gripped onto the edge of her apron. She really hoped that they'd stop trying to guess her family situation.

Instead, Lonnie double-downed and asked, "Artificial insemination?"

"W-what?!" Marianna's jaw dropped and even Bree looked surprised that Lonnie had dug that deep.

"It means your dad donated sperm and–"

Marianna stood up, blocking the TV as she yelled, "My mother is polyamorous! She's with both of them! I have two moms and a dad!" There. Maybe now they'd stop trying to figure out her parents.

Bree was the first to say something and blurted out, "That kind of thing happens in real life?!"

"You shoot green pixels out of your hands, Bree, how is **this** the thing you fumble with?" Lonnie asked.

"How come you've never mentioned this?!" Bree was so surprised by this revelation that she felt the need to jump off the arm of the couch, face Marianna, and point an accusing finger at her. "How could you keep this from me?!"

Marianna gave Bree a tiny, sheepish smile. She wasn't sure why she felt bad. It had to be that lone finger pointed directly at her. "It never came up?"

"Yes it did! You've talked about your family before!"

"Well yes, I did, but only in the context of **magnifiquenoir**. I talked about the attack that paralyzed my mother and how it caused her hatred for magical girls. There wasn't a need to discuss my Mama Yo or my father – who came into the picture later."

"And your Mama Yo doesn't mind?" When Marianna shook her head Lonnie let out a low whistle. "Damn. Ms. Lynn got it goin' on!"

"Lonnie! That's my mother!"

"Maybe she can teach me the ways so I can have two girlfriends..." Lonnie said, a thoughtful look on her face.

"OH MY GOD!"

Bree was glad there was a comfortable chair near the couch because she ended up stumbling back into it as she broke into a huge giggle fit. She was really starting to appreciate Lonnie's presence. Marianna was yelling at her to stop laughing but Bree couldn't stop wheezing as she sputtered out, "This is too good!"

"I can change the subject to something more serious..." Lonnie said.

"Don't you dare!" Bree shouted. "I-I'm not done laughing!"

Marianna tried her best to look angry, but a smile was creeping across her face due to Bree's infectious laughter.

It was odd walking into the gym now that she didn't live there.

Lonnie had to consciously remember to bring her gym bag to class that day since her gear was no longer up a flight of stairs. She also had

Once Upon a Time...

THERE WERE THREE MAGICAL GIRLS WHO WERE AS *STYLISH* AS THEY WERE *POWERFUL!* AFTER A HARD DAY OF ABSOLUTE SLAYAGE, THEY PREPARED FOR BED.

#1: THE LEADER

I ADORE CUTE KITTY PAJAMAS!

#2: THE BACK-UP

I'D RATHER BE NAKED :) ♡♡♡

NO!

#3: THE FIGHTER

JUST GIVE ME SOMETHING COMFY THAT DOESN'T SMELL BAD!

OH! AND MY HAIR BONNET, OF COURSE!

WTF?!

THE GIRLS WERE STUNNED AT THE FIGHTER'S ATTIRE. HOW COULD SOMEONE SO *COOL* AND *MAGICAL* PRESENT THEMSELVES IN SUCH A WAY? THE TWO GAVE THE RAINBOW WARRIOR A FRIENDLY WORD OF ADVICE...

MAGICAL GIRLS MUST BE CUTE AT ALL TIMES!

I HATE GIRLS!*

*SOMETIMES

BUT THE NEXT DAY, THE FIGHTER *FLOURISHED* WITH HER FLAWLESS HAIR AND HER BEAUTIFUL, DARK SKIN. SHE THEN PROCEEDED TO GO ABOUT HER DAY LIVING

Unapologetically Ever After!

LET THE HATE FLOW THROUGH YOU!

SEARCH YOUR FEELINGS YOU KNOW IT TO BE TRUE...

I DON'T HATE ANYONE...

WHAT EVEN IS MY LIFE ANYMORE?

MAGNIFIQUETANGLES (SORRY GIRLS)

A BEDTIME STORY
Briana Lawrence • www.magnifiquenoir.com

to remember that she'd be sleeping in a completely different bed instead of the full-size one she had in her bedroom – *old* bedroom. Even if she'd upgraded to a queen, there had been something quaint about being too tall for her former bed.

Lonnie set her bag down and took everything in. The still cracked floor reminded her that not too much time had passed since that dreadful attack. Some of the holes in the wall had been fixed with a layer of plaster, but the larger ones still lingered and would be tackled in due time.

"Well well well, look who it is."

Ah, there was the welcome she was expecting. Lonnie turned to see Braydon walking over to her. He was slow in his steps and standing slightly hunched over, but still giving her that cocky smirk. Kendra was next to him, holding herself up on crutches to stay off of her foot. "You two aren't here to actually box, right?" Lonnie asked.

"Sure we are," Braydon joked. "Think I can't take you on?"

"You're right, let's go."

"Me first," Kendra said. "Though I may have an advantage," then she nodded toward the crutches she was using.

Lonnie smiled at the both of them. "It's good to see you two in such good spirits."

"Why do you keep saying that?" Braydon asked.

"Huh?"

"*You two.* As if we're... I-I mean..." Braydon looked away from Lonnie, but not fast enough for her to miss his reddening cheeks.

"Did I miss something?" Lonnie asked. "Why are you so-"

"That's not important!" Braydon snapped, his face turning redder at Kendra's soft laughter. "Kendra!"

"Don't pick on him too much," Kendra said, a hint of a smirk crossing her lips.

Lonnie raised an eyebrow at that but said, "I'll hold off. For now," because it was clear that something had happened between the two. If she had to guess, she'd say it was while they were at the hospital. Maybe injuries were the key to getting Braydon to confess his feelings, or maybe Kendra had gotten tired of waiting. Lonnie decided that it had to be Kendra, who was still smirking at Braydon as he tried his best to maintain eye contact with her. "So why are you two here if you can't practice?" Lonnie asked.

"We wanted to visit Rodney and make sure he was doing better," Kendra said.

"Knowing him? He'll tell us he's even more handsome now," Lonnie muttered in annoyance.

"That is so unfair! I look like hell!"

Kendra smiled up at Braydon and said, "Hell's not so bad, you know?"

Now Braydon was blushing so much that it had turned the tips of his ears red. Between Kendra's gentle smile and the knowing look on Lonnie's face, he needed to change the subject. Fast. "Sooooo… how's living your ultimate lesbian fantasy going?"

That shouldn't have caught Lonnie off guard. She should've seen it coming but she still ended up nearly choking on the air around her. "You know I *just* did you a solid by not poking fun at your flustered state…"

"You mean living with two cute girls *isn't* fun for you?"

"No, that part's fine, but you make it sound like we all sleeping in the same bed, wearing cute pajamas while eating cake."

"Is that a thing? Can that be a thing?" Braydon's eyes lit up in excitement at the thought.

Lonnie made a mental note to never introduce Bree to Braydon. He didn't need to know that she came to her door in her underwear. "Shut up, Braydon," Lonnie said, even though a pajama party with cake had definitely been a thing on the first night she'd moved in. Suddenly, a thought occurred to her, and a mischievous look crossed her face. "You know, I should ask Kendra what you sleep in."

"W-what? Why would she-"

"Boxers," Kendra said, her face completely serious. "But I'll break him out of that terrible habit. Sleeping naked is best."

No part of Lonnie found men attractive, but she could definitely appreciate a woman who knew what she wanted. She could doubly appreciate how the red was practically tattooed to Braydon's cheeks. That alone was deserving of a high five to Kendra.

"What's going on out here?"

Lonnie smiled when she saw Rodney walking over to them with Raye. Rodney was, at least, walking around without wincing with every step, but Raye was staying close by in case he got too tired. The man who walked around shirtless as much as possible was now wearing a large top with his loose pants. Long gone were the days of flaunting his injuries, especially when these had been from such a terrifying, personal encounter.

Before Lonnie could answer Rodney's question, Braydon jumped in and said, "They're bullying me!"

Both Lonnie and Kendra laughed while Rodney and Raye tried their best to keep the smiles off their faces. "Ladies, leave Braydon alone," Rodney said.

"Yes, you both know how sensitive he is," Raye added as she smiled over at Braydon.

"Raye!"

"It must be tough since it's usually you who's doing the teasing."

Lonnie poked Braydon's nose like a sister teasing her sibling. "Awwwww, did you think Raye would go easy on you?"

Braydon decided to respond by turning his head away from the group, but Lonnie caught sight of the small smile on his face.

From there, things melted into a happy and well known normal, and it was exactly what Lonnie had come here for. The dusty smell. The feel of the floor mat as she warmed up. The sound of her foot hitting the punching bag as Raye held it in place for her. The obnoxious commentary from Braydon and Kendra telling him to knock it off. Lonnie had known that she'd miss this when she packed a week ago, but she hadn't realized how much.

A few minutes later Lonnie took a break, sitting on the bench and enjoying her bottle of water. Both Braydon and Kendra had moved over to the ring, looking at it fondly, both itching to go back in. Lonnie couldn't hear what they were saying, but she imagined that they were planning for the day they'd be able to box again. As she sat and watched them, both Rodney and Raye came over and joined her, Rodney sitting next to her. Lonnie didn't comment on how he'd grimaced from the movement or how Raye had to help him. Instead, she said, "It's good to see you out of bed."

"It *feels* good to be out of bed."

"It's also good to see those two moving around," then Lonnie nodded over to Braydon and Kendra.

"And you? How's everything going with you?" Rodney asked.

"Good. The girls are very nice."

Rodney raised an eyebrow at Lonnie and asked, "That's it? Nothing about your new room? You got enough room for all them CDs? Is your bed bigger? Anything?"

Lonnie laughed and said, "Yeah yeah, all of that. My new room makes my old one look like a shoe box."

"Well this *shoe box* ain't the same without you."

"I miss it here, too."

"You know, you didn't have to move out. I mean I understand staying somewhere while we were at the hospital, but..."

296 - BRIANA LAWRENCE

It was in that moment that Lonnie realized that Raye hadn't told him anything. Had he spent the whole week trying to figure out the great mystery of Lonnie moving out? Lonnie glanced up at Raye who gave her a small nod in response.

"I saw that." Rodney frowned up at his wife.

"Saw what, dear?" Raye leaned down and draped her arms around Rodney's shoulders.

"You two are keeping secrets from me."

"We would *never*," then Raye kissed Rodney on his cheek.

It was nice to see the two of them bantering back and forth the way they usually did. Back when the attack had happened, Lonnie had to watch Raye cry over her fallen husband. She couldn't imagine what that must've felt like, especially since Raye had seen Rodney take some pretty nasty hits over the years. Nothing could've prepared them for that monster attack or the painfully slow recovery afterwards. But now they were back to being the husband and wife duo who loved each other very much... even if they, occasionally, got on each other's nerves.

Lonnie watched as Rodney made a face at Raye after her kiss, the woman laughing at him as he actually pouted about being kept out of the loop. After a deep breath, Lonnie decided to blame what happened next on her sentimental heart. She leaned over and whispered to Rodney, "I'm Radical Rainbow."

Rodney blinked, then blinked again, then glanced between Lonnie and Raye and asked, "Who?"

Both women looked at each other then laughed. They'd forgotten that Rodney had been in bed for most of the week. He'd missed all the action packed stories of **magnifiquenoir** and their newest member. Raye leaned down and kissed Rodney's cheek again and the man actually swatted her away. "Don't patronize me! Who is that?!"

Raye glanced over at Lonnie who took another deep breath before she began. "Well, it all started with those two girls I moved in with…"

"Is everything okay now?"

Marianna looked up from where she was putting a new batch of brownies into the display case at the bakery. To her surprise, Dana was standing on the other side of the case, hands on her hips as she waited for Marianna to respond. "I didn't know it was possible for you to walk into a building quietly."

Dana let out a shocked gasp at Marianna's comment and yelled, "Hey! I'm checking up on you!"

Ah, there was the Dana she knew, the one who didn't mind that her loud voice always startled the people around her, particularly the few customers in the store who were looking at the case and trying to decide what they wanted. "Everything's fine now, Dana. Honest."

"Well it better be because you haven't talked to me in over week!"

And there was the Dana she didn't want to face, but she knew she had it coming. The last time the two had talk Marianna had been upset about the situation with Lonnie. Dana had taken the time to cheer her up, then Marianna... vanished. Okay, she didn't *actually* disappear, but she'd gotten so swept up in Lonnie that she hadn't had a chance to talk to Dana. "I guess I lost track of time?" Marianna gave her her biggest, most apologetic, sweetest smile.

It didn't work.

"Ma. Ri. An. Na. How DARE YOU not CALL ME after our sleepover. You used me! You're a terrible friend!"

One of the customers was actually nodding in agreement even if she didn't know the whole situation. "Do you want a brownie?" Marianna asked.

"Do you *reeeeeally* think that's enough? Is that all my time is worth to you? A BROWNIE?"

Marianna winced. Strike two. "What about one of the Fabu Cakes? A chocolate one. With sprinkles!"

"Thank you," then Dana pranced over to one of the small tables and sat down, legs crossed as she waited for Marianna to plate up her apology. Marianna was sure to grab the biggest piece with the most amount of sprinkles and frosting.

"I knew something was going on."

Marianna jumped a bit when Ms. Green walked out the back room, armed with a tray full of cookies. "You scared me! I almost dropped Dana's cake!"

"A baker would never do such a thing," the older woman said as she slid the tray into the case. "That's a pretty large slice. Are you in that much trouble with her?"

Marianna looked over at Dana who tapped her wrist as if she were wearing a watch. "Yep."

"Well then you should join her," then Ms. Green grabbed two forks. "You both can share that."

"My break isn't for another hour..."

"Oh? That's too bad. If only there was a boss who could change that..." Ms. Green bumped her wide hips against Marianna's and said, "Go on."

Marianna smiled. "Sure you can handle things while I'm on break?"

"You think I can't handle workin' the counter? Girl, puhleeze! I've been workin' the register since-"

"Since before I was born, right?"

Ms. Green raised an eyebrow and said, "Don't get smart with me."

"You tell her, Ms. Green!" Dana shouted from her seat.

"Hey! I'm bringing you cake!" Marianna shouted back at her, the customers who had been looking at the display case laughing at their banter.

"You're bringing me cake because you *owe* me cake," Dana corrected as Marianna walked over to her.

Marianna set the plate in front of Dana and moved to sit across from her, watching as she took a fork and dug right in. The look on Dana's face was a clear sign of her forgiveness as she let out a happy little hum of appreciation over the cake. As she took another bite, Marianna decided to actually apologize. "Dana... I'm sorry for not calling you. I mean it."

Dana smiled. "I know you are, but I have to give you crap sometimes."

"Well I deserve it this time," Marianna said as she ate a forkful of cake. Good lord, she needed to learn Ms. Green's secret. The chocolate melted in her mouth and the frosting had the perfect amount of sweetness to it.

"Everything is okay now, right? Whatever *everything* is?"

Marianna hesitated. She never did explain what was bothering her to Dana – not that she could. Well, she *could*, but she didn't want to. She had a feeling the other girls felt the same way about wanting to have something normal. Bree hadn't told Ella yet, and Lonnie hadn't told Braydon or Kendra. "Everything's fine," Marianna said. "Between that attack at the mall and getting a new roommate..."

"Wait... you got a new roommate?"

Perfect, the distraction worked. She knew she needed to tell Dana a little bit, and revealing a new roommate would give her enough to gossip about. "I was worried that we wouldn't get along."

"Who in the world wouldn't get along with you?!"

"You'd be surprised, Dana."

"Well she's crazy if she doesn't like you," Dana said, pointing her frosting covered fork at Marianna. "Everyone should like you."

Marianna laughed as she ate another bite of cake. "Well that's certainly not true. I can be hard to get along with. Ask Bree."

"Well *I* had no problem getting along with you. I never will."

"You might be slightly biased."

"H-huh?" Dana nearly choked on her next bite of cake. "What makes you say that?"

Marianna giggled as she tapped her fork against Dana's. "Who else is gonna go shopping with you?"

"Oh… right, that."

There it was again. That same quiet response that made Marianna's heart tingle. "Dana-"

"You know for a second I thought you were gonna say something else."

This was the first time Dana actually kept talking after one of her little slip ups. "What did you think I was going to say?" Marianna asked.

Dana looked down at the plate and slowly moved her fork over a couple of cake crumbs. "I dunno, like… dating, or something? I mean *everyone* thinks we're dating anyway…"

"Well yeah, but-"

"Would it really be so bad?"

"Dana…"

"I'm serious!" Dana looked up at her now, eyes determined to get through what she was about to say. "You're the complete package, Marianna. Looks. Intelligence. Kindness. I get flustered because you're kinda amazing." It was both odd and frustrating. Dana Santiago didn't know the meaning of the words *shy* and *unsure* unless if Marianna was involved.

Marianna let the words process through her mind as she tried to think of something to say. It didn't feel right to say she was too busy to think about this. She'd been mentally using that excuse for months and Dana deserved better than that. "What if... I'm not interested in dating?"

"... huh?" That wasn't the question Dana was expecting. "Do you mean me or... anyone?"

"I'm not really interested in it at all... is that weird?" She remembered bringing this up to Bree some time ago, but her heart didn't beat this fast back then. "I mean I know my friends are dating... *kinda* dating? I dunno, Bree gets so flustered around Kayla and it's really cute but... I don't feel like that with anyone. I never have."

"But you like spending time with me, right?"

"Yeah! Absolutely!"

"Marianna... what's so weird about that?"

Marianna wanted to respond but she was left speechless at Dana's question. In a world where she could create cupcakes that exploded on impact... why did she think *this* was weird? "I... guess I dunno..."

Dana smiled. "Ha. You don't have an answer for everything after all."

"You know... I'm kinda glad I don't in this case." Between school, the bakery, and **magnifiquenoir**, it was kinda nice that she didn't have to have all the answers about some aspect of her life.

"What? You mean my little overachiever actually *wants* to relax?"

"Ha ha. Just for that I'm eating the last bite," then Marianna stuck her fork in the last bit of cake and ate it.

"Hey! That was my apology cake!"

Marianna stood up and said, "How about I get us a new slice of cake, then? A 'Marianna doesn't have to have all the answers' slice."

"Deal!"

"You two can't keep eating up my cake," Ms. Green said from the counter, causing Marianna to stumble mid-step. Had she heard the entire conversation? Marianna swore they'd kept their voices down. Wasn't hearing supposed to be one of the first things to go with old age? Damn that elderly black woman super-powered hearing when it came to gossip.

"It's a special occasion, Ms. Green!" Dana called from her seat.

"Uh huh," then Ms. Green held up another slice of cake and said, "This is the last slice you two get."

"Thank you, Ms. Green," then Marianna walked back over to the table. "So... to our first... um..." Marianna wasn't quite sure what word to use.

"*First?* Girl, this is like the millionth!"

"Fine. To one million *and one*," then Marianna held up a forkful of cake.

Dana raised her fork and clinked it against Marianna's. "To one million and one."

"So explain to me who these boys are?" Kayla asked.

"Wow, Bree, you're so great at dating..."

Bree shot Torrence a look as he rung up her games. Unlike the list she'd emailed her brother, these games were used titles she hadn't had a chance to pick up. "Torrence, I haven't seen you in a week, don't tarnish our reunion by being a jerk."

"I'm fine, by the way. Thanks for asking," Torrence said as he let out a dramatic sigh.

"I asked how you were when we walked in!"

Torrence laughed at the offended look on Bree's face. He hadn't seen the girl since the botched midnight launch. The first couple of days after the monster attack had been an unexpected mini-vacation as the mall had been closed for repairs. It didn't take long for money hungry corporations to complain about a dip in sales, and soon, the mall was open for business – despite the construction required to fix what had been damaged. Since holiday season was right around the corner, work was being done around the clock to make sure the mall was at one hundred percent. The second floor walkway was cluttered with hazard signs and workers armed with power tools and hard hats. The stores that had been effected were covered in long sheets of plastic – but still open for business, of course.

Torrence was sure it would take a while for the general public to go back to their regularly scheduled shopping, but he'd underestimated the power of weekly sales. At least it meant he could see Bree and her blue lipsticked lady friend again. Speaking of which… "You two are on a date, right? Why are you even here?"

Kayla laughed and said, "He does have a point." They'd almost made it to an actual restaurant. Unfortunately, said restaurant was in the vicinity of the mall. Like a beacon in the sky, Bree was drawn to the video game store. To be fair, Bree had asked if it was okay for them to go, promising that it would only take a minute. Kayla had been torn between wanting to go on a real date – she'd even worn a skirt despite the frigid weather – or saying "yes" so she could see that cute smile Bree got when she was near video games.

In the end, the smile had won.

Though the smile was completely gone now as Bree frowned at Torrence one more time. Kayla had to admit that seeing the cashier was making the trip worth it.

"Torrence. Shut up," Bree hissed as she pulled her wallet out to pay for her games.

Kayla decided to give Bree a break and said, "I'm just givin' ya crap. Now, tell me who these boys are," then she pointed to Bree's shirt. There

304 – BRIANA LAWRENCE

were two faces animated in the center of it with the words *Grump* and *Not So Grump* – whatever that meant. Kayla knew enough about video games to get by, but this was new territory for her.

"Surprised you haven't heard about them already..."

To be honest, Bree was too. "Have I not mentioned the *Game Grumps* yet?"

Kayla shook her head. "I don't think so?" Though Bree had a lot of geeky things to keep up with so it may have slipped her mind.

After he finished scanning Bree's reward card Torrence said, "*The Game Grumps* are two Let's Players who Bree is obsessed with."

"Says the one with a crush on Arin." Bree made sure to wink at Torrence when she said that.

"Shh!" Torrence frantically looked around the store as if Arin Hanson were somewhere in the vicinity. No one was paying attention to their conversation, too focused on scanning the walls for the games they wanted to purchase. "Jeez, tell the whole world, why don'tcha…"

"Which one is Arin?" Kayla asked. When Bree pointed to the face on her shirt Kayla nodded and said, "He's cute. I like the blond streak in his hair. You have good taste, Torrence."

"He's had good taste for yeeeeears," Bree teased.

Torrence responded by shoving her bag into her hands. "Go away now, please," but to Torrence's horror there was no one else in line. Everyone else was either deciding on what game to pick up or playing on the demo units. He'd even had time to take care of the traded in games from the day and put their cases out on the sales floor.

"Alas, their love is not meant to be," Bree said as she placed a hand over her heart. "Arin's married."

"It's even worse because Suzy is cool, too!"

Kayla was fascinated at the conversation. It was like they were lamenting on a fictional crush, though she supposed Arin Hanson was a real person. Technically, it was no different than any celebrity crush, and

Kayla had plenty of those if her social media likes were any indication. "I take it that's his wife?" Kayla asked.

"Yep. She also has some YouTube channels where she plays video games and does fashion stuff."

"Now see, I can get into that," Kayla said as Bree pulled out her phone to show her one of the channels.

"Mine too, actually." Torrence leaned over the counter to look at Bree's phone with them. It felt good to be dealing with customers he could admit that to. "Her tutorials are on point," he said as Bree hit play on one of the videos that showed off her style of clothing.

Bree smiled at the both of them, her eyes shimmering in delight. "Awwwww, you two have something in common!"

"Ah, I suppose that's vital, right? Your girlfriend getting along with your friend?"

"Not just friend; Torrence, the provider of my video games," Bree said proudly.

Both Kayla and Torrence exchanged a little smile. Bree hadn't denied the girlfriend label, nor did she get flustered over it.

"Besides, she gets along with all my friends save for Ella, but I only talk to her online until I go back home for break." As Bree closed the video she realized that Kayla hadn't met Trey either, but Trey was too troublesome to introduce her love interests to.

"I suppose that's coming up soon, isn't it? Any big plans?" Torrence asked.

"Besides not telling my mother about my sexual preferences even if my brother thinks I should? Nope."

"Is your mother not accepting?" Kayla asked.

"My mother is religious," Bree said in response, as if that answered the question.

"That doesn't necessarily mean she won't be understanding..."

"I beg to differ. You haven't lived until you've ruined Thanksgiving and your grandparents condemn you to Hell." Torrence gave a solemn nod, speaking from experience.

"Was it before or after the meal?" Bree asked.

"Sadly, it was before. Couldn't even enjoy my aunt's mac and cheese, every forkful was met with judgment. *He even eats his food like a fag...*" then Torrence made a motion with his hand to imitate trying to eat his food. "I still don't know what that means."

"Ouch." Bree hadn't heard that story before. She didn't think her mother would be *that* judgmental, but still judgmental, nonetheless. "I'm sorry, Torrence."

Torrence shrugged his shoulders. "That was a long time ago, I'm over it."

"Well... in case you're not, we can always talk about it or something," Bree said.

"What, you mean hang out *outside* of the store?" Torrence took a moment to gesture around him. "Are you even capable of doing such a thing? You can't even go out on a date."

Kayla laughed as Bree gave Torrence a hard glare. "I WAS TRYING TO BE NICE!"

"I know. I'm cheering myself up at your expense," then Torrence plastered on a sweet smile. Bree was too cute when she was angry.

"You're such a dick," Bree declared before she turned and headed for the exit.

The smile on Torrence's face grew wider. "Awwwww, thank you!"

Bree wished she could perfect that intimidating look that Marianna had mastered. Instead, she looked like a grumpy five-year-old as she stormed out of the store. Kayla followed after her, waving to Torrence as she walked out the door. "It was your idea to go to the store," Kayla pointed out as they headed for the escalator.

"I know. I'm not *that* mad, but I can't tell him that. I have an image to keep, ya know?"

"Ah, of course." The two girls headed for the mall exit and Kayla immediately pulled her coat around her body. The store had been so warm that she'd forgotten how cold it was outside. Damn her need to look cute all the time, but there was no better combination with her boots than the skirt and small top she was wearing. "You know... I'm not sure if our relationship is serious enough to warrant telling your mother," Kayla said, using the conversation to take her mind off the weather.

"It probably isn't, but my brother is always pushing me to come out."

"He does realize that you have to do it when you feel comfortable, right?"

Bree nodded her head. "No, he gets that, I just don't think she'll ever understand. He's convinced she will."

"I suppose I'm pretty lucky, my dad was pretty understanding right off the bat. Told him when I was in high school."

"And he didn't flip out?"

Kayla shook her head as the two walked down the sidewalk toward a cluster of restaurants. Finally, they could do this whole *date* thing properly. "Well... he did think it was a phase, but he's gotten over that."

"And your mom?"

"Dunno, never got to tell her, she left when I was a kid."

"Oh... I'm sorry. If it makes you feel better my dad left..."

Kayla raised an eyebrow and asked, "How is that supposed to make me feel better?"

"You know, because I understand how you feel? Or something? Right? O-or was that colossal titan levels of stupid?"

"Colossal titan?"

"It's an anime reference. Titans are these giant beings that eat people."

"Yum," then Kayla licked her lips.

Bree was so fixated on Kayla that she almost walked into someone who had been walking on the other side of them. After a quick apology to the man she turned her attention back to Kayla. "Jesus Christ!" She was sure her mother wouldn't appreciate her using the Lord's name in vain, but Bree felt that He would make an exception this one time.

"What? It got you to stop being so nervous. I thought we were past the nerves at this point."

"Oh no, never. I'm gonna keep being nervous. It might calm down after the first kiss, I'm not sure."

"Is that an invitation?"

"I dunno... m-maybe?"

Kayla smirked at her, and suddenly, Bree could feel her heart racing. She hadn't meant to blurt out that whole kiss thing, but as Kayla leaned in she realized that it was working in her favor. Bree only had experience with one girl in her eighteen years of life, and that experience had been behind closed doors. The assumption with that girl had been that they were good friends, after all, girls always hugged and complimented each other, right? But this was different. This was out in the open where people could see them, and Kayla didn't seem to care at all. Bree liked the way that kind of freedom tasted, and she wanted more of it, so she closed her eyes and...

...got interrupted by Kayla's phone ringing.

It completely caught Bree off guard. If anyone was going to interrupt this, it would be one of her friends. She was the magical girl of the story, and that always dictated that interruptions be on her part. But nope, it was Kayla's phone ringing, and it was Kayla who was letting out an exasperated sigh before answering it. Bree watched the frustration mount on Kayla's face as she talked on the phone – something about a dancer calling in sick and needing someone to entertain a party of sorts.

Kayla rolled her eyes as she accepted the job. Extra money was nice, but kissing cute girls was much nicer. "Guess it's my turn to cut the date short," Kayla said as she put her phone back in her purse.

"One of us has to do it, right?"

"Someday we're gonna spend an entire evening together."

Bree smiled and decided to embrace the moment of bravery before it disappeared. It was a quick kiss, nothing real concrete to write home about, but it was enough to make her heart feel like it was going to erupt from her chest.

"Congratulations. You kissed a girl."

"I've kissed a girl before!"

"Out in public?"

"...stop teasing me, *Torrence*."

"Oh, sick burn," Kayla said with a laugh. "Still... it was a good kiss."

"Maybe we can do it again sometime?"

Kayla smiled. "How about when we have an actual, uninterrupted date?"

"Deal."

And that was that. Bree watched as Kayla turned and ran for the bus stop, barely managing to hop on before it pulled off. It was like a scene from a romance movie, the free-spirited love interest taking off in the sunset. Speaking of taking off, Bree decided that she should head home, too. There was nothing out here for her save for the memory of a brief kiss, and she could reflect on said memory in the warmth of her own bedroom. As Bree headed toward the bus stop she felt her phone vibrate inside her coat pocket. She pulled it out and chuckled when she saw Marianna's name appear. "Good timing," Bree said when she answered. "I was about to head home. My date got cut short."

"That's probably for the best. We have a situation."

Bree quickly looked around to make sure no one was close enough to hear her. "An attack?"

"Nothing has surfaced yet, but... something feels off."

Bree was about to ask for more details but then, in the distance, she could see that something was happening. It was like a scene from a video game or anime series. The clouds shifted to a dismal gray and Bree could feel a humid heat, her coat suddenly too warm due to the odd increase in temperature. There was an energy in the air, something foul and suffocating that made the breeze feel sticky. If she booked it now, she was sure she could make it to the energy source in a few minutes. "I'm close to whatever it is."

"I think I'm close, too. I'll call Lonnie."

"Got it."

Bree was starting to appreciate the large, bulbous monsters.

They, at least, made their presence known. They took up the sidewalks and indoor malls, making them easy to find and eliminate.

"Anything?" Marianna asked from the other end of the phone. She was a few blocks away from Bree, hoping to cover more ground that way.

"Not a thing," Bree said as she turned another corner. There were still people wandering around outside, commenting on the strange weather but deciding that it wasn't worth going inside for. Bree wanted to tell them to go home, but there wasn't anything to base that on save for a *bad feeling*.

"Ladies. I think I see something," Lonnie said. She had taken a spot on the rooftop of a building, trying to look over the city for any hint of trouble. There was an ugly mass of energy a few blocks away, as if the gross heat was coming together to center on one focal point.

"Where?" Marianna asked.

"Toward Main Street. There's a cluster of energy… and it's getting larger."

Marianna looked ahead. The street wasn't too far from where she was. "Let's meet up there," then she took off running. As she got closer she could see people running toward her, trying to get away from whatever had decided to linger around Main Street. At least she knew she was going in the right direction.

"What the hell…"

Marianna stopped when she heard Bree on the other end of the phone. "What's wrong?"

"The sidewalk is covered in filth," Bree said. She'd started running, too, but she ended up stepping in a pile of what smelled like rotten eggs. It reminded her of the creature they'd faced at the bakery, only it was gray and smelled much worse. Whatever it was, there was a trail of it, and it was leading toward the street Lonnie had mentioned. "This is really gross."

"I'm almost there," Marianna said.

"Me too," Lonnie added.

Marianna arrived first, just in time to see what looked like a shapeless mass of gunk crawl through the city. Not just through it, but over things – trash cans, traffic lights, cars. Bree arrived next, followed by Lonnie, and the three watched as everything it touched was absorbed into its body. "Is it… eating?" Bree asked.

Marianna didn't answer right away. Instead she watched and tried to figure out what was going on. Her eyes widened and she let out a horrified gasp when she realized what was happening. It wasn't just eating. "It's growing."

In seconds, the murky gray matter doubled in size, then tripled, and began to harden and form into something out of a nightmare. To say that it had become as big as the tallest skyscrapers in the city would be an over exaggeration... but not by much. It was a big, meaty thing, with grayish-blue skin, sharp claws, and way too many teeth. Its tail looked especially threatening as it whipped around and cut through a building like butter.

"Holy shit." In the ring, size didn't matter. The bigger they were, the harder they fell, as they say. Lonnie always saw it firsthand whenever tiny little Kendra took on anyone, and whether Kendra realized it or not, she was an inspiration.

That being said... Lonnie had never seen anything this big and it had happened in mere seconds. If they didn't do something now, there was no telling how large it would get.

Marianna took a look around to make sure that no one was around. The area looked clear – small miracles, she guessed. "Shall we, ladies?" Marianna asked as she forced herself to swallow the hint of hesitation in her voice. Bree and Lonnie both nodded in agreement, then all three young ladies took deep breaths before speaking the words.

"galactic purple rise up!"

"cosmic green press start!"

"radical rainbow let's kick it!"

For a moment, the bleak and gray area was lit up in bright colors. Each of their tools snapped apart, the pieces surrounding them and giving off the energy needed for them to transform. Their clothes dissolved into the sparkles as their outfits materialized onto their bodies, their hair shifting to purple, green, and multi-colored braids.

There wasn't time to stand around once the glitter and sparkles finished their job. The gruesome creature immediately set its sights on the three of them and swiped its claws into the air, the movement so swift that a gust of wind came rushing toward them. They moved quickly, each one jumping in three different directions, hoping to divert its attention. The plan worked and the creature looked confused for a moment, then decided that green was a more noticeable color. Cosmic Green jumped around enough to dodge its attacks, its claws scraping across the pavement and cutting into traffic lights instead of hitting her.

"cupcake bomb!"

Cosmic Green rolled out of the way as a wave of purple cupcakes were launched at the monster. They splattered onto its arm and created a mess of purple, Galactic Purple waiting for the acidic frosting to do its job before the inevitable explosion.

Nothing happened.

The girls watched as the frosting and cake combination sat there, the creature letting out an almost amused growl. Soon, the dessert dissolved into its skin, its arm growing thicker with purplish, throbbing veins. "What just happened?" Galactic Purple took a step back. That had never happened before.

"It… absorbed…" Cosmic Green shook her head. She'd seen this attack numerous times. There was supposed to be an explosion big enough to, at least, blow off the creature's arm.

"Watch out!"

Cosmic Green was broken out of her shock by Radical Rainbow's yell. The green haired magical girl barely managed to roll out of the way of another attack, then she pushed herself up and kept moving. She managed to duck inside a building just as the claws were coming toward her. She could hear them scratch the glass doors, then she had seconds to run for the stairs as the monster balled up its fist and punched through the glass to try and get to her.

Galactic Purple launched another round of cupcakes, this time at the huge tail. The tail reacted as if it had a mind of its own and cut through the cupcakes, causing pieces of them to land on the ground near its feet and explode in spectacularly ineffective fireworks. The beast didn't even bother turning its attention toward her, instead, its tail rushed forward, Galactic Purple jumping away from it and watching as the pointy tip stabbed into the ground hard enough to crack the sidewalk. She knew the cupcakes wouldn't work, but she'd hoped that they'd distract it enough to turn away from the building where Cosmic Green had gone.

But it was waiting and ready as she ran onto the roof.

Cosmic Green only had a few seconds to react and quickly held her hands out. Green, square bits surrounded her to protect her as those vicious claws sought her out again. The claws scraped against her green energy, putting a dent into the squares and causing some of them to disintegrate, leaving her open.

"**CUP. CAKE. BOMB!**" Another swarm of cupcakes, but this time they exploded just before they hit their target. This got the creature's attention and it whipped its head around to look down at Galactic Purple. It stomped its foot into the ground, the force so strong that the buildings around it rumbled in protest as the street buckled and cracked. Galactic Purple only had time to raise her arms up to try and protect herself from the harsh gust of wind that smacked into her. She tried to stay standing, but she was sent flying backward, her body slamming into one of the abandoned cars on the road.

"Oh, you are so DEAD!" Then Cosmic Green screamed, "**8-BITS and PIECES!**"

Down below, Radical Rainbow was helping Galactic Purple regain her footing. "It's strong," Galactic Purple warned her teammate.

"Yeah, got it," Radical Rainbow said with a nod. The two girls watched as Cosmic Green's pixels blasted into the creature's back like the square bullets of an old Atari game. They were chipping away at its skin, slowly, but surely. Before it could refocus its attention on Cosmic Green, Radical Rainbow ran forward and delivered a swift kick to its knee, trying to knock it off balance. It let out a sharp cry and stumbled, but didn't fall, a rainbow colored bruise left in its skin as Radical Rainbow prepared to hit it again.

"It's working," Cosmic Green shouted down to the girls as she kept her attacking going, the bits of power raining over their opponent's back. The roar that bubbled out of its throat was loud enough to make the windows in the buildings around it shake. Galactic Purple quietly shook

her head. That wasn't a sound of pain from their foe… it was one of annoyance.

They weren't hurting it at all.

"Get out of there!"

But it was too late. Its foot moved so fast that Radical Rainbow didn't even have a chance to try and guard the attack. She was kicked away as if the large creature were swatting at a fly. Cosmic Green prepared to continue her bullet hell assault, energy right at her fingertips. Before she could do anything the enemy's tail twitched and twisted up like a hungry snake ready to strike its prey. The end of the tail split apart, the gray, smelly ooze from before pussing out like a popped pimple. The gray skin rolled back to expose two curved claws similar to a scorpion as the creature whipped its tail, the two blades detaching and whistling through the air straight at Cosmic Green. Cosmic Green stumbled back with a small cry, holding her hands out as a wall of green pixels barely managed to grow around her in time. There was a loud crack as the two claws embedded themselves in the sheer green bricks. Cosmic Green couldn't remember how to breathe as she scrambled backward, the wall fading away and the skin on the tail rolling back to reveal another blade, almost ready to throw.

"Hey asshole!" Despite having been kicked across the sidewalk Radical Rainbow was on the move, running at the monster with nothing but anger and adrenaline. The monster stepped toward her, its blades gleaming and eager to cut into her, but soon there was frosting smeared across its eyes from Galactic Purple throwing more cupcakes. As the two girls distracted it, Cosmic Green decided to head to the door to the roof to meet with them down below. Suddenly, her legs felt weak, a wave of dizziness sending her down to her knees. She looked down at her hands to see a nasty cut. She hadn't even realized she'd been hit by one of those blades when she'd tried to protect herself. Cosmic Green tried to shake it off and stand, but the movement made her feel woozy. She winced and looked down at the cut again, her eyes widening as she saw the gray, murky gunk around the edges of her skin.

Down below, she watched as the monster held its hand out in the same way she had done, a green energy humming around its gray skin. "N-no…" she tried to yell down to the girls but it hurt to talk, her throat feeling like it was coated with needles. She forced herself to ignore the pain and screamed, "That's cheating! It's going to-"

Before she could finish, large, pixelated squares were sent after Radical Rainbow. The kickboxer stopped in her tracks and quickly jumped away, the bits of energy breaking into tiny squares when they hit the ground. Instead of backing down, Radical Rainbow took a moment to punch her fist into the palm of her hand, her fist emitting the same rainbow glow that enveloped her anklet. "**Rainbow Rush!**" A wave of colorful energy followed her like the wind as she dodged the creature's stolen attacks and set her sights on its split tail. If she could hit it hard enough there was a chance she could stop it from gaining more power. When she got close the tail zipped after her, both pieces coming from opposite directions. Radical Rainbow rolled out of the way of both of them and went after the base of the tail, hammering it with a combination of punches and kicks. The rainbow colors spread across the tail until the monster stumbled away, the separated pieces coming back together and rushing after Radical Rainbow.

While this was going on, Galactic Purple had made it inside the building where Cosmic Green was. Her heels frantically clicked up the stairs as she rushed to the roof. When she got there, she saw Bree laid out on the ground. She'd been drained so much that her magical clothes had faded away, leaving her to rest in a pile of pixel blocks that were disintegrating around her. "Bree!"

Bree lifted her head up when she heard Galactic Purple screaming her name. She looked down at her injured hand and grimaced. Her skin almost looked like it had molded and smelled just as rotten as the creature. When Galactic Purple knelt down in front of her she shook her head and whispered, "Don't worry about me." She felt sick to her stomach and she really wanted to curl up in a soft bed and sleep, but she couldn't tell Galactic Purple that. If she did, her purple haired comrade would focus too much on her when there was a bigger problem to face. "Go help Radical Rainbow."

"But-"

"Go!" Bree watched as Galactic Purple reluctantly nodded her head and leapt off the building. Bree took a couple of deep breaths and told herself to stand back up, but the coldness of the roof below her was so inviting.

It wouldn't hurt to close her eyes for a little while, right?

On the ground below, Radical Rainbow was still busy dodging the creature's tail, waiting for an opening where she could strike back at it. Finally, she decided to throw caution to the wind and punched the sharp piece as it came at her. Her fist managed to put a rainbow colored crack in it, which only served to anger the fearsome monster and send it into a frenzy. Suddenly, there were sharp claws gripping onto Radical Rainbow's hair. She let out a harsh cry as she was slammed down to the ground by her hair, her head hitting the concrete hard enough for her to see spots.

"cupcake Bomb!!!"

Galactic Purple's cry was laced with desperation and anger. Instead of hitting the creature's hand, she aimed for its claws, watching as they broke apart from the impact of the mini-explosion. Radical Rainbow rolled away as soon as her hair was free and forced herself to stand back up, only to be smacked by the back of the thing's hand and sent skidding across the ground. That left Galactic Purple alone with the looming threat as it reached out and grabbed her with the hand that had the now broken claws. She squirmed against it and screamed in protest as she was pressed down onto the concrete.

Radical Rainbow stood up and winced when she felt the pain in her arm. Her skin felt like it was on fire from where it scraped into the pavement, blood starting to escape the cuts. Just like when she was in the ring, she made a conscious effort to ignore the pain. The one thing she couldn't ignore – beyond Galactic Purple's screaming – was the lack of rainbow colors around her. At some point she'd reverted back to her normal state, and she felt far less powerful than she had been before. Had she really been hit so hard that she de-transformed?

Well, did she ever have a surprise for that son of a bitch.

"Hey!" Lonnie shouted at the monster. When it turned its attention toward her she made a grand show of cracking her knuckles as she stepped forward, inviting its next strike. The creature took the hint and let Galactic Purple go. Lonnie noticed that she wasn't transformed anymore, either, as she curled up on the ground in an attempt to remember how to breathe, cupcake frosting crackling at her fingertips before it dissolved in the air. Lonnie took a deep breath and got in a fighting stance. "Let's go," she hissed, and the creature charged forward.

"N-no," Marianna whispered as she tried to stand up. Her entire body protested at her moving, but there was no way she could let Lonnie do this alone. "No!" She hit her wrist against the ground, her bracelet clanking against it. "Galactic Purple Rise Up," she cried out. When nothing happened she hit her wrist against the ground again. "Rise Up!" Marianna could feel her throat getting hoarse from how loudly she was screaming, but now wasn't the time to think about that. Right now, Lonnie needed her, and it was absolute torture to not be able to do anything to help. "Rise Up!!!"

Nothing.

Marianna lowered her head as her tears landed on the ground beneath her. This was what they were supposed to do, what she'd been doing for months, what she'd defied her mother about before she set off to prove how necessary magical girls like her were. They were supposed to deal with threats like this. This was their job as magical girls. While Marianna knew better than to assume that they'd always win...

...weren't they always supposed to win?

To her credit, Lonnie was dodging the attacks, but her arm hurt like hell and her legs were getting tired. She was trying to find any weak spots, throwing punches and kicks when she could and ignoring the pain of hitting the solid, gray mass head on. A punch in the arm as its fist barely missed her. A kick in the knee, no matter how feeble it was. Deep down, she knew she wouldn't be able to last much longer, but she wasn't going to give up. Maybe she could buy enough time for the other girls to recover. Maybe they could find the strength to transform again and finish this thing off. In the distance she caught a glimpse of Marianna trying to get her bracelet to work. If Lonnie could keep at it, she knew Marianna would be able to transform.

Sadly, she didn't have that much time. Her lungs were burning and her moves were getting sloppier with every second. Lonnie finally stumbled and the creature was quick to take advantage of the situation. If Lonnie had to equate the hit to something, she imagined it was like being rammed into by a giant wrecking ball. She hit the ground, hard, and it took everything in her power to not fall into unconsciousness. She could hear Marianna screaming her name but it sounded so far away, like a distant echo at the end of a tunnel. Lonnie's vision was blurry, but she could make out the creature's foot hovering above her.

This was it.

This was the end.

She'd only been part of the group for a week and it was about to be over with just a stomp of a monstrous foot.

"Guess it was fun while it lasted," Lonnie said softly. She almost wanted it to be quick so she wouldn't have to lay here, body aching and voice cracking as she reflected on the situation. She wanted to tell Marianna to stop crying because she knew the girl was going to blame herself for this. She'd been so persistent about Lonnie joining that she'd most definitely shoulder the blame. She wanted to tell Bree to stay down, but she knew that when the girl regained consciousness she'd try to avenge her – or something along those lines. She wanted to tell Raye to not be angry with Blaze, but she knew she would be. Lonnie had chosen this and, in hindsight, she'd probably do it again – maybe even be more agreeable. As she closed her eyes she smiled to herself. At least she'd gotten to tell Rodney. At least she'd gotten to see Braydon and Kendra together. And while she didn't get to tell her grandmother, she at least got to hear her berate her over the phone for not calling in a timely manner and...

...why wasn't she being stomped on?

Lonnie blinked in confusion as she watched the large monster struggle against something. She squinted to try and make out what it was, but her head felt like it was swimming through a muddy swamp as she tried to get her eyes to focus. Soon, she could feel someone gently shaking her shoulder. Lonnie looked over to see a fuzzy image of Marianna kneeling next to her. "Hey you," then she winced, feeling the sharp prickling in her throat.

"Hey," Marianna whispered back, her cheeks wet from crying. "This is a stupid question... but how are you doing?"

"There's two of you... but it's slowly fading to one."

Marianna smiled a little but her eyes were watering again. "I was worried about you."

"I'll be honest, I was worried, too." Speaking of which, her attacker still hadn't done anything. Both Lonnie and Marianna looked up to see that the monster was still struggling against something. After taking a few slow breaths, Lonnie raised her hand so Marianna could help her stand up, the taller girl leaning on Marianna for support. Now that the world had stopped spinning they could both see what looked like thin, pink thread wrapped tightly around the creature's raised leg.

"Who's doing that?" Marianna asked.

"Up here!"

At best, the girls expected to see Bree standing on top of the crumbled building several feet above them, completely conscious and ready to jump into battle again. But last time they checked she was still knocked out and her powers didn't involve bright pink threads. Seeing Blaze would've been a surprise, but it would've made more sense than seeing the stunning young lady in pink. Despite the dismal setting, the mystery girl managed to shine through it all with a gentle smile, glasses, and cute freckles scattered across her face. As her pink and blue hair flowed in the wind, they could see her holding the threads that were keeping the creature from going after them. The girl let out a happy little giggle and tugged on the threads, hard. Marianna and Lonnie watched as the monster let out a startled growl and fell to the ground.

Huh. Apparently, there was a glasses wearing magical girl who was strong enough to make a giant monster topple over. Good to know.

The girls covered their ears from the sound of the loud crash and were thankful that no one was in the creature's way. The same couldn't be said for the traffic lights and the few cars that had been abandoned by people who had run off.

The sound made Bree's eyes snap open from where she was still laying on the roof. She couldn't remember how long she'd been out, in fact, she could barely remember where she was. As she sat up and looked around it all started to come back to her. She had been in the middle of a fight and things weren't going well. Galactic Purple had come to check on her, but Bree had insisted that she keep fighting. And now? Now there was some new girl standing at the edge of the building where she had been laying, armed with sparkles and confidence. The girl was moving her hands in the air, her fingers moving in an almost rhythmic motion. Pink threads moved through the sky and around buildings to tie the frightening beast down to the ground in an attempt to keep it still. Bree slowly stood up, hand still throbbing as she cautiously approached the girl. "Um..."

The young woman turned to look at her, adjusted her glasses, and smiled. "Are you all right?"

"I... y-yeah, I-"

"Oh my goodness, look at your hand! Let me help with that."

Bree tried to speak again. "I..." but she didn't get a chance, the girl carefully taking her hand and holding her other hand over it. The pink threads moved over the wound, actually stitching it shut with cool, pink energy.

"There, that'll do for now."

"Thank you... where are my friends?"

"Down below."

Bree walked over to the edge of the roof to see Marianna and Lonnie standing several feet away from the monster. At least the two of them were okay, at least, for now. "How long can you keep it pinned down like that?"

"Probably a few more seconds."

"W-what?" But the girl was right. The threads were already snapping loose, Marianna and Lonnie slowly backing away. "Shit! We have to-"

"Calm down," then the new girl smiled at her. "I was just warmin' up. Besides, if we work together we can definitely finish the job."

Who in the world was this girl?! The three of them had been struggling during this entire battle. Now there was a new magical girl who'd managed to knock this monster right on its back, tie it down, and heal her hand. It occurred to Bree that she should've been voicing her questions out loud, but before she could, the final threads broke apart and the bulking monstrosity was back on its feet. "Oh god..."

"Don't worry, we've got this," then the girl leapt into the air and actually landed on the creature's shoulder.

Lonnie's eyes widen and she shouted, "What the hell are you doing?!" Normally, Marianna would've been the one to voice any concerns, but Lonnie's body was still throbbing from that thing's attacks. Whoever this girl was, she needed to know what she was jumping into before she ended up as badly hurt as they all were.

But the girl just smiled and said, "Giving you an advantage," then she shouted the words, "**sewn together symmetry!**"

Everyone watched as the pink threads wove together to create a thick cloth around the creature's eyes and mouth. There was a loud growl of protest, but the girl pulled the threads as hard as she could, blocking the creature's sight and forcing its mouth to stay wide open. How she was standing strong on that thing's shoulder was beyond comprehension, but one thing was clear: they could attack it full force now.

But would it be enough?

They'd tried before and all three of them had ended up beaten to the point of losing hold of their powers. The cosmic colors were gone and they were left standing as normal girls faced with a daunting task. Perhaps this was the one that would be too much for them. Perhaps this was proof that they weren't nearly as ready as they thought they were.

"Screw it," Lonnie said as she pulled away from Marianna to limp toward the creature. She'd dealt with blows like this before – a lie, of course, since the ring never had a building-sized monster in it. However, if she kept telling herself that lie, her steps wouldn't be as hesitant. "We have to at least try."

"Lonnie!"

"We knew what we were signing up for," Lonnie said in response to Marianna's cry. "This is what it means to be a magical girl."

"We don't even have our powers anymore!"

"Bullshit we don't!" Lonnie snapped, her voice weary as she made herself push through the pain. "They're inside of us, right? That's what you told me before!" To be fair she hadn't believed it before. She'd chalked it up as one of those after school special speeches that were required at the end of the episode. But as she walked forward she swore she felt her anklet grow warmer. She'd run out of power, right? There wasn't anything left for her to give save for a dose of determination. But maybe, just maybe, that was enough to march onward.

Marianna tried to plead with Lonnie and shouted, "It's not working! Lonnie… please stop!"

"Then we make it work!" This single phrase was the slogan to the life of Lonnie Knox and it was time to dig deep and take those words to heart. So Lonnie slammed her foot down onto the pavement and shouted, "**Radical Rainbow! Let's Kick It!**"

Lonnie could feel the power swelling up inside of her as the colors exploded around her. Her anklet snapped apart and the pieces circled around her the way they were supposed to. She knew she hadn't transformed as many times as the other girls, but this time felt different. The rainbow colors had never felt so intense before, not even when she'd faced off against Jeremy to protect her trainers and her friends. There was something rippling inside her, something that was making those magical clothes shine brighter, the colors vibrant in each strand of her braided hair. Suddenly, she felt like she could do this.

No, *they* could do this.

Together.

The mysterious magical girl smiled before she pulled harder on her threads and said, "Ladies! I could use some help!"

Bree had seen this scenario so many times before, only those times were from the safety of her computer screen and Crunchyroll subscription. She'd watched the heroes who walked into a hopeless situation, fueled by determination and a need to prove themselves. Generally, it worked out for them, but there was a huge difference between anime and real life. Then again... she did live in a world where she could use green pixels as a weapon. She also lived in a world where an entire city was depending on her and, once upon a time, she'd been willing to jump off of a building for it.

It wasn't a matter of *could*, but a matter of *must*. They *had* to do this. So they, most certainly, would. They'd come out victorious and Bree would go back to worrying about visiting her mother... which didn't seem too bad, all things considered.

"cosmic green. press start!"

There was a warm sensation that washed over her body before her bow broke apart. It was as if Bree hadn't been drained of her powers at all, the bow pieces swirling around her body. The green and black outfit was back, complete with cosmic stars lining her hair and skirt. Bree looked down at her clothes in surprise. She hadn't expected it to work, to be honest. She'd felt so weak earlier, but now her exhaustion felt like an afterthought, giving way to that fabled second wind.

Maybe Lonnie was right. Maybe they did have a chance now.

"Mari! Come on!"

Marianna looked down at the bracelet around her wrist. It was scuffed up from how hard she'd been hitting it against the pavement before. She knew what she had to do, but the logical part of her brain was making her second guess herself. They'd already tried before, could they – *should they* – go at it again? As Marianna watched Radical Rainbow and Cosmic Green jump into action she knew the answer to that, and honestly, she wouldn't have it any other way. She chose to wear this bracelet, and now, she had to believe in herself and use it. The power came from the hands that wore the bracelet, not the jewelry itself.

"galactic purple. Rise up!"

It was amazing that everything was happening so easily now. She'd been trying so hard earlier, and her throat still felt raw from all the screaming. But now she was transforming like she normally did, shattered bracelet sparkling in fragments of purple as her power washed away the fatigue and pain like dishes in a fresh sink. She was Galactic Purple again. She knew she had a job to do and she was ready for the next round.

As the cloth was pulled tighter around the creature's eyes and mouth its tail reared up, ready to attack the girl in pink. "Oh no you don't," Galactic Purple whispered before she turned her attention to Cosmic Green. "Blast the tail!"

"You got it," then Cosmic Green jumped into the air, the familiar green bits of power blipping into existence around her hand. Part of her wasn't sure if it would be enough, but the other part focused on the powerful warmth and shouted, "**8-Bits and pieces!**" She didn't remember the attack shooting from her hand so quickly before, but in mere seconds it was blasting into the monster's tail. The sharp piece that had been cracked by Radical Rainbow actually broke apart, pixeled

328 – Briana Lawrence

bits dropping to the ground. The rest of the tail didn't fair much better, chunks of it being blasting off and littering the street around it.

The thick, gray pieces melted back into the black gunk from before, the slimy substance trying to inch its way back over toward the damaged tail. Galactic Purple responded by tossing one of her cupcakes into it, watching as the absorbent goo tried to devour the explosive treat. The blast actually did some damage this time, leaving behind a mess of frosting and foul smelling residue like the stuff that clogged drains.

The creature's movements were becoming more frantic as it reached up to try and swat the new magical girl off of its shoulder. With a loud shout of, "**CUPCAKE BOMB**," Galactic Purple didn't give it a chance. A wave of purple energy formed into a dozen miniature cupcakes, each one slamming into its wrist. There was a loud, satisfying BOOM as she watched the monster's wrist break apart. Before its hand could hit the ground, Cosmic Green blasted it to bits, then manipulated the swarm of green toward the creature's leg. Galactic Purple used her cupcakes at the same time, their powers combining into a magical array of green and purple that shredded into its leg until all that remained was a shriveled stump that couldn't hold the creature's weight. The thread using magical girl kept her balance as their opponent came crashing down to the ground, falling flat on its stomach. She pulled the cloth away just in time for Radical Rainbow to unleash a full-on attack.

The kickboxer hit their nemesis right in its teeth, splatters of rainbow cracking them and bursting through its cheeks. She thought she'd gained a rush of power when she transformed for the first time, back when she'd faced off against Jeremy, but this was in a league of its own. If she wanted to, she could keep punching and kicking the creature until rainbow bruises and dents were scattered all over its face.

So she did just that.

"**Rainbow Rush!**"

Radical Rainbow was relentless in her attack and soon all the monster could do was let out low, pathetic moans of pain. The other girls would've felt bad for the creature had it not destroyed part of the city and nearly killed them. Radical Rainbow hadn't been in many battles with the girls, but she couldn't deal with the fact that they'd almost lost – worst, *died*. Deep down she knew that it was completely illogical to believe that they were invincible, but to her, this was different from being in the ring. In the ring, she knew she had limits, but as a magical girl, she was supposed to be able to exceed them.

Radical Rainbow felt a gentle hand on her shoulder and finally stopped hitting the creature. Its skin was covered in distorted colors, eyes swollen shut and cheeks caved in as a pool of the black ooze dripped from its lips like blood. She looked over to see the new magical girl smiling at her before she said, "I think you've made your point."

Radical Rainbow took a deep breath and stepped away from the now unconscious beast, Galactic Purple and Cosmic Green joining her. Now that the monster was out of commission there was something else to discuss. All three girls looked at the new girl in front of them but Radical Rainbow was the first to address her. "Who are you?"

"The name's Prism Pink," she said. "Nice to meet ya."

"Likewise," Cosmic Green said, after all, the girl had basically saved their lives.

Galactic Purple, on the other hand, was a bit more skeptical. "Where did you come from? Why haven't we seen you before?" She'd assumed that they were the only ones. It had never occurred to her that there may have been more magical girls out there. She knew a little bit about the group Blaze had been a part of, but this girl didn't appear to be Blaze's age. Did Blaze know about her? Did Blaze create her? Was it safe for this *Prism Pink* to know who they really were? She'd watched them transform the second time around and, in the heat of the moment, Marianna hadn't thought of the repercussions of transforming in front of someone she didn't know.

Prism Pink did at least answer one of her questions. "You all had things under control up until this point. When I saw the damage this thing was doing I had to help."

"So you've been watching us?" Cosmic Green asked.

"Kinda, though to be honest, everyone in this city knows who you are."

"So... what happens now?" Radical Rainbow asked.

"Well now I-" But before she could finish her sentence the girls heard a low, weak growl behind them. They all turned to see the creature actually pushing itself up so it could try and stand. There was a trail of that black ooze pooled around its leg, quietly absorbing the debris around it to make its leg stronger. "Guess I'll be answering that question later," Prism Pink said.

Galactic Purple nodded. First, they'd have to get rid of that grotesque slim so that it couldn't absorb anything else, and they'd have to do it fast. She could already see its claws regrowing along with that damn tail. "You ladies ready?" She asked. The answer was *no* but none of them wanted to admit it. They knew it wouldn't matter. This monster wasn't going to cut them some slack because they'd fought so hard and needed a moment to breathe. So everyone nodded. This was what they were here for. They had to take this thing down because there was no one else who could.

Or so they thought.

Suddenly, its skin erupted into hot, blazing flames, the putrid black substance igniting and spreading the fire all around it. All four girls backed away as the creature let out a phenomenal roar as more parts of its body erupted into fire. The group looked at one another, uncertain of who was causing the violent attack. It was Galactic Purple who caught sight of their very own leader standing several feet behind them, dressed in a long coat with a top hat, her piercing eyes looking dead at the monstrosity in front of them. Blaze had her hand pushed out as she clenched it into a fist. That movement made the fire spread all over the large creature until all that remained was a pile of dark ashes.

It was in that moment that Galactic Purple, Cosmic Green, and Radical Rainbow remembered a few things. Blaze had been a part of **magnifiquenoir** before, which implied that she'd seen her fair share of battles. It also meant that she had abilities of her own, and judging by her name, those abilities were most likely fire-based. That being said... none of them expected her powers to be so devastating. Sure, there'd been hints here and there, but this? They'd struggled so much against this creature, but Blaze made it look as easy as a tutorial fight.

"I suppose I'm not needed after all."

The girls turned in time to see Prism Pink smile and wave to the three of them before she jumped into the air. Radical Rainbow was the first to react and shouted, "Wait! Where are you going?!" There were still so many questions they wanted answered, and while Blaze's heroics had been impressive, to Radical Rainbow, it was this woman in pink who was the most remarkable. A leader saving her team was to be somewhat expect, but this new magical girl had come out of nowhere to help. That meant so much more.

Prism Pink gracefully landed on the building she'd been standing on earlier and smiled down at Radical Rainbow and the other girls. "Don't worry, ladies. If you need me I'll be around," and just like that she was gone, leaping across the cityscape, her hair shimmering and flowing around her.

"Are you girls all right?"

Everyone turned toward Blaze, her face no longer holding that hard edge it had during the battle. Though was it really fair to call it a *battle* when she'd ended it so quickly? Galactic Purple nodded her head and said, "We're fine, but you didn't have to-"

"Stop," Blaze said as she shook her head. "Did you really think I wouldn't help you if things got too rough?"

FiNAL BATTLE
Musetap Studios • www.musetapstudios.com
Radiant Grey • radiant-grey.deviantart.com

"But we're supposed to be the ones who–"

"And you wouldn't be able to continue to be *the ones* if you were killed," then Blaze added, "I care about you all too much to lose any of you."

There was something in her voice, something painful and tragic. Galactic Purple wanted to ask but she also didn't want to be that cruel. Leader or not, Blaze needed to share things at her own pace. For now all that mattered was that she was here for them and she always would be.

And apparently... so would Prism Pink.

SEASON FiNALE:

BREAK

"What are you doing for Thanksgiving break?"

"Sleeping. Lots of sleeping. Then eating. Lots and lots of eating."

"Mmmmm, I can't wait to get to the eating part. I need some of my mom's mac and cheese."

"I'll see your mac and cheese and raise you some collard greens."

"Girl. Yes."

Lonnie quietly listened to the girls in class that morning as everyone waited for their professor to show up. This was the exact conversation she had been looking forward to now that Thanksgiving break was upon them. Some people enjoyed Christmas decorations and eggnog, but Lonnie counted down to the day she could bask in her grandmother's cooking.

Sadly, none of that seemed relevant.

The attack from last week was something the city was still recovering from. There were plenty of buildings in disrepair and roads closed until further notice. The day after the attack city officials had decided to invest in some kind of alarm system. This led to all kinds of piercingly loud tests with tornado sirens and various news stories on *proper procedures*. What Lonnie had wanted to do was show up at the Channel 5 newsroom as Radical Rainbow and tell them to do what they always did – run and hide. Of course, she wasn't allowed to do that sort of thing.

Funny how all that precaution still hadn't been enough to shut down campus, not even for a day. All it had done was make the commute unbearably long. Some professors had even cancelled their lectures. Lucky for Lonnie – question mark – this class was still in session. It wasn't the paranoid mayor, law enforcement, and extra hour it took to get to campus that bothered Lonnie… it was the fact that no one around her was really talking about it.

As soon as the attack had happened, you couldn't go anywhere without hearing about the outrageous fight between **magnifiquenoir** and the city-sized monster. Now? It was business as usual with people making plans for the holiday break and ignoring the new alarm tests. It was ironic, Lonnie thought, that she'd been so ready for people to stop talking about her bravery back when she'd took on that creature in the mall. Now all she wanted was to discuss what she'd gone through last week.

Or rather… a *very specific* part of the battle.

"The name's Prism Pink. Nice to meet ya."

Lonnie covered her face with her hands and took a deep breath. No matter how hard she tried she couldn't get that girl out of her mind. Was this going to be a regular thing now? Cute girls appearing out of nowhere to help them in the middle of intense battles? Not just cute girls, *strong* cute girls who made monster slaying look effortless.

Huh.

Was this how Marianna and Bree had felt when she'd defeated the threat at the mall?

"What's her name?"

"Huh?" Lonnie looked up as Kayla sat next to her. "You're late."

"Nope. Mr. Carlson still ain't here. I'm right on time," Kayla said as she took off her jacket and hung it across the back of her chair.

"Guess that attack last week has helped with your attendance record," Lonnie chuckled. Wait, did she just make a joke about the situation? No wonder people had moved on so quickly.

"Hey, I'm not late on purpose. I had a late night."

"This is why you and Bree are perfect for each other." Not that Bree ran late to things – she preferred sleeping in class, according to Marianna.

"I see you trying to mention my future wife to distract me. I'll allow it."

Bree would be thrilled at the title of *future wife*, but Lonnie had a feeling if she told her, the poor girl would melt into a magical pile of goo. "Not trying to distract you, just making conversation. If you must know I'm not thinking about a girl." That was only a partial lie, but Kayla didn't need to know that. "Just... thinking about the holidays."

"Ah. Do you have a crappy family?"

"No. Well... there's some people I could do without," Lonnie muttered, remembering a particular set of cousins and their enabler parents. "But my Grand-Penny is awesome."

"So what's the problem? Is the food not good?"

Lonnie smirked with an air of overconfidence. "Oh no, the food is on point. My grandma starts cooking on Wednesday. *Tuesday* if she decides to go all out on desserts. She's got the best sweet potato pie in the neighborhood."

Kayla let out a longing sigh. "I miss sweet potato pie so much. Pumpkin just doesn't compare, you know?"

Lonnie looked appalled at the mention of a pie that wasn't her precious sweet potato. "Why the hell are you eating pumpkin pie?"

"It's what my dad's family makes."

"...why? That's so..."

"White?"

Lonnie didn't want to say it, but since Kayla had spoken the word she decided that it was okay to nod in agreement.

"The pleasures of having an interracial family," Kayla said.

"I didn't want to assume…"

"Thanks for that. I already get enough 'what you mixed with' questions, or comments about *passing*…" Kayla's annoyance over the subject was obvious in her exhausted tone of voice.

"Is that just from dumb customers when you're dancing?"

"And the occasional overzealous classmate." Kayla nodded toward the back of the classroom where some guy wasn't even trying to hide that he was staring at her.

"Ugh. Do they actually think that works?" Lonnie asked.

"*They*? God Lonnie, you're so *lez*."

Lonnie nearly choked on her laughter as she lightly punched Kayla in her arm. "Let's get back on the topic at hand."

"Which one? Your holiday woes or my white Thanksgiving?" Kayla made a grand show of rubbing her arm where Lonnie had hit her.

"I didn't hit you that hard!" Lonnie was loud enough for the entire class to look back at her. She gave them all an embarrassed smile before she turned her attention to Kayla again. "I don't know what Bree sees in you."

"I'm cute. Duh."

"Whatever," but Lonnie knew she was right. "Anyhow, your white Thanksgiving. I'm sure it's not *that* bad, right?"

"Naw. Fortunately my dad takes us to the person in the family who can cook. I'm convinced every white family has that one aunt who can throw down in the kitchen. My dad used to try and do it himself. It was a spectacular failure."

"Why don't y'all just let your mom cook? Or... is she a bad cook? That happens, you know? Bree can barely boil water."

"Seriously?"

"I'm pretty sure that's why she and Marianna are friends..."

Kayla smiled a sad little smile as she shook her head. "I don't know what kind of cook my mom is cuz she's been gone since I was a kid."

"Oh. I'm sorry, I didn't mean-"

But Kayla waved it off and said, "No worries. It was gonna come up eventually. Holiday season and all. I'm over it, though."

Lonnie had a feeling she wasn't, but she wasn't going to pry. Instead she said, "So if your dad can't cook how did you have sweet potato pie?"

"Old girlfriend. Went to her Thanksgiving. It was like a religious awakening." Kayla sighed a happy little sigh as she closed her eyes and reminisced about the taste of that pie.

Lonnie smiled and said, "That'll do it."

"So... you gonna finally tell me what's buggin' ya? I opened up and everything so it's your turn."

"Yeah yeah." The problem was Lonnie couldn't figure out how to explain it without blabbing about the whole thing. At the same time, it would be good to discuss her feelings with someone who wasn't directly involved. Marianna and Bree were in the same position as her, especially since the one person they all wanted to talk to had gone completely silent.

"Did you send that girl?" Marianna asked.

Blaze shook her head. They were back home now, all in her chambers and trying to settle down after the battle.

"So there's another girl out there." Bree's voice was full of wonder, as if she'd discovered some secret character in a fighting game.

"Prism Pink. She said her name was-"

Blaze interrupted Lonnie and said, "Girls. We can discuss this later." The woman looked exhausted, her hands shaking as she took a seat in her chair. The skies around her were gloomy, and most of the stars had lost their brilliant shine. They could feel the power emanating off of her and had a feeling she could eradicate an army of those creatures if she wanted to, and yet, in that moment, she looked surprisingly vulnerable.

"How can we wait until later?" Now that the danger was over Lonnie was feeling the exact opposite of tired. The adrenaline rush was in full effect. "There's a new magical girl out there!"

"And we just faced the biggest monster we've ever come across," Bree added. All those battles she had embellished for her channel were nothing compared to facing that very real threat. How could Blaze possibly think of talking about this later?

But the woman didn't give in and repeated herself. "Girls. Please. We can discuss it later."

Marianna could hear the desperation in Blaze's voice. It was something she'd never heard from her before and it was a little unsettling. This couldn't be because of the battle, no, not when she'd ended it with little to no effort. This was something else. "This is about us, isn't it?" When Blaze didn't respond Marianna pushed on and said, "Blaze... we're all right. I promise."

Blaze smiled a little. "You didn't call me ma'am."

"I didn't think it would help if I addressed you so formally when you're so worried about us."

"Jeez, Mari. You try to not be formal by being formal."

Marianna turned and stuck her tongue out at Bree before she faced Blaze again. "I mean it. We're all right. You don't have to worry."

Blaze got up from her chair, walked over to Marianna, and rested her hand against the side of her face. "I know you're all right, but for a moment, you weren't all right. I need a moment."

Despite their desire for answers all the girls nodded in agreement. It had been a rough battle, after all, and sleep would be a good idea. A moment wouldn't be so bad.

But an entire week had gone by.

Now Lonnie was frustrated and anxious. A week had come and gone and Blaze hadn't spoken to any of them. She was always sitting in her room and staring up at the stars, Marianna insisting that they leave her be. There hadn't been any attacks since then and it allowed the entire city to move on... but it left Lonnie behind with her unresolved feelings.

"Lonnie?"

"What do you think about that attack?" When it doubt: blurt out your feelings.

"Huh? Oh, you mean from last week? It was terrible, of course. They always are."

"Well... yeah, of course, but this one was huge! There hasn't been one this big before."

"That's true, but **magnifiquenoir** always finds a way."

Lonnie hesitated for a moment as she let her mind latch onto the word *always*. *Always* was certainly a long period of time. "What if they don't?"

Kayla looked surprised to hear the question. "Aren't you the one who said we can't always rely on them to do everything?"

Lonnie mulled those words over. She had said that before, back when monsters were able to fit inside of malls. But this was different. This thing had taken everything out of her, out of all of them. Was that what was really going on here? Maybe she wasn't actually upset about people no longer talking about it. Maybe she was upset because she was scared.

Or maybe it was a combination of both. Ugh, why did emotions have to be so complicated? She could just hear Braydon in the back of her mind, mocking her for showing the smallest hint of insecurity. Then again, after his own monster attack, maybe he'd understand where she was coming from.

Maybe.

"It's just... it's never been that bad before, you know? And it's weird that no one is talking about it. It's weird that no one is worried."

Kayla shook her head as she leaned back in her chair. "Naw, people are worried. They're definitely worried."

"But... shouldn't they be discussing it? Who can possibly think about King's Hawaiian rolls after something like that?"

"First of all **everyone** thinks about King's Hawaiian rolls." Kayla was quick in correcting Lonnie about that. Even her non-cooking father did that part right. "Secondly... it's just people's way of coping."

"What?"

"Think about it," Kayla said as she looked around the classroom. Most of the students around them were making small talk while waiting for their professor to show up. Exams. Thanksgiving break. Black Friday. No one was talking about the attack, but there were signs that it very much affected them. On top of the physical damage to the city, there were a few empty seats from students who hadn't been to class all week. Whether they were too scared or their parents decided that this was not the university for them was up in the air. "We're a city where monsters show up and make a mess of things. People don't want to constantly think about it, so they find things they enjoy so they can focus on that instead of focusing on the reality of the situation."

"Which is?"

"*We're a city where monsters show up and make a mess of things.* Sure, we have a group of women who do something about it to the best of their ability, but what if, one day, it's not enough? What if something bigger than last week comes?" Kayla was moving her hands around now, gesturing upward to try and illustrate the height of some unforeseen creature. "It's much better to think about the potential food coma from Thanksgiving than that."

Lonnie could feel another layer of her feelings reveal itself. Now that she was a magical girl, she was supposed to make it her business to be enough. Last week proved that she wasn't ready. None of them were. She remembered feeling that extra swell of power when Prism Pink showed up. They'd all worked together to put that creature in its place, but it hadn't been enough. Had Blaze not shown up, there was no telling what would've happened next. On top of being concerned for the team, Lonnie had a feeling that Blaze was concerned about the same thing she was: what if something bigger showed up?

In hindsight, Raye would be pleased that Lonnie was actually analyzing her feelings and voicing them out loud. That being said... it sure was irritating. "Isn't it a bit of a cop out to ignore the problem?"

Kayla shrugged her shoulders. "It's not ignoring it if you take a second to breathe so you can come back to it fresh. Everyone needs a break, Lonnie. You're allowed to be excited about your grandmother's cooking and be aware of the fact that your city is full of monsters."

Lonnie supposed that also applied to Blaze. In fact, it may have applied to her more than anyone else. It couldn't be easy to be going through this again with a different set of girls, especially with threats as big as last week's attack.

"Sorry I'm late, class."

Both girls watched as Mr. Carlson walked in. He was out of breath, his hair disheveled since he'd obviously ran here to try and get to class in a decent amount of time. "You should really get up earlier to get here," one of the students joked, the class laughing with her.

"Ha ha," he said as he opened his briefcase to get his lesson plan. "I already do, the commute is a nightmare." He paused for a moment then added, "But it's much better than the alternative."

"Which is?" Lonnie asked.

"Not being here at all."

Player Select

NAME: ?????
AGE: ?????
OCCUPATION: seamstress
FIRST SEASON ATTACK: sewn together symmetry!

THIS FRECKLED FACED, GLASSES WEARING BEAUTY WATCHES THE GIRLS FROM AFAR & IS ALWAYS READY TO WEAVE HER DEADLY THREADS AND HELP SAVE THE DAY... BUT WHO IS SHE, REALLY?

prism
PINK

"I'M JUST AS MAGICAL AS EVERYONE ELSE!"

Lonnie watched the class all nod their agreement as their professor began to write on the board. She glanced over at Kayla who smiled an all too knowing smile. Lonnie rolled her eyes and muttered, "Go ahead. Say it."

"Told ya so."

"I'm so excited that you're coming home!"

"Jeez, Ella, you act like you haven't seen me in years," Bree said as she sat in front of her computer after class, video chatting with Ella.

"Am I not allowed to be excited to spend time with my friend?"

"No, you're allowed, I'm just surprised that you're *that* excited."

Ella crossed her arms and gave Bree an irritated look. "What's with you? I thought you'd be fangirling over the fact that you get to hang out with Chevy."

"I was trying to be cool about it," Bree muttered, puffing out her cheeks in a full-blown pout.

"Well don't be cool! Get hyped! We can hang out! Game! Marathon that anime series with the ice skating! You know, the usual." Ella paused for a moment then added, "You can even spoil that new game you got."

"Huh?"

"You know, the one you went to the midnight launch for? Oh... but that attack happened... did you ever pick up the game after that?"

"Oh... yeah, I did," though she'd almost forgotten to. "You're not counting side quests, are you?"

"No. Main campaign."

"Oh, well yeah, I already beat it..."

Ella leaned closer to the camera and gave it a curious look as if she were looking right at Bree. "...was it that bad? You don't sound too thrilled. It got pretty good reviews, hell, even Chevy liked it... though she kept referring to the cast as a boy band..."

"What? No, it was fun." Bree tried her best to smile, but truth be told, it felt weird talking about video games and potential anime marathons after everything that had happened. She guessed almost being killed by a monster that smelled like a sewer, then being rescued by a warrior in pink really made you re-evaluate your life.

"All right, what's bothering you?"

"Huh? Nothing!" Bree quickly waved her hands into the camera. "Just... things have been kinda crazy here lately and it feels weird to just... leave."

"Define *crazy*."

"City nearly pulverized by a monster."

"Correct me if I'm wrong, but isn't that a normal thing in your city?"

It wasn't a lie, of course. The city was threatened on a normal basis, but this last time... "It was really bad this last time," Bree said, her voice getting softer as she spoke. "It was actually... scary."

"Ah, I get it," Ella said, nodding her head as if she were a doctor who'd discovered some kind of long sought after cure.

"You do?"

"Sure. You all have **magnifiquenoir** to come save the day like some fashionable defenders of love and justice... or is it more like sugar, spice, everything nice, and some random chemical?"

"Um... the first one," Bree said. "Fairly certain it's *magic* and not *chemicals*."

"Damn. The *Powerpuff Girl* formula would be cute as hell in real life. Anyway, my point is your city is used to them being around, so even when things get really bad people expect to be rescued, right?" When

Bree nodded her head, Ella continued. "And I take it this last time they struggled?"

"Yeah…" Bree ignored the dull pain in her heart. It was excruciatingly hard to talk about this as if she were an outside observer who wasn't directly involved with **magnifiquenoir**.

"But they still won. You need to focus on that part. Sure it was a struggle, but they still came out on top, you're still here, and you're coming home soon."

"But… what if something happens while I'm gone? What if I come back and the city is in worse shape?" That was a very real possibility. While Marianna and Lonnie's families were in the city, Bree's was a two hour trip away. If something happened and they needed her, there would be no way for her to get to them in time.

"So what, you wanna stay there now? You don't wanna come home?"

"That's not what I mean! I'm just… I'm worried, Ella! I'm worried I'm gonna be sitting in a church with my mother, pretending to sing along with the Lord, and the city's gonna become a giant crater. I mean like… huge! Like Cell versus Gohan, epic Kamehameha huge!" To demonstrate, Bree positioned her hands as if she were about to blast said Kamehameha, then she spread her arms out to indicate the large explosion.

"That's pretty big…"

"Yeah! Exactly!"

"But… they were fighting in the middle of nowhere…"

"In the middle of a tournament, Ella!"

"Were there even any people at the-"

"I am so beyond done talking to you," then Bree turned her head away from the computer screen.

"Look! I get your fear, you just have to use a different analogy! How about... giant monster who can step on an entire city until a guy beats him in one punch?"

"That. Does. Not. Help. Me!!!"

"What do you want me to say, Bree?!"

"I want things to be normal again!" Bree's eyes widened as soon as she said the words, realizing the weight of them... but it was exactly what she wanted. She wanted to be back in the dorms with her quiet roommate, unaware of destructive monsters and the magical girls who battled them. She wanted her biggest priority to be her channel and the occasional religious jargon from her mother. As she sat in her chair, looking down at her hand where a faint scar lingered from that previous battle, one lone thought circulated through her mind and it made her feel terrible.

She should've never accepted Blaze's offer.

"This is why you should be thrilled about coming home," Ella said. "Things are normal here. Well... I use the word *normal* loosely considering our ragtag group of friends."

"But then... I have to come back here. Back to this city of monsters."

"Bree, that's not all the city has. What about your friends? What about Kayla? They're all there, too. Right?"

That was true. It wasn't like Marianna and Lonnie only talked to her during battle. The three of them had established a friendship. Even if they'd come together because of **magnifiquenoir**, they had spent time together without magic and intense battles. But it felt so contradictory to be in such a bad place about the group. She'd been so gung-ho to join and had even gotten angry with Lonnie for saying no.

"I think you're right," Bree said. "I think a break is very much in order."

"That's the spirit! You're allowed to leave the green wig behind from time to time," then Ella winked into the camera.

"What was that wink for?"

Ella chuckled and said, "Oh nothing. Nothing at all. I'll see you soon, okay?"

"K..." then Bree reached over and shut off her camera.

"She totally knows, you know."

Bree let out a surprised yelp then spun around in her chair to see Lonnie standing in the doorway of her bedroom. "Jesus Christ! You could've knocked!"

"Door was open. I take it you got distracted while packing?" Lonnie nodded over to Bree's bed, which was a mini disaster of clothes, shoes, and video games. "Break is only for a week, not a lifetime."

"Ha ha," then Bree asked, "How much of that did you hear?"

"Enough to know that you're just as hesitant as I am, oh, and enough to know that Ella knows that you're Cosmic Green."

Bree decided to ignore that last part, even if she had a feeling that Lonnie was right. "Wait... you're hesitant about leaving, too?"

"Yeah, a little. I feel a bit better after talking to Kayla but-"

"You talked to Kayla?!" Bree jumped out of her chair and clasped her hands together in excitement. "When?!"

Lonnie had a feeling that Bree's eyes would shift into hearts if they could. "We have class together, remember?"

"Right, of course! So... what did she say?" Bree resisted the urge to ask if she'd said anything about *her*. There was no need to derail the conversation. Yet.

Lonnie stepped into Bree's room and sat down at the edge of her bed, somehow managing to find space among the explosion of clothes. "She said it was okay to take a break."

"Yeah, Ella said the same thing... but I guess you heard that part."

"It's not like I don't want to, believe me, I do, I just-"

Bree interrupted Lonnie and asked, "Wait. You take breaks?"

"Cute, Bree."

"I'm serious. You don't seem to be the type who'd want to get away from the action, I mean you did stand up to that monster without any powers."

"Right, and it went so gloriously well," Lonnie said, her voice dripping with sarcasm. "I almost died. *We* almost died... until Prism Pink showed up. It... scared me..."

Bree lowered her head, not quite ready to look Lonnie in the eye after such an admission. On the one hand, it was comforting to know that she wasn't the only one scared that night. On the other hand... if someone as strong as Lonnie was scared, how could Bree possibly feel secure right now?

"You know... everyone gets scared, Bree. It's something I don't like admitting to, but it's true. Marianna was scared that night. So was Blaze."

"Yeah... but Blaze is our mentor, of course she was scared for us. And no matter how scared Mari is she'd never consider walking away from this," Bree said with a long sigh. "She has something to prove."

"And you don't? I don't?"

"Of course I do! And you do, too! But... is that worth all this?"

Lonnie smiled and stood up to walk over to Bree. Once she was standing in front of her she pulled her into a comforting hug. "I wasn't the only one who kept fighting that night. Me standing back up first does NOT discredit you and Marianna standing with me when you were finally able to."

Bree hadn't even thought of that. All three of them had kept fighting, so much so that they'd all felt a new surge of power. That power that had brought that creature down to its knees. It may not have died, but it definitely suffered, and all four of them were willing to stand against it again. "Man. Hearing that doubtful voice sucks," Bree whined.

"Ugh. Preaching. Choir."

"Oh God, please, do NOT mention choir."

"Huh?"

Bree left the security of Lonnie's arms to walk over to her closet. Once there, she pulled out a long, white dress that had colorful sunflowers scattered all over it. "Hi. Meet Sunday Bree. She'll be sitting in church with her mother and older brother."

Oh right, Bree had mentioned her mother being rather fond of religion. Lonnie smiled brightly and said, "Awwwww, Sunday Bree is adorable!" When Bree glared at her Lonnie responded with a loud fit of laughter. "Come on, it can't be that bad!"

Bree reached into her closet to pull out a large hat and said, "Did I mention there's a hat to match?" Maybe she could *accidentally* leave it in her closet.

"That's actually pretty tame compared to some of the ladies at my Grand-Penny's church."

"Just because it *could* be worse doesn't mean that it isn't bad. Look at all these rhinestones! And this bow!" Bree waved the hat in Lonnie's face, said gems glinting in the light.

"Thought you'd be used to bows and sparkles by now..."

"And here I was gonna let you bitch about having to sit through a holiday church service."

Lonnie shrugged her shoulders and said, "I don't mind it."

Bree stopped waving the hat and gave Lonnie a bewildered look. "What?"

"I don't mind it," Lonnie said again. "My Grand-Penny's church is cool and open to everyone."

"I've heard legends about queer friendly churches, I didn't think they actually existed."

"Now granted, if the church weren't queer friendly, my grandma would raise hell on anyone who tried to mess with me. Best of all? She'd do it in the name of the Lord," and Lonnie made sure to draw out the word *lord*.

Bree smiled brightly and cried out, "Amen!"

"What are you two in there talking about?"

Bree and Lonnie looked out into the living room to see Marianna, who was sitting on the couch and pulling her shoes off. It was the second best thing to do after a long day of work, the first being the all-important removal of her bra.

"We're discussing the upcoming break," Lonnie said as she stepped into the living room and sat next to Marianna. "I also got introduced to Sunday Bree."

Mariana's eyes lit up. "Isn't she the cutest?!"

"Shut up, Mari!"

Marianna giggled as she leaned back in the couch. "I'm gonna miss that frustrated crack in your voice."

"It's only a week, Mari..."

"What can I say? I got used to it."

As the girls were talking to one another, something occurred to Lonnie. She remembered Marianna talking about her family before and the tension between them. While most college students would be more than eager to return home, this couldn't be easy for her. "You know, Marianna, if you need somewhere to go, my grandmother makes pleeeeenty of food." While Lonnie had no problem with having leftovers, she was more than willing to offer a plate to a friend.

Marianna smiled at Lonnie. "I had a feeling you'd invite me to come with you. And Bree, before you ask, I'm fine."

Bree sat down on the other side of Marianna. "Well I was gonna invite you to come with me so I wouldn't have to be in the car with my brother for two hours..."

"I do appreciate the both of you, but with my dad and Mama Yo around, it should be fine."

Bree and Lonnie looked at each other, silently wondering if Marianna was telling the truth. Finally Lonnie blurted out, "You know for someone with such a cute face you are eerily difficult to read."

"That's why she makes a good leader."

All the girls looked toward the front door to see Blaze standing there, smiling at them. All three of them looked surprised to see her. She hadn't been out of her room since the attack and hadn't really spoken to any of them. It was nice to see her walking around and even nicer to see her smiling. Still… it was hard to figure out what to say to the woman. A week ago they'd wanted to discuss the attack, but now? Now they were worried that if they brought it up, Blaze would go back to sitting in her chair, completely motionless and unaware of her surroundings.

When no one said anything Blaze spoke again. "I just came down to say that I hope you girls have a nice break, you all deserve it."

"I'll still be around to make sure things are all right."

Ah, so that was Marianna's plan. Bree and Lonnie gave each other knowing looks as Blaze asked, "What do you mean by that, Marianna? Aren't you going back home?"

"I am, but if I'm needed, I can come back. Home isn't very far, besides, I'll be doing some work at the bakery anyway." Ms. Green was already slammed with orders for the holiday, it would only be more chaotic as they got closer to Thanksgiving. Retail stores had Black Friday, but the bakery had an equally dreadful Wednesday.

"I guess I never thought of that. I can come back, too," Lonnie said.

Blaze gave the girls a stern look and put her hands on her hips. "No. No one is coming back. You ladies are on break. If anything happens I can cover it."

Marianna quickly shook her head and said, "You don't have to do that."

"Do you not think I'm capable, Marianna?"

"N-no! I didn't say that!"

"Damn. That's pretty cruel," but Lonnie couldn't help but be impressed with their leader's tactic. Bree nodded her head in agreement, but she also knew that it was the only way Marianna wouldn't put up that much of a fight.

"Well then it's settled. All of you enjoy the vacation," then Blaze turned and left the girls alone in the living room.

"I should've known she would do that," Marianna muttered.

"Yeah. You should've."

Marianna gave Lonnie a sugary sweet smile and said, "Good luck talking to your Grand-Penny, by the way."

"W-what?"

"You're gonna tell her about being Radical Rainbow, right?"

"...that cute face is so deceptive."

"Been sayin' that for years," Bree said, even if she'd only known Marianna for a few months. Still, that was plenty of time to know that Marianna was queen when it came to having the last word.

She'd felt fine when she got in the car.

She'd even felt fine during the drive, even when they had to drive past broken bits of the city and take all kinds of detours to try and get to the highway.

But now, as Blaze pulled up in front of her old home, Marianna could feel the anxiety bubbling up in the pit of her stomach. If she were lucky, her Mama Yo would be home to be the necessary icebreaker between her and Lynn. Her father wouldn't be at the house until Thanksgiving, so Mama Yo was all she had. One would think that having two parents to balance out the third, unreasonable one would make things easier.

"It'll be all right," Blaze said as she reached over and took Marianna's hand. "You know if it gets too bad, you can call me."

"I wish you could come with me."

"You know that wouldn't go well."

Talking to Raye about Lonnie had been hard enough, but talking with Lynn over the summer had been akin to stepping into a war zone. Yolanda, to her credit, had tried to keep the peace, though it was clear that she wasn't completely on board with Marianna's decision to become a magical girl. Meanwhile, Marianna's father had been on board save for the standard fatherly worries. Then again, Andre hadn't been directly involved the way Lynn and Yolanda had been. He hadn't been around before or during the attack that crippled Lynn, so anytime he tried to offer input, Lynn would shoot it down.

In the end, Marianna had made her decision, and she hadn't really spoken to her parents ever since.

Well... not Lynn, anyway.

"She's just worried about you," Blaze said, and she couldn't blame her, especially after the last attack.

"There's being worried, and then there's being hateful."

"I think it still boils down to her being worried."

"She said she *hated* it." Marianna spit out the word as if she'd been gargling with venom. "Those were her exact words."

"I know. I was there."

"Right. Sorry."

Blaze sighed and squeezed Marianna's hand. "There are a lot of layers behind your mother's feelings on this. It's not just about you joining. We failed her, back then. She's allowed to be angry."

"That was years ago! Why does she have to take it out on me?"

"She doesn't see it like that. She just-"

"Doesn't want me to go through the same thing. I know." She knew better than anyone, especially considering the attack from last week. Now her mother would have extra ammunition to use against **magnifiquenoir**. Marianna glanced out the window to look at the house. Growing up, it had felt so small and claustrophobic. Now, the two story home felt large and overbearing – even from a distance. Marianna had fresh memories of her mother doing everything she could to shelter her from the world. Go to school. Come home. Lather, rinse, repeat. She could barely remember any interactions with classmates beyond cafeteria get-togethers and sitting next to random kids on the bus. It was a miracle that she'd ever connected with Dana, then again, Dana had been persistent. Marianna had tried to warn her about her overprotective mother and Dana took it all in stride. If Marianna couldn't go out, then Dana would come over: simple as that.

It had made Marianna more frustrated with her mother, no matter how many explanations her Mama Yo gave her.

Fortunately, Marianna had weekend visits with her father. Andre didn't live in the house with them, but he and Lynn were still close. They just couldn't live together. They butted heads too many times and Yolanda would always take Lynn's side. Marianna had a feeling that her mother was aware of the freedoms her father granted her – mall trips with Dana, for instance, and a certain part-time bakery job – but, somehow, the man had managed to convince Lynn to tone it down, at least for the weekend.

Until that faithful day over the summer before Marianna went to college when a certain fiery woman in a long, black coat and top hat came into her life. Marianna's parents weren't supposed to believe her when she rushed home to tell them about being rescued from a terrifying monster.

"*This is exactly why I wanted her to stay home!*"

"*Lynn...*"

"*She could've been killed!*"

"Lynn, calm down, she's fine."

"For now. She's fine FOR NOW Andre!"

"Damnit Lynn, you can't keep her locked in her room because of what happened before!"

"Before? Before?! It's happening now!"

"It's been quiet for years, Lynn! There's no way–"

"Get out."

"What?"

"GET OUT!"

Someday, parents would realize that their children listened in on their arguments. Marianna's father hadn't left right away. Instead, he'd double-downed on the yelling. Before Yolanda could enter the kitchen to back Lynn up, Marianna stopped her and asked the question that changed everything.

"What happened to her?"

She'd asked it before, of course, but now there was more weight to it. It was easy to pick up on the clues. Something had happened before, something related to the grotesque monster that had threatened Marianna's life. This time, Yolanda would have to tell her the truth, because Marianna had witnessed it first-hand.

So Yolanda told her everything. Monsters had attacked the city before, seemingly out of nowhere. There was a group of magical women who made sure the city was safe, and those women were always victorious... except for the one time it mattered most – at least, to Lynn.

"She didn't want me to look into **magnifiquenoir**. She told me not to."

"And we see how well that went." Blaze couldn't help but chuckle. Teenage girls were a curious bunch.

"How could I not investigate?"

"I suppose she wasn't making things any better by not telling you the truth right off the bat," then Blaze quickly added, "Don't tell her I said that. I don't need her coming after me."

"Your secret's safe with me," Marianna said in response.

"Had she told you sooner... would you have really stayed away from this?"

Marianna decided not to answer that question. She supposed that by not answering it, that was her answer. Had she found out when she were younger, she probably would've been even more interested in the group. Still... "It would've been nice to know that she wasn't just being unreasonable."

Blaze smiled and leaned over to hug Marianna. "You'll be fine. She'll be happy to see you home. I bet she doesn't even bring **magnifiquenoir** up."

Marianna closed her eyes and rested her head on Blaze's shoulder as she whispered, "You don't believe that at all, do you?"

"No... but hopefully it encourages you to get out the car."

Ah, they had been sitting outside for a while, hadn't they? Marianna pulled away from Blaze and took a deep breath before she slid out of the passenger seat. After she retrieved her suitcase from the back seat, she took one more deep breath before she headed for the front door. She looked back to see Blaze waving to her with a comforting smile. It was only for a week. She could do this. All she had to do was avoid talking about the group that meant so much to her. She'd tuck **magnifiquenoir** away in a closet and stick to conversations about her classes and the afternoon shopping she planned on doing with Dana on Black Friday. She could also find sanctuary at the bakery. She did say that she'd work a couple of hours, so when she thought about it like that it wasn't *technically* a full week at all.

With that in mind, Marianna pulled out her old key and stepped inside, closing the door behind her.

The first thing she heard was the familiar jingle of her cat's collar. Marianna smiled as Snickerdoodles trotted down the stairs with excited little *meows*. Marianna happily picked up her fluffy old friend, letting her snuggle in her arms with a chorus of purrs. She remembered Bree making a comment about her being a magical girl with a cat and being eternally amused by it... then immediately disappointed when Marianna hadn't gotten the reference right away.

"Yolanda? Is that you?"

Marianna felt the nervousness building in her throat when she heard that voice. Snickerdoodles squirmed out of her arms, the calico proving to be easily distracted. So much for her Mama Yo serving as a peacekeeper. "N-no. It's me," Marianna said.

Everything felt so loud as she stood at the front door, listening to her mother wheel herself into the room. Snickerdoodles was now in her lap and accepting any and all pets. There was such a stark contrast between Lynn's outer appearance and her bitter demeanor. She was as beautiful as Marianna remembered, with large, natural curls and a flowy clothing style full of warm colors to match the season. How could this vision of a woman be such a negative person? At least she was smiling. "Good to see you," Lynn said. "Yolanda should be back soon, she went to get groceries for Thanksgiving."

Marianna nodded as she walked over and hugged her mother. "It's good to see you, too," and she meant it. It had been months and it did feel nice to see the woman again, even if Marianna had a feeling that the warmth wouldn't last.

"Let me get a look at ya."

Marianna laughed as she took a step back. "It's only been a few months, mama."

"Looks like you losin' weight, though."

"Mama..."

"What? I can't give you a compliment?"

It wasn't much of a compliment, but Marianna kept that thought to herself.

"So how'd you get here? Caught the bus? I thought traffic would be terrible with all the-"

"Mama. Don't."

Five minutes. It hadn't even been five minutes. Hell, it hadn't even been a full minute.

"Did that woman drop you off?" Because Lynn refused to use her name if she could help it.

"You know the answer to that."

"I suppose I do. Come on, let's go into the living room. We've got a lot of catching up to do."

"Of course. Let me bring my suitcase up to my room," then Marianna quickly walked upstairs, suitcase in hand.

Maybe she could stay upstairs long enough for her Mama Yo to get home.

For some reason her alarm was going off.

Bree groaned and buried her head into her pillow. She was aware that she was on break, but for some reason, her alarm felt the need to wake her up as if she had a class to get to. Had she forgotten to turn it off? Bree reached over to grab her phone and hit the SNOOZE button. She'd figure it out in fifteen minutes.

"Nope. Wake up."

Bree quickly sat up and looked over to see her brother standing by her bed. "Trey?"

"Get up. We have to get ready for church."

Church?

Oh... right.

She'd remembered that she was on break, but had forgotten where she was. No wonder she was wearing a long pajama shirt instead of her nude default or pixelated underwear. She'd have to thank Lonnie for letting her borrow it. "It's too early."

"You knew this was coming."

"Can't I sleep in and wait until the Thanksgiving service?"

"We talked about this in the car."

They'd talked about a lot of things in the car, and technically, church had been one of them. Something about making their mother happy, yadda yadda. "It's kinda weird to be back here."

"Don't waste time, Bree."

"I'm serious! I mean... look at my room!" Or rather, what *used to be* her room. Long gone were the posters and plushies of cute anime and video game mascots. The ongoing manga series and the well-loved video game strategy guides weren't there. It had all been replaced with floral wallpaper and bare bones furniture in an attempt to make a guest room of sorts.

Trey sat at the edge of the bed. He knew this was a stalling tactic, but he couldn't deny knowing what Bree was feeling right now. "I remember feeling like that, but hey, at least your room got turned into a guest room. Mine is full of plastic totes and other random boxes."

"I told you I could've slept on the couch..."

"Eh, it's fine," Trey said with a shrug. "Besides, you're whinier if you don't get a good night's sleep."

Bree would've pointed out how she could easily fit on the couch. Trey was so tall that his legs had to hang over the arm of the couch, but she could tell that he was having one of his older brother moments. That car ride hadn't been completely uncomfortable with comments about her new life, there were genuine moments of him missing his little sister.

They lived in the same city, and yet, they rarely saw each other. There wasn't much time for sibling bonding when she had new friends, a gaming channel, classes, and monsters to combat. It was a wonder she even had time for a crush, then again, Kayla had a slight advantage since they had the same class together.

"Come on," he said as he stood up and yanked the covers off of her. "It's time to praise the lord."

"Awww, come on! I wanted to go and hang out with Ella today!"

"You can go after service is over."

"So tomorrow, then."

"Ha ha," Trey said, voice deadpan from Bree's commentary over the length of black church sermons. "It won't be *that* long."

"That's a damn lie and you know it."

"At least the food will be good when we go over to sister so and so's house."

Well. That was a bit of a silver lining. Even after living with Marianna's cooking, there was something wondrous about the soul food from the eldest member of the church congregation. "All right, all right. I'll be ready soon."

"You better. I'll be back in ten minutes to be sure you didn't go back to sleep."

A few minutes later, Bree stepped out of her room to head to the bathroom to get ready. It was odd to be standing in that space again. It had only been a few months, but for some reason, it felt like an entire lifetime had passed since she'd been there. It was the little things, really. The fact that she had to bring in her toothbrush instead of it already being there. The fact that her shower gel wasn't there, replaced with her mother's standard brand that hadn't come from a mall shop full of fruit fragrances. The fact that her Nintendo themed bath towels weren't there. She'd brought all that stuff with her, and there was something a bit upsetting about it not being in the place she'd called home for eighteen years.

"Bree? Don't take too long, we have to get ready."

Then again, there were some perks about not living at home. She'd had several months of free Sundays, now she had to go back to the religious quo.

"Yes mother," Bree said. Good lord, how was the woman already awake and chipper?

After brushing her teeth and showering, Bree went back to her room – *guest room* – to get dressed. She was surprised to see a text message on her phone. Who else would be up this early?

Mari

Hey.

Your mom driving you crazy yet?

Good timing. I was just about to get dressed.

Today's the day.

LOL! This must be agony for you.

What about you? You doin' ok?

Well enough, I guess.

Kinda wishing I took one of you up on that offer to come with.

Maybe ask Lonnie? Or Blaze? Or Dana?

I'm sorry I'm so far away.

Eh, I'm just complaining.

We'll all be together again soon enough.

Enjoy your Sunday.

Ha.

Ha ha.

Ha.

Bree set her phone down and walked over to her suitcase to grab her dress. In hindsight, she didn't have it so bad. She couldn't imagine having to be at a place where someone so important to her hated what she was doing. Then again, that was kind of her situation, right? If she ever did tell her mother about **magnifiquenoir** she was sure that she'd turn her nose up at it.

Oh, and the whole bisexual thing.

During the two hour car ride home, it had been easy to say that she'd think about it, and truthfully, she had. But now, as she stood in what used to be her room, dressed in her retired Sunday best, her stomach was doing flip flops over the whole thing. She did understand Trey's point of view. After that last attack he'd confessed that he didn't want to be the bearer of devastating news, and if anything ever happened to Bree he'd be forced into that role. That was the last thing she wanted to make him do, but the prospect of telling their mother everything was nerve wracking. Trey thought that Bree's uncertainty was purely based on her assumptions. In all honesty, it'd be easier if that were the case.

But it was also based on Marianna's experience with her mother.

"Bree. Come on, we need to get going!"

"Coming!"

Bree quickly slipped her shoes on and left the room. No sense stressing about it now, not when she was about to deal with her butt falling asleep from hours of pretending to know spiritual hymns.

There she stood, in the middle of the living room. Ahna Danvers. Part of Bree had always wondered if church was just another way to have a fashion show. Her mother's hair was perfectly flattened. Bree had a feeling she was still doing it the old fashioned straightening comb on a stove top way instead of giving into flat irons. The state of her hair shouldn't have mattered because of how outlandish her hat was. The curved headpiece was full of twists and turns that made it look like an exotic flower that had yet to be discovered. The suit was a plain, pure white, but Bree knew that was the entire point: the hat was the real showstopper, and any embellishments on the suit would detract from it.

Bree thought she'd feel the urge to say something snarky, but there was something genuinely comforting about the image in front of her.

This... was normal.

Especially when her mother walked over to her and said, "Girl, put some pantyhose on. And button up that top button, don't have your goods on display like that."

Bree thought she'd be annoyed. She thought she'd want to snap back at the woman about how she was an adult – *sort of*. She fully expected to grumble about having to sit in a place surrounded by overly opinionated people who lumped their judgmental attitudes as *the word of the Lord*.

But that's not what she felt when she saw her mother.

After being away from home her mother's stern frown was welcoming, because she knew there was more to her than that. This was the woman who hummed to her after her frightening encounter. This was the woman who sided with her and reassured her that she'd done nothing to warrant her attack. This was the woman who volunteered to ride a bus to be by her side and broken character to curse her brother out for not answering his phone. Bree had been using her mother's religion as an excuse, assuming that she would be just as unreasonable as the elder brothers and sisters in the congregation. But there, in the hallway, she saw a hint of a smile in her eyes as she went into her normal, motherly routine with Bree.

Maybe she could tell her. Someday. But for now she was enjoying the normality of early Sunday morning so she smiled and said, "Yes ma'am," before she turned to do as she was told.

"...your sister all right?" Ahna asked as Bree closed the door to her old room.

Trey smiled as he, unsuccessfully, tried to tie his tie. "Yeah. She's fine, ma."

"Boy, you STILL don't know how to tie one of these?" The woman let out a long sigh and helped her son, missing the cute smile on his face as she did so.

People who thought that coffee was the best part of waking up clearly hadn't been in her grandmother's house the week of Thanksgiving.

It was only Tuesday and Lonnie could already smell the signs of baked goods wafting through the large house. Lonnie smiled as she got out of bed to head downstairs. The house was still a bit of a maze to navigate, with too many rooms for one elderly woman to have. Once upon a time it had been full of children, then those children had grown up and moved out on their own, having families and bringing them over for every occasion. The rooms were always available to anyone in the family, like a certain kickboxer or that one uncle who took his time moving out. Currently, the house was empty save for her and her Grand-Penny, and Lonnie was enjoying the silence. It would be much louder on Thursday, and she was sure there'd be a cousin or aunt who would need to stay the night.

Lonnie smirked as she headed to the kitchen. It was almost sick how she enjoyed the bit of gossip during the holidays. There'd be someone in the middle of a breakup, or a family member who argued with someone else. Then again, she knew some – *most* – of them would be giving her a hard time. She'd gained a bit more muscle and had had two more girlfriends since the last family gathering.

Then, of course, there was the big ol' rainbow colored magical elephant in the room.

Lonnie had no intention of revealing the truth to every member of the family, but she did remember Marianna's words. She may have said them to give her a hard time, but she was right. After that last attack she needed to tell her grandmother, and if she was going to do it, now would be the time.

"Morning," Lonnie said as she walked over to the fridge.

"Why is my Lonnie-Pooh up so early? You're supposed to be on break."

Lonnie glanced over at the woman and gave the shirt she was wearing a look of disapproval. Ever since she'd started college her grandmother felt the need to wear over-sized shirts with the school mascot on it at least once during her visit. Her hair was all over her head, much to the dismay of the comb she'd take to it later, and she had a comical amount of sweet potatoes lining the counter. Lonnie could already smell a handful of pies being baked, but her grandmother had a tendency of making too much.

Not that anyone was complaining.

"That shirt is so old, Grand-Penny..."

"You think I care? My baby's in college!"

"This is my third year. It's nothing new," but she couldn't help but smile. Her grandmother's pride was so heartwarming even if it was over old news. Lonnie being in college was one of the things she boasted about, especially when anyone in the family tried to come at her. *"I don't see you trying to get a degree,"* she'd say. It was truly a sight to behold.

"Then you ain't gonna stand me when you graduate."

That was a valid point, but Lonnie had a feeling she'd be able to deal with it. She'd probably be showered with so many gifts that she'd be able to finance her first apartment.

Assuming she'd be living somewhere else, what with the whole magical girl thing and all.

Lonnie opened the fridge and nearly wept at the amount of food inside. All sorts of meats and vegetables. A variety of yellow and white cheeses for a truckload of macaroni. A bunch of colored peppers and the all-important collard greens that would be picked and cleaned tomorrow. For now, cereal would do, and when Lonnie opened the cupboard she could see that she had an entire grocery aisle of options. "Um... why is there so much-"

"Couldn't remember what kind you liked."

Lonnie knew that was a lie. She'd lived in this house since childhood. There was no way her grandmother didn't remember anything about her, especially when it came to food. "Do I wanna know how much you spent on groceries this week?"

"Don't remember."

"Grand-Penny!"

"What? I don't get to do this as often as I used to, and I know Rodney and Raye ain't feeding you like this."

"Technically, they aren't feeding me at all."

"What?"

Wow, had they not even told her that she'd moved out? On the one hand, Lonnie was happy that they'd left it completely up to her. On the other hand... how dare they leave it completely up to her! "Oh... I moved out..." Lonnie said as she finally settled on a box of cereal. Something full of sugar and artificial fruit flavor sounded great.

"What?! With who? When?!"

"Well... remember when Rodney was injured? And I went to stay with some friends? I... kiiiiinda never left..."

There was a look on her grandmother's face. It was that patented Penny Knox look of contemplation. Lonnie hated that look. It was hard to tell what she was thinking and no way of knowing what she would say next. Finally, the woman spoke up and said, "What made you wanna move out?"

"I just... I get along with the girls really well, and..." Ugh, that sounded like a lie even if it was partially true.

"Why do you look so nervous? You know you can tell me anything," then Penny walked over and sat at the table with Lonnie.

Suddenly, Lonnie wasn't hungry anymore. The poor looped cereal was going to get soggy, but she supposed that was why there were multiple boxes to choose from. "I know..."

"I already know you like girls, what else is there to know? I thought that was the hardest thing to tell someone?"

"Actually... I didn't tell you..."

"Right, but you could've denied it and called your big mouth cousin and nosy ass auntie a liar."

Lonnie chuckled. It was kind of endearing when her grandmother talked smack about the family members who gave her a hard time. "That's a good point, I guess. But this... this is bigger than that."

"You gettin' married?"

"What? No!" Lonnie was glad she hadn't been trying to eat her cereal, otherwise, she would've spit it right out as she tried to not choke on her milk. "I'm not even seeing anyone!" Well, there was a girl who was on her mind, but not for anything like *marriage*. Though she definitely wouldn't mind bashing monsters with Prism Pink again.

"And you can't be pregnant... right? Unless... are you bi? Did you hook up with some raggedy ass little boy and get pregnant?"

"No!" Lonnie couldn't say no fast enough. The thought of children was more unsettling than the creatures who wreaked havoc on the city.

"Good. We already got enough kids that'll be in this house on Thursday."

Lonnie grinned and said, "I thought that's what all the extra rooms were for."

Penny shook her head and said, "You know I love y'all, but sometimes, I enjoy my peace and quiet."

"Is that so you can yell at the TV louder?"

"Girl. Did you SEE *Hell's Kitchen?* Lord..."

Lonnie was about to continue the conversation but she stopped herself. It would be way too easy to fall into a marathon of gossip about every single reality TV show they watched. If she wanted to get this truth out there, she needed to say it. Now. "Grand-Penny, I... do you know about **magnifiquenoir**?"

"Of course I do. Who doesn't?"

"I... well... I-I kinda... joined them."

And that was it. It was out in the open. Lonnie watched the expressions on her grandmother's face shift from shocked, to concerned, to angry, and finally... amused. "You play too much," she said as she stood up from the table. "I need to check on these pies and-"

"I'm serious," Lonnie said, then she lowered her head to look down at her cereal bowl. "I'm not kidding."

"You mean you're in some kind of fan club or something, right? Do you kids still do that? Have fan clubs?"

"Yes, but they're all online." Lonnie forced herself to look over at her grandmother and face the situation head-on. "That's not the point, though! I'm really-"

Penny shook her head as she turned and pulled four pies out the oven. "If you're not gonna eat your cereal, you can come over here and help me with these next couple of pies."

That was a bad sign. Her grandmother never asked for help when cooking. "Um... sure..." then Lonnie stood up and walked over to the woman. "What do you want me to-"

"Wash the sweet potatoes for me so I can get some more pies going," then she turned and put a new batch in the oven.

It was much too quiet in the kitchen and it was making Lonnie feel uneasy. Her Grand-Penny would at least yell if she were angry with her. Did that mean she was disappointed? Worried? Was she going to treat her to some grand guilt trip speech that made her feel bad for joining the group? *"How dare you worry your poor grandmother,"* she'd say, or rather, that's what the average grandma would do. Her Grand-Penny would probably curse her out and hit her with a balled up first.

"You call yourself a heroine and you can't even wash potatoes."

Lonnie blinked and looked down into the sink. The water was running, but she hadn't even picked up a single potato to scrub. "Oh... sorry."

"Girl, move out the way," then Penny took Lonnie's place at the sink. "This is why I never ask any of y'all for help."

"That's not the reason and you know it," Lonnie said as she set the timer on the microwave.

"What are you doing?"

"Setting the timer so we know when to take out the pie."

Penny looked up at the ceiling and said, "Lord help me, girl moves out on her own with a bunch of magic ladies and now she thinks she knows how to cook."

Lonnie almost wanted to text Bree and tell her that her grandmother was having a conversation with God. "One of them is a baker, you know. And she uses a timer."

"You new school girls need to spend more time with your grandmothers."

"That's what I'm trying to do... but you kinda stopped talking to me."

"Just for a moment. I needed a minute to collect my thoughts," then Penny turned and hit Lonnie in her arm. "That's for nearly gettin' yourself killed."

Well she was right about being hit. "Ow! Do you gotta hit me? I take enough of that at the gym."

"And apparently you take it in malls and on the streets against crazy monsters. Who gave you permission to join these girls? And you better not say Rodney and Raye, you know you gotta talk to me first."

"I know, but... they were kinda there when it happened. It's how Rodney got hurt. The gym was attacked."

"By one of them things?" Penny asked as she finished scrubbing the potatoes. "Check to see if my water's boiling."

Lonnie looked over at the large pot on the stove then shook her head. "Not yet."

"Good, because now we got some time to talk."

"Great..." Lonnie muttered.

It was Thursday, at least.

Tomorrow, she'd go shopping with Dana and lose herself in the entire day.

Then, on Saturday, she'd recover from all those sales. She'd stay in her room, enjoy her bed and her cat, then go back home on Sunday.

So, in a way, this was the last day she had to get through.

"Where should I put this?"

"Ah, on the dining room table."

Of course, the week hadn't been a complete disaster.

Marianna watched as her father walked out of the kitchen to put the fresh out the oven ham on the table. He'd shown up bright and early, armed with the last few ingredients they needed before he and Marianna tag teamed dinner. Yolanda was in the kitchen with Marianna, giving Andre instructions on where to set each dish. Yolanda wasn't much for cooking, instead, she was all about organizing and making sure everything looked perfect. She was a woman who dressed like she was going to a glamorous restaurant even if she was eating at home, from her pristine, pinstriped suit, to her runway worthy heels. Andre was the exact opposite. He lived in jeans and T-shirts, even when Yolanda requested that he attempt to look nicer for the occasion. It was an old argument between the two and deep down she didn't care that he wore beat up tennis shoes and wrinkled shirts. He was the man who worked overtime and braved the grocery store on a holiday just to get the last few eggs.

"It smells too good out here to not be able to eat anything!"

"You gotta wait, Lynn! We'll be done soon!"

It had to be the holiday spirit, but even Lynn had a smile on her face. There were times when Marianna couldn't understand how Lynn had captured two people's hearts, but on days like today, she could see the charm in her mother's smile.

All she could do was hope that it stayed that way.

Yolanda went about setting out the plates and silverware. Lynn was insisting that she could help, moving her chair around to put out the remaining pieces of flatware. When done, the woman smacked Yolanda's behind with a smug, "Told ya so," and Yolanda let out a hearty laugh.

"She's in a good mood today," Andre said, standing behind Marianna.

"Good, because she was pretty lousy when I got here."

"That wasn't aimed at you, you know that."

"I really wish people would quit saying that..."

"I know, kid, but that's just how it is."

"Does it really have to be?"

Andre frowned sadly as he handed Marianna a basket full of dinner rolls. "Here, go put this out there. Let's try to have a nice dinner."

Marianna nodded, because really, that's all she could do.

The meal itself wasn't uncomfortable, but there was something off about it. There was something in the air that made Marianna feel tense. They all partook in the conversations she'd expected: school was going well, the bakery was getting her a lot of experience, and she was excited to go out shopping with Dana tomorrow. Her parents didn't have much to contribute. Life was pretty standard: work, home, dinner, a lovable cat trying to get scraps of said dinner, then bed. Speaking of lovable cat, Snickerdoodles was prancing around under the table, not-so-secretly waiting for someone to drop a juicy piece of ham. Marianna decided to do the cat a solid and drop a tiny piece, after all, it was Thanksgiving. Mama Yo frowned at her, but her eyes looked too amused to actually be angry.

Nothing had changed, and chances were, nothing ever would.

"That's what happens when you get old," Andre said after finishing off his piece of ham. "Life gets mundane."

"Who you callin' old?" Lynn asked, Yolanda laughing as Andre tried his best to backpedal from his statement.

That's what it was. It all felt... fake.

It wasn't that the three of them couldn't get along, in fact, they all got along quite well most of the time. Sure, Lynn and Andre argued – mainly about Marianna – but somehow, the three of them made the relationship work. But this? This wasn't real. It was clear that they were all avoiding a subject: THE subject, if Marianna were honest. She knew what they wanted to discuss, but no one would bring it up. They hid behind plates of macaroni and string beans in an attempt to ignore the obvious.

magnifiquenoir.

Marianna couldn't decide if this was better or worse. She certainly didn't want to spend Thanksgiving fighting, but there was something painful and raw about ignoring it. There'd been a terrible battle, one that could've destroyed the entire city, one that could've killed them all... and here they sat, debating who got the last dinner roll.

"Marianna? Did you want it?"

"Huh?" She looked up to see Yolanda offering her the roll. "Oh, um... sure."

"Something on your mind, kid?" Andre asked.

Leave it up to her dad to try and give her an opening, but could she really answer that? Without worrying about her ticking time bomb of a mother who loved to tarnish the magical girl name? Marianna could remember a conversation with Bree months ago, one where her friend told her to talk about her feelings and not hold them in. But that wasn't something she could do at this table. There was no way she could breathe out any semblance of the word *magnifique* without Lynn flying off the handle, but all three of her parents were looking at her, waiting for a response.

Finally, Marianna answered. "Nothing's wrong."

"But-"

"She said nothing's wrong, Andre," Lynn said as she put a second helping of macaroni and cheese on her plate. "Let her eat."

"Jesus, Lynn," Andre whispered to himself.

Lynn set down her fork and asked, "What was that?"

Andre looked like he wanted to press on, but he shook his head and said, "Forget it," then he went back to eating his food.

It was too late, though, and now Lynn was in the mood to talk. "If you got something to say, say it."

"It's nothing. Can we please just enjoy dinner?"

"You obviously wanna talk about something. Both of you do."

"Lynn," Yolanda reached over and gently took the woman's hand. "Maybe after dinner. Marianna isn't home very often anymore. We should enjoy-"

"She'd be home more if she didn't go to that damn school."

So much for a nice dinner. Andre set his fork down and snapped. "Was she not supposed to go to college? Really? Because of your paranoia?"

"No, no, it's fine, really. She can go to that school. She can be a magical girl and risk her life all the time. She can nearly die. Whatever, it's her life."

"Lynn! That's not-"

"It doesn't matter," Marianna whispered as she stood up from the table. "Don't try to explain yourself, it doesn't matter."

"Sit back down, young lady. We're still having dinner."

"Are you kidding me?! You think we're still having dinner?!"

"Marianna, please-"

Ah, there was Mama Yo, right on time with her attempt at keeping the peace. Normally, Marianna would've welcomed it, but now she was fired up. She'd been quiet for eighteen years of her life. Now that she'd left home, made more friends, and established herself as Galactic Purple, she didn't feel like being quiet. There was an entire city thankful for her presence, but getting the same welcoming reception from her mother was, apparently, asking too much. "Please what? Sit down? Not talk about one of the most important things of my life?"

"You mean that thing that woman tricked you into?" Lynn hissed.

"I mean *that thing* that woman introduced me to that gave me a sense of purpose! Without it, I'd still be upstairs in that room, completely miserable!"

"Miserable? If it was so miserable, why did you even bother coming home?"

"Lynn!" The shout came from Andre, who stood up and actually slammed his hands onto the table.

"If she wants to have an attitude-"

"Speaking up for myself is not having an attitude! I have friends now! And people who care about me! I'm not the quiet, fat girl who sits in the back of the classroom. I'm not the quiet, fat girl who doesn't talk to anyone because of her paranoid mother. That accident happened before I was even born, mama, and things have changed! I'm Galactic Purple, and I'm magical!" Marianna turned and ran upstairs, Snickerdoodles running after her as her parents were left to mull over what just happened.

Marianna wondered if they'd worry about her when they finally went up to her room to check on her. She was sure when her father found it empty, the window wide open, that he'd go downstairs and snap at her mother. Mama Yo would probably try calling her, but Marianna had left her phone behind for a reason.

Marianna sat at the edge of one of the tallest buildings in the city. She'd been here several times, back when **magnifiquenoir** only consisted of Galactic Purple. The height gave her a good view of the city so she could see if any monsters were lurking about. When school started it became more difficult to come to this spot, but she'd still steal moments alone to sit and reflect on her thoughts.

Her mother was never going to agree with her on this.

A small part of her had hoped that with more girls joining, her mother would be more at ease about the whole thing. Marianna was no longer fighting alone, so there was less chance of her being hurt, or worse. With the last attack, she was sure that her mother's defenses were way, way up. Now that they'd had their disagreement, Marianna was feeling a little bad about it. Of course her mother was worried, anyone would be worried if their child decided to do something that was even a little dangerous.

At the same time… it felt so good being Galactic Purple.

She'd spent so much time being insignificant that it felt good to actually be somebody. She was now somebody who protected people and somebody who was worth looking up to. She knew her mother would never see it like that. Her mother had done everything in her power to make Marianna blend in the background, all in the name of *protection*. Lynn would never see that Marianna needed a life that was worth protecting.

"I guess that's just the way it is," Marianna said as she stood up. Part of her had hoped for some kind of attack so she could work out her frustrations, but apparently, the creatures they faced took a break for the holidays.

At least, that's what she thought, until she heard the sound of an explosion.

Marianna turned and leapt off the building, transforming in mid-air, her heels clicking against the ground when she landed. The explosion hadn't happened very far, and Galactic Purple took off running in the direction of the billowing smoke. This was why she was needed. This was why **magnifiquenoir** was necessary. While everyone was at home enjoying the holiday, she was about to face a threat that sought out the destruction of their city. For a moment, she did worry about the strength of this creature, especially considering their last battle, but she'd fought on her own before and she could do it again.

Unless the creature was already burnt to a crisp.

Galactic Purple arrived just in time to see Blaze standing in front of what used to be a fearsome beast, dressed in her black coat with her matching top hat. Blaze turned and frowned when she saw Galactic Purple, the flames serving as a threatening backdrop. "I thought I told you girls to enjoy your vacation."

"I-I was just in the area…"

"Uh huh. Are the others with you? I know Cosmic Green is too far away, but is Radical Rainbow going to show up here?"

"No... it's just me."

"So you came to fight a monster alone?"

"Y-you just fought by yourself!"

There was a look in Blaze's eyes, something dark and terrifying as she stepped closer to her. "We are not on the same level, so don't you dare use that as an excuse for your foolishness."

Galactic Purple lowered her head. She could feel her heart drop from those words but she knew that Blaze had every right to be angry. She'd explicitly said to take the week off, now here she was, putting herself in danger because she couldn't handle her parents. "I'm sorry," she whispered, her voice tight as she spoke.

Blaze sighed and made herself take a calming breath before speaking again. "Don't do that," she said as she put a hand on Galactic Purple's shoulder. "I just... after what happened with that last monster..."

"You don't want us fighting alone. It's too dangerous to fight alone now."

"I understand that things are difficult with your mother, but-"

"I can't do it," Galactic Purple blurted out. "I tried so hard, I really did. It was so uncomfortable. I hate that when we talk about it, we fight. But I also hate not talking about it because it feels like I'm suffocating."

Blaze's harsh frown settled into a sad, sympathetic look. "I know you don't want to have someone else tell you to try and understand your mother's feelings-"

"But that's what you're gonna say, right?" Galactic Purple knew where this conversation was going. It's where this conversation went anytime she tried to be mad about her circumstances. "Why can't I be upset?"

"What?"

"Why am I not allowed to be upset? I know she was hurt before, and I hate that she went through that, but does that mean I'm not allowed to be mad at her for stifling me for years because of her over-protection? Am I not allowed to be mad at her for constantly putting down the one thing I did to stand out?"

Blaze smiled as she shook her head. "This? This isn't what makes you special," then she reached forward and poked Galactic Purple's chest, right over her heart. "*You* do. This power is special because it's yours. You're using it the way you see fit."

It was the same thing Marianna had said to Lonnie, back when Lonnie had refused to join them. Why was it so hard to take her own advice from time to time? Even so, "That still doesn't answer my question about my feelings."

"Your feelings are valid. They always will be. You're allowed to be mad, I just don't want you doing anything foolish because of it."

"You mean like distancing myself from my mother?"

"No. I mean running out here to fight a monster by yourself."

"Oh that." The fire had died down, leaving them in a much too quiet city with faint traces of charred monster bits on the ground. "I can get rid of that for you, you know."

"I can too, dear, but I suppose since you're here…"

Galactic Purple smiled brightly, happy for the familiar action of eradicating a threat. It was a small gesture, but watching the acidic frosting melt the creature away made her feel good, some of her frustrations melting along with it.

"I know you used to fight alone before, but I never want you to have to do that again. My intentions were for there to be a team."

"I know. I was just–"

"Frustrated, and you needed to work out some of that aggression. Believe me, I understand. Just... be smarter about it. At the very least, call me."

"I can do that." After all, it wasn't like Blaze was being completely unreasonable, unlike some women she knew.

Huh, guess some of her frustrations were still there.

"If you want to come back early, you can," Blaze said. "You don't have to stay where you aren't comfortable."

"I thought you didn't want me to distance myself from her?"

"When did I say that?"

"Well, I mean... you want me to understand where she's coming from."

"Sure I do, but just because you understand doesn't mean you have to agree."

And there it was. The one sentence that Galactic Purple – no, *Marianna* – needed to hear. Her magical persona slipped away as she looked up at Blaze. "...really?"

"Yes. Really," then Blaze wrapped her arms around Marianna, holding her close. "You can be as angry as you want."

But now that the words had been said, all Marianna felt was sadness as she closed her eyes and rested her head against Blaze's shoulder. "I don't want to be angry. I want to have a mom who doesn't hate what I've become. I want her to be understanding like my father, like Mama Yo, like Bree and Lonnie... and you. But... that will never happen, will it?"

Blaze ran her fingers through Marianna's hair. Deep down, she knew that the answer was no. Lynn would never see things their way. She was past the point of understanding, but Blaze didn't have the heart to say it out loud. Still, she wouldn't be doing Marianna any favors if she lied, right?

"You're a young lady who can make cupcakes explode. Anything is possible."

It wasn't a lie, but it was as close to the truth as she was willing to get.

"Hey! Happy Thanksgiving! I know you said things would be fine but I wanted to see how things were going. I hope they're going well! And if they're not, well... m-maybe things will improve? Maybe this is an alternate universe with reasonable parents. My mom's been pretty cool and I haven't burst into hellish, bisexual flames yet, even after we went to church on Sunday. But now there's the holiday service, which is an entirely new boss battle to-"

"Bree! Get off the phone and let's go!"

"Coming mom!"

Click.

Marianna laughed as she pet her precious cat, who had decided to turn her pillow into a bed. Marianna imagined that Bree would have all kinds of stories to tell when she returned, each one more outlandish than the last.

"Hey you! Happy Thanksgiving! Sooooo... my Grand-Penny made a bunch of food and it's really, reeeeeally good. You should come over! You know, before my rotten cousins eat it all. Raye can even come pick you up, I just need the address. Unless, you know, things are going okay over there? Anyway... call me back!"

Click.

"MARIANNA! You ready for tomorrow? We're gonna WRECK that mall!"

"HI MARIANNA!"

"That was my mom. She says-"

"MARIANNA! HI!"

"HI MARIANNA!"

"HEY!"

"GUYS I'M ON THE PHONE!!!" A pause, then, "Sorry about that, my family says hi. You know, you can come over if you want. Just call me back and-"

"IS THAT MARIANNA?! TELL HER I SAID-"

"OH. MY. GOD! GET OUT OF HERE!!! Bye Marianna."

Click.

"Marianna? About dinner... look, I know it's hard to-"

Marianna pulled the phone away from her ear as Yolanda went on about understanding how she felt, apologizing on behalf of Lynn, and wanting her to come back home, unaware that Marianna had left her phone behind. Marianna went on to the next message, not at all surprised to hear her father saying something similar. Unlike Yolanda, Andre added words like *unreasonable* when he described Lynn's actions.

Speaking of her Mama Lynn... she'd left no message.

Because of course she didn't.

Marianna set her phone down and scratched behind Snickerdoodles' ear. "You won't be too upset if I leave early, right?"

The cat purred in response: the result of Marianna scratching her in her favorite spot.

Marianna stood up and left the room, heading downstairs to where they had attempted to have dinner. Snickerdoodles followed behind her in the hopes of being pet more or receiving any leftovers. All the food was put away and the dishes done, and Marianna imagined that it was all done in silence. Her father had probably, at most, muttered a few things under his breath until Yolanda shushed him. Meanwhile, Lynn had probably ranted about her disrespectful daughter, or something along those lines. Marianna took a moment to wipe at her watering eyes. It wasn't like she wanted this tension with her mother, in fact, she wanted the exact opposite. She wanted them to get along, but if they couldn't even make it through a delicious meal there was no hope for them.

"We're here live at the sight of the destruction..."

Marianna blinked. Where was that coming from? Snickerdoodles meowed up at her then ran into the living room, Marianna following after her. Lynn was sitting in front of the television, watching a news story about a massive attack that had happened in the city. Marianna winced. She shouldn't have been surprised that some news station would do a holiday story that reflected on the attack that had happened. Marianna knew they weren't on great terms right now, but, "You don't have to watch that, mama."

Lynn didn't listen, didn't even turn to look at her. Marianna walked forward to turn off the TV but stopped when she looked at the screen.

This wasn't about the attack from before.

The picture quality was poor, as if it had been recorded on a VCR, and the destruction was much too great. The monster they'd face had done a great deal of damage, but nothing to this degree. The streets were broken apart like scattered puzzle pieces. The buildings and any billboards were torn apart as if they'd been pulverized by an angry tornado. Traffic lights were hanging limply from their posts, looking ready to fall to the ground and join the rest of the rubble below.

"This is..."

"What happened back then," Lynn whispered.

Marianna looked over at her mother, who was holding a framed picture in her hands. Marianna recognized it as an old college photo, back when her mother attended the university that she was attending now. She also recognized the women in the photo with her as friends of her mother's, *best friends*, to be exact. Yolanda had told Marianna stories about those women, how close they had been to her mother to the point of making sure her mother's suitors were up to par. *"Myself included,"* Yolanda had said with a laugh.

Marianna remembered asking what happened to them. At the time, Yolanda had simply said that they weren't there anymore. She'd taken that to mean that they had moved, after all, people went their separate ways after college all the time. Had she been paying closer attention, she would've realized how tight Yolanda's voice had been when she spoke of them.

"I wasn't just physically hurt that day," Lynn said, her voice shaking as she spoke. "I know I can't stop you, Marianna, but…"

Marianna looked at the television again. Fortunately, the monster she and the others had face was destroyed before it could get too bad. Once upon a time, that hadn't been the case. Marianna and her friends *could've died*, but Lynn… "They died, didn't they?" Marianna asked.

"Three of them did," Lynn said as she held the picture tighter.

"Mama…"

"I know what I've done to you is unforgivable, I just… I was eighteen once… and so were they."

"Why didn't you tell me?"

"Would it have mattered? You still would've said yes to that woman."

So she wasn't just blaming **magnifiquenoir** for her injuries… she was blaming them for the death of her friends. "Mama, it's not-"

"Her fault? That's what you're gonna say, right?"

This conversation was so familiar. Marianna had been tired of people telling her how to feel, so maybe, just maybe, she could give her mother the same courtesy. "No," she said. "I won't do that to you. You can feel however you want. You can say whatever you want."

"No, I've done enough to you."

"Yes, but now I know *why*."

So Lynn took a deep breath and talked to Marianna. She talked to her like a woman who had lost everything in the blink of an eye. She talked to her like a worried mother who knew that she was sheltering her child. She talked about the anger she felt when Blaze spoke to her about **magnifiquenoir** and how Marianna would be perfect, oh so perfect, to protect those who couldn't protect themselves. All those years of trying to protect her daughter had led her to the exact place she didn't want her to go. And she knew, in her heart, that Marianna was perfect. She was strong and kind and would do what the group before her had done, but Lynn couldn't come to terms with it.

And Marianna listened, really listened, as her mother talked and cried and talked some more, the house cat now settled in her lap in an attempt to try and get the tears to stop.

"I'm sorry," Marianna said. She knelt down on the floor and rested her head in her mother's lap, much to the dismay of Snickerdoodles who jumped away and sauntered over to the couch.

Lynn ran her fingers through Marianna's hair, all cried out with nothing else to say. "I'm sorry," Marianna said again, "But... I can't leave them."

"I know," Lynn whispered. "I don't expect you to."

And that was it, both of them lingering at an impasse. Marianna would never do what Lynn wanted her to do, and in return, Lynn would never understand. It should've left Marianna feeling empty, but instead, she felt like she finally understood where her mother was coming from.

"The world needs you," Lynn said. "I just wish that it didn't."

"Sometimes... I wish the same thing."

"Really?"

Marianna nodded. "I think all the girls feel like that sometimes, you know? We know what we signed up for, but sometimes..."

"It's too much."

Marianna nodded again. "But someone has to protect this place, right?"

"There really is no better person to lead those girls."

"You... think so?"

Lynn looked down at Marianna and smiled. Actually smiled. It was so genuine that Marianna could feel the tears stinging the corners of her eyes. "Just because I worry about you doesn't mean I don't see your value, Marianna. You are magical."

Marianna couldn't stop herself from crying even if she wanted to. Lynn rested her hand on the top of Marianna's head and let her cry as much as she needed to. Reaching for the remote with her other hand, she shut off the TV, mother and daughter sitting in silence for the rest of the night.

"So you don't need me to come pick you up?"

"No," Marianna said into the phone. "Not until Sunday."

Blaze smiled as she stirred cream and sugar into her coffee. "I'm not just hearing things, right? It is pretty loud out here."

"Where are you?"

"Out," Blaze said as she watched the restaurant fill up with people. Most breakfast places wouldn't be this full on a Friday morning, but with all the early morning shoppers, the wait staff was constantly on the move. "Today's the day for shopping, you know."

"I didn't know you were going out today, too. Dana and I are going later."

"Ah," then Blaze added, "So I really don't have to come and get you?"

"No, we talked. We still have our differences, but now I have a better understanding about why we have our differences."

"You know, I swear someone was trying to tell you-"

"Yeah, yeah," Marianna muttered.

Blaze laughed. "I'm glad you two worked things out, well... as much as you *could* work things out."

"Me too, actually. She... s-she thinks I'm a good magical girl."

"Well, she's right. You are."

"I just... never expected to hear that from her."

"Well it's about time," Blaze said. "Anyway, my waitress is on her way over, I should let you go."

"All right. Have fun today!"

"You too, Marianna," then Blaze ended the call.

"Ma'am? Are you ready to order? Or are you still waiting for your friend?"

"Oh, I'll order for her," Blaze said. "She should be here soon."

The waitress nodded and dutifully took down Blaze's orders, then quickly hurried off to attend to another table. Blaze took a sip of her coffee and glanced out the window. The sidewalk was full of people going about their day, most of them already armed with shopping bags while others frantically made their way to the next store on their list. Blaze sat back and enjoyed her coffee. Her friend, as the waitress had called her, would be here soon enough. Blaze wasn't terribly fond of being out shopping today, but she was fond of certain friends who insisted on going out to face these crowds year after year. Besides, some of the deals were great, and Blaze could use a new coat for the upcoming winter.

All she had to do was wait. She'd be there soon enough.

ROLL CREDITS

So what exactly was that "strange orb" that Ella was talking about? You can find out by reading her crazy, video game themed adventures in the comic book series *8-Bit*! This comic is by Musetap Studios, whose art has been featured in **magnifiquenoir**! Here's a snippet of what life is like for Ella and her good friend, Chevy!

ART AND STORY BY:
MUSETAP STUDIOS

HTTP://WWW.MUSETAPSTUDIOS.COM/8-BIT

Can't wait to read more **magnifiquenoir**? Well you can indulge in Briana's other book series until then! "The Hunters Series" is a collaboration with her partner, Jessica Walsh, and takes place in the Midwest. In it, Fagan and Alex are a team who keep their city safe by hunting down the things that creep through the shadows, but things take an interesting turn when a creature tells them about *The Storyteller*. This mystical being is said to live in a giant library that is full of books, each book representing a person's life. The Storyteller has the power to change anyone's life with just the turn of a page, and this is the exact kind of power that Alex has been looking for... but how far will he go to obtain it?

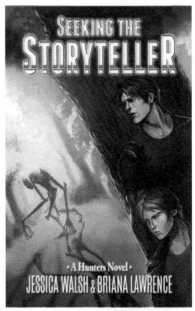

For *Seeking the Storyteller* **Molly Lolly** says: *"The world Ms. Lawrence and Ms. Walsh created was so much fun and absolutely fascinating."*

Rainbow Gold Reviews adds: *"So many of these characters were not what they seemed to be. Kept me on my toes!"*

Crystal's Many Reviews calls *Seeking the Storyteller,* *"A truly unique and well written story."*

For *Beneath the Chapter* **Molly Lolly** returns to say, *"Oh my gosh why did it have to end?! I enjoyed this book and couldn't put it down. The overall storyarc hits its stride here."*

Join the hunt here:

http://www.magnifiquenoir.com/other-magical-works/

MEET THE CREATOR!

Photo by: Elyse Lavonne

At the age of nine, like most kids, Briana Lawrence had a dream. She wanted to be the best "WRITTER" in the whole wide world. Her fourth grade class laughed and wondered how one hoped to become a "writer" if they couldn't even spell the word. Back then her stories were created with crayons and construction paper. As she grew older they progressed into notebooks and colored ink pens of pink, blue, and purple. When she lost her older brother, Glenn Berry, in a car accident, she stopped writing.

Dreams, however, have a funny way of coming back.

Before she realized it she was grabbing her notebook and pens again. She would write stories that ranged from high school romance to her imagination running wild with the likes of Goku, Vegeta, and the other characters of *Dragon Ball Z*. This continued throughout college where she would always end up writing about the space exploits of the pilots of *Gundam Wing* and other works of fan fiction. Soon she realized that she wanted to do more than that. Her head was full of ideas, full of original characters and worlds that she wanted to share with others.

Thus, she stepped into an English Major with some Women's Studies on the side.

She graduated Iowa State University in 2006 and moved to Minneapolis with her partner. Here, she tried to get into graduate school, but things didn't pan out the way she wanted. She ended up working retail, her dream becoming buried by Black Fridays and other busy times of year. Once again, however, that dream returned. She went from immersing herself in geeky fan fiction to actually writing about the geeky things she loved for several anime and video game review sites. However, it was her discovery of National Novel Writing Month that made her go back to creating her own characters and plots.

In the meantime, Briana would cosplay with her partner, Jessica Walsh, and go to conventions with her just for fun. Overtime, the two worked together to create a business that is open to everyone. Their business is a combination of their crafts, written works, and the cosplay that Jessica brings to life. While Briana isn't the one who's doing the sewing, she often speaks about different social issues in the community. This began in 2013 after she was bullied online, and she's been working to promote positivity among her peers.

As an author, freelance writer, and cosplayer, Briana is working to get her works out into the world. Whether it's creating a fantastical universe, writing articles pertaining to social issues in the geek community, or putting together fun scripts for WatchMojo.com, Briana is out to be the best "WRITTER" she can be.

website:	http://www.magnifiquenoir.com/
facebook:	https://www.facebook.com/magnifiqueNOIR/
twitter:	https://twitter.com/BrichibiTweets